MAN-KZIN WARS XIII

CREATED BY
LARRY NIVEN

BAEN

Man-Kzin Wars XIII

Copyright © 2012 by Larry Niven.

"Misunderstanding" copyright © 2012 by Hal Colebatch and Jessica Q. Fox; "Two Types of Teeth" copyright © 2012 by Jane Lindskold; "Pick of the Litter" copyright © 2012 by Charles E. Gannon; "Tomcat Tactics" copyright © 2012 by Charles E. Gannon; "At the Gates" copyright © 2012 by Alex Hernandez; "Zeno's Roulette" copyright © 2012 by David Bartell; "Bound for the Promised Land" copyright © 2012 by Alex Hernandez.

A Baen Books Original

Baen Publishing Enterprises
P.O. Box 1403
Riverdale, NY 10471
www.baen.com

ISBN: 978-1-4516-3894-3

Cover art by Stephen Hickman

First Baen paperback printing, February 2013

Library of Congress Control Number: 2012003332

Distributed by Simon & Schuster
1230 Avenue of the Americas
New York, NY 10020

Pages by Joy Freeman (www.pagesbyjoy.com)
Printed in the United States of America

THE MAN-KZIN WARS SERIES
Created by Larry Niven

Also by Larry Niven

To purchase these and all other Baen Book titles
in e-book format, please go to www.baen.com.

WHAT ARE THE ODDS?

The main kzin force, having gathered in a wide ring around the pillbox, tried to send a team to work through the misty margin between the flank of the strongpoint and the southern hot spring. Weapon fire erupted from the pillbox; two kzinti went down immediately. A third was clipped in the back of the leg as he tried to reach the safety of the tree line again.

The surrounding perimeter of covering brush erupted in weapon fire, all directed inward upon the pillbox.

Smith swung his binoculars back to the kzin flankers coming up his slope. The two who had already been veering away were now sprinting pell-mell back in the direction of the battle. Of the remaining three, their pace slowed, not due to argument, but to indulge in a wistful appreciation of the same martial spectacle.

Which was why none of the three slope-scouting kzinti heard the reports of the elephant guns that fired into them from the rear.

Smith saw one flash and then another jump out of the dark wall of the undergrowth some seventy meters behind the kzin.

Two more flashes licked out of the distant wall of tangled vegetation, and the last kzin fell over, three meters short of the outcropping.

Smith exhaled through a smile.

The fellow next to him in the slit trench—a 'Runner named Tip and their best guncotton brewer—cocked a quizzical head: "What's up, *hauptman*?"

"Our odds of success," Smith replied, "our odds of success."

—from "Tomcat Tactics," by Charles E. Gannon

CONTENTS

CONTENTS

MAN-KZIN WARS XIII

MISUNDERSTANDING

◆ ◆ ◆

**Hal Colebatch and
Jessica Q. Fox**

> *"Remember the Chunquen?"*
>
> *"Both sexes were sentient. They fought constantly."*
>
> *"And that funny religion on Altair One. They thought they could travel in time."*
>
> *"Yes, Sir, when we landed the infantry they were all gone."*
>
> *"They must have all committed suicide with disintegrators. But why? They knew we only wanted slaves. And I'm still trying to figure out how they got rid of the disintegrators afterwards."*
>
> *"Some beings,"* said A-T Officer, *"will do anything to keep their beliefs."*
>
> —From *The Warriors* (recording salvaged from the wreckage of kzin scout ship *Far-Ranging Prowler*'s bridge recorder by the crew of *The Angel's Pencil*.)

The star known to human beings as Altair has a number of planets. Planets are, of course, as common as dirt, so no big surprises there. There are some rings of asteroids close to the star, and then a single planet in what human beings call the *Goldilocks zone*. Not too hot, not too cold, but just right. The planet was eventually called Altair One by human beings, and something meaning pretty much the same by the kzinti. It is a planet similar to both Earth and Kzin in atmosphere, climate and gravity, so would be habitable to both species. It has, however, never been colonized. There are reasons for this.

One of them is the existence of an intelligent species, the Dilillipsans. They are, it has to be said, *different*.

If you asked any one Dilillipsan to choose a number between one and ten you'd get at least a thousand answers, and π would probably be one of them. Dilillipsans call their own world something which might be rendered, loosely, as *Glot*, a tiny fraction of a sound-name which is completely unpronounceable, and which translates, roughly, as *the place we know a bit about and are usually standing on or sometimes moving around on when young and foolish*.

The acoustic part of the Dilillipsan language sounds something like the station announcements at the beginning of *Monsieur Hulot's Holiday* played backwards, or perhaps sideways, and at double speed. *Monsieur Hulot's Holiday*, incidentally, had been quite a favorite with the Dilillies once they began picking up Earth television transmissions, its tragic grandeur never failing to move them.

Unlike human beings, who believe many things, or kzinti, who also believe many things—except when they are of the very high nobility and have become cynical—the Dilillies believe everything, but by different amounts.

Some things they hardly believe at all, and some things they are almost certain about, but certainty is regarded as a mental health issue on Glot. They communicate with each other in five or six languages simultaneously, one involving generating three-dimensional pictures on their stomachs, one involving chemicals that can smell bad, and two, or maybe three, involving making noises. It makes translating conversations just a little difficult. Note the delicate understatement in this remark.

Not many human spaceships or probes have passed near them, but some have been near enough for the Dilillies to eavesdrop on their communications, as they have on radio and television transmissions from Earth, which is a mere fifteen light-years away. They have done this from curiosity, and without malevolent intent. Their knowledge of human culture is both broad and deep, but their insights are fragmentary. The understatement in *that* remark is very far from delicate.

The hell with it. Language reflects culture and a way of perceiving the world, and the Dilillies are so different there's no way of translating anything with any precision. So let's just mangle everything shamelessly. Take it as a parable. Do what the Dilillies would do: believe everything, but not very much.

"You have to face it, those human beings are just so incredibly creative. I mean, what kind of wild mind would you need to have in order to be able to invent the hat?"

"Or a tie."

"Or shoes."

"No, shoes make sense. They have to walk around a lot and they have to walk on hard stuff like pavements and grass and they have very soft feet. So either they wear their feet out or they have some sort of protective cover for them. What I don't understand is why it's called *footwear*. It should be called anti-footwear."

"Or foot anti-wear."

"Yes, they are not very logical. But I still rate the moustache without the beard as the most brilliant joke. I mean, first you go for hundreds of thousands of years growing hair on your face. Then you find a way to get rid of it. Then you get rid of all of it except for a little bit right under the nose. That's absolutely brilliant. You couldn't make this up, none of us could ever get close! But those human beings did it. They're amazing!"

The three-and-a-bit Dilillies brooded on this for a few seconds. They had been vastly entertained by moustaches for centuries now. It had started a topiary cult twice.

"I still think that there's a reason for these things. One that we can't easily grasp, but one that makes sense to them."

"What possible reason can there be for a necktie?"

"Perhaps the top button is obscene. Perhaps the buttons are more and more disgusting as you go up, and the top one is so obscene it has to be covered by something."

"They can't be obscene in themselves. It's only when they are put through the buttonholes. Of course! It must be a symbol for sexual activity! Unbuttoned top shirt buttons must be merely vulgar. And I think moustaches are worn to tell other human beings that the owner isn't really a child or a female. Their young don't have hairy faces, nor do the females usually. I think they mostly want to be mistaken for children, but some don't. Either that or the males feel that the females will feel inadequate for not having hairy faces and they want to cheer them up. So they get rid of most of it, but the insecure ones leave a small bit to prove they are adults."

"Hmm. You think the females suffer from Hairy-Face Envy. I suppose it's possible. But then why don't they all wear false moustaches like the leader of the Marxists?"

"I don't think Groucho was the leader of the Marxists, just the most famous of them."

The bit, which was very young, and bobbed around in a very distracting manner, asked, "Why do they all spend so much time running around? They even invented cars and aeroplanes to do it faster."

"Oh, that's easy. If one of them wants to communicate with another, they have to move very close together. Or they had to until they invented mobile phones."

They thought about this. It made sense. Sort of.

Coco was explaining his recent hobby activities to his friend John Wayne. There had been a fashion for human nicknames in their early years. These are not even remotely like their real names, each of which would run to several pages of text, a dozen cartoons, the sound of a waterfall crunching its gears and the contents of a Spanish *Farmacia*. The term *his* is also not exactly accurate, and *friend* refers to a relationship which on a scale from zero (meaning total loathing) to ten (meaning someone you have a psychotic fixation on and spend all your time stalking) would score approximately the square root of a matrix of imaginary numbers.

"A spaceship? Full of animals that look like tigers? Can I see them too?" John Wayne was thrilled. "Really see them directly, not just on your stomachs?" Ever since *The Greatest Show on Earth*, one of his favorite films, when the tigers escaped during the great train wreck, not to mention *The Jungle Book*, whose name had thrillingly romantic connotations for the Dilillies, John Wayne had wanted to meet a tiger. Since seeing *The Lord of the Rings*, he had wanted to meet a Balrog, but had accepted, reluctantly, that they would probably not make congenial passengers in a spaceship.

"Sure, it's easy. The hielterober can take us there. They won't see us, of course, although I'm working on that. I'm planning a new avatar, just for them."

"Can I have one too? I'd love to have an argument with a tiger. But will it be possible? I've wanted to have arguments with humans, but they're too far away. It would be difficult for them to remember the last move when it was a third of a century ago. The poor things don't live very long."

The Dilillies had been picking up Earth television signals for several centuries. They had discovered its entertainment possibilities with Adolph Hitler opening the 1936 Olympic Games and had never looked back. Whenever some Dilillies felt depression gathering, they'd look at one of the old war newsreels and laugh themselves out of it. Far funnier than Chaplin, and even sillier than *Star Trek* reruns.

"It should be possible, the tigers' spaceships are fairly close. They'll be here in a few weeks. It would be prudent to find out more about what they intend to do when they get here."

"Bring on the hielterober; this I've got to see!"

Coco started the hielterober. It was something between a virtual reality body-suit and a huge wardrobe full of invisible fur coats. After some cursing as he found the current location of the spaceships, Coco and then John Wayne stood, somewhat changed in size, on the bridge of the kzin warship *Far-Ranging Prowler*. The captain, his weapons officer and the alien technology officer were in conference before a very pretty view of space in general and Altair in particular. Coco felt intense pleasure as he looked at the oval outline of his sun. From Glot it could be almost any color, purple to crimson by way of bright pink, but from space it was brilliant white. And that green star next to it, that was Glot. A thing of beauty. He pointed this out to John Wayne, who was studying the kzinti with fascination. John Wayne was more of a people person.

"They don't have much to say to each other, do they?" John Wayne whispered. "And it's so slow."

"Bandwidth limitations in the communication channels. Poor things. Very like human beings, I suspect, but with fur and bigger teeth. They only talk three languages at a time. But each language is handled by a different part of their nervous system and so what they wind up telling each other is anybody's guess. Most of the time, the captain is telling everyone to be afraid of him. It's not very interesting. And the others are telling him they *are* afraid of him, but it doesn't seem to stop him. Perhaps he's worried they might change their minds."

"I'm glad you've got the translations fixed," John Wayne commented. "There's more going in on the making-growling-noises-at-each-other channel. I missed it at first, but the big one with the orange stripes is asking the medium-sized one with the spots whether they are close enough to detect any radio or television signals. They will be ever so disappointed! Can we go back and make some for them to detect? We could pass on the human World War II newsreels. They look as if they could do with a good laugh. Or we could send them my last poem."

"I don't know if they quite deserve that. The tiger people will arrive at Glot long before the end of the first canto, John Wayne. Still, if that's their preferred form of communication, yes, let's try it. And we should welcome them and show them something of our culture, although I foresee problems. I think my new avatar should be ready by now, and we can use that on the television."

"I can use one of my old avatars, I expect. Might have to scale it up a bit so it looks like something they would recognize, though. Some fur, and teeth perhaps. I rather fancy my Jabba the Hutt, the pink one, what do you think?"

"Why not? But teeth might be a problem for the captain. I mean, you have to be horribly insecure to tell everyone to be afraid of you all the time. Something friendly like a moustache might be better."

"Good thinking. Suppose I start with fur and take it off later, to show that we aren't the least bit threatening. That might calm him down a bit."

"We have a signal from the planet, sir." Technology Officer saluted respectfully, claws-across-the-face. "It seems to be a 3-D video, and we are translating it now. And a sound channel as well."

"Call the telepath and get him here immediately! Oh, and the strategist, it will be something for him to think about." The captain snorted with contempt.

He was not kindly disposed to thinking as an activity, considering it some kind of perversion, and he also despised telepaths, as did all right-thinking kzinti. "Bring the image up there, where we can all see it!" he decreed.

The big screen cycled through blue, green, yellow and purple, formed two images overlayed and then separated into a stereo image. It was somewhat surprising that it made any sense at all; some intelligent species had only three-color sensitivity, and their artificial images were incomprehensible.

"Strategist, what are we seeing?"

"Clearly two aliens, sir, and very different in appearance, to be sure. Perhaps different species, possibly merely different sexes. Since the signals originate from the middle continent, and since there are four distinct large land masses, it is conceivable that different species have attained intelligence on different continents. Their technology levels would seem to be at least what ours were some centuries ago. Since they are beaming the signal we may infer that they have detected our presence, which suggests somewhat more advanced technology."

Before them with what might or might not be a toothless smile, a bright pink face with a huge slit mouth looked out of the screen at them. It had gray fur and wore a straw hat on its head, which, although the kzinti didn't know it, was decorated with bananas, apples and a lobster. It wasn't, of course, a real lobster, but it was quite convincing. Next to the pink animal with the big mouth was a skeletal creature with a big green head wearing a morning suit complete with gray top hat. It had two arms with clawless hands on the end encased in gray gloves. The captain found it difficult to tell what parts were artificial and which parts were of its integument. It had its hands clasped on a black cane with a gold knob on the end. It looked into the eyes of the captain and spoke.

"Welcome to Altair One." It spoke in the Heroes' Tongue. It spoke as well as the captain. In fact it spoke in the captain's voice.

The captain's response was not fully articulate, being something between a howl and a roar, but a definite note of interrogation could be detected in it. Coco wondered if he had been misheard.

"Yes, welcome. We are very pleased to greet you and we anticipate with pleasure your arrival from the stars. We are sure you have lots of interesting things to tell us," the big fat pink one spoke. It also spoke the Heroes' Tongue and also sounded exactly like the captain.

Captain looked at them. They appeared to be waiting for a response.

"Is it possible that they can hear us, Strategist?"

"Since they speak the Heroes' Tongue, they have plainly heard Kzin before, and since they speak in your voice, my captain, then they must have somehow heard you previously. It would be prudent, therefore, to assume that they *can* hear us."

"Kill the link!" ordered Captain. "And Technology Officer, ensure that no transmissions from this ship are permitted." It was elementary that the enemy aliens should not hear their Council of War. None of the kzinti were aware that this made no difference to Coco and John Wayne.

"Ha," growled the captain in the mocking tense. "They may not be so pleased to see us when we arrive. I don't know what they taste like, but they look as if they could be made into competent slaves." A new, populated planet! That would mean wealth for him, and a Name! A pity there were not really enough marines aboard to leave a garrison, but that could wait until their return. However, he wondered at the big mouth on the fat one. He had not seen teeth, but there was something unsettling about the implied swallowing power.

Telepath had slumped into a semi-sitting position, hind-legs sprawled out before him. The captain thought of bringing him to his feet and to attention very forcibly indeed, but he knew from past alien contacts that he must be suffering from information overload. Some alien species, like the Chunquen with their nasty undersea boats, were like enough to kzinti in their thought processes to make it relatively easy to get a handle on them. Species on different planets followed broadly similar evolutionary paths, possibly because they had common microbe ancestors, possibly because those were the best way to go. Assuming these were mammalian, the number of teats would indicate the size of their litters. But the sexual dimorphism was more extreme than anything he had ever heard of. He found it hard to imagine either of them being sexually attractive even to each other. Perhaps they were different species. But could different species share a planet? The screen came on again, though no one had laid a claw on the control console.

"Taste like?" the pink one spoke in bewilderment.

Captain's comfortable ideas were turned upside-down. If these enemies had superior technology, and they'd just demonstrated that they had, then not only was *Prowler* in trouble, so was the whole kzin species.

Captain shot a look full of death at Technology

Officer. "They can hear us? They control our communications links! How is that possible?"

"I cannot imagine, sir. They must have some advanced technology indeed."

Alien Technologies remembered, fortunately for him, that stating the obvious to Captain was never a good idea at the best of times, and this was decidedly not one of them. He tried to shift the blame:

"We know, sir, that they have been listening to us, as Strategist pointed out."

Strategist broke in. "And if they deduced our language on only one sample, they are extremely advanced in linguistics. And if they have had other samples, how far-ranging are their probes? . . . or ships?"

That was also not a pleasant thought. If other kzinti had met them, why had they not reported the fact and staked their claim? A reason occurred to the captain and he did not like it. It fitted uncomfortably with the pink one's big mouth.

The pink Jabba avatar spoke breezily. "Never actually met a space-faring species before, Captain, not to speak to. But my friend Coco here has been visiting you by the hielterober for some dozens of days now." Coco lifted his top hat respectfully and put it back. His head appeared fleshless bone, not unlike the skull of a *kz'eerkt*. "So naturally he picked up your languages. But let's get back to this tasting business. What exactly did you have in mind?"

"I have it in mind to find you on your planet, hunt you down, and then rip off your head and gorge myself on the flesh of your body," the captain explained.

"Good Lord, are you serious?" John Wayne asked in astonishment.

Captain snarled, showing a lot of teeth, most of them very pointy. Still, addressing him as "Good Lord" showed the creature had some elementary grasp of decorum. Perhaps, thought Captain, making what was for him an unusual effort at empathy, it was attempting to pay him a compliment—or was it an insult? None of his slaves on Kzin had ever addressed him as "Good," though they certainly addressed him as "Lord."

The big pink creature studied the teeth thoughtfully. "Yes, I see what you mean," he told the captain. "Well, I'm very sorry, but I don't feel that it's a good idea. I can see that opinions may honestly differ on this point, but on balance I'm against it. How about you, Coco?"

Coco, or the avatar that looked like death in a formal costume, considered the matter. Then he shrugged. "It seems a frightful waste to me. But you want—and let me be quite clear about this—you want that *you* should eat *us*?"

"Yes!" snarled the captain, who wasn't used to arguments from food.

"Not that *we* should eat *you*?"

Captain was lost for words. Telepath, who had been struggling to his feet, was knocked down again by the full psychic blast of Captain's outrage, made no less devastating by the fact, which even the other officers sensed, that it also contained more than a hint of fear.

Coco looked out at them from the screen, turning to look at each of the kzinti in turn, another cause for worry. "I'm not wildly keen on that idea either, frankly, but I just want to be sure." Coco was trying to be polite on the off-chance there was a misunderstanding here.

There wasn't. The captain made it very clear that he was expecting to greatly enjoy tearing them limb from limb and feasting on the remains.

"But the plain fact is that we would taste absolutely terrible. Think sawdust laced with lots of small pebbles and nails, with a dollop of jam," John Wayne told him reasonably. "Particularly nasty jam. Made from sour fruit that was stolen from the trees by plague-stricken *sthondats*. We're talking serious indigestion here. And that's the best bit. Coco's body here has got hardly any meat on him by any standards." John Wayne had wanted to say *avatar*, but there didn't seem to be a word for it and had chosen *body* as the next best thing.

If the captain did not understand the meaning of the word "jam," Telepath did. Vegetable reproductive structures crushed to a pulp, fermented with sucrose, and...and eaten! Generally when spread upon a paste of crushed and baked vegetable seeds! He began vomiting convulsively, with barely time to turn away from Captain. Fortunately, the bridge, as in every ship which might encounter aliens and carried a Telepath, was fitted with a disposal unit for just such emergencies.

"Then he and his kind will make slaves." The captain was not in a good mood, but he saw that what the enemy said was probably true enough. It was plain from Telepath's behavior that here was a horribly perverted race...or races. Further, he had to admit to himself, neither of them looked particularly appetizing. One more-than-vaguely resembled a long-dead and sun-dried *kz'errkt*, the other a very large version of something that lived under a rock.

"Slaves. You mean fetching and carrying and dying in the arena, that sort of thing?" John Wayne asked.

"That sort of thing," Captain agreed. "I see you've got the idea." It was interesting that they were showing some sense. Two questions rose at the back of his mind. *Where* did they get the idea? And *who* had told them about the arena? True, dying in the arena was a criminal punishment by which disgraced kzin nobility might regain some honor, far beyond a slave's aspirations, but the fact that these aliens were aware of it suggested that they had the rudiments of culture. They did, of course, but in this case it came from watching old broadcast versions of *Gladiator* and *Spartacus*.

"Well, I suppose it could be interesting," John Wayne said reflectively. "What do you think, Coco?"

"Only for a week or so," Coco told him. "After that, I should think, it could get rather tedious. And those who got to die in the arena might very well object. It would be a terrible waste, some of those bodies have been around for decades. I think they'd quite possibly refuse, frankly. Not really much of an improvement over being eaten, when you come right down to it."

"You will obey in all things, vermin," Captain told them with emphasis, the kzinti words for "alien," "enemy," "slave" and "vermin" all being much the same, though the Heroes' Tongue was remarkably rich in suggestive insults otherwise. The idea of a slave, or a meal, refusing a command was too alien to be digested easily. It had happened, from time to time in the past, but to say the consequences had been drastic would be putting the matter altogether too mildly.

Then Captain asked: "Can you keep records? Do you have good record-keeping devices?" He had not had a good record-keeper since he lost his temper with his Chunquen slave for spilling the ship's ceremonial jar of the Patriarch's urine during a sudden maneuver.

"Well, with all due modesty, I think I have a good memory," John Wayne told him. "And so does my colleague here. Weather now, and rainfall . . . I think I can recall the weather-patterns for most of my lifetime so far. Or do you mean by 'record' those round things humans previously placed on turntables to make sounds? Coco thought-skibbed it was to make music, but I fropgrievened to him that that was not possible—not once you heard it."

"Do not presume to trade on your usefulness!" Captain snarled. *"Trade"* in the Heroes' Tongue was in most contexts one of those many deadly insults. Still, good record-keepers would be useful, he admitted to himself. He was in no mood to track down the meaning of the various strange words the creature used.

"I skrieg that you are using the speaking-to-slaves tense already. But I think you're wrong about that," John Wayne told him soberly, using the tense of equals, a breach of etiquette which would certainly cost any slave his tongue and shortly thereafter his life if he was within reach of Captain's claws. "I hate to be the one to break the news to you, but we're not very good at obedience. And frankly, we don't often even try."

For the unfortunate Telepath, it was as if the control-room turned white as Captain's rage washed over him. At least it blotted out the alien thoughts, even of the . . . jam . . . for a time.

"Some might manage to learn it," John Wayne went on, "but only if they want to. And I doubt if anyone would. There's always the odd nutty eccentric of course, but not many that odd. Or that nutty. Still, we do hope you'll come soon and talk it over with us. Or perhaps we shall come to see you, in person, so to speak. Yes, we'll visit tomorrow sometime, if that's alright with you, Coco?"

Coco nodded, looking slightly bored, though equipped with very little by way of facial expression to manage it with.

"Nutty"... that seemed to have multiple meanings. Captain knew what nuts were—seed-pods of certain vegetable matter. He did not know he was being offered a fleeting clue to many things that would bewilder him.

"There you are then, we'll drop in tomorrow." John Wayne waved nonchalantly at the kzinti. "Bye-bye for now." And the picture vanished.

"What do they mean *drop in*?" the captain asked Alien Technologies and the rest of the Bridge Team.

"I interpret it as meaning that they will appear on *Prowler* some time within an eight of hours. Some sort of teleporting by the sound of it. They said 'tomorrow,' and that would seem to mean a day away. Their planet, like their sun, rotates very quickly."

"Then we must be ready for them. They clearly have some advanced technology, but they may not be expecting an attack. I, of course, shall lead my Heroes. Follow me with whatever weapons we can use without damage to the ship. Technology, Weapons, you will prepare every weapon we have that might be useful in conquering them. Oh, and make sure Telepath is awake. It might get us useful information from their minds."

Strategist was not consulted. He was used to that. He had long ago concluded that his captain, although undoubtedly brave and aggressive, was not very bright. Telepath might, of course, detect that thought; but Telepath was intelligent enough to work out that Strategist would know that he might. Simply doing nothing made a certain kind of alliance there. Alliances were something which had occasioned Strategist a good deal of thought. They did not come naturally to the kzinti, for whom the largest natural group was the pride, and packing hundreds of them into a spaceship caused stress. Clans were, of course, much larger than prides, but essentially an alliance of prides. Alliances of individuals was a radical idea. Exploring new and radical ideas was a part of how Strategist saw his job description.

Far-Ranging Prowler was heading for Altair One under the full thrust of its gravity-motor. Coco and John Wayne appeared on the bridge as promised the following day. They were not images on a screen, but three-dimensional and apparently solid, and they glanced around with keen interest, looking fearlessly into the eyes of the captain and each of the bridge team. It would have been considered the most appalling insolence in any species, including the kzin. Captain held his instinctive reaction in check.

"Captain," John Wayne said, "I understand you mean to land on our world. We call it Glot, by the way. At least, that's as close as we can get in your spoken language."

"You understand correctly," Captain told him grimly. With remarkable self-control, not to mention an unadmitted hint of caution, he had decided that he would not scream and leap at them just yet.

"Well, we've given the matter a certain amount of thought, and this is really rather embarrassing, but, frankly, we don't feel a meeting would be a good idea. We had hoped for an exchange of ideas, but you don't seem to have many. Of all the possible relationships we might establish in principle, you don't seem to get beyond eating us or enslaving us. Neither of which, after extended reflection, look to be a whole lot of fun. And if you tried your ideas, you might damage us. Or, much more likely, we might have to damage you. So we have reluctantly come to the conclusion that the best thing for you to do is to copulate off."

Captain, not for the first time when dealing with the Dilillipsan, was rendered speechless. Telepath, unable to stop himself, howled in terror.

"We shall land, whatever the results of your *thinking*," the captain told them contemptuously. "And then I shall hunt you down and rip your entrails out with my bare claws."

Coco and John Wayne looked at each other.

"Oh, you won't find us, you know," John Wayne told him brightly. "We shall simply move to a different time. Our religious studies require us to do a certain amount of time-travelling, so we shall just all move somewhen else. A few thousand years in the past should do it. That will avoid unpleasant complications all round."

Coco gave him an odd look but didn't speak.

"You . . . travel . . . in . . . time?" Captain ground out the words with difficulty.

"Yes, just like Rod Taylor. Don't you? I thought everybody did it. Even the humans do it."

Had Captain thought to pursue what the Dilillipsan meant by *humans*, subsequent history might have been very different. He was, however, too preoccupied with this matter of insolent slaves, an idea comparable to his earlier thoughts on insolent food.

"How?" He demanded.

"Well, that would be rather difficult to explain," replied John Wayne, cheerfully. "In any event, I don't think your primitive physics has the terminology to express it."

Many things in the Heroes' Tongue are insults, but "primitive" is generally regarded as a compliment. It implies connection with the *sthondat*-defeating progenitors of Old Kzin.

"You will reveal it under torture," Captain told him, a little calmed by the compliment.

"Oh, I don't think so," John Wayne told him. "You see, we won't be around."

They disappeared. The captain's scream and leap ended in empty air and he landed on the deck in a somewhat less than dignified manner. He surveyed his officers, hoping one of them would laugh. None did, and they turned to preparations for the landing.

Down on Altair One, Coco and John Wayne were discussing their first contact. "You don't think they are semi-autonomous avatars of something with genuine intelligence, do you? Sort of avatars made of meat?" Coco asked. John Wayne thought about it.

"We made that mistake with the human beings for a long time. No, I think they are more like wasps. There is a sort of hive-mind, which is extremely stupid, and the individuals are a bit brighter. Brighter than the hive-mind, that is. Brighter even than wasps. The hive-mind directs them to go out in spaceships and make slaves of other species and also to make their young. Using sex, I expect, just like the human beings."

They both laughed boisterously at the thought. There's nothing quite as funny as a pornographic movie made by a totally different species. Coco and John Wayne had watched dozens of human porno-flicks, or what they thought were porno-flicks, before the joke had begun to pall. Still, they liked straight comedy best. *Dunkirk* had been particularly hilarious. (The moment when the Stukas dived on the artillery battery was positively convulsive. They watched it again and again.)

"No, seriously, if their hive-mind wants them to run around to different planets and eat whatever they can find palatable and enslave everything intelligent, I can't believe that they have much to offer us." Coco was thoughtful. "And I am sure you were right in thinking that they assumed our avatars were like them. Sort of autonomous and intelligent on their own."

"Yes, it's a considerable disappointment," John Wayne admitted. "But perhaps we should have given them a chance. They might be prepared to trade. Human beings do it quite a lot, with each other."

"I don't remember Shere Khan trading in *The Jungle Book*," Coco said. "Maybe tigers don't. These certainly didn't give any sign of it."

"These tiger folk can't have met human beings yet," John Wayne said reflectively. "But it won't be long before they detect their television signals. I wonder what will happen then."

"I suspect the human beings won't much want to be eaten either. And probably they won't want to be enslaved. It will be interesting to find out, there could be some really complicated arguments for both sides,"

Coco said, recalling *Spartacus*. "Possibly involving those gun and bomb things the human beings used with each other. I never thought that showed much feeling for logic, you know."

"Their hive-mind is too stupid for logic. So is that of the tiger people, I am afraid. Not the one on the spaceship, anyway. At least there are some signs the human one has developed a bit recently. But there's a good chance that the tiger folk will be the same as the human beings used to be. And if one side uses logic and reason and the other side uses guns and bombs, it's not altogether clear that the logic will win. Which makes being illogical quite logical really."

"I don't expect it will work out that way," John Wayne objected. "If the tiger folk look like winning with guns and bombs, the human beings might use them back. They were pretty good at killing each other before they saw sense. The tiger folk may need a bit of guns and bombs argument before they see that logic is a lot cheaper. I don't recall Shere Khan ever used a gun...These might be different, of course."

"I don't think the human beings have come to logic for logical reasons. They seem to have got there by telling each other lies. They've rewritten their history so as to make people think that they can't use guns and bombs without being intensely bad mannered. It's not much of an argument. Better than guns and bombs perhaps, but not really convincing."

"True," John Wayne admitted. "You know these lies are fascinating. It's all a matter of bandwidth. The lower the bandwidth, the easier it is. You'd think evolution would make it harder to get away with it."

"I expect it does. Give them time. Just a few of

our lifetimes and they'll have evolved enough to see the awful waste involved."

"In the meanwhile, I must say I could get to really enjoy it . . ."

When, like the Dilillipsans, you have no natural enemies on your planet, and when there are certain problems with movement once you have matured, communication becomes very important. So does fun. They worked overnight preparing a city for the kzinti.

A new star shone in the sky that night: *Far-Ranging Prowler* descending on chemical rockets. Before long the details of the city became visible from the kzin ship, but they were puzzling. Rocking with laughter, the Dilillipsans reabsorbed most of their avatars. All of them, planetwide. Unlike human beings and the kzinti, they didn't have to be close to each other, or rely on mobile phones, to pass the word around. They warned their children not to move for the next few days, explaining that it was a matter of life or death.

The children wanted to know the details, of course, and took some convincing, but the arguments were flawless and backed up by comprehensive records. The children would watch carefully and see for themselves. They weren't big on trust, but the hypotheses had high *a priori* credibility.

Captain led his Heroes in the landing, of course. They descended on a number of well-armed gravity-sleds, and spread out on foot, weapons at the ready. They had discovered only one city on the entire planet, which seemed strange, particularly as it was not a very big one. The captain had landed close to the city, which is where the action might be expected, others had landed further afield to find out if there were outposts of single homes scattered about hidden by the trees, of which there were a lot.

Captain recalled the conquest of Chunquen. Rich industrial cities, bordered by wide blue seas. The locals had been feeling proud of themselves because, despite the fighting between the sexes, they had just sent a rocket to the nearest of their moons. Telepath had translated their excited and boastful broadcasts to one another. *Far-Ranging Prowler* had been scout for a squadron of dreadnaughts then.

Gutting Claw and the sibling dreadnaughts, *Spine-Cruncher*, *Sthondat's Leg-Bone Crusher Leaving it Crippled* and *Careless Blood-Spiller,* had landed infantry and put a stop to their boasting.

They had been passing over the seas to the next continent when the Chunquen missiles rose from their undersea ships. *Spine-Cruncher, Crusher* and *Careless Blood-Spiller* had closed to destroy the primitive devices. Another missile was detected heading toward the main encampment which the kzinti had established on the first continent. The kzinti, having only encountered peaceful space-faring races in the Eternal Hunt up the Spiral Arm, had had little experience of war.

Captain had been at a conference aboard *Gutting Claw* at the time, dealing with the agreeable subjects of dividing up land, loot and slaves, and the recommendations for the award of Names to appropriate Heroes, and he remembered Feared Greiff-Admiral's puzzlement that the enemy had fired only one missile rather than a volley at each of the ships and at the kzin ground installation.

The reason had occurred to Greiff-Admiral and to

Captain simultaneously. Captain remembered leaping to the com-link, screaming to his ship to boost out of orbit. *Gutting Claw* did the same. It was too late for the other ships and the ground troops. When the electromagnetic pulses from the thermonuclear explosions cleared, three kzinti dreadnaughts and several thousand Heroes had been converted to unstable isotopes, their very atoms dying. Greiff-Admiral himself had gone to the arena over that blunder, when the Supreme Council of Lords heard about it, and Feared Zrarr-Admiral had taken his place. Captain had sometimes thought that had he been in Feared Greiff-Admiral's fur he would have gathered together what remained of his fleet and headed beyond the frontiers of the Patriarchy; but presumably, when one was an Admiral, honor prohibited such a course.

It was, the episode had taught him, unwise to assume anything about a new world, or to take even an apparently easy Conquest for granted.

Then he wondered if these new aliens could overhear his unspoken thoughts. Perhaps they were telepathic. The Ancients had had telepathy, as they, apparently, had used faster-than-light travel. Some students had speculated on a possible connection between the Slaver power and the telepathic ability which kzinti possessed to a greater or lesser degree, even though the two species were not contemporaries by billions of years.

What if this new species had FTL technology? To discover such a secret would give him more than a Full Name, let alone a mere partial Name (why, even particularly distinguished NCOs might hope for partial Names). It would mean adoption into the Riit Clan itself!

◇   ◇   ◇

Strategist looked around. The sled he commanded had come to rest in a long valley, the far end of which twisted out of sight. The sky above was a darker, purpler shade than he was used to, with long stringy clouds streaky and fast moving. There were groves of trees in the valley and long grass blowing in the stiff wind. In fact it was almost a storm by kzin standards. That would be the rapid spin of the planet, of course, transmitting unusually high levels of energy to the air masses.

The trees tinkled. Their leaves seemed almost metallic, and moved constantly, as did the branches. Each grove seemed to consist of three or four large mature trees and a greater number of smaller bushes. Higher up on the slopes of the hills, the trees were much denser. There was no sign of animal life, except for insects, some of them flying. Creatures like wasps, as big as his head, flew around and made an irritating deep drone. Some of the trees had fruit on them, which the insects seemed to be feeding on. Strategist's nose quivered with disgust. Clearly very low-grade life forms.

"I want infrared detectors for picking up animal traces," he instructed his sergeant. "There must be some. All this vegetation must be food for the very primitive animal species, and they in turn food for the less primitive. And we know there are some advanced life forms on this world. The less advanced ones must therefore exist. Find them. I want to know of anything bigger than a *strovart*. And I want a fence of wires around our position, able to stun or kill anything that attacks us."

His reasoning was essentially sound, but there

were, unfortunately for him, some false assumptions buried in there.

Strategist sniffed the air. High in oxygen. Much too high for convenience, one could get intoxicated on it at this level. And it was strange that there was so much. Forest fires usually turned it back into carbon dioxide at levels lower than this. Continent-wide forest fires had happened in the remote past on his own world. And wind rates like this should make thunderstorms and lightning strikes happen a lot. So he had a problem here which merited some thought. Oxygen, of course, was a waste product of plant life. And a source of energy for animal life; outputs joined to inputs to produce an ecology. His forehead wrinkled. He would need to consult Technologist to see if some plausible ecological modelling could be done as they started to get results on animal types. They would, of course, slot into roughly the usual collection of ecological niches, but they might be physically different from anything known to the Heroic Race, and there might be some strange niches never seen before. Modelling would make nasty surprises less likely. Strategist didn't like nasty surprises.

He sneezed. A good deal of organic particulate matter in the air; they might have to take shots against allergy reactions. Some of these things could be mistaken by the immune system for a virus.

The captain and his troops approached the city with what was unusual caution for kzin warriors. The superior technology of the Dilillies had the effect of making the captain take precautions, so the troops advanced in small groups, others covering them, until an ambush seemed unlikely. There was nothing like the collection of tall buildings they had expected.

The city, when they entered it, was weird even to those kzinti who had seen alien architecture on different worlds. It seemed to consist of little more than ribbons of metal, with Mobius strips a frequently occurring feature, with vegetation growing through it, and a few tall trees, planted in scenic locations. A plinth with a most peculiar statue on it occupied their attention for some minutes. Then they found the rails. They were a pair of some sort of metal, possibly aluminium, less than an arm span apart, and disappearing behind the strips of metal and the trees in both directions. Some sort of road?

"We follow them, that way." The captain ordered. They had gone only a few hundred paces when they heard a whistling sound and a curious regular pounding. Coming around the bend was some sort of monster with eyes and a face wearing an imbecile smile. It bore no resemblance to the creatures they had seen, and it puzzled the kzinti, who were of course unacquainted with Thomas the Tank Engine. Possibly, they thought, it was a local god, something like a moving idol. It ran towards them on wheels connected by rods, mouth agape, and screaming with apparent excitement. They opened up with massive firepower, and it exploded, leaving almost nothing behind.

The captain pondered the ineffectual attack, and inspected the remains of the monster. The absence of blood worried him. The absence of almost *anything* worried him. Even a war machine should have left more than this, a quantity of what a human being would have thought looked rather like the result of scraping the burnt bits from overdone toast. And which, moreover, was being rapidly dissipated by the ever present wind. They went back to following the rails in the direction from which the thing had come, to find the track terminated in a large but empty shed.

Exploring from the shed in different directions led to more inconsequential discoveries. There were lakes and canals, one of which contained a small replica of what an informed human being or Dililly would have recognized as the *Bismarck*, though the armament in its turrets, which the kzinti had taken at first to be rail-guns, turned out to be dummies. When the metal of these various artifacts was analyzed, they turned out to be common alloys, with a large amount of the aluminium which was found in ordinary clays on many worlds. There was nothing the automated mining and factory facilities of the big carrier could not easily synthesize. Sitting forlorn and solitary in another shed they found a copy of the British State Coach. This yielded some small amount of gold, which the kzinti valued as ornaments and a source of coinage, but of course their physics had enabled them to synthesize it for generations. The coach was too small for adult kzinti, but Captain could, he supposed, present it to Feared Zrarr-Admiral as a plaything for his kittens. Working out what were the seats and doors enabled him to make an estimate of the occupants' size. Unfortunately, this had no relevance to the Dilillipsans—a fact he could hardly be expected to guess. There were no rare earths in worthwhile quantities.

Captain was more than a little disappointed. One totally pointless attack didn't appear to be much ground for glory, he hadn't lost a single kzin. Losses in battle were taken to be a mark of success, so he could hardly claim one. He doubted any kzinti would want to settle on the planet, even if game were imported: it was too far away from anything. Population pressure was not a problem on Kzin worlds, given the kzinti's predilection for death-duels. Its alien industrialization, such as it was, seemed useless. The search continued but no trace of the natives or their advanced technology was found. They had gone . . . somewhere.

Captain concluded heavily that there was little worth bothering with. There were the insects, probably existing in some symbiotic relationship with the vegetation, and some small animals, according to Strategist, but nothing to make a worthwhile hunt. They seemed to feed on dead and decaying vegetable matter, and there were not many of them. They had a peculiar metabolism that led them to excrete what was, for their size, very large amounts of carbon dioxide. Without that, Captain thought, the oxygen levels on the planet would be even higher than they were. Telepath reported they were not sentient. Alien Technologies Officer dissected a couple with the aid of an electron microscope, and reported that he *felt*—he could not give precise reasons—that their cell structures had been artificially altered to give them this peculiar metabolism. This was also disquieting in a vague, undefinable sort of way—another indication of a science beyond Kzin's own. Why would the natives—if it was indeed their handiwork—want animals whose only use seemed to be to produce carbon dioxide? It hinted at unpleasant potentials for bio-weapons, but no facts into which one could sink a claw. There was still no trace of either of the life-forms which they had seen previously. No footprints, no factories, no houses, no nursery areas, no cemeteries or crematoria for their dead. Only the one strangely ineffective god or war-machine.

There were considerably more animals living in the sea and rivers. These were also not sentient, and their dead bodies washing ashore (they floated with the aid of bladders, also filled with carbon dioxide, which they apparently extracted from sea-water), seemed to provide much of what proteins the ecosystem contained. The people, it seemed, would be the only profitable product of the planet. Kzinti tended to have a fairly high turnover of slaves, and there was always a demand for them on kzin worlds.

But the people were nowhere to be found.

Kzinti on a hunt are nothing if not thorough. Had any sentient animals been lurking in hiding, they would have been found. Had they burrowed underground, kzinti tracking devices would have detected disturbed soil or rock. There were a few caves, but they were empty. There was one curious detail about the caves in limestone areas: the stalactites and other calcium carbonate formations seemed to have been removed. Contemplating this, the alien's boast that they could travel in time came back to Captain. Was there . . . *could* there be . . . some connection? He dismissed the thought.

They searched the ground with high-resolution cameras from space, and visually from the highest parts of the strange buildings. They set off small bombs such as a human geologist might have recognized to detect any hidden subterranean chambers. Using technology developed to deal with the Chunquen, they explored the contours of the seabed. They flew to the tops of hills to survey the country around, and they explored canyons and valleys.

Finally, Alien Technology Officer reported to Captain, "They've gone."

Captain thought hard. He did not want to end up in the arena, and the more spectacular, prolonged and expensive his failure here, the greater the chances of that became. At present, things had not gone too far: he had landed on a planet which turned out to be uninhabited. He had not wasted too many resources yet, or cost the Patriarchy any assets. No one could blame him for making a mere reconnaissance-in-force of the planet, particularly if the bridge recordings of the alien conversations were quietly destroyed.

The locals must have disintegrated themselves. The disintegrators would be valuable weapons, but where were they? The idea they had really travelled in time returned, and again he dismissed it. There were too many paradoxes involved. Or he *almost* dismissed it. Better not to dwell on such things...for a race that really had time travel would be a threat indeed...It was impossible. But the Ancients had had FTL, and that was impossible, too. And the inhabitants of this planet, whether one race or more, were without doubt very clever. He remembered the strange, leering smile on the face of what he did not know was Thomas the Tank Engine. It seemed to mock his perplexity.

He had done his duty in ensuring there was neither threat nor treasure on this world. His report would presumably be filed and forgotten in the Imperial bureaucracy (the kzin were terrible as bureaucrats, which was the main reason why they were always looking for slaves with record-keeping skills). He urinated formally on the ground to claim it for the Patriarch, and gave orders to return to the ship.

"There is a problem, Captain," Strategist informed the bridge team as they gathered in the control room. "The ecology makes no sense. The only animal life is either insectoid or things that scuttle around in the detritus of the forest, nothing bigger than a paw. There are larger things in the sea, but on land, absolutely no carnivores."

"And the aliens who came here. There was something strange about their minds, they were not in the right *place*," Telepath said shrilly.

"Why is that a problem, Strategist?" Captain asked dangerously, ignoring Telepath.

"Because evolution works in predictable ways. If there is a huge supply of food, then creatures evolve to devour it. If there is a huge supply of vegetation, as on this world, then there are inevitably lots of herbivores. And when there are many herbivores, there are carnivores. But there are few if any herbivores, and no carnivores. It is absolutely impossible. Further, there is the single city with no real signs of housing and certainly none outside. We are missing something. I recommend a closer study until we find it."

This settled things for the captain. Anything this intellectual idiot wanted to do was obviously a stupid idea.

"Overruled, Strategist. We have higher priorities than solving academic problems of no interest or importance to the Patriarchy. We leave immediately." He hoped for some kind of argument, which would have justified his taking Strategist's throat out, but there was none.

"Delete those absurd so-called communications records, Technology Officer. They were obviously some sort of malfunction of the computing machines. I've never trusted them, and I was right. Prepare for takeoff. We shall log our experiences on the planet and pass the reports back, but we have no reason for delay. That is all."

Strategist watched him stalk from the bridge and shrugged internally. Not all captains of small warships were fools, but for some reason he had been cursed with one of the more foolish. Quick reactions, yes; courage, enormous. Brains and capacity for thinking, zero. The usual story, high birth beat brains. One could only hope he never got promoted. He'd be a menace were he to command a proper fleet. Telepath caught his eye and nodded almost imperceptibly but said nothing.

Back on Glot, the children were allowed to move again. They'd been good except for the one that had started Thomas, and who had lost his toy in appropriate punishment. Everyone started extruding avatars for various reasons, including keeping the numbers of animals down.

"I do feel a bit sad about it all," John Wayne told Coco. "A whole culture, with all its splendor and wonder, all gone. Look how much we've been enriched by exposure to the human beings, even when we've only seen them on their old movies. And another species, it could have had so many insights for us, so many puzzles, so many interesting things to think about."

"We wouldn't have had much from this lot," Coco argued. "They'd want to eat our avatars, and enslave them. Face it, they just wouldn't have been fun. And something that's been puzzling me, how on earth did you say what you did?"

"What did I say?"

"That stuff about travelling in time. I think he took you seriously."

"Yes," John Wayne sounded very pleased with himself. "It was a lie. I've always wanted to tell a lie and of course we can't do it in the ordinary way. I mean you need a barely intelligent alien to tell it to; one of those low-bandwidth ones, if you can call them intelligent at all. So there he was, and there I was, and I thought, this is my big chance, and I might not get another anytime soon. So I did it. I lied like a human." He gave the Dililly equivalent of a beam of pride. "It's not even particularly difficult. But I hope we meet up with some more aliens soon, because I think I could get to quite enjoy telling lies. We'll have to make one of those spaceship things so we can go looking for them."

Coco thought about it. "That's an interesting idea. It will take a few hundred years, of course. No time at all by our standards, but the human beings and tiger folk will have done new things by then. And it will have to be quite big. Lots bigger than the ones which just left."

"Oh, there's no hurry. It will be an interesting problem. We couldn't extrude a whole spaceship, but we could do it in bits. The lifting and carrying and sticking things together will have to be done by avatars. But if the kzinti and human beings can figure it out, it can't be too hard."

The wind blew, and the wind blew, and the wind blew, as it always did. And the bushes and the trees with their crystalline leaves moved in the wind and tinkled like a billion tiny bells. The leaves flashed and glittered. Just for a moment, one of the bigger trees had some of the leaves flash what looked remarkably like a picture of a spaceship balanced on a tower of flame. And the tinkling sound was a little bit like laughter.

TWO TYPES OF TEETH

◆　◆　◆

Jane Lindskold

Jenni Anixter was one of the happiest people in the universe. Born at a time when aliens had been little more than a matter of speculation and rumor, she had seen them become a reality in her lifetime.

Her happiness showed in the lines lightly etched into her round face, in the way she moved her plump body as if dancing, in the bounce of short, untidy mahogany curls. That happiness might keep someone from noticing the thoughtful expression of her dark gray eyes. Certainly, this aura of happiness meant that, despite her numerous academic degrees, Jenni was often dismissed as just a wee bit frivolous.

Now, Jenni herself was among the first to admit that the kzinti hadn't proven to be a very *nice* reality. They might be real live aliens, but they were also war-like, focused on conquering and enslaving any sentient race they encountered. Non-sentient species gathered in along the way were a bonus, like sprinkles on an ice-cream sundae.

But, nice or not, the kzinti were a reality. Due to them, Jenni Anixter, who had studied medicine because there simply weren't scholarships and grants for those

41

who wanted to specialize in hypothetical alien biology, found herself in much demand.

She was courted by a branch of ARM that very carefully didn't name itself but had "Intelligence" (itself a euphemism for other, less genteel-seeming activities) written all over it. The members of this agency who came to speak to Jenni in her cramped little lab had clearly read all her papers. Jenni was flattered. Not many people bothered to read speculations on alternate biologies and the psychologies that would evolve along with them.

But these agents had done so. Moreover, they wanted to give Jenni a very big, very fancy new lab. Along with the lab would come lots of resources, an extensive budget, and even a few assistants.

There were, of course, conditions that went along with this largesse. Jenni would need to relocate to a very isolated Intelligence station, a base with an address so secret even Jenni couldn't have it. Instead, she was assigned a postal drop and a new e-dress. She was assured her correspondence would be rushed to her. Needless to say, she had to agree to having all her correspondence—in-going and out-going—reviewed and censored.

None of these conditions bothered Jenni. Her last serious relationship had ended in an argument over silicon-based life forms—specifically as to the likelihood thereof and would humanity even recognize such unless they bashed into or rolled over our collective feet.

Jenni's family had long grown accustomed to hearing from her only through short notes on holidays and birthdays. Jenni didn't doubt that her relatively introverted personality had been a major factor in causing

Intelligence to select her over one of the handful of co-professionals who shared her esoteric interests.

Time passed. Jenni settled happily into her new home. There, in addition to her new lab and extensive budget, she was given three assistants: Roscoe Connors, Ida Mery, and Theophilus Schwab. She rather suspected that at least one of them, if not all three, reported to Intelligence, but that didn't bother Jenni in the least. After all, so did she.

Not very long after Jenni was established in her new lab, she was given access to information that was unknown to the majority of humanity. What she learned about the Slavers and Protectors was fascinating, but since both these ancient races were unlikely to ever interact with humanity, what she learned was also largely inapplicable to the current problem.

More importantly, Jenni was also sent files containing raw data taken from study of wrecked kzinti ships. (There was no other kind. The kzinti did not surrender.) She voraciously read this material, then set Ida Mery to constructing data bases. The one thing Jenni refused were files containing speculations about the kzinti.

"Such information," she explained, "would pollute my own conjectures. Perhaps later, but for now give me raw data. If my conclusions match those of other researchers, all the better for you."

So Jenni was sent raw data, some of it very raw indeed. First there were tissue slices, already mounted on slides. Later there were entire limbs, flash-frozen and untampered with (beyond, of course, the circumstances that had contributed to the death of the source in the first place). Eventually, she was sent whole corpses—or mostly whole. Kzinti extended their violent natures to themselves, suiciding rather than accepting surrender or capture. Therefore, the corpses Jenni received were rarely all in one piece.

Here her practical medical experience—for she had worked both as a diagnostician and a surgeon, archaic skills that had all but died out with the coming of the autodoc—came in very handy. She dissected corpses, humming as she inspected organs and bone structures, comparing these to other samples.

From her studies she slowly built a database representation of a "typical" kzin. She discovered that—at least among humanity's attackers—there was minimal variation within the species. Kzinti seemed closely related, as the "races" of Europe had been closely related. Certainly, there was no such variation as there had been between, say, an African pygmy and a strapping Nordic Viking.

Kzinti males (she had yet to see the corpse of a female) were uniformly large—almost three meters tall. Their fur was usually a deep orange, adorned with a variety of tabby patterns that ranged from tigerish black on dark orange to paler orange on marmalade orange, to almost yellow stripes also on orange, although in this last the undercoat was sometimes of a pleasantly pale hue. Their long tails were pink and hairless. Their ears were complex, furling and unfurling in response to a wide variety of stimuli.

Yet, despite the human tendency to call the kzinti "cats" or "catlike," kzinti were no more cats than humans were monkeys. Jenni went out of her way to stress this in her reports, but she didn't know if anyone was paying attention.

In fact, what use her reports would be to Intelligence, Jenni did not know, nor did she care. She was happy learning new things every day, unhampered by mundane constraints regarding equipment or funding. In some vague sense, she was even happy to know that she was helping in the war effort, especially since she herself did not need to go to war.

Then came the day when they brought her a live kzin.

Somewhat alive might be a better way to put it. The kzin was floated into her largest lab, still encased in what looked like a ship's emergency freeze unit. Beneath the frost, he appeared to be wearing a spacesuit of peculiar configurations.

"Fix him," was the order that came with this surprise delivery.

Jenni, slightly less happy than she had been, agreed to try.

Human voices wakened him.

The listener remembered the explosion. He remembered how the bulkhead had come at him, how he'd held up his hands, claws extended in a vain attempt to stop armored metal from smashing into him. There had been pain, then darkness. He'd thought he was dead.

When he came around, he wished he were dead. This wasn't because of the pain, although that was considerable. However, a warrior of the Patriarchy did not admit pain as a consideration in matters of life and death.

No. What made him wish he were dead were the voices.

Later, the listener would realize he was hearing through the open communications unit on his suit's helmet, the default setting of which was to fasten on any active channel. At the time, he was not capable of such coherent thought. He simply heard voices, human voices, speaking Interworld, a language he had learned because it was always useful to know what your enemy was saying.

"We're down in what looks like a combination engineering and gunnery deck, Captain. It's a real mess."

"Survivors?"

The captain's voice was strong and firm, but its pitch and timber identified it as female. The concept of a female as captain of what must be a warship was still a strange one.

"Doubt it, Cap. Looks as if someone set off explosives. What didn't boil away from contact with vacuum has painted the walls with fur and guts."

The listener felt pleased at this confirmation that he might indeed be dead. He was even more pleased that the self-destruct had worked. The Patriarchy's policy was that neither ships nor crew should be taken. As the Patriarchy knew from experience, much could be learned even from a damaged ship or an uncooperative prisoner.

Reassured that he was dead, the listener drifted on background waves of alien speech, not even trying to understand what was being said. Then an excited burst of speech roused him.

"Captain! We may have found a live one! He's buried under a bulkhead. Looks like it came down and protected him from the worst of the explosion. He doesn't look good, but the telltales on his suit show live."

"Careful! He may be playing dead to lure you in."

A coarse laugh, a sound that didn't express humor as much as disbelief.

"Maybe, but it's not going to do him much good. The bulkhead kept him from getting smeared, but he's not a pretty sight."

"Can you capture him?"

"Well, Captain, I don't think he's going to be running anywhere anytime soon. In fact, I doubt he's going anywhere under his own power for a long time—if ever."

The listener felt himself being shifted. Pain shot through him.

Human hands lifted him. Something was attached to his suit. He felt himself being moved, but try as he might, he could not break free. Had they actually gone to the trouble of restraining him? He felt a surge of pride that they recognized him for the danger he was.

He was aware of being examined as he felt a sequence of jolts of pain so acute that he lost his ability to follow the alien language. Words washed over him. Some, at least, he thought, were directed at him.

Human voices had wakened him. Now, smothered by their babble, grateful for the darkness that claimed him, he drowned.

"The prisoner was found after a battle," the man from Intelligence explained, leaning in a proprietary fashion against the large freeze unit that now dominated Jenni's largest lab.

After he had come to stay at the research station, the man had told Jenni to call him "Otto Bismarck." This was so obviously a pseudonym that Jenni still tended to think of him as "the man from Intelligence," or "MFI," transformed into "Miffy" for short.

She thought the name gave the man a certain distinction he otherwise completely lacked. He was so neutral in appearance as to be completely forgettable: brown eyes, light-brown skin, brown hair cut to average length, average build, average height, average features. The one thing that would set him apart in a crowd was his exceptional physical conditioning, but Jenni had no doubt that Miffy could make himself look soft and flabby if the need arose.

Miffy went on. "Usually a kzinti crew suicides and a self-destruct takes out the ship. Best as we can reconstruct, this one would have followed protocol, but he was already down and out. Between his suit—he was wearing a hardened vac suit—and the bulkhead, he survived. The self-destruct did take out key areas of the ship, but not the compartment this one was in."

Jenni nodded. Taking this as encouragement, Miffy continued.

"The ship's doctor was worried she couldn't keep the prisoner alive, so they popped him in a freeze unit. It wasn't built to hold a kzin, but the hope was his suit would take up the slack. Best as we can tell, it did. At least the telltales haven't shifted to indicate a deceased occupant."

Jenni didn't ask how the man from Intelligence knew which indicators meant what. Knowing things like that was part of his business.

"If you can read that suit panel, I'll need a translation," she said, "as well as anything else you've learned about the suits, what they do, how the hardened variety differs from the standard."

She pretended not to notice how Miffy stiffened. She could almost hear him saying, "That information is classified, released on a Need To Know basis only." Then, as clearly, his automatic conservatism was immediately countered by the realization that if anyone "Needed to Know," it was the doctor that Intelligence hoped could save this improbable patient.

Miffy cleared his throat to swallow his automatic response. "I'll have the information downloaded to your terminal at once."

Jenni studied the figure in the freeze unit, wondering how severe his injuries were, if she could even bring him out of the freeze without killing him in the process.

"How much time do I have?" she asked.

"As much as you need," Miffy said. "Of course, the sooner we can talk to him, the better, the more lives that may be saved."

Jenni nodded again. "I'll do what I can."

"That's all we can ask."

Fiddle-faddle, Jenni thought. *You do realize that what you're asking for is little short of a miracle?*

The Kzin came conscious. As soon as he was certain he was alive, he tried to kill himself.

This proved to be impossible since he was strapped down so securely he could hardly move a finger. However, he felt better for having made the attempt.

Now that he had resolved that he could not kill himself, the Kzin set about assessing his surroundings without giving away that he was conscious. Knowing how sight-dependant humans were, he did not open his eyes. His ears were slack against the pillow on which his head rested. He struggled against the impulse to unfurl them in order to hear better.

Sound told the Kzin that he was the only creature breathing in the room, but it was likely there were several recorders, both visual and audio, trained on him. He attempted to hold his breath and learned that his breathing was being mechanically assisted. After ascertaining that, he next isolated the sounds of several devices and tried to guess what they did.

When he shifted, he heard one device begin to beep more rapidly. This was the sound he had heard when he had attempted to kill himself upon waking. A monitor of some sort. Likely he would have company soon.

The Kzin flared his nostrils. Most of the scents meant nothing to him, registering as vaguely "medical." He sought the scents of urine and feces, for both would tell him something about his condition. He caught neither. This indicated that he was probably being fed via tubes, the nutrients carefully calculated so that his waste production was minimal.

That was interesting. He had not thought humans knew enough about kzinti biology to devise such formulas. Perhaps they had been able to analyze what was contained in his vac suit. That wasn't good. He wondered what else they had captured.

To divert himself from this uncomfortable train of thought, the Kzin analyzed his own body. He didn't feel a great deal of pain, but then again he didn't feel a great deal of anything, especially below the waist. He suspected a spinal block or some similar technique.

The alternative was too horrible to contemplate. It would mean his limbs had been amputated. How could he escape then? Could he even kill himself? Was he fated to spend the rest of his life, long or short, as a captive torso impaled upon the claws of the enemy?

The sound of a door sliding open, the feeling of fresh air moving against the fur of his face, interrupted this unhappy train of thought.

A human voice—male, the Kzin thought, although in the higher registers—spoke quickly, with great animation. "We thought we should wake you, Dr. Anixter. The monitors seemed to indicate that the captive had come conscious at last."

A sound the Kzin recognized as a human yawn. A scent, vaguely floral, mingled with that of several humans. Less distinctly, a rank odor he associated with weapons and those who carried them.

"You did right, Roscoe," came a voice, human female, heavy with drowsiness that did not completely mask a note of authority. This, then, was someone accustomed to being in charge. "I'll review the tapes in a minute. Let's take a look at the patient."

Fingers touched the Kzin at various pulse points. As these points were different on a kzin than on a human, the assurance with which they were located told the Kzin that this Dr. Anixter knew something of kzinti physiology.

The sensation of being touched helped the Kzin to focus on his body in a way he had not been able to manage before. The body tends to neutralize sensations that are not being actively stimulated, otherwise no creature could do anything other than feel.

He decided that other than the possible spinal block (or amputation?) he was not receiving any pain-controlling medication. This made sense, since most of these caused drowsiness. The "at last" included in Roscoe's initial speech would seem to indicate that the humans wanted him conscious.

"Is he awake?" Roscoe asked. "The readings from the monitors are conflicting."

"I think he is, but probably he is disoriented," Dr. Anixter replied. "Let's stimulate his senses."

The Kzin fought not to tense his muscles. He knew what sort of stimulation the interrogation officers at a kzinti base would employ. None of them would be in the least pleasant. Torture was dishonorable, but it was astonishing how far the definition "stimulation" could be stretched.

Braced against pain, the Kzin was surprised when instead he heard the rush of water interwoven with the sound of the wind sighing through tall grass and the flapping of leaves. Involuntarily, his ears twitched, so did his tail.

"Ah . . ." said Dr. Anixter. She sounded pleased. "There's been a shift in brain activity."

"I saw his ears move, too," said Roscoe helpfully.

"Yes. But we've seen that before," Dr. Anixter said, not so much in reproof, rather as if she valued accuracy, "and some muscular response and nostril flaring. However, at no other time have the physical motions been accompanied by this much brain activity."

"So is he playing 'possum'?" Roscoe's tone was guarded, tense.

"Perhaps. Perhaps he is merely coming conscious, but not fully alert. Let us not assume malicious intent where what we are encountering may be nothing more than confusion."

Roscoe gave a sort of dry laugh that had nothing to do with humor.

"This is a kzin, Doctor. A live kzin, a trained member of a warship's crew. Of course it's malicious!"

"Perhaps . . . I'll sit here for a while with him, see if he comes around and tries to communicate. Would you bring me a reader and the tapes of his vitals over the last couple of hours?"

The Kzin recognized that although this was phrased as a question it was actually a command. So did Roscoe. Immediately, there was the sound of feet against a floor made from some hard material.

Roscoe paused. "Shall I bring you something to eat, Doctor? Some coffee?"

"That would be nice."

Roscoe's feet moved again. The door slid open, then shut. The Kzin heard breath indrawn then exhaled in a long sigh. Of annoyance? Frustration? Some other emotion?

Recorded birds sang. Water splashed over rocks. The wind joined the doctor in a duet of sighs.

"He's been conscious for a week," Miffy said, his voice tight with frustration, "and he hasn't spoken a single word. We've interrogated him in both Interworld and the Heroes' Tongue, but not a single word. Why won't he talk?"

They were seated in Miffy's office, he behind his desk, Jenni in a comfortable chair, a cup of spiced chai in her hand. Despite the tension radiating from the man she supposed she must consider her boss, Jenni was enjoying the opportunity to relax. There had been very little time for such since the Kzin came around—nor, now that she considered it, in the weeks before while she had struggled to save his life.

There were times Jenni longed for those days when all the kzinti had been to her were slices of tissue on slides and dismembered body parts. Dealing with a living alien was much more complicated.

She thought Miffy's question had been rhetorical, but he was glowering at her impatiently, so she said the obvious.

"Well," Jenni replied patiently, "why should he talk? You wouldn't expect a human captive to speak to interrogators in a similar situation, would you?"

"Not if he was a trained soldier, no," Miffy admitted. "And all the kzinti we meet are trained soldiers. Tell me, do you think he understands Interworld?"

"I do, actually," Jenni said. "I've studied the tapes and the spikes show activity similar to when he is spoken to in the Heroes' Tongue. I can show you..."

She reached to activate her portable screen, but Miffy waved her down.

"I'll take your word for it. This isn't a case where the squiggles will mean more to me than your interpretation."

He thumped his fist against his thigh, a gesture Jenni suspected he thought was hidden by the bulk of his desk.

For all his skills in reading others, Miffy forgets that the body's muscles are connected. I wonder if he's a very good poker player or a very bad one? This led to another question. *Or does he expect me to interpret the gesture and react? Does he expect me to be frightened by his impatience?*

Jenni decided that Miffy did expect her to be afraid. Now *that* was interesting. Why did he think fear would get him anywhere?

What should I be afraid of? Physical violence? Not likely. Losing this job? Possibly. However, Intelligence

*would find me difficult to replace, and even if they
did, what would that matter? I have material enough
for dozens of papers. While they could keep me from
publishing, they can't stop me from sharing the information with the small handful of people who would
actually be interested.*

After a time, Miffy broke the silence. "Do you
think there has been brain damage? Perhaps the Kzin
understands but cannot frame a reply?"

Jenni considered. "I think not. There was not significant damage to the cranial region. His helmet did
an excellent job of protecting it. Kzinti also have very
interesting skulls. I believe the brain would be better protected from impact than our own in a similar
circumstance..."

She was about to go into more detail, but Miffy
raised a hand to forestall her.

"Do you have any idea how to make him talk?"

Jenni considered. "It's possible that eventually we
might synthesize a cocktail of drugs that would make
him more persuadable, but that could take quite a
while."

"Quite a while, as in months?"

Jenni shook her head. "Oh, no! Nothing like that."

The man started to smile, but the smile faded as
Jenni finished her statement.

"Quite possibly years. You forget. He may be conscious, but he is hardly 'well.' We'd be searching for
a drug that would make him persuadable without
compromising his health, although after one such
dosing his continued health might not be an issue."

"Oh?"

"Well, I think it's likely that you'd only get one

attempt. The next time he had the opportunity, he'd probably do something like bite out his own tongue. I suspect the only reason he hasn't tried to at this point is he can't see an advantage to be gained."

Miffy blinked, but he did not protest that this was unlikely. They both knew it was all too likely.

Jenni continued. "You've tried interrogation. That has gotten nowhere. He is our only kzinti prisoner, so you cannot put him in with another such prisoner and hope to learn something from their conversation. We have discussed the pros and cons of drugs. As I see it, there really is only one remaining option."

"Letting you dissect him?"

Jenni let her horror show. "Please! Don't even joke about that. There is a great deal I could learn from a fresh corpse, but nothing that would outweigh the greater loss of having a functioning metabolism to observe."

She suspected that Miffy thought of the loss in his own terms. To him, the Kzin was most useful as a source of information, not of scientific knowledge. She felt glad that, unlike the kzinti, humanity did not routinely employ telepaths. Miffy might not like the disdain for him he would find in her thoughts.

Of course, humans haven't found the means to create telepaths as we suspect the kzinti can. Our psi talents are wild. I suspect most human telepaths would take care not to let those like Miffy know of their ability.

Does Miffy realize that, unlike him, I do not think of "loss" in terms of the information we might force from this prisoner, but of life? Has Miffy forgotten that I am a medical doctor as well as a researcher?

Has he forgotten that some of us still believe that rational answers can be found for any problem?

"I'm sorry, Dr. Anixter," Miffy apologized. "My comment about dissection was in bad taste, especially given your extensive labors to keep the prisoner alive. Do you have any suggestions as to what we should do next?"

"We could continue in our efforts to let the prisoner regain his health," Jenni suggested. "There is only so far we can go with him strapped to a bed. Despite electrical stimulation, he will have suffered muscle atrophy. Also, we are feeding him intravenously. After a while, his digestive system will cease to function. With a human patient, I could recondition it, but I have no idea whether similar techniques would work with a kzin."

"Why wouldn't they?" Miffy asked.

"For one, kzinti are carnivores. Among earthly carnivores a prolonged fast can have devastating consequences. If the domestic housecat, for example, undergoes a prolonged fast, eventually the liver shuts down. Other organs rapidly follow. For now, we're getting nutrients into the prisoner, but he is also burning his own body fat. When that is gone, those nutrients alone may not be sufficient."

"That doesn't sound promising. What do you suggest?"

"We continue in our rehabilitation efforts. The prisoner must be permitted out of bed. I suspect exercise is more crucial to kzinti than it is to us, both for physical and mental well-being. With exercise will come appetite."

"It's risky," Miffy said, his tone considering rather

than dismissive. "What's to keep him from committing suicide?"

"He understands Interworld," Jenni said. "I suggest we explain matters to him. Do kzinti have a saying equivalent to 'Where there is life, there is hope?'"

"I have no idea," Miffy said, "but I can think of a few sayings that might get through."

He considered options for long enough that Jenni was actually beginning to drowse in her chair.

"Very well," Miffy said. "We'll give your approach a try. In the condition the Kzin is in, you say we can't risk drugs—even if we knew which ones would work. Right now he won't last long off life support, and that rather limits other options. We might as well try the carrot and keep the stick in reserve."

"Not the carrot!" Jenni exclaimed. "Never the carrot. Rather we must try the flash-heated steak."

With consciousness, the opportunity to think, to meditate, had returned. This was not at all pleasant. Hour upon hour, the Kzin considered whether he might have managed to somehow get himself free, if once he was captured he might have done something to end this dishonorable state.

Eventually, he decided he could not have done so. That settled, next he considered what to do. He was tightly strapped down. The straps were padded and not unnecessarily uncomfortable, but they were also quite unbreakable. Perhaps if he had not been injured . . . but he doubted if he could have broken the straps even then.

For a time after he came conscious, the Kzin had managed to fool the humans into believing he was not quite alert. During those days, he had learned a few useful things, including that he was the only captive and that wherever he was being held was within human-held space.

This period of listening inactivity ended when Dr. Anixter stated quite clearly—and the Kzin wondered if the statement had been for his own benefit—that she was certain he was shamming. That ended the usefulness of such a charade for, thereafter, nothing of any significance had been said within his hearing.

When at long last the Kzin had shown himself conscious, a male human who called himself Otto Bismarck had come to speak to him. Unlike Dr. Anixter, who struck the Kzin as rather soft, even for a human, Otto Bismarck was all corded steel cables. Despite his muscles, Otto Bismarck did not act like a warrior, yet the Kzin thought he knew precisely what this human was. The Heroes' Tongue did not have a single term for such a position, but humans used one simple word: spy.

Despite his skinny frame and lack of weapons, this Otto Bismarck was dangerous, a warrior whose weapons were information rather than claws, edged weapons, or firearms. Many kzinti would have scorned the human's profession, but the captive could not. His own professional field was too close for him to dismiss spycraft without dismissing himself.

Shortly before the disastrous voyage that had ended with his capture, the captive had been selected to train as an Alien Technologies officer—specifically as a Human Technologies officer. If he was fortunate and showed himself willing and capable, he would eventually be instructed in the lore of various captive races, even that of the long-vanished Slavers, whose technologies were occasionally found, and once understood, had dramatic impact upon those lucky enough to discover them.

As a Human Technologies officer, this particular kzin had been taught Interworld and drilled in various aspects of human culture. Unlike the kzinti, who never permitted themselves to be taken prisoner...

(This particular kzin had to remind himself that he had not *permitted* himself to be taken captive. Circumstances beyond his control had led to this shameful situation.)

...humans were taken captive with disturbing ease. Even the bravest could be interrogated by means of telepathy, although this option had to be used with prudence lest the telepath—never stable at the best of times—be rendered useless for the immediate future.

Despite his training in human cultures, the Kzin was surprised when, following his routine physical a few days after his first meeting with Otto Bismarck, Dr. Anixter dismissed her assistant. Usually, the humans came to see the Kzin in pairs. If one of the straps that bound his limbs needed to be loosened for some reason, a veritable army attended the procedure.

The Kzin took these precautions as a compliment.

But today, following an examination that had become so routine as to no longer be humiliating, Dr. Anixter pulled a chair close to the bed on which the Kzin was bound and waved her assistant away.

"No, Ida, I don't need any moral support. I'm just fine. Besides, you don't think I'll be alone, do you?" She gestured vaguely at the ceiling and walls. "Otto Bismarck wouldn't miss this interview for all the raw resources in the Belt. Besides, I'm certain the usual guards are standing by."

Ida—a severe-looking woman who reminded the Kzin of a narrow-bodied burrow hunter—sniffed, but departed as ordered. When the door swished open the Kzin caught a whiff of male sweat, metal, and mineral oils. Dr. Anixter had been perfectly correct. Guards were indeed standing by, more than usual.

"Very good," Dr. Anixter said, settling comfortably into her chair. "Now, we're going to have a talk. I've studied your readouts extensively and I'd bet my life—in fact, you might say I *am* betting my life—that you understand Interworld."

The Kzin was fascinated. As part of his training, he had spent some time with captive humans. Dr. Anixter smelled excited. Yes. There was a touch of fear, but this was outweighed by something else . . . Anticipation?

He wished his training had been more extensive, but even his teachers dismissed humans as a slave race rather more annoying than otherwise. Understanding the subtleties of their emotional landscape was not a priority. It was enough to know how to control them.

Dr. Anixter paused as if to give the Kzin an opportunity to confirm or deny her speculation as to his ability to understand Interworld. When he did not react, even to a twitch of his ear, she sighed and shook her head. Her gentle smile—so unlike a kzinti snarl that it did not raise even a faint attack reaction in him—did not leave her rounded features.

"Very well," she continued. "I have spoken with Mif . . . Otto Bismarck, and he agrees with me that it is unlikely you will regain your health if you remain strapped to a bed. Otto is very eager that you regain your health. I, of course, would hate to lose my star patient. Therefore, as of today, we are going to begin a course of physical therapy—physical rehabilitation."

The Kzin had to fight not to unfurl his ears in astonishment, but he thought that Dr. Anixter might have noted a twitch. She did not comment, but went on with her explanation.

"You would probably be interested in knowing how well you are healing."

Again the pause inviting him to agree or disagree, but this time the Kzin managed to suppress even an ear twitch.

Smiling gently, as if they had just shared a joke, Dr. Anixter continued. "I have promised not to tell you how long you have been here, so forgive me if my references to time are vague. When you were brought in you were in terrible condition. Long bones in your legs had been broken multiple times by something falling on them. Your hands were in bad shape as well. From recordings I was shown later, you'd apparently tried to hold up a bulkhead.

"You'd lost a considerable amount of blood, but internal injuries were less severe than we had first imagined. Your vac suit was hardened. That, combined with the angle at which you fell, preserved you from damaging organs beyond our ability to repair them. The worst was some damage to your lungs, but that marvelous basketwork rib cage of yours is so much more nicely designed than ours—no rib-ends to poke into the lungs. Your head was protected by your suit helmet—and by your singularly tough skull."

She paused and looked thoughtful, doubtless reflecting over her labors.

"Our efforts to save your life were helped because the crew that rescued you—or, as you doubtless prefer to think of it, 'captured' you—also salvaged some medical gear before a back-up self-destruct mechanism took out the remainder of your ship."

The ship was gone then, the Kzin thought. Well, at least his family had the comfort of thinking him honorably dead—not that there would be over many to mourn him, a nameless junior officer. His father had many sons and, in the manner of traditional kzinti, saw the promising ones as much as rivals as ornaments to the household.

"Cosmetically," Dr. Anixter went on, "to be honest, you didn't do too badly, since you took more crushing damage than cutting. Your helmet protected your ears and face. We did need to shave areas of your fur to facilitate surgery, but most of that is growing back nicely."

She smiled, this time not so gently. Although the fur on the back of his neck rose, the Kzin felt instinctively that this teeth-bared expression was not intended for him. Dr. Anixter's next words confirmed this impression.

"Otto Bismarck said I should tell you that you were shaved repeatedly, so that you cannot use the rate of fur-growth as a means to calculate the time you have been in our custody."

This Otto Bismarck may be her supervisor then, the Kzin thought, *but not one she particularly likes. Yet that does not fit the interactions I have witnessed. Perhaps they are more rivals than master and slave or commander and soldier. She reigns in the medical areas, he elsewhere—and in matters such as how much I may know, Otto Bismarck is the master.*

"As of this date," Dr. Anixter said, "your condition is no longer critical. However, as I have painstakingly explained to Otto, you are also not 'well.' Indeed, it is likely you will begin to decline. Already, despite the use of electrical stimulus, you have suffered considerable muscle atrophy. New bone must bear weight if it is to develop properly. With a human patient, I could employ a wide variety of technological aids. Doubtless my assistants and I could design the same for kzinti, but that would take time...time I do not believe you have."

Again the Kzin was aware of a tightening around Dr. Anixter's eyes, a tension in her muscles.

This "time" she feels she lacks is not then completely dictated by the deterioration of my body. There is another factor as well. Impatience on the part of Otto Bismarck, no doubt.

"Therefore," Dr. Anixter said, "we're going to fall back on older methods. Already you have been eating some solid food to condition your gut."

(The Kzin winced a little at this. He had tried to resist, but the hot meat had smelled so very good... After the male called Roscoe demonstrated how they could use a muscle relaxant to make it impossible for the Kzin to lock his jaw, resistance had seemed not only futile, but foolish.)

"Now we must condition your body. We will begin with upper-body exercises while you are still in bed. Soon, very soon, I hope, you will graduate to walking about."

The Kzin considered what he would do when Dr. Anixter unstrapped his arm. Perhaps he could make amends for being weak enough to eat the hot meat.

"My people have a saying," Dr. Anixter said as she

rose from her chair and moved to unfasten the straps that held the Kzin's right arm. "'Where there is life, there is hope.' I don't know if you have a similar saying. In any case, I think you should see the logic of this one. Someone who could break his hands attempting to hold up a bulkhead is not immune to the value of being alive."

She paused with her fingers on the strap. "However, although I would like to believe you are capable of listening to an appeal to reason, I must warn you that precautions have been taken to assure that you do not exploit this opportunity. You will not be killed or punished, but you will be prevented from acting in any fashion counter to what is suitable for your continued healing. Do you understand?"

The Kzin resisted either nodding in the human fashion—a mannerism quite addictive—or twitching his ears in the kzinti equivalent of the gesture. His heart was beating very quickly, his breath coming fast and short in excitement. Doubtless the humans could read this on their monitors, but could they interpret it? He doubted it. The obvious interpretation would be that he was excited, overstimulated by the proximity of the doctor and the fact that she was apparently about to release him without the presence of guards.

No. They could not know.

Those swift and dextrous human fingers—weirdly clawless though they were—moved to undo catches. He felt the strap loosening, sliding down. Heard the fastener click against the hard material of the floor.

Quickly, Dr. Anixter stepped back out of reach.

"Why don't you try flexing your elbow?" she suggested.

He did, but not in the fashion she might have expected. Although his arm was stiff and weak, he moved with what for a human in similar condition would have been incredible speed. Claws extended, he went for his own throat.

Swift as he was, his weakness betrayed him. He was too slow, the grip of his formerly broken fingers surprisingly flaccid.

Dr. Anixter pointed a finger at him. Too late, the Kzin saw that a tranquilizer gun had been attached directly to her hand. Shaking her head ruefully, she shot him.

"I was so hoping you'd choose to listen to reason."

A few days later, Dr. Anixter once again dismissed her assistant—this time the eager young male called Theophilus—and pulled a chair next to the bed in which the Kzin was strapped.

"Now, we're going to have a nice talk again. I'm going to assume that not only do you remember what I said about your receiving physical therapy, but that you also remember what I said about the conditions under which you would receive that therapy."

When the Kzin did not respond, Dr. Anixter sighed deeply and her ever-present smile faded.

"I know you understand me, but if you prefer one-sided conversations, very well. I suppose you think of your silence as resistance, but I think the need goes deeper. Refusal to speak is the only freedom you have..."

The prisoner nearly unfurled his ears in astonishment. This human thought so very strangely, yet there was something of truth in what she said. Did that also mean there was truth in that odd idea that life and hope were inseparable?

He had thought the idea an outgrowth of the human's strange creed of pacifism, for every kzin knew that life was only of value when it was spent for glory, honor, and, possibly, advancement.

Despite himself, he found he was listening—not merely hearing—for the first time.

At that moment, a siren went off. So did all but the emergency lighting and power to the medical monitors. Dr. Anixter's smile returned and she began to speak very quickly, her voice hushed.

"We should have a moment's privacy. You doubtless think your only value to us is a source of information, but we've already learned a great deal. Miffy—I mean Otto—is becoming impatient. I have heard rumors that kzinti consider torture dishonorable—although I've heard other stories, about humans being eaten piece by piece while kept alive, that make me wonder. Whatever your interpretation, many humans don't view torture of an enemy as wrong. If you work with me, we may be able to save you from that, but..."

The lights came back up. The door to the corridor slid open, bringing the shrieking sound of the siren closer. Two men in battle armor, holding guns, came rushing in.

"Dr. Anixter, are you all right?"

"I'm fine. What is that racket?"

"Something went..."

The soldier stopped. Looked at the Kzin. Obviously decided not to speak in front of him.

"Ask Otto Bismarck."

"You may report to him that I'm fine and so is my

patient," she replied. "The lights dimmed, but the Kzin is no longer dependant on life support. Thanks to Otto Bismarck's forethought, his restraints are quite primitive, nothing that could be affected by a power outage."

"Will you leave now?"

She rose, nodding. "I think so. I think trying to begin physical therapy after this break in routine would be impractical. I could tranq him again, but repeated doses in a short time would defeat the purpose of making him stronger."

Without another glance at the Kzin, she departed. She did not return that day nor the next, giving the patient a great deal of time to think over his options.

Jenni knew she'd been taking a risk when she'd altered the station's power systems, but she'd had to do something to permit her to say a few words to the Kzin without Miffy hearing. She thought she'd been quite clever in how she'd worked it. Futzing one of Miffy's own bugs so that not only would power be cut, but any bugs with independent power sources would also be messed up had been very neat. And how could Miffy complain without admitting how extensively this facility was bugged?

She sighed contentedly. The funny thing about Miffy was that although he had hired her for her intellect, he actually thought of her as rather stupid. She supposed this was because he had bought into the stereotype of the absent-minded professor, maybe because he worked with specialists of various types who really didn't know much beyond their own field.

However, Dr. Jennifer Anixter, M.D., Ph.D. (this last so many times over that all the B.A.s and M.A.s had been discarded as superfluous), was a generalist. How could she be otherwise when she was studying something that—until the advent of the kzinti—even she had not known existed?

Savoring her minor triumph over the snoopers, Jenni walked back to her lab. If her kzinti patient persisted in attempting to commit suicide, she supposed she'd have no choice but to let him. The other option was to hand him over to Miffy for torture. She couldn't do that. The reason wasn't just that she felt such an act would be a violation of her Hippocratic oath to do no harm. Quite simply, she didn't like Miffy.

There was a lust for dominance in the man from Intelligence that stank. True, the kzinti had beaten humans in battle over and over again. The kzinti had destroyed or looted human ships, making slaves or food animals of those humans they captured. She understood that humanity needed an edge or they were going to end up just another slave race. But what Miffy wanted was something more than an edge, something more than victory. He wanted to get one up on the Patriarchy personally. If he got the opportunity, he'd do something just to show himself as better than her patient.

She didn't know what she'd do about the problem of Miffy in the long term. First her kzin had to be gotten healthy. The rest must come later.

The next time his arm was unbound, the Kzin didn't take a swipe at Jenni or, more importantly, at himself. Dutifully, he exercised the muscles, then permitted the arm to be restrapped, and exercised the other arm. There were more exercises for the legs.

After three days—far more quickly than anyone else thought wise—Jenni decided to let the Kzin get up and try walking. He still wasn't speaking to her, but she kept chattering at him anyway.

"We have a full machine shop here," she said, trundling in before her a gigantic walking frame, "and I had one of the machinists put this together for you. Your upper body simply isn't strong enough for you to use crutches."

She grinned impishly at him. "Anyhow, Otto was worried you'd use the crutches for clubs. This walker is heavy—and bulky—enough that you'd have trouble lifting it."

The Kzin had answered Jenni's grin with one of his own, showing a mouthful of needle-sharp teeth. For a moment, Jenni was delighted. Then she noticed that his hackles had risen and his ears were folding tight.

"Sorry," she said. "I didn't mean to make you feel defensive. Funny, funny... Big, mean you reacting because little me shows you my flat, boring omnivore teeth. Really, I wonder that enough kzinti survive to adulthood for you to put armies into the field."

He glowered at her. Defiantly, she gave him a closed-lipped smile.

"I have an idea," she said. "Maybe you'd feel less defensive if you could talk to someone. Since you won't admit you know Interworld, well, then, I'll teach it to you. After all, it's possible I'm wrong about your linguistic capabilities."

"However, first we need to get you on your feet. Here's what we're going to do. I'm going to call in Roscoe and Theophilus. They're going to help you stand upright. You, in turn, are not going to bite or claw either of them. I suspect you're actually going to need to put your full concentration into balancing. You've been on your tail—quite literally—for . . ."

She'd been about to say how long, then caught herself. "For quite a while."

Getting the Kzin to his feet was easier than anyone but Jenni herself had expected. Even her medical staff tended to think of the Kzin as a sort of furry human— when they weren't thinking of him as a monster.

Jenni didn't make either of those mistakes. She thought of the Kzin as what he was—an alien, descended from a race of predators, from a culture where even a show of teeth was considered a challenge that could lead to a fight to the death. Such a species would not survive very long if its members did not heal fast and cleanly.

Still, Jenni permitted the others to think she was as surprised as they were. Best Otto did not realize how much closer to recovery the Kzin was. She wasn't really lying. Certainly the Kzin had been able to stand, but he was still weak—she couldn't resist the image—as a kitten. Certainly, he was far weaker than he himself had expected to be. His fingers had curled very tightly on the handgrips of the walker and he had shuffled forward as carefully as any geriatric case deprived of his float-chair.

While they walked, Jenni had started very simple vocabulary lessons, focusing on concrete nouns such as "door" and "floor." She avoided names. From the minimal information that had been gathered from humans who had escaped the kzinti and from the kzinti themselves, names were a complex matter within kzinti culture.

She wondered by what name or title her patient thought of himself, wished she could ask, but knew that he would never reply. That would mean admitting how much he actually understood.

This first walking/language lesson session had not lasted long. The Kzin had seemed relieved to get back into the hospital bed. The next day, he had to be hurting, but unlike a human patient, who would probably have complained, he was evidently eager to try again.

And so it went. Eventually, even the guards didn't immediately tense when the gigantic orange-furred, black-striped creature went by, his pink, hairless tail twitching with the effort involved in every step. This was foolish, of course, because the Kzin was far stronger and more mobile than he'd been on that first day he'd teetered to his feet, but humans were like that. The familiar was far less terrifying than the strange.

Perhaps the kzinti are wiser than we, Jenni mused as she walked alongside her patient, his only escort, for as she had pointed out to Otto, why should they put more humans at risk? *Kzinti do not forget what bared teeth mean, nor that an enemy is an enemy. Perhaps they are wiser. Perhaps...*

She did not fool herself into thinking that familiarity alone had led to this reduced attention to her patient when out and about. There was another reason the sight of a kzin shuffling behind a gigantic walker did not attract as much attention as before. Something had changed at the base. Something new had been brought in and captured the attention and enthusiasm of Miffy and his cohorts.

Jenni had managed to gather only fragmented

rumors, but from what she could piece together from these, she thought the new prize might be the wreck of a kzinti ship.

The Kzin found himself looking forward to his daily physical therapy sessions. He knew he should not. Getting stronger and healthier was the last thing he should desire in this place where there was no hope for escape. As long as he was unwell, he was in Dr. Anixter's custody. After he was well, she would have little excuse not to turn him over to the human she sometimes referred to as Otto Bismarck, but more frequently (although never when the man was present) as "Miffy."

The Kzin wondered at the significance of these different names, but he did not ask. To do so would be to give away how much he understood. Already, he had grown to fear his own eagerness to talk. Dr. Anixter's language lessons had robbed him of the excuse to not speak at all.

She had explained to him that although human mouths and throats often had difficulty shaping the rasps and gutturals of the Heroes' Tongue, humans had learned that kzinti could easily master Interworld. She framed this as a compliment, praise of the kzinti race's greater abilities. However, the captive soon realized that her words were also a warning that he should not resist these lessons.

On the evening following the deliciously memorable day she had taught him the words for "meat," "steak," "chicken," and "fish," her assistant, Roscoe, had used these words when arranging for the evening meal. When the Kzin refused to use any of the words for more specific types, settling on "meat," instead of giving him the hot steak that had been usual to this point, Roscoe served him fish—cold fish at that.

The Kzin did not need the lesson spelled out twice. At the first meal of the day, he requested "steak." At lunch, he was given the choice of "chicken" or "fish." Neither was his preference, but he selected chicken, since this, at least, was usually served warm. Later, a similar procedure was used to get him to employ adjectives such as "hot," "warm," and "cold" or "large" and "small."

It wasn't that the Kzin could be led so easily by his belly. He admitted to himself that he hated being taken as stupid, even as brain damaged, as Roscoe had suggested more than once. For all they fought among themselves, kzinti were social creatures, and this particular kzin (Human Technologies Specialist, if he ever would have given the title that was the closest he had to a Name) was not immune to needing praise.

Subconsciously, plump, soft little Dr. Jennifer (Jenni) Anixter was filling the place in the Kzin's mental landscape where more usually his father or war leader or ship's captain would fit. He could stonewall the others, but her approval or disapproval was becoming essential to his mental health.

He knew he was entering dangerous territory, that he should try again to take his life, but, alone among the humans, Dr. Anixter was the only one who never seemed to forget that he was a danger to himself as well as to others. When he was permitted the freedom of his hospital room/cell, she demonstrated to him how quickly the chamber could be flooded with a gaseous form of the same tranquilizer she had used on him before.

"Someone is always watching on the monitor," she said, smiling her gentle, closed-lipped smile. "They know I'll have their heads if anything happens to you. Understand?"

Pretending to understand only part, and that mostly from the physical demonstration, not the words, the Kzin nodded.

He found himself deeply impressed. In situations where a reprimand was exacted, kzinti supervisors usually settled for taking an ear. Dr. Anixter must be more ferocious than he had thought if she insisted on an entire head.

Jenni had just returned from one of her long walks with the Kzin when Otto Bismarck knocked at the door of her office. Even as she admitted him, she assessed the information he had wordlessly given her.

He came to my office rather than summoning me to his, so he wants something from me. However, he did not call ahead for an appointment, nor did he wait long after my return. The one shows that he expected me to admit him. The other . . . Impatience, perhaps? Or is it something more subtle? A signal that he does not think anything I have to do would be more important than seeing him?

Motioning her visitor to a chair, she took a long pull on the drink bulb Theophilus always had waiting for her on her return. Today's choice was hot cocoa, no doubt an acknowledgment that her walk had been through some of the longer internal tunnels cut into the asteroid in which this base was made, areas that, while not cold, were not precisely warm either.

"Hello, Otto," she said. "What may I do for you?"

She wondered if Miffy was conscious of the subtle distinction in her use of "may" rather than "can." She swallowed a laugh. She was always like this after a session with the Kzin, hyperconscious of the many meanings of words and actions, of messages that went beyond mere dictionary definitions.

The Kzin tended to be highly literal in his use of words. Was this a reflection of how kzinti thought or was it his effort to hide that he knew a great deal more Interworld than she had "taught" him?

Otto's reply was not what Jenni had expected.

"What do you know about the other project we're working on here at the base?"

Jenni blinked, covering her surprise with another pull on her drink bulb. "You mean the mechanical one? The one that has to do with some scavenged kzinti technology?"

"That one."

She decided against admitting she knew the technology in question was a ship. After all, she wasn't certain. She'd deduced it from the types of injuries that had come into her office—the base did have numerous autodocs, but some injuries were best looked at by a human medico. There had been a few verbal slips as well. She didn't want to get anyone in trouble.

"I don't know much more. I've been assuming it's something scavenged from a kzinti craft either before the self-destruct went off or after an incomplete destruction."

Miffy let slip—or was it a slip?—a look of satisfaction.

"It's better than that," he said, "or should be."

He paused, doubtless considering—or appearing to consider—how much he should tell her. Then he continued.

"We actually have an entire intact ship. It's not a very large one, but with some repair it should be functional."

Jenni made surprised and astonished noises. So encouraged, Miffy unbent further.

"From studies of past wrecks, we had gathered a fair idea of where the kzinti tended to mount their self-destruction packets. There are usually several—near the drives, near the bridge, and suchlike. A plan was evolved in which an effort was to be made to disable these packets. I won't bore you with the details of our near successes and flat-out failures, but in the end we succeeded."

Jenni knew that by "we," Miffy meant the widespread arms of Intelligence, not him personally. As far as she knew, he had never left the base.

"The ship was brought here. When I say it was 'intact,' I should probably qualify. It is intact compared to other kzinti ships we have taken, all of which—as far as I know—have been complete wrecks."

A touch of bitterness in that "as far as I know," Jenni thought. *Competition then between the spooks? Yes. I think so.*

"This ship has a functioning drive and functioning life support. The computer systems appear to be fried, as are the weapons systems."

He looked at Jenni and seemed to interpret her expression as one of disapproval when all she'd been thinking was how nice it would be if Theophilus came in with more cocoa. She really was very tired. Walking a kzin up and down corridors for hours was more demanding than others might imagine, since she never dared be anything but completely alert. She knew that her finger on the tranquilizer gun stood between her life and death—and quite likely the life or death of her patient.

"Yes," she said, trying to sound as encouraging as possible. "I can imagine it would be impossible to take a kzinti vessel without disabling the weapons systems. Computers are fragile at the best of times."

Otto seemed satisfied. At least he now zeroed in on the point of this interview.

"Without being able to access their computer, we're having difficulty figuring out how the ship works. From escaped captives, we've learned a little of the written version of the Heroes' Tongue, but, frankly, we don't have a strong technical vocabulary."

Jenni could see where this was headed and decided that seeming cooperative and eager was her best move.

"And you're wondering if the prisoner might be able to help," she said. She sucked in her lips, considering. "He might. I've gotten him using a limited Interworld vocabulary, but I will admit, it's not heavy on the technological stuff."

"I thought you said you thought he already spoke Interworld," Miffy said suspiciously.

"I did and I do," she said carefully. "However, I think he may not have had as wide a vocabulary as I believed. I think what I was seeing was an awareness of patterns and a few words, rather the way you can watch a movie with subtitles in a language you don't know, catch a few familiar words, and so 'hear' meaning that you couldn't actually translate."

Miffy blinked, then nodded. "Yes. I see what you mean. You've been teaching him Interworld. Do you think he knows enough to explain to us how parts of the ship work?"

"I'm not certain," Jenni replied. "You'd need to make your questions very concrete—not 'What does this do?' or even 'What does that red button do?' You'd need to show him—and I fear that you'd also need to permit him some hands-on opportunities to demonstrate."

"Maybe," Miffy said. "Maybe eventually. I believe at first we could manage with a holographic reproduction. No need to let him near the ship. No need to take undue risks."

The Kzin could smell a new tang—Was it fear? Was it tension?—in Dr. Anixter's sweat when she came to his room. When the door into the corridor swished open and shut, he caught another scent, that of Otto Bismarck. Something unusual was about to happen.

He learned what this was when their walk—which was along some tunnels he did not think he and Dr. Anixter had ever visited before—terminated rather more quickly than was usual at a room that managed to simultaneously seem both cramped and quite large.

The reason for this contradictory sensation was that while the chamber—a natural air pocket, the Kzin thought, within the metal ore of the asteroid that the humans had adapted and converted into this base—was ample and spacious, the only part of the chamber that was lit was a relatively small area near the center.

Without the natural olfactory and auditory cues on which he usually relied, it took the Kzin a moment to "see" what was represented within that lit area. When he recognized what he was being shown, his heart began to beat so furiously that his head swam and his tail lashed wildly.

There before him was depicted the cramped confines

of the cockpit of a kzinti scout ship. The detail was so perfect that the Kzin felt no doubt the humans had access to an actual ship. Immediately, as he might have leapt after prey in a hunting park back home, the Kzin's mind came to what he was certain was a correct conclusion.

The humans had captured this scout ship. Not the crew, he determined... Even with the scrubbers that efficiently cleansed and recycled the air in this contained environment, he thought he would have smelled another kzin. No. Not the crew, but the ship, definitely the ship.

A low growl rumbled in his throat and before he could stop himself, he turned to Dr. Anixter.

"What?" he asked. "Why?"

"A ship," she said simply. "Or rather part of a ship, a picture of part of a ship. Otto Bismarck wants you to help him understand the controls."

Most of these words had been introduced in their language lessons. Even "controls" had come up in the context of permitting him to use the food dispenser and waste disposal facilities in his room. There was one rather glaring omission and he addressed it.

"Ship?" He sketched the rounded lines of a non-atmosphere-entry-capable vessel with one claw, then the more disk-like lines of ships used for surface-to-space transit. "Ship?"

"Ship," Dr. Anixter agreed.

She held up her holopad. A parade of vessels—all human-make, the Kzin noted—glided across.

"This ship," she went on, lowering the pad, "is a kzinti ship. Otto Bismarck is interested in learning how it works."

The Kzin's mind raced. He could refuse. He *should* refuse. However, if he did so, he would be pressured to cooperate. He had begun to understand the relationship between Otto Bismarck and Jenni Anixter. He thought that in this particular situation, Otto Bismarck's will would dominate. Therefore, Dr. Anixter could only protect her patient to a point. After that...

The Kzin's spirit shrunk from the idea of hiding behind the protection of a soft, weak human—a female human, at that. He knew this last response was irrational. Human males and females operated as equals in their society, but he couldn't help his ingrained prejudice that females were weaker.

He dismissed that train of thought as irrelevant. Very well, in most cases, refusing to cooperate, even if that meant submitting to torture and even execution, was the right choice. However, this was not most situations. Suicide had been the best choice when he had thought there was no opportunity for escape. Now, however, it appeared that the humans might indeed have a ship, a ship he could fly, a ship he could use to escape.

Surely, it was now his duty to live; not only to live, but to remove the ship from human claws. What he did after that... That would have to wait. Escaping into kzinti-held territories would be his best choice; however, he had no idea if that was possible. He could crash the ship into this asteroid, in one move eliminating two of their prizes: himself and the ship. If he was lucky, he might seriously damage the base.

Jenni Anixter was staring up at him, her omnipresent smile vanished. He wondered if she could guess what he was thinking. He hoped not...

Hope. He hadn't felt that for longer than he could remember. What had she said about hope? Something about life and hope? Very well, Dr. Anixter had assured him that he would live. Now he would do what he could to assure that he had reason to keep hoping.

Unfortunately, he thought the first step of his program was likely to be rather painful. For the first time in a very long while, he found himself hoping that he would survive.

Initially, the Kzin refused to have anything to do with the holographic representation of the kzinti ship's bridge. He would not even step into the room. He did so after a time, partly coaxed by Jenni herself, partly prodded by a couple of Otto Bismarck's beefiest security officers. Then he sat and refused to answer any questions.

The next part was very unpleasant. Jenni was told to absent herself. She did so, but judging from the Kzin's reaction when later she went to check him over and take him for his usual exercise, Otto Bismarck's methods of persuasion had not been solely verbal. There were no obvious marks or scars, but a blood chemistry reading showed a high level of stress hormones. The Kzin was also quite jumpy—something not exactly pleasant in a creature nearly three meters tall and increasingly muscular beneath the loose orange-black-striped fur.

So matters continued for several days. Jenni found mild burns beneath the Kzin's fur, making her suspect some form of electrical stimulus was being used. The Kzin's appetite began to slacken. Then, on the very day that Jenni had resolved she must protest, a sleek and satisfied Otto Bismarck summoned her.

"I thought," he said, leading her down the tunnel toward the cave in which the holographic representation of the kzinti ship's cockpit was displayed, "you would like to see this. We have sound-dampening screens up, but still, keep your voice low."

Jenni did so. She didn't know whether to feel relieved or saddened by what she saw. The Kzin sat restrained in an oversized chair in front of the display, obviously attempting to answer the questions put to him by the member of Otto's staff who sat in a much smaller chair next to him.

"Why the restraints?" Jenni asked. "He seems cooperative enough."

"We had a bad moment when one of my team members forgot himself and smiled after the Kzin offered the solution to a problem we'd been stumped by for weeks. The Kzin only nicked him, but it was a warning. I think the Kzin actually prefers being restrained to otherwise. I believe he sees it as being protected from himself."

Or from what you'll do to him if he slips up, Jenni guessed, but didn't vocalize her thought. There was something uncomfortable in Miffy's body language, a sense that because he believed himself in control, he was more dangerous than before.

She'd seen the like back in pre-War days. Earth's culture had followed a creed of pacifism, but although a combination of acculturation, psychiatric counseling, and judicious use of chemical cocktails had maintained this creed, still there had been those who kept big pets—huge dogs or spirited horses—and clearly found an outlet for forbidden aggressive behaviors in their ability to dominate their pets.

She looked at Miffy. Not a horse person. In any case, making horses do precisely what you wanted was more a female kink. She decided that before the war, Miffy had probably had a dog or two, probably Rottweilers or pit bulls, maybe Doberman pinschers, but she suspected the more overtly muscular breeds would have been his type.

And now he has a kzin of his very own...How long before he begins to resent my relationship with the creature? I've overheard some of the guards referring to me as the lion-tamer because the Kzin will walk with me. I had better take measures...

So she said, "I think using restraints is very wise. The Kzin's bloodwork shows that he cannot take too much more of the tranquilizing drugs without suffering a setback. At the very least, his mental processes would be dulled, and you need those. I'd been thinking about changing my own safeguards during physical therapy."

Miffy nodded, clearly pleased by her approval.

If I'm not careful, he's going to come after me next. How better to deal with the lion-tamer who is making you feel inadequate than by taming her? I've got to be careful.

And for the first time, Jenni was not completely happy with her lovely labs and the isolated base, for she realized she was at the mercy of a man who would be ruthless if his dominance was threatened.

The Kzin had not enjoyed being tortured. However, since submitting had served his purposes, he behaved as he hoped was expected. First he had fought, then he had cringed, finally, he had begun to do as his handlers directed. It helped that he understood more

Interworld than Miffy and his assistants believed was the case.

He found himself thinking of Otto Bismarck by Dr. Anixter's nickname for him, as if renaming his tormentor gave him a measure of control. It also was a small matter of revenge for the names they called him. The favorite was "ratcat," a reference to two Terran creatures. He'd heard "warcat" as well, but while this held a degree of respect, "ratcat" was the purest insult.

He pretended ignorance and suffered, mostly in silence, although not completely. Once, he'd gotten a good swipe in at Miffy, a solid hit where the man's tail should have been. Miffy had bled most satisfactorily, almost enough to balance the pain he inflicted on the Kzin afterwards.

The strike at the smiling human had not been quite the accident they believed. Over the long days of his captivity, the Kzin had learned to discipline his response to that particular human mannerism, but *they* didn't know that. He took some satisfaction in the straps that bound him after that, proof that while they considered him humbled, they did not consider him tamed.

When he began to show them how the control panel of the scout ship worked, he was careful not to tell too much, but also not to directly lie. Not only was a lie dishonorable (although he ascribed to the creed that said lies told to a captor were not dishonorable), but also if he was caught out in one, his entire plan would be jeopardized.

First, he established that he was not a pilot. These humans apparently had some idea that kzinti society was structured around hierarchies and specializations. He gave out that he was nothing more than an infantry solider, what he heard Miffy refer to as a "grunt." However, he admitted to some second-hand familiarity with how space-capable vessels were operated. After that, matters went smoothly enough.

"So," Miffy asked, "how many are needed to operate this craft?"

The Kzin considered. The actual answer was "one," for no kzin would wish to be left operating a machine when he could be fighting. However, the cockpit was furnished with three chairs, so that during slow times duties could be shared.

He decided to lie. "Two."

"But there are three chairs," Miffy called up holographic representations. "What do these do?"

The Kzin took refuge in his presumably limited vocabulary. "Operator," he said, pointing to the pilot's chair. He pointed to the next. "Operator assistant." The third chair, "Operator assistant assistant."

This led to a heated discussion between Miffy and a couple of his own assistants. In the end, they decided—or rather Miffy did—that what the Kzin meant was pilot, co-pilot (possibly a navigator), and back-up. Such redundancy was apparently common among humans. Their discussion explained to the Kzin, who had once been a Human Weapons Technology expert, the high degree of back-up systems and safeguards in human machinery.

So it went. "What does this button do?" "What does this one do?" "How do you operate this lever?"

Mostly, the Kzin answered truthfully, for his goal was to be taken to the actual scout ship. The minute some device operated other than he had said it would, that opportunity would be lost.

The hologram was useful, but only to a point. Since the handgrips and levers had been designed for kzinti hands, which were much larger than those of humans, the Kzin could only mime how the grips and levers were pulled or pushed or shoved into position. (Kzinti liked to handle their equipment. The smooth pressure pads humans usually employed were not for them.) Moreover, kzinti equipment had been designed to be operated using a manual attribute humans did not possess—claws. Overall, human fingers were more delicate and dexterous than those of kzinti, but claws changed that equation. They could be extended to make fine manipulations, to extend reach.

The humans, accustomed as they were to having fingers that stayed one length, conditioned by experience and comparison with Terran species (such as the frequently mentioned "cat") to thinking of claws merely as biological weapons, had a great deal of trouble adapting to this view.

Only after they had gone to the trouble of dismounting a control panel and bringing it to where the Kzin could demonstrate how the various shifters and buttons worked when one had claws, not merely fingers, did they believe he was not misleading them.

"Fascinating," said the man called Roscoe, a man who the Kzin had first met as one of Dr. Anixter's assistants and who he now realized answered first to Miffy. "Where we would put in a spring or some other sort of release, they simply employ a claw-tip to pull the key back into position. For many years, it has been speculated that body form would influence how problems are approached and solved, but this is an elegant demonstration of the proof of that theory."

"Write your paper later," Miffy grunted. "Right now I want to know how much more the ratcat can teach us from holograms."

"There should be more," Roscoe assured him. "We haven't even touched on the weapons systems—of course, those were pretty badly slagged. I must say, however, if you're interested in their piloting and navigation, eventually, we're going to need to take the ratcat to the ship."

"I wonder if he can tell us anything," Miffy said. He seemed to have forgotten the Kzin was there. "He says he was just a grunt."

"Still," Roscoe said, "I would think the effort would be worth it, even if we only learned a little, especially with the computers down . . ."

He trailed off. Miffy nodded. The Kzin struggled to hide his fierce joy. He had not invited torture for nothing. He was going to see the ship.

The captured scout ship was being kept in a hangar scooped from the asteroid's outer surface and fitted with sliding doors that were smooth and shiny on the inside, but did a remarkable job of mimicking the exterior of the asteroid when they were closed.

When the Kzin saw the ship—most especially when the doors into the interior of the craft were opened, and odors, stale but still present, wafted out—the Kzin found himself overwhelmed with the last sensation he had expected: homesickness.

Through all of his long captivity, the Kzin had been so acutely aware of the shame of having been captured by humans that his main emotion when he thought of those he had left behind had been apprehension.

He had dreaded the scorn and reproach he would certainly meet if other kzinti learned that not only had he been captured, but that these weak, furless, fangless primates had kept him captive. Nor had he thought that scorn would be undeserved.

Now, however, as familiar shapes and smells assailed him, he had to fight against the contradictory urges to rush forward or to shrink back. He longed for the feeling of furniture designed not only for his size, but for a backside equipped with a tail. His gaze feasted on color schemes and shapes designed around the aesthetic values of his people, his culture.

But most of all he drank in the scent of his own kind. Some of these were not pleasant—old blood, least of all—but even the rankest and most foul odors belonged to his own people.

He had forgotten the humans, so when Miffy spoke, only the restraints the Kzin wore kept him from wheeling around and taking off the man's head. The Kzin found himself grateful for the restraints. Killing Miffy—at least now—would not suit him at all.

"We've patched the holes in the hull," Miffy said, "but other than that, we've not tampered with anything. Time to earn your kibble, kzin."

Eager to stay in this place, the Kzin did his best. He demonstrated how various hooks and levers operated—using this as an opportunity to check that they still functioned. The humans had disabled power to the systems, so nothing actually did anything, but as far as he could judge, if power was restored, they would work.

The first day, they concentrated mostly on the bridge. The second day, they moved to engineering. This was not a separate deck as it would be in a larger vessel, but a compartment. Here the Kzin was forced to disappoint his captors. Although he could show them which telltales indicated what readout, even translating the commas and dots of kzinti script that labeled various devices, he could not tell them anything about how the engine itself functioned.

Miffy pressed, asking the same question in several different ways, almost certainly hoping to catch the Kzin in a lie. The result was the same. He couldn't tell them, because he really didn't know.

Roscoe finished making a note, then shrugged. "Really, boss, the ratcat's done better than we expected. I mean, except for Belt miners, who knows how every part of a ship works? We already know that the kzinti go more for specialization than we do."

Miffy reluctantly agreed and they moved on to the next section—the badly damaged computer system. Here the Kzin felt glad that they'd looked at the engines first and the humans had grown to believe he knew little or nothing about complex technical matters.

The computer was indeed damaged, the main system completely ruined. However, he was able to ascertain that some of the back-up systems connected with engineering and navigation were untouched. They would need to be manually activated, but if he did somehow manage to steal this ship, he wouldn't need to fly blind.

For the first time, the Kzin allowed himself to entertain the idea that not only might he steal the ship, he might manage an escape. Up to this point, the best he had dared realistically hope for was destroying the scout ship, himself, and hopefully a section of this base. Now . . .

Surely his first duty was to get back to areas held by the Patriarchy. He had learned a great deal about humans. Moreover, he had a good idea how much humans had learned about kzinti. All of this would be useful.

Yet the desire for revenge was strong in him. He imagined the hot battle lust that would flood his veins as he aimed the nose of the scout ship directly at the asteroid. Although the base was neatly contained, still there would be equipment on the exterior. He knew the humans augmented their power with solar energy gathered from whichever star this asteroid orbited. They captured and processed comets as well. All that equipment would be on the surface, concealed, yes, but vulnerable.

Or he might hit a thin place, near the hangar doors, perhaps, and shatter the asteroid's integrity. He imagined atmosphere rushing out, life-support desperately struggling to replace voided air and water, spilling more of this vital material into barren space. If his crash created a large enough hole, many humans would be killed. Within the base, only the guards routinely wore pressure suits, and these were not worn closed and sealed.

Overcome by panic—for the Kzin had seen that humans panicked easily—many would forget the drill. Humans were not kzinti. They were new to war. Most of the staff on this base were from Earth herself, not from the colony worlds, the Moon, or the Belt. Flatlanders were remarkably complacent, often ignoring the dangers involved in living in an artificial environment.

He remembered hearing a story about a human woman on a tour ship who had complained to the ship's captain because the windows in her cabin didn't open . . .

The Kzin was jerked from these lovely reveries by Miffy asking more questions. Obediently, he answered.

Carefully, because now there was so much to lose, he played the part of a slave, but he was a slave who scented freedom.

Over the days that followed, the Kzin was regularly taken to the scout ship. He participated in various drills meant to check to what degree the scout ship was functional.

Miffy had what he believed was a foolproof way of assuring the Kzin's cooperation. While he and his staff members wore pressure suits, the Kzin was left naked to vacuum. This was supposed to assure that he did not do anything foolish, for if he did, he would be among the first to die.

As if a kzin would fear death if duty or revenge called, the Kzin thought.

But he wondered if he had caught some infection of human caution. There were several times when he might have damaged the scout ship or some of its key components, but each time he held back. He told himself that this was because he did not wish to settle for half-measures. The humans had shown themselves quite good at repairing both damaged machines and damaged kzinti. If he were to act, the act must be final.

Self-doubt crept into his dreams. Was he really trying for the final measure or was there something else? He did not believe he feared to die, but was there something he feared more?

Did he fear going home?

Jenni watched as the Kzin grew first stronger, then, with a sudden change of mood and health, ragged and weak. His appetite was reduced so that even his favorite steak hardly seemed to tempt him.

"You've been overworking him," she said to Miffy. "I demand complete rest or I will not answer for the consequences."

Miffy glowered at her, but he could not disagree.

"We have enough information that it will take us weeks to process. I wish he'd been able to explain the gravity polarizer to us! Still, the documents he translated, especially the print manual we found, give us some idea."

"But not enough to figure out how to make one?" Jenni asked sympathetically.

Miffy shook his head. "No. Too much information is assumed. What we found was more like an operator's manual. It tells you how to use the machine and even how to do basic repairs to various systems, but it doesn't go into the theory of construction."

"Stick your arm in the autodoc," Jenni agreed, "and send me the readout. Simple to use, but providing no idea how the device itself works—much less how the human body the 'doc is diagnosing works."

"Right."

"So you can do without my patient for a few days?"

"I suppose."

This last was said grudgingly, even distractedly. Jenni decided to take a risk.

"I'd like to go over the ship myself."

"Why?"

"Did it occur to you that the Kzin might have caught something? You had the environmental systems up and running, but if there was an infection in the scrubbers... As I recall, the original crew did not survive."

"No. They were pretty much squished."

"And that could have released something nasty. I want to take a bioscanner and see what I can gather, compare it to my patient's bloodwork, do some other tests."

"Wouldn't it take a hardy bug to survive vacuum?"

"Microscopic life has survived in worse environments than within a ship, even a ship open to vacuum," Jenni reminded him. "And it's likely that some areas remained sealed."

For a long moment, she thought Miffy was going to refuse her, then his expression grew thoughtful.

"That would be a hardy bug," he said. Then his tone became casual. "Oh, why not take a look? Let me know the results?"

"Of course," Jenni replied, thinking, *Why doesn't he just write "Let me know if you find something I can use as a bioweapon" on his forehead for me to read?*

She went down to the scout ship with Roscoe. They spent enough time there that the guards got distinctly bored. However, by the time they left, she felt fairly certain the ship could function with a single pilot.

Later, Jenni drew blood from the Kzin and gave it to Ida with detailed instructions as to what she needed to look for. She asked Theophilus to do an analysis of hair, urine and fecal samples.

Then she went and took the Kzin for a walk.

"I have arranged some privacy for us," she said. "Anyone monitoring us will hear me questioning you about your recent lack of appetite and the like. Innocent conversation."

The Kzin flickered his ears in a manner that was— Jenni now suspected—an expression roughly equivalent to a human raising her eyebrows. That is, indicating surprise and perhaps a small element of doubt and incredulity.

People with fur on their faces must employ other visual clues, she thought. *I suspect there are a host of olfactory ones that I'm missing.*

She swallowed a sigh of regret. There was so much more to learn, but the time for study had ended.

"You must take that kzinti ship and flee," she said. A flaring of nostrils and flattening of ears caused her to amend her words. "Or if 'flee' is too cowardly a term for you, then say 'escape.' Whatever term you choose, I will help you."

The Kzin's ears flattened, his hackles rose, but although his body spoke of tension, his words indicated a high measure of trust. For the first time, he did not speak in the abbreviated, staccato version of Interworld he had used to this point for communication with humans.

"Why?" asked the Kzin. "Not why must I escape, but why will you help me? Strange as you are, I have never fancied you a traitor to your people."

Jenni smiled her gentle smile. "No. I also do not think of myself as a traitor. Rather, during these long months over which I have cared for you, I have had much time for reflection about humans, about kzinti, about those other aliens of which I have been told, although I am not likely ever to have an opportunity to study them. I have come to certain conclusions."

The Kzin gave a brief, human-style nod of encouragement, and Jenni went on.

"There are humans—Miffy among them—who believe that in order to defeat the kzinti, we humans must

become more kzinti than the kzinti themselves. We
must become more ruthless than our worst imaginings
of you and your culture: more brutal, more bloodthirsty.

"Miffy and his type would say that long ago, humanity took a wrong turn when it slowly embraced a creed
of pacifism. They forget how close humanity was as
a species to destroying not only ourselves, but our
native biosphere. I suspect many of Miffy's sort have
not been cleared to learn about the horrors included
in the historical record of that time, not only about
wars, but about industrial accidents that occurred
because humans channeled their aggressive natures
towards achieving their goals, rather than trying to
see the larger impact of such actions.

"Yet, even though I personally disagree that pacifism was a wrong choice if humanity was to survive
without destroying itself, there is some truth in what
Miffy and those like him believe. We humans learned
how not to destroy ourselves, but this was achieved
at the price of creating a false history, a history full
of outright lies and clever omissions.

"When, with our meeting with the kzinti, the need
to fight came again to the human race, we were shocked
to discover how very easy killing was, how quickly we
adapted the technologies of peace and prosperity to
those of war and destruction. Then, too, rumors came to
some ears that our Golden Age had in itself been a lie,
created not by our own cultural and spiritual evolution,
but seeded and enforced from without."

The Kzin bent his whiskers forward in interest,
but Jenni went on without further explanation. She
did not know how much the kzinti had learned about
Brennan and the Protectors. Not knowing this, she did

not think it was her place to spread that particular bit of information.

"So, is our pacifistic nature a lie and the warlike true?" She smiled, deliberately baring her teeth and touching first the front incisors, then the side canines. "We have two types of teeth: those designed for the eating of plants, those for the eating of flesh. No one rejects their teeth, yet we keep rejecting one or the other side of our natures: the hunter or the gatherer. One must be right, the other wrong. The truth is less easy to accept. We are both warlike and peaceful, hunters and planters, ruthless and nurturing.

"If I let those such as Miffy have their way, then I am denying what is most real. That is why I am going to help you. Not because I am a traitor, but precisely because I am not."

"I have but one sort of teeth," the Kzin growled.

"Do you?" Jennie said. "But your claws retract. Think on that. Now, here is what we must do..."

They laid their plans with great care, not only that day, for if the physical therapy session extended too long, suspicions would be raised.

Happily, the Kzin's nature was impatient rather than otherwise. Had he possessed a human's cautious desire to plan, to cover any and all contingencies, Jenni feared she might need confide in him his new value to Miffy.

Bioweapons had not been a real possibility to this point in the conflict between humans and kzinti because too little had been known about the kzinti's biology. A great deal can be learned from genetic scans, but in the end, a test subject would be needed.

Jenni knew that her patient thought his value would end when every bit of information had been extracted from him. She suspected he thought that he would then be killed. She did not think he had any idea that more likely Miffy would keep him alive so that various infections could be tested upon him.

Jenni herself would refuse to participate in such tests. She thought that Theophilus would also refuse. Ida and Roscoe, though, were of a different sort. Roscoe was Miffy with a background in medicine, rather than in espionage. Like Miffy, Roscoe enjoyed power and domination. She knew he had found it difficult to work as her subordinate.

Ida was a more complex person. A great number of her family members had been on a ship when the kzinti had taken it. Moreover, she knew without a doubt that many of them were dead. Ships with holes like that in their hulls didn't usually preserve the passengers. It was hardly any comfort for her to imagine them enslaved.

Morevover, Jenni did not trust herself to become an accomplice at one remove. Could she really refuse to try to keep the Kzin alive if he was infected with something deadly and painful? Could she keep from trying to create a cure, even if she knew that cure might be used to blackmail the Patriarchy into a surrender?

Her only choice was to get the Kzin away before he could be so used. It would be a small victory, but if one only thought of winning a war, not individual battles, then there could be no hope for victory.

So while the Kzin made certain the scout ship was capable of flight, she did her best to learn what she could to facilitate the escape itself.

There were many small details, but she was quite good at details. As she gathered codes and set trails, she was aware that Roscoe was cooking up a horrible brew in a lab she wasn't supposed to know about, that experts were coming to take a closer look at the drive of the scout ship, that time was, in fact, running out.

Had it not been for his long captivity and the practice he had acquired in suppressing his immediate response to behaviors to which most Heroes would have reacted with fang and claw, the Kzin did not think he could have kept from giving away his intent during the days that led up to the planned escape.

It was not only his own tension he must suppress— although he thought that if Roscoe came and drew any more of his blood he would have the man's ears and accept the consequences. No. He must also hide his awareness of increased tensions among the humans themselves.

Externally, Dr. Anixter seemed her usual placid, smiling self, but to anyone with a nose, she reeked of anxiety. The reasons for this, the Kzin quite understood. Not only was she taking risks in assisting with the escape attempt, but afterwards there would be consequences.

What concerned the Kzin more deeply were the changes he sensed in some of the others. Roscoe's body language had shifted. Did Dr. Anixter realize he no longer deferred to her except in form?

Miffy was more moody, some hours almost merry, others so tense that he lashed out—usually verbally—at whoever was closest. From snippets of conversation he overheard, the Kzin gathered that specialists were coming to look at the scout ship. This had made Miffy very happy. It had been the later news that someone important from ARM would be coming along with these specialists that had triggered the mood swings.

The Kzin understood, actually. In a detached fashion, he almost sympathized with his enemy. The arrival of those above one in the hierarchy was always a mixed blessing. On the one hand, they had the power to grant promotion. However, they were more likely to hand out punishment or reprimand.

And my departure, the Kzin thought, *will surely make this a visit Miffy will long remember.*

Assuming the Kzin actually made it onto the scout ship and got it out of the hangar, he was left with one dilemma. Did he try to escape as Dr. Anixter intended or did he take advantage of his opportunity to try and damage this base?

The first was full of uncertainties. He might escape the base only to be shot down later. He might be recaptured. He might make it all the way to Kzin only to find himself reviled.

Taking out the base would be so much more certain. Taking out the base would provide death with honor. Some day in the future, if word of his deeds reached the Patriarchy, he might be awarded a posthumous Name.

Really, the more he considered it, taking out the base was his best option.

But always beneath that certainty came a niggling doubt: *Or are you simply afraid to return?*

The day came or rather the night. In an artificial environment like the base, night and day could be eliminated, a shift schedule established. Advocates of efficiency often argued in favor of such plans, but even if night and day could be eliminated, the human need for sleep could not.

Yes. There were sleep sets that reduced the need for rest. Drugs that did the same—although these had colorful side effects. However, especially for those engaged in creative endeavors, there was no replacement for seven to nine hours of good, solid natural rest.

As more and more substitutes for actual dream-filled sleep had been developed, a side effect had been found. Much creative work was done in the subconscious mind. The subconscious mind used dream time to organize material, to rearrange it, to move toward that "Eureka" moment.

So it was, in some professions, where creativity and questioning were not valued, ersatz sleep was actually a preferred alternative. However, in the research and development branches of the arts and sciences, sleep had proven irreplaceable.

The base was, as such things went, a relatively small community. This was another reason that the continuous shift model did not work well. Best to have the majority of staff awake at the same time, so they would be able to interact.

The final reason was as old as human civilization. No one liked to be inconvenienced by routine maintenance. This had probably been true when such inconvenience meant dealing with the sweepers who cleaned out the cart ruts in ancient Troy. It was certainly true in the modern era.

So the base had night and day shifts. It was during the equivalent of the deepest, darkest night that Dr. Jenni Anixter and the Kzin readied themselves.

Jenni's preparations had begun earlier that day, with the baking of twelve dozen chocolate chip cookies. As might be expected of one possessed of her rounded and jovial figure, Dr. Anixter was an excellent baker. Of course, the majority of the food at the base was provided by auto-kitchens, but scientists have always surpassed themselves in finding ways to create the rare and strange.

In another day and age, this might have been a still for the distillation of forbidden liquor, but on the base, nonreconstituted food was valued more highly than any amount of alcohol. Long ago, Jenni had rigged her oven and figured out how to get the auto-kitchen to produce the equivalents of flour, sugar, butter, eggs, and the like.

Her cookies were very popular, even with those who claimed to disdain sweets, such as Miffy. She made certain to hand deliver cookies to the guards who were on watch during the late shift. They were quite grateful. Her kindness was widely known.

Later, when questions were asked about why everyone had slept so soundly that night, why the guards on duty hadn't been overly attentive to the feeds supplied to their various monitors, the cookies would certainly be remembered. For this reason, Jennie made certain to have a dozen or so set by in her private cookie jar.

She was completely confident nothing out of the ordinary would be found in those cookies, because there would be nothing to find. The drug that had contributed to that lack of attention had only been partly contained in the cookies. The rest had been in the drink dispensers—very few will eat fresh cookies without a beverage of some kind.

This last had been a bit trickier to pull off, but Jenni had been confident. In any case, all the drug components were engineered to break down within eight hours. Jenni might be determined to help the Kzin escape, but she was not suicidal enough to point a finger directly at herself. Of course, if she was questioned under proper circumstances, she would give it all away, but that would take time, and time was what the Kzin needed.

She had acquired the passcodes to the various doors (including that of the hangar) and supplied a data loop that would show empty corridors during minutes when the Kzin would pass down them. However, the Kzin had insisted she do nothing to actively help him depart.

"You must be safe in your bed when I make my escape," he'd said. "My honor insists that you have that much opportunity to clear yourself from complicity in my escape."

And Jenni had agreed. Now she lay curled in her bunk, eyes closed, breathing regular, but wide awake, listening for the sound of the klaxon that would indicate that everything had gone wrong.

At the appointed moment, the Kzin opened the locked door to his cell. The guard who stood outside was awake, but his reflexes were slower than they should have been. Even at their best, they would have been no match for those of a trained kzinti warrior.

As the guard swung his weapon around, the Kzin clipped him hard to one side of his neck, using a subdural stroke perfected when someone pointed out that killing slaves that bred and matured as slowly as did humans was a waste of resources.

The man crumpled. The Kzin paused only long enough to use the man's own tranquilizer gun to make certain he would not wake again for many hours. Dr. Anixter had assured him the drug meant for the Kzin would also work on humans, that the concentration would not be sufficient to be fatal.

Holding the tranquilizer gun in one hand, the Kzin loped down the passage. He wondered why Dr. Anixter had wanted to reassure him that he wouldn't be killing anyone if he used the tranq gun. Did she think he cared or was she really reassuring herself?

Unerringly, he headed in the direction of the hangar. His escorts had attempted to confuse his sense of direction, but they had no idea how well he read Interworld. Moreover, in a facility where there was only one kzin, tracking his own trail was easy. As a last assurance, in a few places where he might be confused, Dr. Anixter had left a small scent marker, a tiny spritz of something floral.

Three times more he had to disable guards. Each time, he used the tranquilizer rifle. The trigger mechanism was too small for his fingers, but his index claw worked admirably. Each guard was down before he—or in one case, she—was aware someone had entered his (or her) zone.

At the door to the hangar, a human would have been stumped, for the pressure pad used to enter in the passcode was behind a section of wall. The Kzin was unfazed. Extending the claws on his right hand, he inserted them into a barely visible seam, then pulled back and ripped. He'd spent a great deal of time reconditioning his arm muscles and was now rewarded for the effort. The wall material, tough stuff that would have resisted a human's best efforts, tore back.

He entered the keycode—the one Miffy himself used—and the door slid open, automatically closing once it sensed he was through. So far, all was going according to plan. However, as he loped over to the scout ship, he realized that something was wrong. The hatchway stood open and light was coming from within.

The Kzin scented the air, isolating fresh scent traces from the older ones that eddied about. One person, male . . . The Kzin's hackles went up. He had to swallow a growl. The scent was Miffy's!

Unfurling his ears, he listened, trying to ascertain whether Miffy was present or if he had been here recently and might return. Humans had an annoying tendency that way, always running off to use the 'fresher or grab a snack or drink bulb. What would he do if Miffy wasn't there? It would be very inconvenient to be warming up the drive in preparation for departure and to have the man come walking in. That period of time had always provided the most uncertainties, for the Kzin needed time not only to get the drive powered up, but to put various systems on line.

The Kzin stood poised, listening, sniffing, then slowly prowling forward, tail lashing behind him as he fought down an urge to rush forward and end the suspense. But although kzinti were known to be impulsive, they were also descended from plains hunters. Every cell in their bodies contained the knowledge that a successful hunt began with patient stalking.

He was a few meters from the open door when he heard it, a faint clink as of a tool being set down or a panel shifted. Miffy was in there, then. What was he doing? The sound was slightly muffled, so probably he was not in the airlock, nor in the cockpit.

The Kzin leapt in through the door, rifle ready. His bare feet landed soundlessly on the deck. No one. He paused and listened. Again another click and clink, this time a slight tuneless whistle. Definitely Miffy.

The Kzin began to smile. He readied the rifle. Flashing around the frame of the airlock, he placed himself so that the cockpit was at his back, the short corridor that led back to the engines and life-support systems in front of him.

Miffy sat on the floor next to one of the access hatches into the engines. He had apparently been taking images, projecting them onto a small screen. The Kzin could see schematic diagrams. He didn't wait to see more. Eschewing the tranqulizer rifle, he leapt forward, his attacking scream perfectly silent and the twisting of his features all the more horrible for the self-restraint silence demanded of him.

His hand came down. Miffy crumpled. The Kzin inspected the man quickly. He should come around in a few minutes, time enough to restrain him, then to make certain no one else was expected. There had been no other fresh scent, but that didn't mean someone wasn't coming. It was unlikely that Miffy was sending images to someone else. The Kzin had learned during earlier visits that the hangar walls were thick enough to prevent broadcast communication and that the humans had not gotten around to laying cables.

The Kzin stepped over the unconscious human and closed the panel into the engines. Then he moved into the cockpit and tapped in the sequence that would start the engine warm-up. Miffy was beginning to stir when the Kzin returned. That didn't stop the Kzin from picking him up, dropping him into a chair, and securing him.

His own previous training, combined with careful observation during these long days of captivity, meant that he knew how to inspect Miffy for communications gear. There was surprisingly little. Apparently, the watcher did not like being watched, the one who made others talk did not care to say much himself. The Kzin also shut down the small recording unit Miffy had been using.

The Kzin was fastening himself into one of the spare pressure suits when Miffy came around. To the human's credit, he did so quickly and without the usual disorientation.

"You! What..." he began, but the Kzin cut him off. "What are you doing here?"

Miffy pressed his lips firmly closed. The Kzin pricked out the longest claw on his right hand and stroked it across Miffy's face, raising a line of blood. A kzin would have felt this as unworthy of notice, but Miffy had all too much awareness of what he'd done to the Kzin. A guilty conscience is a wonderful prod. Miffy began talking.

"You'll never get out of here, so why shouldn't I tell you? Something Dr. Anixter said this evening made me realize we'd been overlooking some aspects of the gravity polarizer—seeing them with human logic, rather than kzinti. I came down here to check and she just could be right..."

He trailed off. The Kzin felt his rising growl shifting into a purr... Dr. Anixter, eh? An accident? A bit of nervous babbling? He didn't think so. What then could she have intended?

Glancing over at the piloting readouts, he saw that the engine was halfway through its warm-up routine.

"Are you alone?" he said, activating the life-support system and the back-up navigation.

"I . . ." Miffy's words came slowly, but his sweat reeked with fear.

The Kzin looked at him. "I am committed to my course of action. If you wish an honorable death, that is all one."

Miffy swallowed hard. Like many people who deal out pain and death to other people, he never really contemplated that the same could come to him. In his little world, he was the only real person, the rest were supporting cast.

"You're speaking," Miffy said slowly, "very good Interworld."

"Yes."

"I suppose you lied about other things as well? Such as how many people it takes to fly this vessel? Perhaps only one pilot is needed?"

"Yes."

"Then why should I talk to you?"

"I told you. You don't need to." The Kzin turned his head and smiled slowly, showing an expanding array of teeth. "I believe the auto-kitchen is still operational, but I cannot be certain it will remain so. Living or dead, you will be of use to me."

Miffy started talking. Fast. He had come down to the hangar alone. Dr. Anixter's comment had been provocative and he had wanted to make certain that he was the first to confirm the accuracy of her insight. Implied in this was that he also planned to claim her insight as his own.

"And now," the Kzin said, "you are ruined."

"Ruined?" Miffy's voice broke. "You mean you're going to eat me?"

"No. I would just as soon bring home a prisoner," the Kzin replied. "What I mean is that I am about to escape—or at least attempt to escape. If I am recaptured, I will explain how your carelessness—talking in front of me in Interworld although Dr. Anixter had assured you she thought I spoke the language, letting me move about the base under my own power, permitting me to see you or members of your staff enter in codes—permitted me to craft this escape attempt."

Miffy shrank into himself, his eyes widening in horror.

The Kzin twitched his ears, laughing as he had not laughed since he came semi-conscious in the wrecked kzinti war craft. Dr. Anixter had provided him with the means to send out the code that would open the hangar doors, but now he used Miffy's own unit. If the humans could trace the device's signature, it would further seal Miffy's doom, further ruin his reputation.

Miffy understood. He began to keen in wordless panic.

The Kzin watched as the hangar doors slid smoothly open. The navigation program read the stars and told him he was closer to a contested border than he had dared imagine. He entered in the command to launch. The scout ship slid out into the void.

Now was the time for decision. Did he wheel the scout ship around and crash into the base or did he attempt to get himself and his very interesting prisoner home again? Before he had seen no value in his continued life, but now... Not only did he have what he himself had learned, he had a very special prisoner. His status would go up.

The equation had changed in favor of life...of that strange intangible, hope.

As the Kzin set his course, he knew his escape was not certain, but at least he would die free, not a prisoner, no longer a captive. Miffy had fallen silent, foam flecking his lips, his eyes wild and bloodshot as he contemplated his future.

The Kzin wondered. Had Dr. Anixter all but sent Miffy to the hangar? Had she manipulated the situation so that not only would the Kzin have a hostage and a prize, but also a reason to escape rather than wreck both himself and the base? He wouldn't be surprised if she had.

Two types of teeth...If he survived the journey home, he would need to try and explain about humans and their two types of teeth.

Jenni napped until she was awakened by the klaxons. Without leaving her bunk, she activated a subroutine that would put some interesting information into Miffy's files, information that indicated how deeply he had feared the kzinti, how he had contemplated changing sides if by doing so he could buy a position as a collaborator working under kzinti masters.

Miffy would not be the first human to do this. He would not be the last.

She'd had to keep this final touch until late in the game, for Miffy must not be permitted to see these interesting additions to his files in advance. Now, however, either he was dead, taken by the kzinti, or, at the very least, a base commander who had just permitted his most valuable prisoner to attempt an escape.

Miffy's protestations of innocence would not hold up, especially since Jenni would be there to gently explain how this quite fit the psychological pattern of a man who chose to name himself Otto Bismarck.

Belting her fluffy pink robe over her flowered pajamas, Jenni moved toward the door, reacting just as she would if this was an emergency she knew nothing about. As she hurried out, she swallowed a smile, knowing that now was not the time to show either type of her teeth.

PICK OF THE LITTER

◆　◆　◆

Charles E. Gannon

2367 CE: Proxima Centauri System, Outer Belt

With the bright red disk of Proxima Centauri growing quickly in his forward screens, hn-Pilot rose from the kzin smallship's co-pilot seat. He stretched as much as was possible for an eight-foot felinoid in a cramped cockpit.

The second helmsman—rr-Pilot, who was currently flying the tiny craft—sniffed deeply as his nominal commander twisted his spine to work out the kinks of a long immobile watch. "Boredom has its own scent, evidently."

hn-Pilot stopped in mid-stretch: rr-Pilot's undeniably accurate observation was also borderline insolence. But then again, hn-Pilot's authority was borderline as well: neither had true Names, only differentiation-prefixes, and, therefore, his superiority in rank and seniority was marginal. They were also closely matched in height, weight, and speed, so neither one could be confident of victory in a formal challenge. rr-Pilot's oblique challenge was, therefore, quite canny: without contesting hn-Pilot's official command status, he signaled that he would not accept any matching assumptions regarding personal dominance.

hn-Pilot's fur rippled faintly: the kzin expression of modest mirth or amusement. rr-Pilot was stalking his objective—status—with all the canny indirection that hn-Pilot would have used, had their situations been reversed. Which was good: aggressiveness was the hallmark of any worthy Hero. But, inversely, if hn-Pilot did not effectively respond to this subtle challenge, it would mean *he* was too docile: doubly so, since he was technically the commander of the smallship dubbed *Incisor-Red*.

hn-Pilot finished his interrupted stretch in a leisurely fashion and then stooped forward, resting his arms down on the back of rr-Pilot's seat with a jarring thump. He tilted his weight forward; the seat shifted and squealed in protest.

He watched as rr-Pilot's pink, white-ribbed, scalloped-edged ears half-folded back against his neck fur: annoyance, readiness to fight if further provoked. rr-Pilot asked, "Do you need to remain in that place?"

"Yes," sighed hn-Pilot. "Yes, I do. I want to make sure you are performing your duties properly, rr-Pilot. That's part of my job as commander."

rr-Pilot's ears retracted a millimeter more, quivering. "And are you quite satisfied with my performance?"

"It is too early to say. I haven't finished observing you yet." hn-Pilot made the sardonic amusement clear in his voice. He saw rr-Pilot's jaw sag open, the points of needle-like teeth showing: the kzin "smile" was a prelude to combat, or at least, a readiness to engage in it. hn-Pilot leaned even more of his weight into the chair, which groaned under his mass. "What? Do you disapprove of my command prerogatives? You're not challenging me, are you, rr-Pilot?" Said in the mildest of tones, it was a sarcastic gauntlet waved in the air between them.

"I do not question your command, or its prerogatives. But your scent is overpowering, hn-Pilot."

"As am I." He felt rr-Pilot's body tensing against that boast, but neither the circumstances nor his physical position made resistance prudent. Since the in-flight monitors were running, there would be plentiful evidence that he had initiated violence, which could endanger the mission. And besides, rr-Pilot was seated, facing away from his commander, who was already on his feet, behind him, eyes and claws ready. rr-Pilot's ears folded back fully, taut, then relaxed: he had found a mutually acceptable path out of the confrontation: "hn-Pilot, you might want to use some of your power to tell ms-Pilot of *Incisor-Yellow* to keep properly formed up on us: he is drifting wide again."

The comment not only defused their own tense situation, but was inarguably true: in the sensor scope, the blip signifying their brother craft was allowing the gap between them to widen. hn-Pilot toggled the ship-to-ship: "*Incisor-Yellow*, eyes on the trail! Do you sleep even as you stalk?"

ms-Pilot's response was bored, but the blip indicating his ship began to close the distance: "Surely, this is not stalking. It seems to me that we are simply dragging our paws from one dry watering hole to another."

Which hn-Pilot had to admit was a most adequate description of their current mission: to escort the human robot transport—*Euclid's Lasso*—on its first post-invasion cycle from the main Centauri system to its distant trinary component Proxima, and back again. Why they were loping dutifully after this pointless,

brainless beast of a hull was beyond hn-Pilot's compre-
hension. It shipped food and other necessary supplies
out to the sparse human population of the Proxima
system; it returned with their marginal ore finds. So
far as he could tell, the human miners of Proxima
had a rather desperate paw-to-maw existence, and
were strategically and economically insignificant due
to both their poverty and astrographic position.

But that was hardly any of his concern. hn-Pilot,
like the rest of his species, was of the opinion that
there was nothing to be gained in trying to improve
the productivity of slave races through intervention.
Such intervention always—*always*—cost more than it
was worth. This was the result of language barriers,
of radically different approaches to similar problems,
and of the inevitable resentment of the enslaved locals.
But just as often, it was because those same locals
knew their own systems better than the conquerors
did. As long as the tribute required was paid promptly
and in full, the slaves could use whatever methods
worked best.

And so it was here. However, with the invasion now
in its fifth month, the kzin were admittedly having
more trouble than they had expected. When originally
encountered in deep space, the humans had not only
proven to be (mostly) leaf-eaters, but thoroughly unacquainted with the waging of war. Only later did it
become evident that their societal ignorance of fighting
and violence was a recent phenomenon, a consequence
of three-century-old mandates promulgated by their
government back in the Sol system.

But, for reasons of which hn-Pilot had no awareness, and in which he had less interest, these pacifistic

lessons—despite having been imposed pervasively and powerfully by their homeworld—had been less completely embraced by the humans of Alpha Centauri. The humans of its one habitable planet, Wunderland, and the even less conformist Belter population that was densest on the much-modified planetoid, Tiamat, had all shown surprising will, innovation and tenacity in their resistance to the kzin. However, their desperate attempts to hold back the Fleet were coming to an end, according to the routine updates hn-Pilot had been receiving. Tiamat had been thoroughly pacified now, and the belt known as the Serpent Swarm was secure enough that the Fleet no longer had to worry about surprise attacks upon its rear while pressing the offensive against the main world.

Apparently, the leaf-eaters had built their doomed defensive sphere around Wunderland in order to buy time to launch four generation ships—immense slower-than-light arks—that they were readying there. hn-Pilot did not understand that: only a tiny fraction of the system's inhabitants would be able to flee on those craft. But evidently it was a project which held great significance for the humans: they had fought tenaciously for five months now. It was, therefore, obvious that they were capable of recalling much of the Warrior's wisdom that they had forgotten. hn-Pilot and many, if not most, other kzin, took this as a mixed omen. It meant the humans had enough spine and courage to be a truly useful and self-directing slave race. But it also meant that they had a primal nature that, once awakened, remembered the bloody lessons of their evolutionary struggles. Although omnivores, they had nonetheless proven to be the apex predators of their own world. In consequence, they promised to be the most useful slave race in the kzin stable, but also the one in which lurked the greatest seeds of danger. They would have to be watched closely.

And hence, this largely pointless mission: to monitor the *Euclid's Lasso*, even though it was simply a robot barge, riding its plume of fusion fire from the Serpent Swarm belt of the main system out toward the binary. It began its journey by almost dancing into the gravitic clutches of Alpha Centauri B before the slingshot effect of sweeping close to that orange star's mass sent it on its way with an extra boost, out into the cold and the dark. Accelerating for weeks, it finally reached eighteen percent the speed of light and then cut engines, coasting onward toward the small red dot that was its destination: Proxima Centauri. Where, four months later, it arrived after more weeks of counterboosting that slowed it just enough for rendezvous with the Proximans' own intrasystem cycling robot ship. That smaller automated craft swung perpetually between the Proximans' various cargo transfer points and a trajectory which enabled it to mate and exchange payloads with *Euclid's Lasso*. After which, the bigger intersystem vessel began its return journey to Alpha Centauri, starting the same process all over again.

There were rumors that Fleet Command had considered sending a single missile at *Euclid's Lasso* to terminate its journey to Proxima, whose inhabitants would then have obligingly died off without the kzin having to lift a paw in further effort. But, probably because the leaders wanted kzin violence to be seen as deliberate rather than arbitrary, this path had not been chosen, and now hn-Pilot's two ships were trailing along in the *Lasso*'s wake, ensuring that its contents, as well as their recipients, were benign. Initial intelligence had established that there was no military presence out at Proxima, and so there had been no reason to waste the resources or time journeying out to officially subjugate it. But now that complete investiture of the main system was imminent, the higher and the mightier had decided that the time had come for Proxima's humans to meet, and make appropriate gestures of obeisance to, their new kzin masters.

rr-Pilot pointed at the *Incisor-Yellow*'s sensor blip. "Now he's too close. He's not going to earn a Name for piloting this way."

hn-Pilot could not keep his fur from spasmodically rippling at the sardonic quip. Not only was ms-Pilot botching the simple job of staying in formation, but Names were not earned for routine tasks like piloting, any more than they were for running swiftly or shooting straight. Perhaps, if one were to pilot the Patriarch's own cubs to safety through a swarm of enemy fighters, then, maybe, the honor and achievement would be great enough to earn a Name of one's own. But the monotony of the daily routine reminded both of them just how far away they were from such glory. Worse still, since each smallship had two pilots, the kzin had been compelled to resort to differentiator-prefixes. These subvocal sounds distinguished one from another just as numbers might have. For the Pilots, rr-, ms-, zh-, and himself, hn-, nothing highlighted the lack of a personal Name so much as having to use these tags.

hn-Pilot watched as the second craft in his formation now drifted too close. "*Incisor-Yellow*, maintain the correct distance and attitude."

There was no reply, but the blip moved back to the correct distance. Then, a hesitant message: "*Incisor-Red*, I am detecting some out-gassing from *Lasso*'s outer ring of cargo containers. Do you confirm?"

hn-Pilot glanced at the sensor plot, saw no gross abnormalities; he tightened the scan field while increasing resolution. Sure enough, there was a modest cloud of gas and minor debris vectoring away from the *Lasso*, the signatures emanating from each compass point of its round, head-on profile. hn-Pilot grunted, aimed the viewers at the closest sensor return, and increased the magnification to maximum.

He saw a diminishing puff of vapor and small parts—a metal plate, and possibly the cap-heads of several explosive bolts—rushing away down the sides of the *Lasso*. It was a strange visual effect: since the *Lasso* was counterboosting, the debris was already moving faster than the slowing ship from which it had been expelled, and so, as the detritus swept outward, it also "fell forward," in the subjective parlance of both human and kzin's spacefarers.

hn-Pilot toggled the ship-to-ship. "*Incisor-Yellow*, did you see what that rubbish was? Did something fail on the human craft?"

"I do not think so. The signatures were simultaneous and at perfectly equidistant intervals. In each case, it looked like a short explosive burst, and then modest debris. I could make out nothing more."

Reducing the screen's magnification, hn-Pilot stared suspiciously at the human craft. Its primary hull was an immense central cylinder for large-volume cargo items. Its bow—currently facing *Incisor-Red*—also housed the guidance and robotic elements of the craft.

This main hull was ringed by tubular containers, giving it the appearance of being a baton girdled by a tightly packed bandolier of long metallic frankfurters. Loaded with smaller cargo items, these containers were detachable: the Proximan communities swapped tubes of ore for tubes loaded with comestibles and other essential trade goods. But having four of these containers malfunction simultaneously, and in a cruciform pattern, did not sound like an accident; it sounded like a prelude to—

"Sabotage!" yowled rr-Pilot as the sensor plot was suddenly choked with a spreading cone of small, dense signatures spraying out from each of the four ruptured tubes. However, at second glance, it was evident that this growing debris cloud was not really a cone: it was a funnel. And the only way to escape the junk rushing at them was—

hn-Pilot pointed urgently. "Get into the open space— there, at the center of the funnel."

rr-Pilot growled, complied—and with one sharp jerk, they were in the eye of the scree-storm, unscathed. *Incisor-Yellow* was not so lucky: judging from the com-chatter and the hull's now-wavering course, its portside gravitic polarizer drive had been damaged and the crew-section breached. The craft was losing atmosphere, and a piece of junk the size of a small ball-bearing had punctured the bridge, killing the co-pilot where he sat.

"What treachery is this?" rr-Pilot's growl was low, with a hard, fast vibratory underbuzz: the sound of a barely suppressed kill instinct.

hn-Pilot was still trying to make sense of the ambush. Clearly, the humans had preprogrammed this event into

Lasso's automatic routines. But why here, so far inside
the Proxima system? And why an explosion of junk, jet-
ting out of the four containers that had obviously been
sealed with illegal explosive bolts? To destroy the kzin
escorts, yes, perhaps, but then why not ensure that the
spread pattern would create a full cone of debris, rather
than this empty-cored funnel? Simply moving to the
hull's lengthwise center-line had allowed the two kzin
craft to escape the worst effects of the—

"hn-Pilot, there is more activity."

He looked up at rr-Pilot's tone: puzzlement edged
with dread. The dense, encircling halo of debris was
beginning to fall forward around them, but less quickly,
according to the scanners. That meant that the *Lasso*
had stopped counterboosting, and they were matching
speed to maintain distance—but why was the human
craft not continuing to decelerate?

The answer was in rr-Pilot's next report: "*Lasso* is
tumbling, commander."

A tumble meant that the human ship's engines
were no longer slowing her, so the debris would stay
with all the craft slightly longer, now, continuing to
hem them in. Indeed, the human ship's spin about its
considerable longitudinal axis would ultimately bring
it end-over-end, so that the fusion drive would be in
a position to exert forward thrust.

Or, in other words, the drive's exhaust plume would
rotate straight back into the faces of the two debris-
encircled kzin smallships.

hn-Pilot saw it before the others. "One-eighty tumble
and counterboost—max gees! Now! Do it now!"

But as the last word left his wet, spittle-spraying
mouth, the blinding blow-torch tail of the *Lasso*'s fusion

drive completed its one-hundred-eighty-degree spin: hn-Pilot watched a literally blinding sun rise swiftly into his viewscreen—

—a split second before he and every other object in the two-ship kzin escort were stripped down into subatomic particles by the shaft of blue-white radiance that shot almost fifty kilometers behind the *Euclid's Lasso.*

By the time the inner hatch of the secret asteroid base finally opened, Dieter Armbrust presumed he would find himself staring down the muzzles of at least half a dozen recoilless assault rifles. What he found instead was a single slim woman of indeterminate age and Far East Asian descent. "Welcome," she said. "I am Miriam Yang."

The thirty-year-old lieutenant from Neue Ingolstadt nodded. "Yes, ma'am. You were one of the two specialists I was told might have sent the request that was the catalyst for this mission."

"Which you have carried out quite well, *Herrenman* Armbrust."

Dieter was partly flattered, partly insulted. "I am not a Wunderlander aristocrat, Dr. Yang. I do have my degree from the Uni in Munchen, and I was educated in a private school. But I am not the child of a wealthy family."

"No? Then I suppose you must be quite talented, to have received state assistance to attend a private school."

"Actually, I was not the truly gifted one. That was my older brother, Wulf. He received a full scholarship to go to the private school from the time he was a *bub*. Which meant my parents were able to save enough to send me, also."

Dr. Yang's gaze was unblinking, assessing. "Since you were not born into the *herrenman* aristocracy, I doubt your parents could afford more than half the tuition."

"Exactly half," confirmed Dieter.

"So, the Colonial Branch of the Amalgamated Regional Militia has sent me a half-genius." Yang's momentarily impish expression became severe once again. "Would you like some tea?"

Dieter nodded and followed her gesture into an adjoining room.

Dieter had expected that Dr. Yang's offer of tea had simply been an invitation to nothing more than a shared cup. But he had been mistaken. As he now redid his collar button, still stunned at the events of the preceding half-hour and the stamina of the much-older Miriam Yang, he cleared his throat.

She looked over at him: her face was composed, serene, maybe a bit defiant. "It has been a long time for me." Her tone was matter-of-fact. "And it may be much longer from here on."

Dieter cleared his throat again. "Dr. Yang, about that tea—"

She seemed to laugh; it was a muted sound. "Of course. The tea has been steeping; I hope you like it strong."

Right now, thought Dieter, *the stronger the better.* "Yes, Doctor."

She proferred a delicate china teacup. "So. You have brought the supplies I requested?"

"Yes. And we deposited the disguised reentry vehicle at the specified coordinates in the Serpent Swarm."

"It is encased in rock, to look like the other asteroids?"

"Yes." Curiosity got the better of Dieter: "Is it a delivery vehicle? For dropping a warhead?"

"In a manner of speaking. More tea?"

Dieter had not realized that he had already drained his cup. "Yes, please."

Yang spoke as she poured. "That was quite a clever trick you pulled on the kzinti escorting you. Was it your idea?"

"Partly."

Yang obviously knew false modesty when she heard it. "Not just a half-genius, are you, Lieutenant?"

"I was never sufficiently bookish, Doctor."

"Ah. A man of action." She smiled at him, glanced so briefly at his muscular thighs that he almost missed it. "How was it that the kzin did not find you and your team's habitation module within *Lasso*'s main cargo hull?"

"We were already underway by the time the escorts caught up with us. When the kzin took over the facilities that handle the *Lasso*, the documentation there indicated that her cargo was routine."

"And they believed that?"

Dieter shrugged. "Evidently. After all, they had little reason to fear a single automated transport. Just how much military gear could it carry? And what would it achieve out here?"

"So, the kzin approach problems head-on. And foresee threats in the same way."

"Hmm. I suspect it's their first inclination, but I

also saw evidence that some of them can learn to be a bit more, well, devious. Particularly if they are forced to contend with human sneakiness on a daily basis."

"Not surprising. Indeed, I was worried that they might simply eliminate *Euclid's Lasso* outright."

"I did not share your worry, Doctor. Judging from events in Serpent's Swarm, the kzin mostly observe a hands-off policy when it comes to local economies, even before a formal surrender. They have a keen understanding that damage to infrastructure means a reduction of tribute. And since *Lasso's* payload was already outbound by the time they caught up with her, they probably concluded that we had not had enough time to put a military cargo in her. They presumed it was business as usual."

"A presumption which they will now realize was erroneous."

"Well, they'll know something went wrong, but those two kzin smallships did not get a signal off. And once we take *Lasso* outsystem to rendezvous with the generation ships launching from Wunderland, the kzin will never be sure of just what did go wrong, even if they come out here to investigate."

"If there's anyone left alive by the time they come out here, that is."

Dieter swallowed and nodded. That had been the hardest part of approving the operation: knowing that it might very well condemn the population of Proxima Centauri to slow death. Because when Dieter and the rest of his team rode the *Lasso* out into the void between this system and Earth, how would the needs of Proxima be served? What would happen to the men, the women, the children? *The children . . .*

Dieter opened his eyes, belatedly realizing that he had closed them. Yang was staring at him intently. "It may not be so dire, Lieutenant. The kzin will want to know what happened out here, so they will probably come quickly. When they arrive, they will find no evidence that the locals were involved in foul play. Presuming that they will leave the fate of Proxima in human hands, either a new cycling vessel will be tasked to provide for the system, or it will be evacuated."

"But we don't *know* that's what will happen."

"None of us ever know what is going to happen, Lieutenant."

"You seemed to, Doctor."

"What do you mean?"

"I'm referring to your research proposal, Doctor. An eighty-page experimental précis doesn't get whipped together in three days. But that's how much time elapsed between the first news of the kzin invasion and the time you sent the proposal insystem by tightbeam relay."

"That is because it was already written. As you surmised. But that did not require any powers of prophecy on my part, Lieutenant, simply reasonable deduction."

"Deduction based on what?"

"Why, on the first warnings of alien contact we received from Sol's high-power lascom array. The news that the kzinti had almost destroyed one of our deep-space STL ships years ago provided me with enough information that I was able to construct a research program to help us win a war against them. In concept, at least."

"So you designed a multi-tiered set of research

initiatives based on those first sketchy reports from *Angel's Pencil*?"

"Yes, that is exactly what I did. And you must take them to Earth. And must give the Amalgamated Regional Militia's leadership the necessary information for maintaining communications with me."

"Which is to be accomplished by—?"

"Reception and transmission on my end will be by phased arrays, with the individual components embedded on native rocks that have been adjusted to maintain absolute position in relation to each other during their orbit of Proxima."

"And how do you intend to send your signals to Earth without the kzinti detecting you?"

"The components of the array will send separate, intermittent bursts, usually no more than a few per month. These will mimic the local background noise, except that the frequencies and wavelengths are rare for this region of space. It should be undetectable as a message, since the time intervals between the signals will be hours, or even days. Now, tell me: how much longer until the slow boats at Wunderland are ready to launch?"

"A month, maybe five weeks before the general exodus begins. *Lasso* will be on its way now, so as to match their vector and velocity. Once we've rendezvoused, we'll transfer our hab module and join everyone else for a long, cold nap as we return to Earth. At which point your plans can be put before the Amalgamated Regional Militia. Although I confess, I'm not exactly sure how to do that."

"What do you mean?"

"Dr. Yang, how do I get the ARM brass to listen to

me long enough to ensure that your rather expensive project is delivered to people with enough clearance, and enough clout, to make it happen?"

"You will give them my name. That will be enough."

"Just your name?"

"Yes." She filled their teacups again. "Have you ever wondered how it was that the ARM managed to exert so much control over weapons and technology development out here in Centauri?"

Dieter smiled. "I have indeed wondered about that, since ARM supposedly has no *official* presence out here."

"Just so, Lieutenant. You see, ARM has no way of working unobtrusively in a frontier environment the way it does on Earth. Back there, the entire solar system is under constant observation, and since all technological *innovation* is actually technological *evolution*, ARM's observers know what precursor innovations to look for. They simply preempt would-be inventors before they achieve their goal."

Dieter nodded, understanding. "But out here in Centauri that model doesn't work. The population is too dispersed, too disparate."

Yang shrugged. "The preferred method here is to wait, to watch, and to intervene selectively and secretly."

"So you are ARM."

"As much as one can be, beyond the Sol System, yes."

"And the research team you indicated you were gathering for this project is already assembled—?"

"—and safely hidden on another rock."

"A rock that's big enough to store at least twenty years of consumables for you and your staff."

Yang shook her head. "No. We, too, shall be in cryogenic sleep during your trip back to Sol."

"And this place?"

Yang looked casually at the walls around her. "By sidereal midnight, it will be permanently abandoned. It will appear to have been ransacked by raiders."

"Let me guess. Any records of either facility have already been erased from all files in the three Centauri systems."

"Correct. Which means, of course, that if anything happened to us now, no one would know. So at this point, I suppose we are entirely in your hands, Lieutenant Armbrust."

From her tone and unblinking gaze, Dieter wondered if Dr. Yang had meant that phrasing to obliquely prepare the ground for another intimate interlude and fresh pot of tea. He decided to interpret her words more literally: he drew his automatic and laid it beside him on the table. Yang looked at it; for the first time since he had entered her asteroid retreat, he saw an emotion pass across her supremely composed face. Well, technically, it was the *second* time he had seen the doctor without her façade of absolute composure—

She raised her eyes from the gun to meet his gaze, searching. "That is a most unusual gesture, Lieutenant."

"As you said, you are in my hands."

"And so?"

"And so, it seemed to those of us on the *Lasso* that however much good you would do here in the Centauri system, you would be infinitely more effective contributing to the war effort back on Earth. There you would have complete safety and the very best facilities in which to—"

Yang's appraising eyes became distant, cold. "A half-genius, after all." Her comment was not quite a pronouncement, was not quite spat out like bile, but it was close on both counts. She sat up very straight. "Lieutenant, I will guide you through the flaws of your conclusion. And you will not interrupt, because I sincerely doubt you have anything to add that I have not already considered."

Dieter shrugged, leaned back. And being a creature of habit, he made sure that his change of position did not increase the amount of time it would take for him to reach his sidearm.

"Lieutenant, when you awaken in the Sol system, you will indeed be in the safest, best place in which to conduct a scientific experiment. Except in this one, crucial particular: there will be almost no kzin test subjects on Earth. The kzinti are here. This is where they will work, where they will 'play.' Where they will live, die, mate, make war, make mistakes—and will occasionally go missing. A resistance organization is already being laid out quietly on Wunderland. And so the kzin will experience ambushes there. There will be hunting accidents that claim both their young and their old. There will be trips that go awry, there will be lost castaways, renegades, adventurers, wanderers. In short, the kzin will suffer the losses that are inevitable during an extended occupation. And during the years you and I are sleeping, select agents will take advantage of these unlucky kzinti. They shall provide us with our first samples. If you are squeamish, you might not want to hear what is involved; if you are vengefully minded, you might savor the details. No matter: we are fighting for our lives and we do not have the luxury of gentle methods.

"Consequently, when my team and I awaken, we

will remotely access the data compiled from these samples and from long years of observing kzin behavior and practices. And from that information and from those samples, and with the aid of the research you will cause to commence on Earth, we will eventually design weapons specially tailored to eliminate the kzin invaders."

"You mean a selective bioweapon, a tailored virus?"

"Our ambitions go well beyond that, Lieutenant. However, suffice it to say that whatever weapon is to be used against them, it will be far more effective if it is produced, and readied, here. You will have live kzin subjects on Earth eventually, but probably never enough to amass as diverse a sample base as we will have accumulated here. And besides, what good is a secret weapon if you cannot be sure it will survive deployment? If it must cross space to get here, traveling in a ship, how could we be sure that it will not also be destroyed with that ship in battle? On the other hand, if the weapon is already here, and ready to deploy in proximity to the most sensitive enemy targets—"

"Yes. I see. But why do you think we will have any live subjects on Earth at all?"

Yang raised one pencil-thin eyebrow. "Do you really doubt the kzinti will attack our home system? Be assured of this: they will. They must. Indeed, I suspect that the first attacks on Sol will have occurred before your own voyage has ended. Their gravitic polarizers should allow them to make that same journey in five, six years, at the most."

Dieter had a sudden vision of taking a shuttle down for his first visit to Earth, to the homeworld and womb of the human race, watching the disembarkation ramp lower—only to reveal a smoke-plumed panorama of devastation. He swallowed: "That's a disturbing concept, Dr. Yang."

"Perhaps. But remember: the kzinti leap before they look. I suspect Earth's defense fleets shall take advantage of this repeatedly. And with every defeat, the kzinti will leave behind new technology that we will reverse-engineer. Imperfectly, of course, but we will narrow those gaps that exist. And in the course of such clashes, you will also have the opportunity—if you are very careful—to gather experimental subjects. Not many perhaps. But you will be able to examine the kzinti in ways that even I cannot, because you will control their environment absolutely. Conversely, I will have access to an immense social sample, but must observe it surreptitiously, from hiding. However, working together, we will be able to find the strategic pearl of great price: the answer to what makes a male kzin—a *kzintosh*—tick."

"I presume you are not referring to anything as simple as biological imperatives."

"You are on the verge of redeeming yourself, half-genius." Dr. Yang smiled; Dieter wished she hadn't. The expression was so unsuited to her face that it looked more like a rictus. "We must learn about their psychology, about their inner lives. Not just what they will show us in the course of our normal interactions with them; we must have knowledge of their emotions and thought patterns."

Dieter nodded. "Of course. And when they invade our home system, we will undoubtedly take some prisoners. And with an unlimited amount of time in which to conduct interrogations—"

"No!" Dieter was startled by the loud, sharp mono-syllable that jumped out of Yang's small mouth. "I am not referring to interrogations. That would be completely counterproductive. What we must acquire is a command of their true, seminal psychology. And to do that, we will need to observe them without the trappings of culture and training. You will be in a position to separate their nature from their nurture."

"What?"

Yang sighed. "Let me put it this way: what we learn from our society shapes us, prepares us to live in a particular cultural milieu, but it does so by coercing us to privilege some instincts and behaviors over others. That is the nurture component of our maturation process."

"And nature is what we get from our genetics and epigenetics."

"Exactly. And that is where the key of the primal kzin is to be found. To put this into terms that bear upon the outcome of this war, it seems urgent to answer this question: how would a kzintosh behave, think, feel if he was *not* raised among his own kind?"

"Who knows? Perhaps they are more extensively 'hard-wired' than we are, less dependent upon cultural shaping."

"Perhaps," agreed Yang, "but I suspect we will find that they actually have a very carefully controlled cultural environment."

"Why?"

"Because what little we have learned thus far suggests that the females of the species are not merely protected and hidden, but sequestered from their own male cubs within mere months of giving birth to them."

"What's your point?"

"Let me put it in familiar terms: if you take humans away from their parents when they are toddlers or younger, they will not develop as most other children. This would be particularly true if they are put in an environment filled with daunting physical requirements, harsh discipline, and rich rewards for properly focused violence."

"So you're saying that, without their current upbringing, kzinti would be just big, cuddly housecats?"

"Nothing could be further from what I mean. They are what their evolution has made them: superb killing machines. But as in all successful societies, adult kzinti will shape their young by amplifying their optimal traits with behavioral training and encouragements."

"Perhaps all this is true, Dr. Yang, but tell me: why do we need to know what they'd be like without the cultural shaping? It's not like we're ever going to meet a kzin without it."

"No, but we might create one ourselves."

"To use in further experiments?"

"No: to use as a political liaison. Either this will be a war of extermination, or it will eventually end, through victory or exhaustion. And when that moment comes, it would be most helpful to have a kzin who considers us its mentors, its parents, its family."

Yang leaned forward, tilted the teapot toward Dieter's cup: nothing came out. "And so," she finished, putting down the pot and folding her hands in her lap, "that is why I must stay here and not flee to Sol. I must remain to perform the research that can only be performed here. And that is why you must take the details of the research agenda back to Earth: so that we may isolate and identify the key features of the kzin nature." She looked meaningfully at the handgun that was still resting on the table.

Dieter picked it up and returned it to its holster. "It seems you are needed here after all, Dr. Yang."

She nodded, her eyes unblinking once again. "We all serve different needs, Lieutenant. Do be so good as to help me prepare another pot of tea." She rose, hips swaying slightly more than necessary.

Dieter, shrugging, rose and followed her.

2396 CE: Sol System, Rearguard of the Third Kzin Invasion Fleet

Thrarm-Captain panted in open-mouthed hatred: the viewscreen showed yet another spray of glittering sparks that sought out and then converged upon the dim mote that marked the location of the rearguard's last *Slaughter*-class battle cruiser. After a moment of darkness, there was a flicker, a flare, and then a white-blue sphere, expanding sharply from a brief pinpoint brilliance, a radiant halo chasing outward before it.

"Thrarm-Captain, *Defiant Snarl* is confirmed lost. The van continues to pull ahead of us, and—"

"—And that is a good thing, zh-Sensor. The van of the Fleet is *supposed* to gain more distance. We are the rearguard: we are accomplishing our task."

"Without question, Thrarm-Captain, but were we not told to detach from the rearguard and rejoin the van when it had attained a distance of thirty light-seconds from the human flotillas?"

Thrarm-Captain's ears became more rigid but pushed downward: zh-Sensor was correct. Of course, they should never have been in the rearguard in the first place. The unexpected arrival of the second half of the human fleet, converging as scores of cannily hidden squadrons, had made a ruin of the kzinti's penultimate attack formation. The human surprise had put them swiftly and entirely off-balance: the kzin left flank had become the front, and the front had become the far right flank. Auxiliaries were suddenly in the line of battle; dreadnaughts were occluded by their own craft, unable to bring their firepower to bear with maximum effect. The third kzin fleet to attack Sol had studied and learned the bitter lessons the monkey boys had taught them during the two prior invasions. And this time, the kzin had been on the verge of defeating the spindly leaf-eaters—or so it had seemed.

Now, in the few spare moments between coordinating anti-missile fire and swatting away single-ships equipped with crude equivalents of kzin gravitic polarizer drives, Thrarm-Captain reflected upon how the outcome of this battle recalled the human martial art known as judo. The monkeys had not defeated this third invasion of their homesystem by meeting force with force, but by using the kzinti's offensive momentum against them. The Heroes of the Fleet had broken the first human formations and had pressed on, eager to bring their weapons to bear upon the great prize: Earth itself. But that had been a baited trap. The real human defenses—smaller, lighter, unthinkably numerous craft—had materialized from various points of the battlesphere, and in so doing, caught the kzinti off balance. The kzin firepower was all on the line, which is precisely where the humans did not strike. And by the time the Fleet's deployment could be altered, and the weapons of its battlewagons brought to bear, the regrouped heavy elements of the human main fleet had returned, and the rout of the kzinti had begun.

Thrarm-Captain wanted to call it a retreat, but that would have merely been a self-flattering fiction. True, the kzin had been able to throw together a rearguard to cover the withdrawal of the most important Fleet assets. And true, they had inflicted horrible losses upon the humans. But there were so many of the small enemy ships, and they spent themselves so freely, that there had been no chance to reform properly. The situation was so chaotic and fluid that it was no longer a true battle: it had devolved into a scattered collection of desperate brawls.

Thrarm-Captain knew zh-Sensor was waiting for his response and, gallingly, also knew that zh-Sensor was right: it was time for them to abandon the rearguard. The terrible strength of Thrarm-Captain's hull was not intended for hunting or attacking, but for protecting. Only chance and dire need had put his ship, *Guardant Ancestor,* in direct engagement with the enemy. His job, and his hull's very design, dictated that he keep his precious passengers out of harm's way. But, today, the humans had made nonsense of everyone's supposed missions: now, simple survival would be accomplishment enough.

"zh-Sensor, I need a close sweep of surrounding space. Helm: plot a course—shortest possible—to rejoin the main van. Communications, open a channel—"

"Thrarm-Captain." It was zh-Sensor again, but his

voice sounded different. Intrigued. Maybe puzzled. Possibly both.

"Yes, Sensor?"

"There is a Raker-class escort approaching from our aft port quarter low. It seems to be heavily damaged, Thrarm-Captain. It is venting volatiles and its energy output is irregular."

A Raker-class? Well, there still were some in the Fleet, but not many. They had been far more numerous in the formations of the Second Fleet, but very few of them had come back. Designed for stealth and swift action, they had been optimal hulls for conducting operations within the peripheries of the Sol System's asteroid belt. Unfortunately, their speed and diminished radar signature had been acquired at the expense of armor and protective screens: the Rakers had ultimately proven far too vulnerable to the humans' weaponry. "Can you establish communications with it? What is its transponder code?"

zh-Sensor shook his fine-boned head. "No response to our hails, Thrarm-Captain. Their transponder is only transmitting intermittent characters."

"Can you verify that the characters are in the Heroes' Script?"

"Yes, the symbols are clearly *Kzanzh'ef,* but the sequence is too broken up for us to know if they are part of an authentic Third Fleet identification sequence."

Thrarm-Captain felt a tinge of caution war with the stronger desire to save any of the other true Heroes of this fleet, particularly those who had fought a delaying action with weak ships against an overwhelming enemy. "How badly damaged are they?"

"Unclear, Thrarm-Captain. But energy spikes indicate

thermal flares, probably from internal fuel explosions. There have been several combustion plumes—hydrogen, we presume—that support this analysis."

"And other than the transponder signal, no communication whatsoever?"

"None, Thrarm-Cap—wait." zh-Sensor's ears stood up rigid, like wind-filled half-parasols. "They have shut down their fusion plant and are running off capacitors. Which they are turning on and off. Repeatedly."

"So?"

"Sir, the pattern of the on-off sequencing: it is the Scout's Tapping, Thrarm-Captain!"

The Scout's Tapping? Thrarm-Captain's lower jaw hung slightly; his angry, tooth-lined maw reflected faintly in the glass of an inert display screen. The humans had rarely, if ever, encountered the archaic code known as the Scout's Tapping, so it seemed increasingly likely that he stood in a position to rescue Heroes who had fought well from ships that were outgunned and outdated. But until the other ship could officially prove its identity, he had to ignore it. He knew he should not feel a simmering rage against those protocols—the monkeys' tendency toward guile and deception had made these precautions necessary—but still, they were now keeping him from doing what his instinct and the Heroes' Creed told him to do: save a ship that was obviously manned by his brothers.

zh-Sensor cleared his throat. It was a sound like a small motor starting. "Thrarm-Captain, are we to return the Raker's signal?"

"What are they Tapping?"

"That their hunt is over, Thrarm-Captain. They must abandon their ship; they ask us for lifeboats."

"Lifeboats? Why?"

zh-Sensor's voice was low. "Because their commander knows that, with his transponder damaged, we cannot authenticate his vessel as belonging to the Fleet."

The gesture was either the mark of a truly brave Hero—willing to take his chance among the leaf-eaters in lifeboats—or of a truly audacious deception. Maybe, reasoned Thrarm-Captain even as he recoiled from the implicit weakness of the act, it would be best to simply send over some lifeboats...

"Thrarm-Captain, human small-boats inbound."

Thrarm-Captain swiveled toward the targeting screens. "Where?"

"Approaching us from the lee side of the Raker, Thrarm-Captain. Our firing solution lies directly through it."

"Fire self-guiding seekers," Thrarm-Captain yowled, but knew it would not be enough. The defensive batteries of three human smallships, coordinated in interlocking fields of fire, would certainly defeat his anemic missile attack. At most, he was buying the Raker some time.

zh-Sensor swallowed. "The Raker is turning about to engage them, sir. It is re-starting its fusion plant, but it seems to be having trouble."

Well, of course; they had to shut down the fusion plant so that their on-off power pulses would come through as the Scout's Tapping. The output of a live fusion plant would have drowned out the fluctuations in the smaller energy signature, much as the roar of nearby waterfalls had, in primeval times, made the original Scout's Tapping useless. But, from a cold restart, that same fusion plant would take some time before rebuilding to optimal output.

On the main plot, the small vermillion speck of the Raker was gamely trying to come about and intercept the three leaf-green lancets bearing down on *Guardant Ancestor*. Thrarm-Captain felt his gorge rise in frustration: frustration at not turning to fight, at failing to lend his aid and firepower to the stricken Raker, and above all, at not having immediately offered to rescue his fellow Heroes.

zh-Sensor started: "The Raker is firing beams and missiles—many missiles! Large-warhead drones, evidently. Two human craft have slowed their approach, and one has been damaged and broken off. The drones are slowing, though—"

Thrarm-Captain narrowed his eyes, felt his vocal chords vibrating, quaking, as he held back a scream of impotent rage. "Those are not drones. They were his lifeboats."

"Thrarm-Captain, the lead human craft has been hit and destroyed. The second is damaged, but now reapproaching." zh-Sensor blinked at his relays. "And—and you were correct, Thrarm-Captain; the Raker discharged its escape pods and lifeboats along with its missiles—"

"—thereby making it look, for a moment, like it had superior armament. Which disrupted the coordination of the human attack. Buying more time for us, but dooming themselves when the humans resume their attack. And see, they do so even now. This time, the leaf-eaters will finish the job. And the crew of the Raker has no way left to escape."

But the Raker's fusion drives surged to life and it discharged its beam weapons in the same moment that two human missiles hit the spindly hull, along with a brace of X-ray laser bursts.

The lasers hit the Raker's tankage sections, but without any free oxygen, the result was simply a profound out-gassing of most of the remaining fuel. The human missiles, however, hit the gunnery decks, which fell suddenly and ominously silent. The interior explosions seemed a bit smaller than Thrarm-Captain might otherwise have expected, but for all he knew, the Raker's racks were dry, and one of the human warheads might have been a dud. Either way, the Raker was now all but dead: fuel already low, and its systems evidently failing, the fusion plant died out again.

But the brief fire by the kzin ship's full-powered beams had destroyed one of the two persistent attackers. The last flinched back, withdrawing along with the first one the Raker had injured. Powering its gravitic polarizer drive from capacitors only, the Raker struggled to come back about and keep up with the rearguard—but would clearly not be able to do so much longer.

"More Scout's Tapping in power pulses," zh-Sensor murmured. "They send *'Hsna'zhao.'*"

The ancient *Kzanzh* byword of resolve, even in death, *hsna'zhao* meant, roughly, "on with the hunt!" It was the exhortation of a dying Hero to his living companions: to fight on, to not risk themselves by tarrying beside one who was already as good as dead.

Thrarm-Captain growled: he could take no more of this. "Helm, distance to the van?"

"Twenty-two light-seconds, Thrarm-Captain."

Good: they could afford a little time. "Reduce acceleration to one-half. Hold steady so the Raker can come alongside."

zh-Sensor looked up: contending emotions warred

in his eyes. "Thrarm-Captain, I mean no insolence. I simply remind you of the protocols."

The kzin captain reared to his full height. "Since the Raker appeared on our screens, I have chased my tail around that very issue, zh-Sensor. I can abide these overcautious dictates no longer. This is clearly one of our own craft, crippled, but brave in our defense. The humans attacked it and they destroyed one of the leaf-eaters' smallships: we saw it with our own eyes. And they speak our language, know our Tapping, act as we would ourselves."

"A clever foe might learn all these things."

"Yes, they might, but to squander such a ploy here, in the midst of this chaos? No. That is not possible. And they have no way of knowing what we carry on board *Guardant Ancestor*, so we may safely set aside suspicions that this is a trap laid especially for us. Which leaves only one reasonable explanation: that every second we waste debating the obvious, our brothers remain in mortal danger of another attack like the last."

zh-Sensor's hide rippled sharply, once. Clearly, he had wanted to go to the aid of their fellow Heroes every bit as much as his captain. The captain turned toward his Helm and, as he gave instructions for allowing the Raker to dock, thought *it is good to lead Heroes worthy of their title*.

The kzin troopers, beamers held in a comfortable assault carry, straightened when Thrarm-Captain came around the bend in the main passageway. The squad leader made the stylized submission gesture that was a salute among them. "Thrarm-Captain, we had no word that you would be joining—"

"I sent no word: I did not wish to disturb your preparations. But I wish to see the Raker's crew for myself."

The squad leader's eyes narrowed. "Uncertainty persists regarding their identity?"

"Uncertainty will persist until I have seen their commander, have accepted his salute, and have had you search every cubic meter of his ship. Which we will evacuate and then scuttle. But I am equally eager to be the first to welcome him: if it was mine to bestow upon him, I would give him a Name."

"Sir!" The squad leader stood very straight, almost presented arms.

The floor jarred softly under their broad, well-padded feet. "Hard dock completed," announced the junior squad leader, who checked his wrist comp. "The hardwire links are mated, but still no coherent data, and no video-feed from the Raker's airlock. Their commo system is down, apparently."

Reasonable, thought Thrarm-Captain, *but in no way reassuring*. "Visual check?"

The junior squad-leader had undogged the inner hatch of the *Guardant Ancestor*, entered its airlock, hunkered down to peer through the small, thick-paned porthole that should have looked through a similar window into the airlock of the Raker. "Again, no visuals, Thrarm-Captain. The glass is smoke-smudged, and it appears that their airlock has only one emergency light functioning."

"Are they sending *anything* through the docking hardwire?"

"Yes, sir. They are pulsing it in the Scout's Tapping. They are asking if our side is secure, sir. They have no sensor function to determine that the hard dock is complete, or that we stand ready on our side."

Again, perfectly reasonable, given the circumstances. And again, not in the least bit reassuring. "Seal for vacuum ops." Thrarm-Captain's own actions suited his orders. "First Squad, force manual entry into the Raker. Stand ready to attack or assist."

The kzinti so instructed loped into *Guardant Ancestor*'s airlock, worked at the manual access to the Raker's outer airlock door, gave up, popped an access plate in its surface, revealing, among other things, a simple hand-crank. The largest of them spun the crank while the others waited. The door eventually gapped a bit, allowing the others to wedge in pry-bars and open it fully.

"The Raker is outgassing, even here in the airlock," one of them reported, consulting his paw-held sensor.

"Atmosphere?"

"Standard, but a lot of hydrogen mixed in. They must have fuel leaks throughout the ship."

A leak which Thrarm-Captain didn't want entering his own ship any longer than necessary. Hydrogen's flammability was the least of his worries: its monoatomic ability to undermine solids—metals, synthetics, composites—by simply passing through them led to a condition called brittlization. After enough exposure, gaskets disintegrated, steel sheeting crumbled like desiccated plastic. "Move quickly, then. What about their inner airlock door?"

"Battle damage, but I can hear someone pounding behind it."

"How bad is the damage?"

"Bad enough, Thrarm-Captain."

"That answer is no answer, Corporal. Tell me what needs to be done to open the door and how long it will take."

"Beam-torch: three minutes, maybe four."

"Then do it, and quickly."

"At the run, Thrarm-Captain."

Within seconds, the sparking glow of a beam-torch flickered inside the airlock. Satisfied, Thrarm-Captain caught the squad leader's eye and made a grasping "to-me" hand gesture. The kzin noncom came immediately.

Thrarm-Captain leaned their space helmets together. He muted his radio feed and said, "This concerns me, squad leader."

"The amount of time this is taking, or the possibility of treachery?"

"Both. I want you to summon two more squads to this area, but do not deploy them around the airlock. Keep them back, in staggered positions, protecting all junctures, all the way back to the main passageway and command bulkheads."

"Yes, Thrarm-Captain." And then the troop leader was gone, already summoning in the squads and preparing a defensive network with multiple fallback positions.

Thrarm-Captain toggled his radio open again. "zh-Sensor: report."

"We are now twenty-four light-seconds behind the van. This puts us abreast of the leading elements of the rearguard, now."

"Yes. And the Raker?"

"Sir, no activity at all, except that its power output continues to diminish steadily."

"The human ships?"

"The ones which attacked the Raker fell back and have merged into the front rank of the leaf-eating harriers that are pushing us before them. But nothing else: no sign of heavier human hulls inbound."

"Very well. Inform me at once of any changes."

"Yes, Thrarm-Captain. I will—"

That was when, with a shrill screech of high-pressure atmosphere, the beam-torch team cut through the Raker's inner airlock door: a brief wash of low-pressure flame flared up as it did. The operator quickly switched off the torch.

"What the Patriarch's entrails just happened?" demanded Thrarm-Captain, instinctively moving closer to the source of the surprise.

"Thrarm-Captain, the atmosphere on the other side of the door is under tremendous pressure." The high-pitched keening of the in-pouring gases almost made his report inaudible.

At that moment, a toxicity alarm started yowling and the specialist with the wrist comp looked up sharply. "Thrarm-Captain, the gas from the Raker: it's pure hydrogen. Coming in at a rate of—"

But Thrarm-Captain wasn't listening: he no longer needed to. He was too busy damning his own gullibility and rapping out orders: "Torch team, immediate return to our hull. Seal our hatches behind you. Bridge, jettison the emergency docking ring—"

The world seemed to tear itself apart around him. Before the torch team could exit the Raker's shattered airlock, its inner door was blasted off its hinges with terrible force, killing two of the team outright, disabling a third.

Following that blast so quickly that it seemed to

be part of the same event, flame came gushing into the passageways of *Guardant Ancestor.* The first roaring rush of white fire was the hydrogen combusting, knocking the kzinti down or spilling them sideways against walls and bulkheads. But hard on its heels came a thicker yellow-orange conflagration: clearly, a pressurized fuel-air explosive gas was being pumped in at immense pressure, right behind the hydrogen. The unit patches on the kzinti's spacesuits began to burn. The battery of the beam-torch cooked off, detonating with a blue-white flash and a double-toned thunder-clap.

zh-Sensor's voice was screaming reports as Thrarm-Captain picked himself up off the deck. "Launches from the Raker. More lifepods—no, not lifepods. Can't be: they are maneuvering, moving straight toward our hull—"

Of course. The leaf-eaters are going to cut *their way into my ship: why use an existing door when you can make your own?* "zh-Sensor, engage the pods with all weapons; they are breaching craft."

"Trying, Thrarm-Captain. They are too close; our weapons will not bear."

That's when the shooting started. The screaming buzz of a human heavy-coil gun was audible through Thrarm-Captain's supposedly sound-proof faceplate, along with images of hellish carnage. The squad leader, who had been racing around the corner toward the airlock, caught a full flight of the electromagnetically propelled four-millimeter, tungsten-cored steel needles. One moment he was there; the next, a vaguely bipedal mist of plasma and body parts was falling backward, a diffusing red smear. Following close behind him, a newly arrived junior squad leader was blown aside by just two of the projectiles, each one opening up a red crater on the left side of his torso.

Thrarm-Captain had his own handgun up as a reflective object rolled swiftly past the tee-intersection where the two kzinti had been riddled. Thrarm-Captain sent three fast rounds after it, may have hit the device, which, he now discerned, resembled a large metal ball propelled by four roller-rings on interpenetrated axes.

The full implications of what Thrarm-Captain was witnessing sunk in. The leaf-eaters were on his ship, with specialized combat 'bots. Somehow they knew what he was carrying, why his ship was built for defense, not offense. It was impossible to conceive of *how* they had learned it, but they had, and their intent was now clear: they did not want to destroy his ship; they wanted to take it.

Unthinkable.

Thrarm-Captain had his mouth open to order his bridge crew to override all local controls and autoseal all bulkhead doors when there was a muffled blast from aft; the lights flickered and the faintly crackling carrier tone of the command channel died away. It came back after a moment, along with approximately half of the lights.

zh-Sensor's words were tinny in the helmet's compromised speakers: "Thrarm-Captain, power in Engineering is out. Apparently the humans have already sent some automated EMP bombs on ahead to—"

There was a dull explosion from the direction the robot-ball had gone—and zh-Sensor's words died along with the rest of the lights. *Leaf-eating spoor-spawn humans: they didn't even have the courage to board themselves and—*

Thrarm-Captain, changing his handgun's now-malfunctioning power-pack, heard and then saw the approach of a new human robot: a floating oblong that bristled with weapons, one of which was clearly the hopper-fed coil-gun that had already killed two of his Heroes.

Screaming rage, seeing the spittle spray in a fine mist against the inner surface of his helmet's face-plate, Thrarm-Captain seated the power pack, and brought up his weapon.

Which operated slightly longer than he did: the grav-chassised robot fired a stream of needles into the big kzin's center of mass. Dead instantaneously, Thrarm-Captain's finger remained frozen around the trigger: the gun fired a few rounds of futile defiance before falling to the deck in imitation of its wielder.

The autocutter—an expensive, purpose-built, one-use device derived from reverse-engineered kzin weapon technology—finished slicing into the hull of the kzin auxiliary cruiser that Lieutenant Commander Dieter Armbrust had determined was his op team's target.

"Holding at two meters standoff," announced the boarding pod's steersman.

"Deploy charge; detonate at will," responded Dieter.

The gravitically tamped charge—which cost a small fortune—spat out of the boarding-pod's nose. It sunk snugly into a small depression that had been burned into the hull. It was ringed by a three-centimeter-deep groove that the autocutter had sliced fifteen seconds earlier.

"Three seconds." Dieter checked his gear: mostly non-lethals. However, for entry, he was carrying a retrofitted kzin beamer: a carbine and, therefore, right-sized for him.

"Fire in the hole," warned the gunnery sergeant in charge of the heavy weapons.

One sharp jar, and then the steersman was moving the pod in quickly, making his confirmations as he went: "Charge was successful: One-point-five-meter breaching hole established." A soft bump as the pod kissed the holed hull: "Pressure gasket is deployed and holding; we have hard dock."

The gunnery sergeant pressed a few virtual buttons on the heavy weapons control console. "Deploying proximity security packages." Almost inaudible through the layers that were still between the boarding team and the interior of the kzin ship, there was a long ripping sound like an oversized popcorn popper in overdrive. "Cluster munitions have cleared ingress point. Releasing hunter-killer ROVs."

Dieter nodded, turned to the six men in Alpha Team. "It's easy to forget your training because of the excitement." *Or fear. But I can't use that word, not here, not now.* "So, one more time by the numbers. We enter in twos, we fan out, using the maps that are being uploaded by the ROVs to our helmet processors right now. Once we have located the target, we move toward it directly, leapfrog advance. A pair of ROVs will cover our six. Watch for friendlies; all teams are converging on the same point. Lethal systems are 'weapons free' until we reach and confirm the target. Then, only designated sharpshooters remain 'weapons free' with lethals: all the rest of us shift over to non-lethal systems. As soon as I signal 'objective achieved,' we reverse our path and fall back upon our pods. Watch for ambushes on the way out." Dieter checked his watch. "Any questions?" Heads rotated tightly from side to side. "Gunny, are the ROVs done?"

"Almost, skipper. Ran into a few big bucks in terminal defensive positions. They took out one of my 'bots. Damn, but the ratcats have good night vision, even unaided. But that's the last of them. I think I'm seeing the objective ahead. I'm labeling its location as Zone Cougar on your maps."

Dieter glanced at the forehead HUD in his helmet. "Got it. And they've lost power in there?"

"Sure looks like it. Seems like this ship doesn't have any more defense against internal EMP weapons than the other kzin battlewagons."

Although I'll bet today's escapade might change that. Dieter nodded to his team. "Ready, team. Steersman, we go on 'three.' Cycle the valve in one, two, THREE—"

The iris valve at the front of the boarding pod contracted out of the way with a shuddering hiss— and they were in tiger-country. Dieter revised that assessment after a quick look through his thermal imaging goggles: they were in *dead* tiger country. To an unpracticed eye, it would have appeared to be the aftermath of a fevered abattoir nightmare, but knowing the sequence in which the hull had been breached and entered, Dieter had a precise forensic understanding of what he was seeing.

The lowest layer of kzin corpses, barely visible under the others, had been the first to die: they were both blasted and pulped. These were the ratcats who had been tasked with intercepting whatever came out of the human pod that had been sighted boring through this part of their hull. God knows what they expected to achieve beyond suicide. The gravitically tamped breaching charge had blasted in against them with the force of a 250-kilo bomb, then there had been explosive decompression tugging them right back out an instant later, until the pod made its hard dock. There wasn't much left of that first kzin welcoming committee.

The second scattering of corpses was piled atop the first. These were more conventionally riddled and dismembered: the late responders, or maybe simply those with enough self-control to hang back around a corner until all the carnage of the initial boarding was over. They had, however, come face to face with the first packages to emerge from the small payload bay at the front of the pod: small, self-propelled cluster-bomblet robots, most of which, like bees, had destroyed themselves in making their attack.

The third, less numerous and more scattered, group of corpses were those that had run into the gunnery sergeant's remote-operated attack drones. More responsive than simple robots, these partially autonomous systems had gunned down any remaining defenders, and were now watching Dieter's flank and rear.

He glanced up to check his HUD's objective locator guidon and aimed his hand aft. "This way. Follow me."

Despite all the precautions and the support robots and ROVs, Alpha Team still had some problems. About halfway to their goal, they had a short, sharp meeting engagement with a trio of kzinti who had evidently been moving aft to protect the objective area. It had been a point-blank firefight, the muzzles of the contending beamers and coil guns almost touching as they discharged. The humans got off the first shot, accomplishing that only because the point man's thermal-imaging goggles showed a split-second haze of approaching body heat before the lead kzin came around the corner. The savage fight lasted four seconds, and Dieter's one casualty wasn't even inflicted by weapon fire: it was a melee kill. The unfortunate trooper's coil rifle had taken off the gun hand of a kzin only two meters away. It had also punched a hole, big enough to see daylight through, through his right lung. But without breaking its stride, the kzin closed and scooped out the trooper's Adam's apple with one sweep of his remaining, claw-sprouting hand. Then the rest of Alpha Team reduced him to a riddled and seared mélange of orange fur and red blood.

Just before reaching their objective, Alpha had another gunfight, which lasted longer due to the team's intentionally decreased firepower. Rather than take any chances, Dieter had already ordered that two of his remaining five men go over to non-lethals. It simply didn't make any sense to get so close to the objective, only to destroy it themselves.

But the kzinti facing them—either because their communication was down, or because they were still trying to adapt to the rapidly changing scenario—did not anticipate that there would be a whole new contingent of human boarders converging on the objective. So when the six commandos of Gamma Team arrived, unbloodied and alert, they made quick work of the remaining kzinti defenders.

Dieter now cautiously scanned the wide, high-ceilinged objective area: it looked vaguely like a gymnasium. "Report."

The response "clear" came from the four point men moving gingerly among structures that looked like a cross between jungle gyms and torture devices.

Dieter toggled his open channel. "All teams, Alpha and Gamma are at the objective. Beta Team, continue toward rendezvous. All other teams, converge into defensive positions ringing objective, as per op order 'Sierra.'" Dieter used his chin to choose his own team's tactical channel, and discovered that there was already too much chatter on it. "Pipe down. Sergeant Aquino?"

"Yes, sir?"

"On me. Let's see what we'll be dealing with."

As it turned out, there wasn't much to deal with at all. They easily found the door leading into the terminal objective: it was completely unlike the efficient naval architecture and fittings that surrounded it. The doorway was an irregular frame of crude, hand-beaten brass, distressed to impart the impression of great age. It was what Dieter would have expected at the threshold of a dragon's lair. Which, on reflection, pretty much defined the room his team was about to enter.

Naturally, it was locked and he had no doubt that the mechanism was sturdy. But not sturdy enough to shrug off his gravitically tamped charges. His demo specialist was almost done with setting the four-point package when Aquino, whose ears probably rivaled those of their kzinti opponents, held up a hand. "Wait. I hear something."

"What?"

"I don't know." He looked at the brazen-bound portal. "Almost like—rabbits screaming."

Dieter felt the hair on the back of his neck stand suddenly erect as a chill washed through him. "Finish and blow the package."

"But, sir—"

"Do it. NOW!" Dieter scrambled back. "Fire in the hole!"

Three seconds later, as the demo specialist dove past him, the charge went off with a shuddering roar, followed by a metallic clangor as the brutally twisted doorframe went cartwheeling away.

And in the wake of that sound arose mewling cries of confused, mortal terror—counterpointed by what sounded like a ragged chorus of snarling sobs.

Dieter leaped up and toward the deformed, blackened doorway. "On me, all numbers!"

Aquino and one of his troopers were through the door before Dieter, but they lagged to a halt as they crossed the threshold, not understanding what they were seeing at first. But Dieter had anticipated this, had argued with the command staff to have it included in the training materials, had worried about it from the moment he had been given the clearance to see Dr. Yang's full report. So he was the first to act.

He brought up his needler and dumped half a clip of its tranq-gelatin wedges into the closest kzin female, who was about to tear off the head of her own kit. She swayed, but the drug didn't take effect fast enough. Her raking claws were off the mark, but still lethal—just not clean and swift. The small kit, no more than four weeks old, dropped to the deck, shriek-mewling, one of his lungs and most of his intestines spilling out.

Damn it: they're too strong to succumb to the drugs immediately. Now if they'd given me the high-octane non-lethals I'd asked for—but that was all spilt milk. And Dieter had no time to cry over it. "Switch back to lethals. Double-tap the females—all of them." He dropped his needler and snatched up his coil gun, already tracking across the loose throng of kzinretti and putting two rounds in each one that danced through his sights.

A moment later, his men followed suit. Some, lately arrived, did not understand the nuances of the situation, and actually shot a pair of kits. Aquino knocked their muzzles aside and shredded them with oaths as pointed and lethal as the projectiles of their own coil guns.

But critical damage had been done to the nursery's precious population, overwhelmingly inflicted by the female kzin themselves. Walking through the litter of bodies, Dieter called out to the xenomed specialist every time he found a live kit. He did not call out very often. He worked deeper into the collective safehold of the harems of the senior flag officers.

At the very rear, in an alcove that was shrouded and almost completely unlit, Dieter saw faint signs of movement. Was it the admiral's mate, perhaps: is that why she was in what looked like a specially secluded boudoir-bower? But no, he realized as he came closer, although it was a special place, set aside for privacy, it also permitted discreet observation. It had not been arrayed and appointed for mating.

It was for birthing.

Dieter parted the roughly spun gossamer blinds with the barrel of his gun, cautious but also feeling a sudden, deep spike of guilt. The female, stretched on her side, moved listlessly: one coil gun projectile, probably a stray, had gone through her neck. The wound, not arterial but severe, had created a puddle of blood beneath her: she was still alive only because of the immense vitality of her species. Under her paws was a newborn female kit. It had been slain with a single claw-slash across its tiny neck. The kzinrett's bloody paw hovered over it, alternately protecting and caressing the little corpse.

Her other paw strained fitfully after the second kit of her litter, a half-black male that had not wriggled closer to her deadly embrace. What had stopped him? Had there been a subtle warning in the tone of his littermate's desperate cries as the milk-rich body which had just given them life suddenly turned tender claws of death upon them? Had it been the smell of blood? Had it been the sight and sounds of devastation with which the strange hairless bipeds had shattered the quiet of the harem-nursery?

The kit's nose wrinkled, turned uncertainly in Dieter's direction, and his eyes blinked open as he made a small sound: "Meef?"

The sound roused the mother. Her eyes roved, her claws slid out of their beds, her arm came back; she even managed to raise her body slightly, to lean her torso forward...

So that she could reach far enough to kill her last kit.

Dieter brought up his weapon and squeezed the trigger once.

The female's left eye imploded. She collapsed, as limp as old rags.

Dieter looked back at the kit; it blinked up at him through milky, and probably still blind, eyes. He reached down, scooped it gently into the crook of his left arm. He could swear that its eyes were fixed upon his.

"Meerf," it said. And then the kit's eyes closed, and it nestled against him tightly.

2396 BCE: Subject age—less than one year

Despite the scenes of carnage that she had been watching for the past minute, Dr. Selena Navarre flinched anew at the scene of a kzin female being bisected—literally bisected—by the screeching sweep of a commando's coil gun. The image froze.

A freshly minted UNSN captain by the name of Armbrust came from behind the lectern. "Had we listened to Dr. Yang's warnings, this outcome might have been averted. Instead, because the approved non-lethals were too weak to instantly drop an adult kzin in its tracks, we had to resort to lethal weapons. And you can see the results." He waved at the frozen tableau behind him. "In addition to having to kill all the females, twenty-five percent of the kits were killed by our fire, as well. They were too close to their mothers, and the situation was too chaotic to take more time or better aim.

"This outcome is compounded by the loss of sixty percent of the kits through the infanticide carried out by the mothers. This leaves us six kits. Of those, one was severely wounded. Your personnel have informed me that it has subsequently been euthanized."

"It would not have been useful to us, anyway," objected Director Pyragy's rather snappish voice from the darkened auditorium behind Selena. "It was a female." So, the team director had finally spoken up. In an attempt to minimize the scope of the disaster, of course. A disaster for which he, it was rumored, was primarily responsible: he had resisted almost every special tactical contingency the mission planners had placed before him for approval. Including the double-strength tranq rounds.

Captain Armbrust stared. "The female kit would not have been useful? Director Pyragy, at this point I would have thought that *any* kit would be useful. After all, as Dr. Yang pointed out in her research précis, there is nothing that proves that the females are inherently subsentient. It may simply be that—"

"Captain, your heroics in securing these live subjects are admirable, as was your rather baffling ability to identify the rumored harem-protection cruiser among the rest of the kzin ships." Pyragy pompously sniffed distaste at the very things he had praised. "But the value of your speculations on the mental capacities of the kzin are directly proportionate to your qualifications in xenobiology and xenobehavior. Which are nonexistent."

Armbrust smiled up toward the source of the voice at the back of the darkened auditorium. "That is almost entirely true."

"'Almost' entirely? You have an uncompleted degree lurking somewhere beyond the margins of your resume, perhaps?"

"No. I had the good fortune of being briefed by Dr. Yang herself, and have subsequently been granted full access to her research proposal."

"Your first point is a non sequitur. The second is valueless." Rumor had it that the director had argued vehemently against granting military personnel access to the full text of the proposal. A strange vehemence, Selena reflected, considering that access to it was, in his current statement, "valueless."

Armbrust apparently detected the same contradiction. "Valueless, Director? Then why did the command staff need to make repeated requests for access?"

"I wonder if sharing it with your command staff was deemed a breach of the project's secrecy protocols, Captain," mused the voice of Marquette, a member of the project's Steering Board and an inveterate toady.

The captain's smile widened. "Actually, I believe our overall clearance rating was higher than yours, in regard to the relevant data. We were actually going on the operation, after all."

The director's own voice rolled, archly mellifluous, over Selena's head. "The reason we resisted granting you access was noise, Captain. The pointless, distracting noise that would have been generated by providing unqualified persons with enough information so that they could start their own pointless theorizings, which, out of sheer good manners, we would have had to listen to—rather than dismissing them out of hand, as was warranted. So: you have your answer. Continue your report."

Armbrust had turned his back and was heading toward the lectern before the director had finished speaking. Selena quelled a sudden impulse to cheer the captain.

"So, to conclude," said Armbrust, "we have only five healthy specimens, two of which are females of less than two weeks. Leaving us three males. One would soon have been removed from the combination harem-crèche-playground: he is at least three months of age. The other is approximately a month old and is not particularly pliable, according to your own researchers. The last one—"

"—Is no concern of yours, Captain. You can hardly know anything about a creature you held for less than two minutes."

"True. But it is also true that it may have been a very important two minutes."

"Yes, yes: I've heard all the amateurish tripe about kzinti possibly having a first-imprinting reflex such as many higher terrestrial mammals, and some species of birds. But at this point, that is only unwarranted and rather romanticized speculation." The director's voice slowed, deepened, became subtly dangerous: "I have it on good report that you have even shown up to look in on the littlest one, from time to time." Selena did not know how a pause could be smug, but Pyragy's was: "Perhaps some imprinting did take place, Captain, but perhaps it is not the kit who was imprinted."

Armbrust shrugged. "Time will tell, I suppose. Now, allow me to show you how we came across our unexpected find as we withdrew."

Selena sat forward: she had only heard the faintest whispers about this when she was posted to the team three days ago, but if the rumors were accurate, it would put a whole new spin on kzin gender socialization.

A new video clip flashed on the screen. The camera motion was jerky. The muzzle of a gun was perpetually visible in the bottom center of the dancing screen: typical scope-view footage. Then, whoever was holding the gun panned around and aimed down a short corridor. He zoomed in on an open doorway there: as the image swam and focused, it resolved into serried ranks of inclined glass cylinders, all over two meters long. And in each was—

Selena breathed in sharply. Her gasp was mercifully drowned out by the director's abrupt, "So these are the cloning tubes? The vats, as I believe you nicknamed them?"

"Yes, sir. I'll advance the recording, so you can see a few more."

The view on the screen sped forward in time, seeming to race down the corridor until it reached the threshold of the long, dark room: female kzinti, encased in dimly lit gargantuan test tubes, stretched to the far wall.

"And when you took samples, did you—?"

"You will appreciate, Director, that we had to improvise everything from this point on."

"Including dividing your forces in the face of your enemy?"

"Sir, this was an unexpected discovery made during a hot exfiltration. I made sure that our primary objectives—the kits—were all removed to safe holding ASAP. Then we set about rigging two of the ROVs to carry one of the tubes in its entirety, as well as gathering genetic samples from all the others, and taking samples of every fluid being pumped into or out of them."

"Crude," commented the director. "Marginally effective, at best."

Had there been any room to doubt that Pyragy disliked, personally disliked, Captain Armbrust, it was gone now. To Selena's mind, and most of the other researchers with whom she could talk about these results, Armbrust had shown considerable presence of mind and ingenuity getting out what he did. That he had then lost an additional five men when another wave of kzinti showed up was hardly his fault: the increased time required to transport the clone tube and samples had made another engagement a near certainty. But in light of what humanity had gained with those additional samples—

"And then you destroyed their ship?"

Armbrust nodded. "Yes, Director, as per my orders. As much to prevent the kzinti from learning of our presence and activities aboard their cradle-cruiser as to strike a further blow against them."

"And your own ship was still operable enough to effect your escape?"

Armbrust unsuccessfully attempted to mask his smile; even Selena hadn't been so gullible as to have believed that the damage taken by the captain's Raker-class decoy ship—salvaged during the defeat of the Second Kzin Fleet—was genuine. "Director, my ship was not damaged at any point, except by the intentional beam hits upon the fuel tanks. In the staged fight that the kzin witnessed between us and our own smallships, one of which was automated and convincingly destroyed by our fire, all the missiles were duds. The apparent internal explosions were prepared charges, already on-board. Our fusion plant was fully operable; it was just rigged to allow us to simulate irregular function and battle damage. As was everything else on the ship. The actual lifepods and lifeboats were replaced with cheap shams, leaving enough room for us to use their launch tubes to deploy our short-range breaching pods, once the kzin ship slowed to match course and come alongside."

The director sniffed again. "A wonderful display of how satisfactory results can result from the suitable use of low cunning." Armbrust smiled instead of taking the bait, leaving the focus clearly upon the director's own ignorance of military operations. Selena was sorely tempted to snicker but thought the better of it. She was lucky to have received this assignment at all. Until she had securely established her experimental schedule, the loyalty of her personnel, and had made herself indispensable, her semi-autonomous position as leader of the Behavioral Team of the Kzin Research Project was far too tenuous.

There was an extended silence in the darkened room. Then the director's voice: "Captain, that will be all."

Armbrust came around the lectern one last time: he was, Selena noticed, a handsome enough man, although hardly the classical vid-hero. For that, he would have needed an extra six or seven centimeters and longer proportions in general: light-legged and fine-hipped, the bottom half of his body was that of a dancer; the top half was broad, hard, flat: a laborer or a weight-lifter. He looked up into the dark, along a trajectory that tracked back to the source of the director's voice. "I wonder if I might ask a few questions. As a personal favor."

The long pause was not promising, but then a new voice—that of the positively ancient board member Boroshinsky—broke in, heavy-accented and quavery:

"You may ask your questions, *gospodin* Armbrust. It is the very least accommodation we can make in appreciation of your fine service." The director may have grunted impatiently; Selena could not be sure.

"*Spasebo*," Armbrust said into the dark with a slight, deferential nod. "My first question is: have you completed the radio array for establishing communications with Dr. Yang in Proxima?"

"We have," Pyragy replied. "Although it will be some years before we know if she is still there to receive it. It seems the kzinti, if impatient, are also thorough hunters."

"Indeed they are. With any luck, Dr. Yang has not attracted their attention. That was her plan."

"And to the best of our knowledge, she has kept to it: we have had no signals from Proxima since the kzinti first attacked twenty-nine years ago."

Armbrust's shoulders seemed to relax. "My other question is about the behavioral component of her research plan: will it in fact be funded?"

"I do not know what you are referring to." The director's tone belied his words: he might as well have said, "I will not share that information with a troglodyte like yourself."

Armbrust was undeterred. "I am referring to her suggestion that, if possible, a promising kit should be raised to adulthood not merely to observe the details of its speciate development and distinguish the influences of nature from those of nurture, but also to breed him as a possible liaison to his own people."

The lights in the room snapped on; the director was on his feet, and very red. "How did you learn of this? Yang specifically stated in the appendix to her proposal that this part of it had been separately ciphered and kept apart from the rest."

"I know. But I also spoke to her directly. And she made her intentions quite clear."

Pyragy aimed a shaking finger down at Armbrust. "Yang's suggestion is an optimistic delusion that ignores one obvious and decisive fact: a kzin raised by us would be rejected by those which are natural products of their own society. Given a reasonable chance, they would retroactively do to our subjects what their mothers were trying to do to them when you first took them from their nursery a few weeks ago."

"So you have not funded Dr. Yang's behavioral research initiative?"

"Oh, no: we most certainly have funded it. We have simply revised its objective."

"How so?"

One of the other board members—Marquette, the toady—waved an age-gnarled finger in time with his pedantic drone: "It is our intent to show that the kzinti can be rescued, saved, from their own base nature."

Selena Navarre almost spun around in her seat to stare. *Really?* Really? *Could they possibly be serious? In their arrogance, they had decided to* rehabilitate *the kzinti? The Board could not be so blind, so stupid— could it?*

"Professor Marquette speaks somewhat metaphorically," Pyragy amended. "Let us say that we wish to explore the possibility that the kzinti need to be liberated from the eugenics programs that their one-time masters—the Jotoki—apparently imposed upon them. And, having followed down that same path themselves, we must further explore what would happen if the modern kzinti were freed from their own hide-bound genetic tyranny."

"Genetic tyranny?"

"Of course. Veiled references to the routine euthanization of intelligent females, and the cloned breeders you found are proof enough of that. Having the knowledge we now do, we can liberate the kzinti from their own self-perverted evolutionary growth, from the senseless violence in which they have immersed themselves. Even more deeply than we did. Until the ARM brought peace and order to our society."

Good grief, thought Selena, *he's a true believer.*

Armbrust muttered a guttural curse in some Wunderlander dialect and stared up at the director. "So you will *correct* the aberrations in the kzinti, the same way you did with humanity for the better part of three centuries? I'm tempted to dismiss it as impossible, but then again, you so pacified humanity that it took a near-genocidal wake-up call from the known universe's apex predator to shake us out of that lotus-eater's dream. But evidently even that hasn't taught you that the universe is not inherently aligned with your cherished notions of nonaggression. So, now you're going to try to make pacifists out of the kzinti? Good luck—and send the kzinti my regards and sincere commiseration."

"They will no doubt appreciate such sympathetic wishes, coming from a warrior like yourself." The director was smiling again. "Set a beast to catch a beast, I always say. And so we did, apparently. I thank you for bringing a set of beasts back to us, Captain. I am quite sure we can handle it from here, your own lofty cosmological warnings notwithstanding."

Armbrust collected his papers and data chips, all the while glowering at the director. In the captain's eyes, Selena saw a more profound, unconstrained variety of her own Belter sensibilities: the ARM had never managed to bring her people as completely under the yoke as they had the rest of the system, and particularly Earth. And now stalking from the room, mouth rigid, was the living evidence that the colonial ARM had been even less successful completing its pacification campaign in the Centauri system.

Which for some primal reason suffused Selena Navarre with a feeling of deep relief and reassurance. And then she understood why: *we always had some real warriors left. But we still came awfully close to being utterly defenseless when it really counted . . .*

"Dr. Navarre, tell me, what did you think of Captain Armbrust's presentation?"

Selena nearly jumped: the director wasn't wasting any time determining if the Wunderlander had any secret allies in his own camp. Particularly that part of the camp which was entrusted to assessing kzin behavior. In short, her camp. She schooled her features to bland compliance, and turned to look at him.

Pale blue eyes, so pale that it was momentarily difficult to discern where the white of the eye ended and the iris began, stared down at her, patient and cool. The mouth beneath them was smiling in benign receptivity. "Director Pyragy, the presentation was informative. It is unfortunate that the transmission of information became entangled with the expression of opinions, however."

As she had hoped, Pyragy seemed very pleased by the response, construing it to fit the context he preferred. "It is refreshing to hear such sanity today," Pyragy commented, casting a self-satisfied glance at Boroshinsky, who smiled faintly, eyes almost twinkling as he stared at Selena. His expression widened into an amused grin before he looked away, leaving her with the distinct impression that although he was quite old, there was nothing wrong with his ears or his mind. He had obviously understood that Selena had crafted her response so that Pyragy could construe it as he wished. *Huh, leave it to a Muscovite to instantly perceive plausible deniability in action: Communism and the commissars have been gone for almost four centuries, but the Russians still remember the lessons.* Besides, Selena was glad that Boroshinsky had seen through to her real reaction. As the Project Manager of the Biological Research Initiative, he would be a useful ally and could be trusted not to knuckle under if Pyragy brought his considerable weight of influence to bear.

Selena let her eyes slide over to the director himself, who was busy reviewing the agenda of the rest of their meeting. Shwe Pyragy was known for being utterly practical in his pursuit of greater institutional power: he was a career bureaucrat who had managed to get himself assigned to the Kzin Research Project simply as a matter of prestige. He did not have the credentials to be a primary researcher or even team manager, but he did have a nose for politics, a vast collection of owed favors, and a taste for high-profile assignments. This one certainly fit the bill, and might also be the last chance he had to prevent his career from a final, irremediable slide into back-office mediocrity and anonymity.

Pyragy was something of a failed prodigy within the Life Sciences Directorate of ARM. He had been a promising young star whose rise had staggered and slumped just when it was poised to become meteoric. It was impossible to say why this had occurred, or at least, Selena did not know anyone with access to the files that might have explained his surprisingly underwhelming career. It was whispered that Pyragy's sexual tastes had been so wide and so injudicious that he spent an inordinate amount of energy—and took inordinate risks—in satisfying them. Along the way, he had evidently experimented with not merely a broad range of practices and partners, but with profound, and ultimately unsuccessful, changes to his own body. Both facially and physiognomically, he had been left stranded in a zone that was not so much androgynous as it was an arresting amalgam of distinctly male and distinctly female features.

Selena knew her negative reaction to be a function of her generation—the first of the post-Golden Agers—who, growing up with the threat of kzin-effected extinction hovering over their heads, reflexively considered such experimentation with inherited physical characteristics to be frivolous. She knew it was not—at least, not for *all* who pursued it—but the flip side of the peace and unprecedented personal liberties of Earth's Golden Age had, all too often, verged over into egomaniacal license. In the decades just prior to Earth's first encounter with the kzinti, increasing numbers of individuals, lacking purpose, had been caught in a growing undertow of ennui and hedonism, their self-indulgences masquerading under labels such as "unfettered exploration of the self." She often wondered if this was what humans did when they did not have urgent matters to attend to: what historians, speaking of other empires and epochs, had frankly labeled "decadence."

Well, the peace of the Golden Age, and the world it had spawned—good, bad, indifferent—were gone. Blood and sweat were back, and, if not exactly stylish, were accepted as the price of speciate freedom, perhaps survival. That made Shwe Pyragy a *de facto* anachronism who had outlived the cultural immediacy of his own choices. He looked down at her again: "Tell me, Dr. Navarre, do you feel that you can synchronize your research phases with those of the biology group?"

Selena nodded. "Yes. From what I've been able to deduce, kzin maturation is not only faster than ours, but has comparatively sharp developmental boundaries. Some of that may be simply because their growth stages are compressed into a shorter span of years. It simply seems their physical and behavioral development evince greater synchrony. It is also possible, however, that their physical and behavioral changes march to a much more powerful, chemically governed drumbeat than that which drives development in young humans."

Pyragy nodded. "Reasonable. Do you foresee special challenges at any particular stage?"

Selena smiled, but not too widely: just enough to look modestly charming. "I foresee special challenges at almost every stage, Director. However, the stage we've labeled 'infancy'—birth to one year of age—will probably be the simplest, since few complex cultural variables will be in play yet. On the other hand, the next stage—two to three years, or what we've crudely labeled as 'childhood'—may present us with some of the greatest challenges."

"Why?"

"Because we may not yet have the relevant information from Proxima Centauri by that time. Dr. Yang would certainly have received our wake-up call and request for information by now: we sent it almost six years ago. However, depending on how long it takes for her to gather and then send the data that was compiled in Centauri, we might not have received it when the kit enters that developmental stage."

Pyragy shrugged. "Perhaps, but we should have all her data at the end of that stage, and so, be well-prepared for the next one. Which the Biological Research group has labeled the 'training stage.' What I don't understand is, why 'training' instead of simply 'puberty'?"

"Director, the kzinti don't really have a word for puberty: their closest term is 'trainable age.' And it should be understood that, from what we can determine, the training received by these four-to-six-year-olds is more like junior boot camp. Other than basic math and language skills, the focus is on physical readiness and combat."

Pyragy stared at her for some time. "There is some merit to your label, then; we shall take it under advisement."

"Thank you, Director. The 'maturity' stage—seven to eight years—will bring with it clear, sharpened interest in females and mating, even though natural kzinti have no access to either at this age. However, because whatever socialization we provide will lack the nuances, compensations, or distractions that make male kzinti manageable during these years, I am afraid that this is where we must expect to lose a great deal of control over our research subjects. We can only hope that Dr. Yang's data will include some useful insights on how kzin culture handles the onset of full sexual awareness and maturity.

"Through some lucky finds, we know that the kzinti themselves call the age of nine to twelve the 'trekking years.' It seems to be a period of wanderlust and itinerancies: they try their hand at many trades. It is unclear whether this is to give them a broad base of competencies, or an attempt to affix them as journeymen to a particular field of endeavor. Finally, they call the age of thirteen, of full maturity, the Name Year—not because any kzin *will* get a Name that year, but because this is the first point at which they *may* earn a Name. Although usually, it takes place much, much later. If at all."

"And do you think we should be trying to make our test subjects liaisons to the natural kzinti, or exemplars of what the whole species might become if they were freed from the yoke of genetic and behavioral conditioning?"

Selena kept herself from swallowing nervously; this would have to be the most politic response of her career. "I think that it is too early to set our final objectives in stone. But I will hasten to add this proviso: whatever we plan upon, our objectives should remain conservative and maximally attainable ones."

Pyragy smiled benignly. *Because you interpret "conservative and maximally attainable" as synonymous with "what we humans can understand, control and inculcate in a kzin."* Selena returned his smile and tried not to feel sick at having to curry favor with him. *But in actuality, the most conservative and attainable of all objectives will be to let a kzin be a kzin—and to see what that means and watch how it happens. And if we're lucky, to inherit at least half of his loyalties.*

Pyragy strolled down to the lectern, set his presentation materials before him, and began: "The kits will be remitted to the care of Dr. Boroshinsky's secure preserve in ten days . . ."

2397 BCE: Subject age—one year

When Selena came back down the inter-biome walkway, she was surprised to see Captain Armbrust in the observation hub. She was more surprised still to see the youngest of the kits, the one he had rescued, with its nose hard against the glass, a small halo of mist coming and going with its breath. The little male was displaying all the now-well-known kzin behaviors of affinity: his ribbed ears were fully deployed, each like one-half of a toy pink teacup. His eyes were wide open and the pupils very large. His fur displayed a slow, rhythmic rippling that ran from the base of his skull down to the end of his spine. While Selena watched, a tentative paw came up to rest on the part of the glass near the captain's face.

She was tempted to just stand and watch, but protocols—and manners—demanded otherwise. "I'm sorry, Captain. I didn't know you were coming. Of course, I didn't know you were allowed to come in here at all. And next time, I'll thank you to check with me before allowing any of the subjects to see you. Particularly that one."

Armbrust stood straight; the kit propped himself up, blinked, sought the human face that had been pressed close to his own through the plexiglass. "I'm sorry." Armbrust waved a hand at the doorway into the habitat dome. "Once I got through security, I tried to find someone to report to." He shrugged. "There was no one around. No way to contact anyone, either."

Selena sighed. "Yes, we're pretty spartan back here. Up until now, all our emphasis has been on getting these habitats set up as quickly as possible. Our little kits were getting a bad case of laboratory cabin fever. Particularly the oldest one."

"How are they doing, if I might ask?"

"You might, if I can find out how you got in here at all. As far as I could tell, Director Pyragy would have been happy to banish you from the planet, let alone our primary live research facility."

"You're probably right about that. But the director doesn't have more authority than the admiral I report to, and the military wants to keep a pair of eyes on this project. Much to Pyragy's chagrin, I'm sure."

"Yes, be sure of that. Pyragy is old-school: 'pills, not pistols; conditioning, not cannons.' You represent more than just a diametrically opposed set of opinions; you embody the destruction of his world."

"Huh. Thought I was protecting it."

"No, you are protecting the planet. But on that planet, there are many worlds, and Pyragy's world was predicated upon the notion that we as a species had finally done away with violence." She shrugged. "It was all swap-water, of course. But his generation of ARM administrators grew up thinking it was gospel." The captain was smiling broadly. "What?" she asked.

"You said 'swap-water.' That's a Belter expression: potable water recaptured from urine. Not always one hundred percent clean when the systems get old, I'm told."

"Yeah? So I'm a Belter. So what?"

The captain's smile got wider still. "I find Belters... well, refreshing. Here on Earth everything is a little too tidy for me. Out where I grew up, on Wunderland, things are messier." He frowned. "These days, a lot messier."

Selena barely restrained the urge to reach out and touch his arm. She had heard rumors that he was the only one of his family who had managed to escape the system on a slowship. They weren't of *herrenman* stock, and so remained on Wunderland, under the watchful eyes and ready claws of the kzin. It was surprising that he had any room left in his heart for anything, let alone a tiny kzin kit.

Instead of touching his arm, she stepped a little closer. "I think we're pretty lucky to have you here, making your own messes, Captain."

Armbrust looked up with a sudden smile. "My name is Dieter."

"And I'm Selena, not Dr. Navarre. So the admiral gave you a 'get into jail free' card?"

"Something like that. After seeing the report about my debriefing by Director Pyragy, there was some concern at the higher echelons that the research project could be in danger of being compromised by personal and political agendas."

Selena looked sideways at Armbrust. "Everyone has an agenda, Dieter."

"True enough. But in this case, the top item on

everyone's agenda should be 'save humanity.' The rest is about method. In the case of your director, it seemed he was more interested in using young kzin to prove something about universal morality."

Selena did not say anything; she did not dare. The problem was not that she disagreed with Dieter, but rather, that she agreed with him. Fervently. But even if the walls didn't have ears, some things were simply too risky to discuss freely in public. And besides, she didn't want to take any chances of being associated with the military agenda, because if Pyragy suspected that, she'd be off the project. Faster than spitting out swap-water. In another six months, maybe a year, her position would be much more secure, possibly invulnerable. But until then...

"Let's walk, Dieter. You've a lot to see." As they began strolling out of the observation hub and down one of the tubes that both separated and provided a means for observing the different habitats on either side, Selena noticed that the kit had padded away from the observation glass and was now paralleling them on their walk. "It seems you have a friend, Dieter," Selena observed, nodding to indicate their tiny escort.

Dieter looked over; as he did, Selena quickly accessed her wrist-relay's primary control program and deployed three of the near-invisible roving sensors in the kit's habitat to triangulate, close and follow him. It was the strongest independent behavior she'd noted thus far, and if it was what it seemed—a post-imprinting affinity—that could be a major factor later on: both a variable to investigate and use as a positive stimuli and reinforcement.

If Dieter noticed what she was doing, he was too

polite to mention it. "Yeah, I'm some great friend of that little kit's, cheating him the way I did."

"By cheating, are you referring to the fact that he only needed saving because you had already—er, destroyed his world?"

Dieter shrugged. "Yeah, that too. But I was thinking more about how I brushed against one of the dead females shortly after entering the nursery. I didn't even consciously think about it at the time, but it was one of the possibilities we had discussed at the command level."

"You mean, to coat yourself in a familiar, comforting scent?"

"Yeah; as far as we knew, the mere smell of humans, being so different, could have made the kits unapproachable under any circumstances."

"That doesn't sound like cheating, Dieter; that sounds like quick thinking."

"It was just a trained reflex."

"The others didn't do it."

"That's because I mentally trained for it on my own. I thought through that assault again and again and again. And, of course, it didn't work out anything like we planned. They never do."

"No, but because you had rehearsed the alternatives so many times in your head, you were able to adapt, quickly and well, when reality went off in a different direction than any of the ones you'd planned on."

Dieter shrugged and glanced back at the kit. "And now I feel kind of responsible for Hap—for him—I guess."

Selena looked sideways at the Wunderlander. "Did you just call the kit 'Hap'?"

Dieter seemed almost embarrassed. "Yeah."

"Why 'Hap'?"

"Well, it hardly seemed right to call him 'Lucky.' Yes, he survived, but we did kill his mom and sister and hijacked him to live among hairless aliens."

Selena smiled sadly. "No, 'Lucky' just wouldn't work."

"But, in some ways, chance was on his side. And has continued to be. So, caught as he is in the hands of Fate, I thought 'Hap' might do. Mayhap, Hap-less, Hap-py: there's no telling what Fate will deal him, but deal him it will."

Selena looked at the half-black, half-orange-furred kit that was becoming weary following them. Hap. A simple monosyllable. That was good. Furthermore, all its phonemes were easy for kzinti: they were basic sounds in the Heroes' Tongue. And if the kit came to know that it had been named by the human for which it felt such instinctual affinity, that might be the influence mechanism that—

Dieter's voice interrupted her thoughts. "How are the other kits doing?"

"The oldest male has proven entirely intractable, as we suspected he might be."

"Too old?"

Selena nodded. "That's our best guess. He's not particularly sociable with the one that's two months younger than he is, but we can't tell if that's normal, a post-trauma reaction, or just a personal quirk." She smiled. "He's the only one we've named, so far. Partly because he's older, partly because he had such a distinctive personality."

"Dare I ask what you've named him?"

"Cranky. Some insist on the longer version: Cranky Cat."

Dieter raised an eyebrow. "Something tells me you never expect to establish communications with him, giving him a name like that."

"It's hard to see how we would forge a communicational link with him: he cannot be safely approached, and he is resistant to both positive and negative operant conditioning. Surprisingly so, for a young creature."

"Although that could be the norm, for kzinti."

"Absolutely so. And I could see several ways in which it would be a necessary survival trait. The kits are ferociously competitive with each other from a very early age. In Cranky, what we perceive as stubbornness and irascibility might well be tenacity and aggressiveness, now warped by being penned up in an alien, aversive environment."

"And the second oldest male?"

Selena shrugged. "Hard to tell; he's had a lot of trouble."

"Why? I thought he was fine when we got him."

"He was. But although he was probably too young to remember any of the trauma of his capture, he was old enough to feel it, for it to leave an emotional scar."

Dieter clucked his tongue. "Kind of hard to think of kzinti having emotional scars."

"I understand, but they can and do get them. In his case, I don't think it would have been too bad: they are very resilient. But without a mother as a source of basic mammalian reassurance, I suspect his mind tucked the experience under his growing consciousness, and is now experiencing its side effects.

"From the beginning, he rejected food until he became desperately hungry. We had to feed him intravenously twice to ensure his survival. Of course, it doesn't help that the damn milk substitutes just don't appeal to the suckled kits."

"I thought it was genetically reengineered from samples, that it was an exact match for their real milk."

"Oh, it has all the right chemicals in all the right proportions, but something is still missing. As a lab-tech in the biology group put it, 'ersatz is ersatz.' And we should hardly be surprised: we've done no better with our own foods."

Dieter smiled ruefully. "True enough. I've had tasty non-alcoholic beer, except it never really tastes like beer."

"Yes, and given how much more acute the kzin senses of smell and taste are—about thirty thousand times and one hundred times, respectively—it's hardly surprising that they reject the substitutes we've created."

"And so the younger kzin male is weak from starvation?"

"Yes. It will be good when we can move him to unprocessed meat, about a month from now."

"But Hap looks pretty robust."

"That's probably because he was newborn when he was taken."

"What? Wouldn't that make him weaker? More vulnerable?"

"No. He hadn't been suckled yet. So, apparently, if newborn kzinti haven't yet had natural milk, they tolerate our synthetics much better."

"So he's feeding well?"

"I don't know that I'd call his intake anything more than 'adequate.' He's still not a fan of our version of kzin food, but he doesn't find it particularly aversive, either."

"And the female kits?"

Selena nodded. "One is having an easier time of it; the other is in the worst shape of all. I expect we'll lose her within the week."

"What's wrong with her?"

Selena shrugged, jammed her hands deep in her lab coat pockets. "Damned if I know. But my gut level instinct is that she has no will to live. I know that sounds bizarre to say about so young a creature, but it's been true from the first. Listless, limp as a wet rag. She's been on IV for the past three days; we had to catheterize her this morning. Nothing we do matters: she just keeps fading away, further and further. The other female is the exact opposite: some think she's the most promising of all the kits. She's certainly the apple of the director's eye, and is surprisingly friendly to most of her handlers."

"So, that's good."

"No, that's bad. Or rather, it's too much of a good thing. Now Pyragy has started exploring the possibility of making the females the primary focus of the research program, with the intent of increasing their intelligence and using them as a long-term weapon against the natural kzinti males. Kind of kzin Mata-Hari Delilahs that are secretly working for the good of humankind."

Dieter rolled his eyes. "Please tell me you are making that up."

"I wish I was. Unfortunately, it's just further proof that the entire project is being administrated by a scientific illiterate."

"What do you mean?"

"I mean that he's still talking about this after Boroshinsky delivered his preliminary reports regarding the cause of the females' lack of intelligence. And Boroshinsky's preliminary reports are often more meticulous than papers presented at the Royal Academy."

Dieter lagged behind; the orange-and-black ball of fur that he had dubbed Hap had flopped down in a histrionic excess of weariness. Dieter crouched down to be closer to him: through the glass, the kzin's eyes narrowed happily, his torso pumping deeply and only a little more quickly than normal. "And what are Boroshinsky's preliminary conclusions?"

"Firstly, the cause of the females' semi-sentience is clearly genetic. So no amount of rehabilitation is going to work. But secondly, Boroshinsky also confirmed that the genetic constraints upon their intelligence are not merely a matter of a single, sweeping alteration to the original female genetics: they involve an ongoing program to maintain that genotype."

"I don't understand."

Before she could stop herself, Selena had her hands out of her pockets, punctuating and emphasizing. "The kzinti had those clones on their ship—and probably near all breeding sites—to ensure that their females remain subsentient. Each of the clones belongs to one of sixteen different gene patterns, which, despite a great deal of diversity in other particulars, have two genetic traits in common: diminished development of the higher-function brain elements and neurochemical deficiencies. Both of which are sex-specific."

Dieter stood, looked more puzzled. "Okay, I get the part about diminished brain development. I'm guessing that this trait keeps their equivalent of the cerebral cortex from becoming large enough to support sophisticated thought?"

"Correct. Whereas the neurochemical deficiency works by reducing how frequently and effectively the synaptic gaps are resupplied with the necessary bioelectric transmitters."

"So the brain is smaller and slower."

"Right. But that's arguably not the most important fact uncovered by Boroshinsky. The kzinti have taken another eugenic step to ensure that female cognitive impairment remains permanent: the clones."

"How do the clones fit into this?"

"Boroshinsky's guess is that despite the genetic alterations, there are occasional regressions to the original, undiminished female genotype. So what the kzinti are doing with the clones, at least on interstellar voyages, is constantly refreshing the desired genetic signal with fresh copies."

"And that's important because . . . ?"

"Because it tells us how primitive and imperfect their genetic science is. The genetic fix they've imposed must not hold too well if they are constantly having to inject direct copies of the modified gene line back into the population all the time. Boroshinsky suspects, and I concur, that they probably couldn't create a more absolute genetic alteration without risking that some of the effects would spill over into the male genome as well. That suggests that their genetic alterations are subject to considerable drift. That's probably why they put in the neurochemical modification, too: being an entirely different gene modification, it's an insurance policy against any reexpressions of full female brain development."

Dieter frowned. "It's hard to imagine the kzinti relying on such a complicated matrix of changes."

"I agree, but a truly permanent solution would require one to be very good at genetic manipulation. From the looks of it, the kzinti never got to be very good at genetics: just pretty good."

Dieter nodded. "Well, I guess that's to be expected. Brandishing a test tube and wearing a white coat: hardly a Hero's garb, I suspect."

"Yes, there's probably an inbred behavioral disinclination, as well. The life of a scientist might be suitable for the faint of heart, but *not* for the short-tempered."

"Which is why the kzinti seem to rely on their slave races to provide many, or even most, of their technicians and bean-counters."

"Yes. The kzin males have a glandular system that keeps them awash in a cocktail of hormones that functions like testosterone in human males, except about one hundred times stronger. Obversely, the females have an almost complete lack of it: another development of their highly selective breeding, apparently."

"So the females are not merely bred for low intelligence, but for docility, as well."

"Yes, but that creates a problem, too. Calm is the handmaiden of cooperation. And patience. And patience generally assists learning. So ironically, if the females were not cognitively suppressed, they would be likely to outperform the males in terms of education and organization."

"Which the males would take extra steps to prevent."

"Exactly," affirmed Selena. "I suspect that's why their neurochemical alteration to the female genome induces a kind of kzin ADHD syndrome."

Dieter stared. "A kzin with ADHD? Given their normal behavior, how could you tell?"

Selena smiled. "This is even more extreme: it significantly impedes language acquisition, deductive reasoning, symbolic and abstract thought. All those tasks would simply feel like too much work to a being with this genetic trait. This pretty much predicts that the females will not only be incapable of learning complicated tasks, but ensures that they will be most adept at activities that are instinctual, and that they will derive most pleasure from sensory stimuli. And that, in turn, means that their self-awareness will be rudimentary, akin to that of a mentally sluggish three-year-old."

Dieter scratched the back of his head. "Rather like me, then."

Selena stared at him frankly. "Tell me, Captain, does that self-deprecating humor act usually work on women?" She smiled.

The smile he returned was both sheepish and genuine. "Sometimes."

Four meters away, Hap yawned, flopped prone again, allowing his eyes to stay closed as the sun approached its zenith. He rolled slowly, presenting his belly for the bright orb to warm...

2398 BCE: Subject age—two years

Hap, who was at the age where his posture only rarely reverted to the quadrupedal, was literally bouncing on all fours as Selena's team led him toward the outer paddock. Sometimes she found it hard to remember that this endearing little fur-ball would evolve into a two-and-a-half-meter apex predator that was the scourge of her species. As if in reminder, Hap's mouth gaped open as he panted in eagerness, revealing rows of surprisingly long, densely packed sharp teeth. No, he was a kzin all right.

Selena crouched down, face to face with him. "Are you ready, Hap?"

Hap nodded, having picked up the gesture from the humans around him. His nose was twitching eagerly; despite the supposedly hermetic seals, he could smell the natural biome beyond the paddock door. Then he stopped, looked around. "Deeder?" he asked, his ears flattening a bit in the kzin equivalent of a frown.

"Sorry, Hap. Dieter can't be here today. He wanted to be. But he's away."

Hap's nose twitched once, mightily. "No, he not. I smell him."

"No, Hap; I'm sorry, but Dieter is not here—"

"Not here, but I smell him." Hap pointed. "On you."

Oh. Each member of Selena's staff suddenly discovered that their routine tasks and instruments now demanded unusually close scrutiny. Well, her relationship with Dieter was going to get out eventually, anyhow. Probably half her team already knew or at least suspected. But, to coin a phrase, the cat was well and truly out of the bag now. "I understand now, Hap: you can detect his scent. But Dieter had to leave a while ago; the person I work for asked him to—"

The small wet nose twitched again. "Selena, no. You wrong. Smell is new, fresh. Very Dieter." He wrinkled his nose. "Very strong Dieter smell." His eyes drifted down, below her waistline.

Oh, good God. "Hap, listen: Dieter couldn't come. He wanted to but—but some other people wanted him to be somewhere else today." Selena imagined herself punching Pyragy in his supercilious mouth. Again and again. "But Dieter will be back soon."

The kzin cub's fur flexed once. Was that akin to a shrug? A similar reflexive gesture had been observed in the other three cubs, and in circumstances that suggested the same social valence. "Okay," acceded Hap. "We go now?"

Selena smiled, careful to keep her lips over her teeth as she did so, and nodded to him, then at her staff.

They opened the paddock door, and Hap looked back quickly at Selena, his eyes very wide. "No harness?"

Selena shook her head. "No harness; not today."

Whereupon Hap performed a prompt, skittering, one-hundred-eighty-degree turn and was through the open doorway in a shot. Selena followed at a more leisurely pace.

By the time she emerged into the open air—and this time, it was truly open air, not an enclosed habitat like the others Hap had been in—the small cub was racing to and fro, moving so fast that he was a blur. He sped from bush to tree to flower to insect to rock and finally, to what was apparently an especially fragrant Mystery Groovy Spot in the middle of the grass. Where he stopped, panting, rolling in luxurious abandon.

Selena approached him slowly, carefully, mostly because she did not want to impinge upon his first experience of The Wild, but also because she was not quite sure what he would do next, and he was already big enough to be modestly dangerous, albeit not deadly.

Hap had evidently heard her approach. "Smells!"

he purr-gasped. "Smells! All around! In my head, all over! It...it...." He stopped suddenly, sat up, a quick and terrifying gravity in his eyes: "No more walls. I want here. Always."

Selena nodded. "Not yet, but soon." She looked up, squinted into the distance: just a kilometer away, a high-security fence—three of them, actually—traced a dim line that paralleled the horizon. She wondered how long that restraint would be a sufficient guarantee against his already-awakening instinct for roving, for wanderlust.

"How soon?" Hap's query was uttered in such a flat, matter-of-fact tone, that she couldn't keep herself from glancing down at him. The cub that looked back—orange belly fur tremoring against the surrounding black of his pelt—suddenly seemed much older than two.

"I'm not sure how soon. The man I work for said that maybe, if you like the new food we have for you, you can stay here right away. Would you like that?"

Hap didn't even nod. "Where is new food?" His eyes roved purposefully.

Selena schooled her face to impassivity as she motioned one of her staff to bring in the sealed plate. Hap's nose was immediately hyperactive. "Meat?" he purred eagerly.

"Yes." Selena kept her voice calm. "Try some."

The plate was placed before Hap; the lid was removed. He started at the sudden puff of steam, the pungent smell of seared beef. "Meat," he agreed. "But burned."

"No: cooked. It brings out the smells, the tastes," explained Selena, wishing she had authority in this matter. "Try it."

Hap's nose wrinkled dubiously, but he gamely seized and devoured a small chunk of the sirloin. He chewed for a moment—then his eyes went wide and the meat came out in a rush, propelled from behind by a veritable torrent of vomit.

Pyragy looked cross. It could have been for any one of several reasons. Rumor had it that his ongoing hormone therapy was interfering with his cardio meds. If so, his choice was between tiring easily (perhaps fatally) or verging into a cascade of implant and transplant rejections that would likely render his body alarming to all but the most open-minded of partners.

Perhaps no less distressing to him was the presence of Admiral Coelho-Chase and the ARM's Associate Chief Executive, Maurizio Dennehy. Their presence was a clear indictment of his handling of the Kzin Research Project. And probably the recent episode involving the cooked meat had caused the long-standing official uneasiness to reify into a full-blown investigation.

But perhaps most frustrating of all to Pyragy was that his two most senior researchers—Boroshinsky and Selena herself—had been summoned by those same powers to explore a possible redirection of the program's research goals. For a man who hungered after preeminence and prestige more than anything else, this was indeed a most annoying turn of events.

The admiral looked up from the reports and toward Boroshinsky. "So you confirm that you made these multiple recommendations against attempting to feed cooked meat to the kzin cub named Hap?"

"*Da*, Admiral. Some of our studies suggested that it might be mildly toxic to him. For kzinti, eating cooked meat would be analogous to us eating a mix of carbonized and denatured meat. Either upsets our stomach. Cooked meat has the equivalent effect upon the kzinti, causing the cub's projectile vomiting: his system was purging itself of toxins."

The admiral and the associate chief executive stared at Pyragy, who shrugged: "This was not known before we tried."

"According to the collected reports and testimony, this outcome was suspected."

"Suspected, but not known," Pyragy persisted.

"Even if we were to concede that possibly specious point, why did you feel that it was important to attempt to get the kzin to eat cooked meat?"

Pyragy spread his hands wide. "Is it not obvious? To see if he could be weaned away from the taste of the fresh kill."

"To what end?"

"Why, to put distance between himself and his more primal instincts. Admiral, Executive, if we are to successfully pursue our most basic mandate—to raise a kzin with whom we might have meaningful communication—we must ensure that he views us as fellow discussants, not possible entrées. If he retains a taste for raw meat, he will probably retain a taste for our own uncooked flesh, too. An independent board of animal behaviorists validated my concern that our relationship with him will remain forever compromised until and unless that association is broken. He will not see potential food creatures as fully sentient and equal to himself."

"And do you agree with this independent review of kzin behavior, Dr. Navarre?"

"I do not know, Admiral, since I have not seen it."

"Why?"

"Because the existence of the external review was not revealed to us until this week."

"Very well, so you are not in possession of the particulars of the report. Given that proviso, and speaking off-the-record, Dr. Navarre, do you feel that the ability of the kzinti to conceive of creatures either as *persons* or as *prey* is as polarized as Director Pyragy is claiming?"

Selena shifted awkwardly. "It seems unlikely, Admiral."

"Why?"

"Because there is plentiful evidence that, after defeating a fellow kzin in an honor duel, the victor will consume a least some parts of the loser. Perhaps much more. But honor duels can only be fought between Heroes, between kzin *persons*. So it seems that the kzinti can operate socially without such an absolute distinction between prey and persons."

"I concur, and consider this further evidence that the research project must be careful not to overanthropomorphize the kzinti," added the associate chief executive with a stern look in Pyragy's direction.

Boroshinsky cleared his throat. "In one way, however, we have determined that the kzinti are, unfortunately, similar to us. The biology group can conclusively report that kzin biochemistry is too similar to humans' for the safe military use of toxins or biological agents. Although some are more injurious to kzin systems than homo sapiens, the margin of difference is completely insufficient for the creation of a tailor-made toxin lethal to kzinti but harmless to humans. Insofar as bacteriological and viral agents are concerned, preliminary tests suggest that our biochemistries are close enough that some pathogens could 'hop' species. On the other extreme, if the organisms are dependent upon specific genetic interfaces, then of course the kzinti are immune to all of ours, just as we are immune to theirs. But so far as we can determine, the kzinti have acquired absolute immunity to all the strains we find latent in their system."

"Even their own digestive flora?"

Boroshinsky nodded at the admiral, a faint smile suggesting he appreciated the intelligence of the question. "Even that. The kzin digestive process is far more robust than ours. The first part is almost sharklike in its capacity; the lower portion simply retrieves moisture and desiccates the wastes. Also, their digestive process is more reliant upon glandular secretions than resident bacteria." He sat back. "I am afraid my group has failed in its primary task."

Associate Chief Executive Dennehy shook his head emphatically. "You have not failed, and your labors are not over, Dr. Boroshinsky. In fact, we are glad to learn this so early in the research process. By removing one alternative from our suite of strategic responses, we can focus on the remaining options. And quite frankly, we considered the possibility of finding a kzin-specific bioagent a longshot."

"You did?" Boroshinsky and Pyragy were an unintentional chorus in expressing their surprise.

Dennehy nodded. "Once we learned that the kzinti had already enslaved races possessing advanced technology, it seemed likely that they would have either genetically amplified their resistance to biological weapons, or that, during an earlier conquest, another race taught them this lesson. The hard way. As far as simple toxins are concerned, we presumed that since they can metabolize our flesh, that our biochemistries would prove too close for either of us to remain wholly immune to what was toxic to the other. But there was no way of being sure without your research."

Boroshinsky rubbed his pointy jaw. "Then, sirs, I am afraid I do not see what you hope we might yet discover as a weapon against the kzinti."

Dennehy smiled. "I wish we could take the credit for the answer to that, but it comes from Dr. Yang. She anticipated all these deadends, observing that if there was any weapon to be found in the kzin biochemistry, it would not be something as inelegant as a simple poison or disease. Rather, the key was to find some way we might be able to turn their own natural secretions against them. And since the kzinti have so many more glands than humans, she thought it possible that there might be something resident in the endocrine system that we could exploit. Do you agree, Doctor?"

But Boroshinsky had not heard the final sentence: he was already scribbling notes on his datapad.

Dennehy smiled, then returned his face to impassive neutrality. "We trust this will provide appropriate new directions for the Research Project. Dr. Navarre, you are specifically instructed to keep your group focused on establishing the cognitive, behavioral and social objectives necessary to facilitate positive, long-term communication with your subjects. That is not your primary concern: it is your *only* concern. Is that clear?"

"Very much so, sir. However, I must report that I consider only two of my subjects—the surviving female and the youngest cub—to show any probability of willing communication with us. Unfortunately, the female's mental capacity has been conclusively demonstrated to be very low; she will probably never become more capable than a human child of three years of age. Less, when it comes to language."

"We understand. So, aside from the kit named Hap, the other kzinti will provide you with bases of both biological and behavioral comparison. In time, we may also need to use them to generate cell lines—samples for the synthesis of kzin scents, hormones—that might be required by either your group, or the biology group. Before we adjourn, is there anything else?"

Pyragy made a huffing noise.

"Yes, Director?"

"Admiral, Executive, in light of these proceedings, I am uncertain regarding my own role in this project."

"What do you mean, Director?"

"Is it not obvious, Executive? You have apparently made me redundant. My group leaders disagreed with my orders and policies and you have intervened on their behalf, overturning all my directives in a public forum. You could have chosen to do so in a more private venue with me, but you did not. So I must wonder: am I still in charge of this project, or have I been reduced to a mere figurehead?"

Selena had to hand it to Pyragy: he might be authoritarian, unctuous and ingenuine, but the bastard had guts.

The two senior officials exchanged long looks before the executive turned dead eyes upon the Pyragy. "You ask a reasonable question, Director. Here is the response: it depends."

"Depends upon what?"

"It depends upon your ability to follow the ARM's

mandate for this project at least as well as your group leaders do. And to date, that has not been the case. So let us put it this way, Director: your position on the project is entirely up to you. Does that answer your question?"

The look on Pyragy's face said that it did and that he wasn't at all pleased with it.

While he was still engaged in his angry staring match with the executive and the admiral, Boroshinsky looked over at Selena slyly, and actually winked. She smiled, nodded faintly in return, and resisted the urge to get up and dance on her desk.

At last: now we can get some real work done.

2399 BCE: Subject age—three years

"This is a funny language, but I like it." Hap practiced the long, linked vowel strings of another of the Heroes' Tongue's compound verbs: in this case, *eaooiiasou*, or, "to seek-while-leaping." He looked up at Dieter, blinking in the sun, and made the sound again, almost as if he were singing it: *"Eaooiiasou!"*

Dieter smiled back, keeping his lips closed as he did so, as Selena had taught him. If Hap learned the open-mouthed smile of humans, he'd be unintentionally sending a challenge every time he met a kzin he liked or found amusing. "He's learning very quickly. And very well."

Selena nodded, mindfully keeping an extra few inches between herself and Dieter as she drew him away from Hap. No reason to give her group any more reason to gossip than they already had. "Yes. He's very clever. I just wish we had a better way to teach him the Heroes' Tongue."

"He seems to be doing well enough with what you've got." Dieter listened as the next interactive learning program began, and the cub began getting corrective oral pulses from the biosensor implants when his pronunciation of unfamiliar phonemes veered off.

"Well, the problem is with what we've got of their language: not much, and not the right kind of lexicon."

"What do you mean?"

"All we know about kzin speech is the comm traffic we've picked up when they invade, almost all of which is heavily encrypted and non-verbal. We got a bit more from debriefing you Wunderlanders who came in on the slow boats from Centauri. But most of what we have was harvested from the few military wrecks that were intact enough to do us any good. Like that Raker-class small-boat you modified for snatching the kits."

"So what's the problem with the information from the wrecks? Were their computers corrupted?"

"No, we got very clean data. But it was the wrong data. Normal speech and military comm traffic may overlap, but the latter is really just a word-poor, albeit highly specialized, dialect of the former. We don't have very much in the way of domestic vocabulary, or terms that describe states of being, or emotional or philosophical concepts. And we won't have any access to informal idiom until we get Dr. Yang's first response. If she's still there."

Dieter nodded. "I see. And the kzinti don't use voice recognition software?"

"Very little. In place of voice recognition software, they depend upon ocular tracking. And since their physical reflexes are much faster than ours, the differential between their 'look-and-blink' systems and our voice command programs is pretty low."

With the next lesson over, Hap flopped backward, sprawling in a manner that somehow mixed the boneless repose of early adolescence with "limp as a kitten." Then his head swiveled slightly, his nose flaring after a peripherally detected scent. His ears shot out to full extension, his shoulders tensed.

"What's that?" asked Dieter.

"That," Selena explained, feeling a bit of inexplicable melancholy as she did, "is Hap detecting the scent of other kzinti."

"Females?"

"Males. We can't start with females. Every bit of data we have suggests that once the male cubs are separated from the mothers, they are not allowed further contact. We suspect that the scent of females could—um, confuse them."

"How long have you been piping in the scent?"

"Just today. And just a few whiffs. Nothing very—"

Hap rose slowly, his head turning, searching. Then he looked at the teaching module and turned his back on it. This left him facing Selena directly. "Where are the others?"

Damn it, he distinguished it that quickly. At one part per million, he—

"Where are they?" Hap's tone, while not quite imperious, was crisp and no-nonsense. "Where are the others like me?"

Selena kneeled down: he had grown so large that

she hardly needed to anymore. "They are in other paddocks, in other spaces."

"Why? Why are we not kept together? Why have I not met them?"

"Well, that's a long story—"

Hap promptly sat down; he looked up at her. "Tell me. Please." He looked at Dieter. "When you come and then go—sometimes for weeks—I start wondering 'why do I have to stay here? Why can't I go with Dieter?' But I know I'll get the same answer as when I ask to go somewhere else: not yet. Always 'not yet.' It doesn't make sense. All of you—without hair—you go other places. Places beyond the walls, beyond the fence. But I don't. I stay here. It's a big space, but I can't go anywhere else. You don't let me." He looked back at Selena. "Why?"

Selena looked at Dieter and then took a deep breath. Before she could start speaking, Hap leaned forward. "Before you start telling me, I need to know something."

Selena blinked. "What?"

"This language you're teaching me: that's my language, isn't it? I mean, the language that people like me—kzinti?—speak. Right?"

"That's right."

Hap nodded. "So I'm going to meet some other kzinti soon, right?"

"Eventually. Why do you think that?"

"Because with the language and the smells, it's like you're getting me ready. That's it, isn't it?"

Selena thought how many ways that was true: getting him ready for the rest of his life, actually. "Yes, that's it."

"I knew it! I knew it! So I'll meet them soon."

"Meet who soon?"

Hap blinked, surprised. "Why, my mother and my father." He stared at her expression. "I do have a mother and a father, don't I?"

As Dieter moved further off, Selena felt her eyes becoming wet. Hap's face was suddenly tense as he watched her fighting against the tears. He blinked twice, rapidly: the kzin equivalent of a nervous gulp. "Tell me," he said. "I can take it."

2401 BCE: Subject age—five years

Selena entered the paddock slowly, carefully. She waited to see if Hap could detect Dieter's scent, despite her extensive efforts at cleansing.

"So, Dieter is back for a while?"

How did he—? "Yes. I know that his scent disturbs you. I tried to—"

"Oh, I can't *smell* him."

"Then how did you know—?"

Hap stood, flexed his prodigiously growing limbs: they were long, rangy, distinctly immature, but already quite deadly. "I knew because you don't smell like anything, not even yourself. And that's how you smell, now, when he is back for a visit. Completely without scent." Hap wrinkled his nose, which was now more angular, less button-like. "It's not natural." He tossed the last of his automated chase-toys from paw to paw. "Of course, nothing is natural around here."

Selena looked at the toy: it had been a self-powered,

semi-autonomous fuzzy quadruped. Originally quite fast and agile, it was now defunct and shredded beyond recognition: one of the rear limbs was missing, the other had been stripped down to the metal servos and armatures. The front limbs had been broken so that they now reached around behind the pseudo-creature as easily as they did to its front. Which was consistent with the apparent theme of physiognomic reversal: the neck coupling had been snapped, allowing the creature's featureless head to stare backward over its shoulder blades. It wasn't the result of play; it was bloody-minded, fixated destruction. Hap had done the same with the other objects provided for his amusement; in fact, over the past three months, he had systematically reduced all of them to so much junk. Starting with the far simpler, slower "chase-and-chomp" toys that he had played with since he was two, he smashed every play/training 'bot he had been given. And now he had finished by mauling the most sophisticated model available, specially designed to hone hunting and stalking skills during his "training years." Whatever modest challenges this 'bot had presented to him, he had caught it within two hours. Now, he set its remains aside, carefully putting it on the end of what had come to be known as Death Row: the queue of toys he had methodically destroyed, one after the other.

And it was Selena's job to find out why.

Fortunately, Hap's next comment provided a convenient way to segue into the topic. "I was wondering when you'd finally ask me about the toys."

"Hap, the toys are just part of something larger. I know that." And how could she not? For the last

year and a half, cheery, affectionate Hap had been
on an emotional and behavioral roller-coaster ride,
more than had been observed in the other two males
as they entered the human equivalent of the terrible
teens. No surprise there: neither of the other two
had experienced the sudden, rude awakening to the
peculiarities of their existence as stranded orphans
the way Hap had, twenty months ago. It made matters worse when Hap's introduction to the next oldest
male ended with that kzin shunning him suspiciously.
The oldest one had been downright hostile. All these
events had initially pushed him closer to Selena. He
frequently sought the comfort of her patient lap, his
eyes wide but seeing inward, and seeing nothing but
uncertainty. Uncertainty about his origins, his nature,
his future. At first, he spoke about it frequently, then
in fits and starts, and finally, not at all. At which
point he ceased to seek her lap. That change had
been permanent.

Hap sat at some distance from her now, didn't even
look directly in her eyes. "Yes, it's more than the toys.
It's so much more than the toys that I don't really
know how to think about it all at once. But the toys
seemed like a good place to start."

"Why?"

"Why do you think?"

Selena wondered: was this kind of insolence a common feature in kzin maturation? Probably not: their
relationship with the older males would be a very
businesslike affair. Open insubordination—for that is
how their culture would almost certainly view such
a testy response—would no doubt be met by a sharp
cuff and dire threats of more. At the very least.

So, by elimination, this was an example of how human upbringing was changing him. Like Boyle's Law of Gases, the contentiousness of his age was expanding to occupy any space that it was not soundly, physically, beaten back from. And even if they knew enough to imitate a true kzin upbringing, that would do no good, not anymore. He was what his upbringing thus far had made him: insightful, reflective, self-determining, curious, and capable of many intensities and shadings of affection for any number of humans. He was no more a natural kzin than a cockroach was, and never had she realized that so clearly as now.

His tone was exaggeratedly patient. "I said, 'why do you think I started with the toys'?"

Selena set her shoulders back a little further and withdrew her emotions from her eyes. "I'm not here to make guesses, Hap. This is not a game."

"Really? Then why these?" He gestured at the broken playthings. "Toys are for playing games, aren't they?"

"They're not just toys, Hap."

"No? Then what else are they for?"

"For training you. For making sure you can exercise all your physical abilities."

Hap sat back; the kzin smirk was surprisingly similar to its human equivalent. "Tell me about my physical abilities, please."

"You don't need me to tell you what you can see by looking in a mirror."

"What I see and feel is *not* what I'm talking about." He stood, and Selena thought: *my god, he's become so big, so fast.* She felt, and quickly pushed down, a pang of fear. Hap was either too caught up in his own thoughts to have smelled it, or very possibly, would not have known what the smell meant: kzin senses were hard-wired to read the emotional states of the prey-creatures of their home world, not Earth. "What I'm talking about is what you *expect* me to become. What you know about my species, my birth, my family. Yes, you've told me I'm an orphan, but not why or how. Yes, you've told me that I'm a kzin and that I'm from another world, but not how I got here, or why. And every time I ask, you—what is the term?— you *redirect* me." He sat down again, reclined. "You know, it gets pretty tiresome, being redirected all the time. And pretty insulting, too: I can hardly believe you didn't expect that I would eventually catch on to what you were doing."

"Oh, I knew you would, Hap. I knew."

"Then why did you keep doing it? Why didn't you stop redirecting, and just talk to me?"

What a wonderful question. And what a shitty answer I have: because I didn't have the clearance to do that. Because once we start down this road, you won't accept anything less than complete answers. And you shouldn't. But no one can agree on when to drop the big bomb on you, Hap: no one can agree that the time has come to level with you about all the dirty truths of how you came to be here. That your race and ours are at war. That we slaughtered your mother and sister. That we don't keep you here out of love, or even kindness, but bloody-minded strategic benefit.

Hap's stare was quizzical, the same look she remembered from when he was a kit. Then, his eyes opened wide: "You weren't *allowed* to tell me, were you?"

Selena had no clearance for any of this, but the

situation had gone beyond concerns over clearance now. If she shut down this conversation, Hap would never trust her again. The relationship would be proven to be a sham. And suddenly, everything Selena had ever done for, or said to, Hap would become suspect; at the very least, he would know it had only occurred because it had been permitted by higher powers, that Selena's own feelings and motivations were secondary to the dictates of others.

So Selena shook her head. "No. I was not allowed." She smiled ruefully. "And to be honest, I'm not allowed to reveal that I was not allowed to reveal things to you."

Hap frowned and then grinned. "That statement took me a moment to work through. *Zzhreef'f!*" Which, Selena knew, was the Heroes' Tongue equivalent of "I'll be damned." He looked at her for a long moment. "So you're going to break all the rules, now?"

"Hap, I won't. I can't."

"Why?"

"Oh, Hap, because if I do, there will be consequences."

"For you?"

"For you, too."

"Such as?"

"Well, in all probability, the same people who haven't allowed me to speak openly to you would probably keep me from coming back here. Ever again. It would be the last time we see each other. And there's nothing I could do about it."

Hap's ears had laid back tightly against his increasingly angular skull. "They'd do that? Really?"

"Really. Look, Hap: you were right when you said that nothing here is natural. But the unnaturalness goes far beyond the fenced-in range, the lack of contact with your own kind, the refusals to let you see the rest of the world, the carefully edited books about history and current events, and these insipid toys." He smiled happily when she spat out the words "insipid toys." Clearly, that admission of repressed fellow-feeling restored much of his confidence in her. "I can't tell you about all of that unnaturalness, not yet. But I think that is going to start changing now."

"Why? Why should it start changing now?"

"Because of you."

"Me?" Hap sat up: curiosity and pride—the pride of an adolescent being told that their input has made an impact in the inscrutable world of adults—was clear in his expression. "What did I do?"

"This." She gestured to the rank of mangled toys. "And the impatience you expressed with your current information limits. It will show the people who have resisted telling you more about yourself, and your origins, that the matter is really out of their hands, now. They can hardly counsel patience anymore, because there's nothing to be gained by it. Your comments today show that you understand that you're living in the middle of a stilted game, not the real world."

Selena had the impression that Hap was trying very hard not to look smug: he was failing miserably, and didn't much care. "Did they, whoever 'they' are, really think I could get to be this old and not ask myself, 'Hey, does everyone grow up alone in a special enclosure? Why are there only two other kzinti and why do they hate me? Where does all the stuff around me come from? Why are there so many questions that never get answered?' Perhaps they thought that since I never knew any different, I wouldn't see anything strange in all that?" His last point rose on a note of incredulity.

At which Selena smiled, because Pyragy had insisted that Hap would remain just that ingenuous. According to him, "the subject, knowing no different, will be unable to adequately frame doubts for some time yet, and will therefore, not be distressed by the peculiarities of his condition."

Before she could respond, Hap sat erect again, surprise writ large on his wide face. "They did! They really thought I wouldn't notice anything wrong? I can't believe anyone would be that stupid."

"You'd be surprised. But Hap, I'd like to start making things better for you, less unnatural. So tell me: if you could change one thing about your life here, right now, what would it be?"

"You mean, other than having to live *here* at all?"

"Yes, other than that."

"Well—" he stared at the savaged toys again "—I'd like to change all that."

She looked at the mauled bits of pseudo-fur. "You mean, you want them removed?"

"No, no." He seemed uncertain for a second; his pelt shook with annoyance. Then he looked her square in the eyes. "I just want to know this: when can I kill something?"

Selena felt the equivalent of a snowball materialize in her gut. Two years ago, he had still been her cheery, cuddly little Hap; now he was asking her about killing as matter-of-factly as a human teen might have asked when he or she could start dating. It was as natural to him as the pelt covering his body. And just as alien as that to Selena. She felt as if, in a single second, he had dwindled into some impossible distance, an invisible speck beyond the heliopause.

Selena swallowed, and said calmly, "You want something to chase, I presume?"

"Well, of *course* I do!" Hap smiled, stared at her indulgently. "What do you think, that I just want to slit a throat? Like *snick*—?" and he demonstrated in the air with a single, suddenly unsheathed claw. "Come on, Selena; where's the thrill in *that*?"

Selena managed not to blink or retch. "Where, indeed," she agreed.

After Selena completed her report, Pyragy looked away, sat silent for a full ten seconds. Then: "Thank you, Dr. Navarre. This is important information. And we will take your recommendations under advisement."

Boroshinsky goggled at the director but said nothing. Poor Mikhail was starting to show his age a bit, despite the anti-senescence cocktails they had him on. He didn't jump into fights like this one with the same alacrity that he used to.

Which left it to Selena. "Director Pyragy, I'm the one in direct contact with the subject. Who now knows that I take orders from a higher authority. If we put this off—if I am not allowed to give him certain minimal assurances about our increased forthrightness—then we will lose him. My personal relationship with him will be shattered beyond repair, and I am quite certain he will have nothing to do with anyone else. Not at this stage, and not under these conditions."

"I was not aware your relationship with the subject had become an indispensable part of our project, Dr. Navarre."

"This was outlined as a high-probability outcome before we even started, Director Pyragy. It has come to pass. As everyone—well, *almost* everyone—expected it would."

He turned to look at her. "So what are you requesting?"

"It's not what I'm requesting; it's what Hap is requesting. And it is utterly reasonable."

"What? That he be allowed to kill creatures?"

"Yes. More specifically, to hunt them down and eat them."

Pyragy shuddered. "It is barbarous even to suggest it."

"Director, we are not talking about a human. We are talking about a kzin. This is part of their growth process. It is only natural that he express this desire, this need. Indeed, it is a sign of our profound cultural influence upon him that he chose to wait—could *force* himself to wait—this long."

Pyragy was silent for a long time; Selena watched a variety of emotions contend on his face. Stubbornness, prudence, distaste, pragmatism, willfulness, cunning. "Small animals," he said at last. "Rodents only."

Selena tried to think where she could find the largest, fastest rabbits. Squirrels, too. "That won't work for long. The references we just received with the rest of Dr. Yang's first reply all indicate that the kzinti bring down game many times their size and mass, and nearly equal to them in ferocity."

"For now, this will have to do. We will cross the next bridge when we come to it."

"I think we've already reached it, Director Pyragy. The subject has also asked about killing sapients."

Pyragy swiveled to face her, his face rigid with horror. "He has asked about killing humans?"

Selena shook her head sharply. "No, no; his questions were philosophical in nature. In particular, he focused on the concept of justified homicide: he is having a hard time understanding that."

"What? He wants to slaughter bunnies but he has a hard time understanding justified homicide? That is such a bizarre juxtaposition that I frankly suspect him of playing a joke on you, Doctor."

"Director, I am afraid you are misconstruing my statement. The subject does not have a problem understanding the 'homicide' part of 'justifiable homicide.' His confusion stems from what he considers the endless and overfine moralizing that informs the extreme constraints our society imposes upon sufficient justification for killing another sentient. He called our attention to the ethics of killing 'obsessive, pointless and unnatural.'"

"And I presume you informed him of his error?"

"Director, for him, that opinion is not an error: that is the voice of his nature speaking."

"Nature be damned. We were killers, once, too. But we have trained ourselves to be otherwise. So can the kzinti. This is the moment when his inclinations must not be indulged: he must be conditioned away from an easy acceptance of wanton slaughter."

Selena stilled her drumming fingers. *Here's where the real fight starts—unavoidably.* "Director, I'm sorry, but this is simply not a question of behavioral training. It is a matter of his nature, and it is not subject to our nurture, as so many of the ARM's idealists presumed when this project started. Sapience is not a guarantee of ethics that evolve around a universal core of pluralism or sanctity of life. For the kzinti, there are worse things than killing, and that's true for them no matter which end of the equation they find themselves on: killing or being killed. What we need to realize is that it *had* to be that way for them, that there wasn't any viable alternative. For them, the impulse to hunt, chase and kill is a positive evolutionary trait. It's how they survived as a species. Every part of both their inbred impulses and early social construction was determined by increasing their chances of success in taking on big, lethal prey animals: the only kind that could sustain a tribe of kzinti, given their immense appetites."

Pyragy's eyes had narrowed. "We suspected as much when we began this project, Dr. Navarre. And we proceeded with a moral resolve to mitigate this behavior, both so that the subjects could eventually become liaisons for us, and so that they could be used to civilize the kzinti." He studied her carefully, clearly giving her enough time to realize that the pause implied the importance of what he was going to say next. "Are you proposing, Doctor, that we—including the ARM's oversight personnel, such as the admiral and the executive—have all made a fundamental error?"

"I'm proposing, Director, that many of us were not well-prepared to face the challenges of this project squarely. And I am not referring to the methodological challenges, but the implicit ideological challenges."

"What do you mean, ideological challenges? Do you mean the conflict between our system of values and the kzinti's?"

"No, sir; I mean a conflict between the realities of our own existence and the ideologies under which we had buried them. Hindsight suggests that, during the last century and a half, during our Golden Age of Peace, there was a tendency to slip into a moral anthropomorphization of the universe."

Pyragy's ever-thickening brows lowered further. "I warn you, Dr. Navarre, if you cannot trouble yourself to be clear, I will be forced to censure you."

"Okay, then, how about this: for the last one hundred and fifty years, many of our leaders were so pleased with how we supposedly purged violence from our natures that they generalized that lofty state of existence into a universal constant: it became the presumed zenith of social accomplishment for any civilization. And no one dared raise a hand in objection or doubt, for fear that they'd be reprogrammed due to their recidivistic sympathies, for aiding and abetting primitivism. From top to bottom, we all drank the Kool-Aid with blissful smiles on our wan little faces."

"'Drank the Kool-Aid'?"

"It's an old reference to sheeplike behavior that got people killed back in the twentieth century. It was a group phenomenon not unlike the one we observe in lemmings, except that we humans leap to our deaths following ideologies, not instincts. Everyone goes over the cliff because they're too busy staring at and complimenting the emperor on his new clothes."

"I asked for pellucidity, not insolence."

"You got the truth as best I know how to say it. And since you didn't seem willing or able to get my earlier hints about how our own social conditioning blinded us to the real challenges that we'd experience working with the kzinti—"

"Silence. I will not be schooled by you, Dr. Navarre."

"Fine—but then you'd better find someone who you

are willing to be schooled by, because your present policies are going to ruin our relationship with the test subject."

"How? By compelling him to initially restrict his murderous appetites to rodents?"

"No: by retarding his development, by withering away those essential parts of him that don't fit into the pacifistic procrustean bed that you've constructed not merely for him, but for all of humanity." When Selena was finished, she realized that her voice had become sharp and that she was panting with suppressed rage.

Pyragy's smile was small, but very smug. "I regret that I will have to report this outburst to our overseers, Dr. Navarre."

Boroshinsky's voice had risen even before the Director had finished: "Yes, Director, do. And add to your report that the entirety of the biology group supports Dr. Navarre's findings and handling of this matter."

Pyragy considered the back wall over steepled fingers. "Well, in light of your unanimity of opinion, I suppose a report might be precipitous. I shall therefore desist—"

"Too late," Boroshinsky snapped. He tapped his wristcomp. "I've just sent a message to Admiral Coelho-Chase and Associate Executive Chair Dennehy that independent assessments from all the project's group leaders are forthcoming."

If looks could kill, Pyragy's would have slain Boroshinsky on the spot. "That," he almost whispered, "was very ill-advised."

Boroshinsky shrugged. "Then fire me." He smiled, sent a sideways wink at Selena. "But I suppose we'd all need to report that too, wouldn't we?"

Selena had never had an impulse to kiss a man so old that his lips had a perpetual quaver in them.

But she did now.

2402 BCE: Subject age—six years

Down in the scrub-covered defile that wove its way into the preserve's boundary ridgeline, there was a burst of dust. It told them that Hap had brought down the mule deer at last. Had he not exhausted himself earlier chasing a particularly nimble springbok, the current pursuit would have been much shorter.

"He's a pretty impressive hunter," Dieter commented, looking away. "But then again, they all are."

Selena did not know what to say, and if Boroshinsky did, he didn't offer it. But they all knew what Dieter meant, and they were all thinking the same thing: Dr. Yang's reports—now distributed to all the members of the research project, as well as select military personnel—made repeated, ghastly mention of the kzin habit of hunting humans on Wunderland. It wasn't done at random, and it wasn't done in a cavalier fashion, but the fact remained: traitors, rebels, criminals, malcontents, and incompetents were not punished or incarcerated on Wunderland. They were the foxes in the horrible hunts whereby kzin officers amused themselves, and the higher ranking ones trained their young males. It was all too easy to stare at the settling puff of dust down in the ravine and imagine that it was not a mule deer thrashing beneath Hap's teeth and claws, but a human.

"It's necessary," Selena blurted, reaching to turn off

the camera on the hoverbots which followed Hap. The three more distant bots—which completed the irregular, changing tetrahedral pattern around him—mercifully did not provide the gory details of the kill. "Without these instincts and these capabilities, any genuine kzin would reject him."

Dieter nodded. "They still might."

Boroshinsky looked sideways at the Wunderlander. "Why do you say this, Captain?"

"Just Dieter, please. Hunting is just the opening ante for being accepted as a Hero. If he is to have any standing among them—if he is to be a liaison who is respected, rather than scorned—he will need to know how to fight. Not hunt: fight."

The air suddenly felt colder to Selena; she rubbed her arms vigorously.

Boroshinsky looked puzzled by Dieter's assertion. "*Shto*? Maybe they have some form of martial art?"

Dieter shrugged. "Maybe; we don't have any intel on that. Most of their combat moves seem to be a direct inheritance from inborn instinct. I suspect they spar, to hone those moves and improve their reaction time. But there's no evidence that they have a special discipline for personal combat." Dieter looked at the almost-vanished dust smudge. "Can't say they seem to need one, either."

"No," said Selena. "They don't. And he doesn't. What he needs is competition."

Dieter looked at her. "What do you mean?"

She sighed. "Hap has been asking questions about new additions to the preserve."

Boroshinsky looked at her closely. "You mean like water buffalo? Rhinos? Maybe elephants?" He laughed.

Selena did not. "Yes. And more."

Boroshinsky's eyes widened. "What kind of *more*?"

Selena looked away. "Lions. Tigers. Bears. Oh my."

Dieter nodded. "Now I know why he was asking me about the new breakthroughs in archeogenetics."

Boroshinsky reared back. "*Bozhemoie*! No! Even if you get clearance for it, some of those creatures are too dangerous. Even for him."

Dieter kept looking at the defile. "Too dangerous for him now, yes. Later? I wonder."

Selena stared at the man who was in and out of her life, along with whispers about the special detachment that he was assigned to: it had no address, no known permanent base, no official name. He got a month Earthside every year. Usually. So she knew him, or at least she thought so. "Well, this is new. A week ago you were worried about us bringing in the caribou. Now you're okay with him taking on raptors?"

Dieter's lip twitched. "They don't have a gene code on raptors. No dinosaurs other than the pieces they can pull from current reptiles."

"Okay; a cave bear, then. Those they've got."

Boroshinsky stared narrowly at her. "And how do you know that?"

"Same way you do, Mikhail. Insatiable curiosity coupled with inappropriate use of my clearance rating."

Which made the older man laugh thinly. "Okay. You win."

Selena kept staring at Dieter. "Well? What made you change your mind?"

Dieter nodded off in the direction of the ravine. "Him."

"Hap?"

"Yes. He spoke to me today."

"He spoke to *you*? After all this time?"

Dieter nodded. "Yes. It was nice. But very strange."

"I'll bet," Selena concurred.

Boroshinsky frowned. "I know I'm not supposed to know anything about this, but I do. I know he stopped talking to you about a year ago. Why?"

Dieter turned to face him. "Because I told him about what I did on the kzin ship. How I snatched him. How I killed his mother."

Boroshinsky stared at Selena. "And you—and the director—approved that?"

Dieter looked off in the distance. "I didn't ask permission. No time, anyway. He'd mostly figured it out on his own, asked me questions that put me in a position where I'd have to lie, avoid the topic, or tell him the truth. So I chose the truth. And he ran off."

"To grieve."

"That. And maybe to keep from killing me."

Selena stood slightly closer to Dieter. "Or maybe because he couldn't bear knowing that the person he's always trusted, even loved, had been the cause of all his misfortunes."

Dieter blinked. "Maybe. Anyhow, today he seemed to have all those emotions well in hand. He was really very frank about it: 'you killed the kzinti who were supposed to raise me. So I would appreciate it if you could help me get what I need in order to truly grow up.'"

Selena wished she had been there for that conversation and was simultaneously grateful that that bitter cup had passed her by. "And so what he asked for were . . . monsters?"

"Pretty much, yes. Prehistoric monsters. I agreed to support his request."

"Out of guilt?"

"Out of common sense. Let's face it, Selena: if he's going to survive among natural kzinti, he has to know how to fight back, how to respond to a challenge. He knows it, feels it in his bones. It has to happen, and it has to start soon. Not with the big creatures, but at least some smaller ones."

Selena found herself wondering how one went about procuring dangerous animals for slaughter: *"Hello, Dial-a-Beast? I would like to order one each of the following creatures for next month: one hyena, one wolf, one cougar, one black bear, one—yes, that's right. I'm interested in an ascending lethality rating..."*

Dieter hadn't stopped. "But I told him I would not support his other request."

Selena felt her brain slide to a halt. "What other request?"

"Can't you guess?"

They stared at each other for a long time. Then she got it: "Females?"

"Of course."

Boroshinsky snickered. "What else?"

Selena shot him a look that she hoped would scald the old man's conscience; he seemed serenely unperturbed by it. "Well, at least you didn't promise him the start of his own harem."

Dieter sighed. "Look, Selena, just because I'm not a scientist doesn't mean I'm stupid. He's six, so in his natural environment he'd be tussling with other male kzinti, and maybe some of the fights would even be getting serious. But there's no way he'd have access to a female of his own for another fifteen or twenty years, minimum. He has to earn a Name first; at the very earliest, that means age twenty. Right?"

"Okay, so you've read the reports. But that doesn't mean you should have—"

"Enough!" Boroshinsky was both frowning and smiling at them. "You argue like old married people. So why don't you make it official and be done with it?"

Boroshinsky's glee at playing matchmaker faded quickly; he saw the uncomfortable look on Dieter's face, saw what was no doubt a similar expression on Selena's. He had the good sense not to say anything else. Maybe later, Selena would reassure him that he'd done no harm, had no way of knowing that the two of them had been over it many times, but could not find a way to turn what they did have into a marriage. They were apart too much and had profoundly different lives, particularly since his was founded on the principle that, at any second, he might get called to defend the system, and die doing so.

Dieter pointed down into the defile. "Hap's moving again."

And so he was: there was a brief flash of black and orange which shot across the valley floor and disappeared into a dense cluster of Mediterranean pines. "He says that when he dreams, he can actually smell females, more clearly than he sees them."

Selena nodded. "That's my doing."

"What?"

"We've been piping in a small amount of their scent into the paddock at night."

"Good grief, why?"

"Well, in case you've forgotten, this is an experiment,

too. Mikhail and his people have found so many hormone secretion systems in the kzin it boggles the mind. So we were trying to get a measure of which ones are released when Hap detects the scent of a female."

Dieter's left eyebrow raised. "Wouldn't the answer to that be a foregone conclusion?"

Boroshinsky shook his head and waggled a corrective finger. "Not so obvious as you might expect. In human males, aggressive behavior of all kinds is associated with testosterone. But this is not the case with kzinti. After all, how do the adult males that lack females manage *not* to go murderously insane without mating access?"

Dieter nodded. "I don't know: how?"

Boroshinsky held up his hands. "We don't know yet. But some preliminary results suggest that the impulse to rut and the impulse toward violence do not seem to be created by the same hormone, although the presence of the first may change the hormonal cause of the latter."

"What?"

"Let's start with what we know: the kzinti are always ready to fight for honor, *da*?"

"Yes."

"But they can control and mitigate that impulse. However, we also have evidence that they become utterly uncontrollable and primal when they are fighting over females, particularly if the females are physically present. So this suggests that there are two different intensities or kinds of violence hormones, the first of which operates without regard to the presence of females, the second of which operates only in their presence, when the male's rutting-drive hormones

are released. And for kzin society to remain intact, some such mechanism *must* be present: if both drives were generated by the same hormone and the same conditions, the intensity and frequency of the males' routine dominance struggles would be indistinguishable from the mating combats. Meaning that there would be constant, irrepressible carnage. There would also be no way for the twenty percent of males who possess females to retain control over the other eighty percent who do not. The frustrated rutting urge would compel the eighty percent to sweep the others aside, regardless of the costs and casualties."

Selena shook her head. "But maybe the difference between dominance and mating aggression levels is simply a matter of cognitive selection; since mating is the primary drive, the male kzinti *choose* to risk everything to satisfy it."

"That was our first hypothesis, but some of my researchers discovered what we believe are different kinds of violence/aggression hormones. If we are right, this would mean that different external situations trigger the release of different hormones, which in turn generate different intensities and types of aggression."

Selena shrugged. "Evolution constantly reveals the universe's infinite capacity for creative solutions to adaptive problems."

Boroshinsky winked. "Or provides a playground for its more advanced species."

Selena stared. "What do you mean?"

"I mean, is this very nuanced hormonal arrangement a result of evolution or engineering?"

"What have you found?"

"Nothing, and I probably won't. Because if the kzin

hormonal matrix is a geneering job, it was both too good and done too long ago for us to be sure that it's artificial. In fact, if it is a construct, it's become so integral to the kzinti that their genome has evolved around it."

"Then why do you suspect interference at all?"

Boroshinsky shrugged. "Now that we've got Dr. Yang's data, we have access to full genetic analyses on the kzinti's native food animals. A close comparison of the genomes indicates that, like us, the kzinti evince a better-than-ninety-percent match to other chordates from their homeworld. But the kzinti's extraordinary diversity of secretions and hormones is a distinct break from their homeworld's dominant evolutionary paradigm."

Dieter shrugged. "But every species has differences, developmental departures from the shared gene code. That's why we don't look like dogs. Or lobsters, for that matter."

"True, but mutation from a common root stock also implies a basic constraint upon the rate of variation. Genetic change does not manifest as the sudden appearance of unprecedented structures, but as gradual variations upon a theme. And this isn't; the kzin hormone structures come out of nowhere. They just doesn't fit in with the rest of their world's evolutionary paradigms, so far as we can tell."

"Well, maybe you don't have access to enough of their homeworld's species. We just might not have the samples that would show the natural progression which produced this mutation." Boroshinsky nodded at Dieter's insight, but did not look convinced. Dieter smiled. "But you don't think that's the answer."

"No, I don't."

Selena turned back to look out over the preserve. On the ridgeline that rose up behind the forest, she saw a fleck of black-orange ascending its jagged protrusions, spiderlike. The movement was sure, swift, even a little frightening. "Wherever their hormonal equipment came from," she breathed out slowly, "it seems to work pretty well."

2405 BCE: Subject age—nine years

For the first time since they had brought Hap to her as a tiny black-orange puffball, Selena was scared, physically scared, to enter the same space that he was in.

He was no longer a little puffball now. Slightly more than two meters in height, Hap had also begun to fill out. His chest was deeper and wider and his haunches were so angular with muscle that they almost looked like a cubist's rendering. And what she had to tell him was not likely to improve his already dubious mood. Dubious because it was impossible to know exactly how or what he felt anymore.

He looked up as she stepped down from the floater, eyed it closely. What was he looking for? A means of commandeering it and escaping? Whether the humans' growing fear of him had pushed them over the line into carrying guns?

But all he said was, "N'shyao, Selena."

"And hello to you, Hap. It seems like you're not finding the bears too challenging anymore." She managed not to look at the lump of savaged black fur and exposed flesh, from which Hap had already carved out a sizeable lunch for himself.

"No, they're very slow. Maybe it's time to move to one of the bigger species. Or the more aggressive ones." He got up and stretched: the men in the floater sat up much straighter. Hap smiled, his mouth opening ever so slightly as he did; it was not a pleasant expression. "Now, as much as I am pleased to see you, Selena, this wasn't one of our regularly scheduled visits. Which I'm sure are all part of a careful interval of observation or conditioning or whatever it is you're doing with me."

She shrugged. "Probably some of both, which is no different from what a parent does as they nurture a child's process of maturation."

Hap's fur rippled sharply with amusement. "Now that was a great answer, Selena. And I suppose it's true, too. But tell me: what's gone wrong? Why are you out here now?"

Selena collected herself. "I've told you we have a female kzin in our keeping, as well."

"Yes, of course. Not like I'd forget that fact." He sat down, looked at her a long time. "She's dead, isn't she?"

"I—I'm afraid so, Hap."

"Why? Didn't she do all the tricks you asked?"

Selena forgot Hap's physical size, blinded by the greater enormity of his callousness, his facetiousness. "That's revolting in so many ways that I don't know where to start."

"Then don't start. And while we're on the topic of revolting, please spare me any claims of regret or commiseration. We kzinti are your lab animals, pure and simple. You just had to put one down. Oh, I know you probably get attached to some of them, but that comes with the job, doesn't it?"

Selena stalked over to look him in the eye. "We didn't put her down. Your own brother kzin did that."

For a moment, Hap sat mute. Then, faster than she could really follow, he was on his feet, crouched, ears halfway back and quivering, mouth slightly open.

And Selena didn't care. Instead she looked him up and down with an appraising glance: "And yes, they say he looked just about like that when he did it."

Hap looked down at her, then looked away. "I'm not angry at you, Selena. I don't know what I'm angry at, exactly. I just know that anything that happens to me—to us kzinti—is because of humans. You killed our mothers, you fight wars with our fathers, you brought us here and you watch us grow. And measure and observe and make all sorts of guesses. We're lab rats."

"No. It's not supposed to be that way. There have always been better intentions than that."

He looked at her for a long moment, measuring. Then he sat. "Oh. So Dieter was telling the truth after all, last month."

Selena had known that this encounter could go in many possible directions. But this surprise—that Dieter had obviously visited Hap last month, without authorization or escort—had not been on her list of anticipated outcomes. "What?" she said.

"Ah, so he never told you about visiting me? Well, so he kept his promise to keep it a secret. Another truth he told that I presumed was a lie." For a split second, Hap might have looked guilty or wistful, but the expression was gone as quickly as it had arisen.

"Dieter told me that most of you were hoping to allow me to go back to the kzinti. To function as a mediator, maybe."

That son of a bitch of a meddling Wunderlander—

"No, Selena, don't be angry with him. In fact, right now, the fact that he shared that with me—and that it was the truth, and didn't tell you about doing so—well, it makes me think that maybe you're not all faithless after all."

"You really think that? That humans are all faithless?"

"Well, why wouldn't I? Yes, you've provided most of what you've promised, but what you've promised is only a tiny fraction of what I've requested. And why can't you provide the rest?" He leaned back until he was supine. "Because I am the enemy, because I'm your prisoner." His tone became extravagantly sarcastic. "If you let me out, who knows what havoc I might cause? What secrets I might learn?"

Selena nodded. "Right. Well, I can see coming out here was a mistake. I'll see you next week, Hap, as per the schedule." She turned on her heel and made for the floater with a brisk step.

"Selena, wait."

She paused, turned.

Hap was staring at her and she couldn't read his eyes, not because they were guarded, but because the mix of emotions and impulses was so tangled and contradictory that it defied delineation. "I'd like to know what happened to the female. 'Pretty,' you called her, right?"

Selena folded her arms but did not reapproach. "That is correct."

"And one of your researchers decided to see what would happen if she was put together with one of the other males, now that they are sexually mature."

Selena felt her stern demeanor slip. Come to think of it, Hap was right: they were just lab rats, after all. At least that's how Pyragy had acted: playing god with his specimens...

Hap's voice was patient: "You didn't approve."

Selena shouted, thereby overriding what started as a choked sob. "Of course I didn't approve! I fought him—the decision—every way I could."

"But you weren't in charge."

"No. And the person who was normally in charge had a heart attack and was still recovering." *Please, Mikhail: get better quickly, for your sake, for my sake, for Hap's sake.* "So the decision rested with someone who is not involved in our work directly."

"Ah. An *administrator*?"

She nodded, both at the word and the way he said it: with a healthy measure of parodic hauteur. "He gave the orders and I tried to get them overturned. But there wasn't enough time. He wouldn't wait."

"Is he a...a..." Hap struggled for the word; although infinitely more mature than a human nine year old, he still had a lot of language learning to do. "...a sadist?"

"No." *Although sometimes I wonder...* "He wasn't motivated by sadism."

Hap thought. "He was trying to use mating as a reward mechanism, then."

Selena felt her mouth snap shut, stunned at the canny insight of the almost-mature kzin before her. Yes, he might be young, but like all his breed, he learned quickly; he had to, if he was to survive. The kzin genotype did not breed many geniuses: the species was inherently unsuited to long periods of reflection. But the genotype also didn't breed many idiots: in accord with the old axiom that there were two kinds of combatants, the quick and the dead, the kzinti survived by having quick reflexes, quick wits or both.

Hap pushed for confirmation of his conjecture. "So it *was* an attempt at creating a new reward mechanism?"

Well, why not answer? Hap had figured it out on his own, anyway. "Yes. And I wouldn't let him use *you* as the test subject. I had that much authority over the process, anyway."

"Hmm. Perhaps I wouldn't have killed her, either." A sharp, territorial glint danced briefly through Hap's eyes and was gone, or maybe just quickly concealed.

Selena sighed. "Perhaps not. Probably not. But if I had given him access to you, that would have just been the edge of the wedge. I could have lost control, might no longer have been able to—" She dragged to a halt, not knowing how to explain.

"You might not have been able to continue to protect me," he finished for her.

Selena nodded. "I know it sounds absurd, that I have to protect you from a colleague who wants to give you the opportunity to mate. But—"

"No, actually, I can see it very clearly, Selena. I may not like the restrictions on my life—and I'm coming to see that you don't, either—but you've been as consistent, and also as humane, as you can be in maintaining those constraints. But this administrator seems rash. Which I find odd: aren't administrators supposed to be the more cautious persons in an organization, the ones who keep the workers from running off in all directions, acting without authorization?"

Selena smiled. "Yes. And he certainly does that. But—"

"But what?"

"He had very different ideas about how you were to be raised. Several of us, his lieutenants you might say, had to appeal to *his* superiors to keep him from treating you kzinti in . . . questionable ways."

"Torture?"

"No. Well, yes, in a manner of speaking."

Hap frowned, then his eyes opened wide. "Oh, I see: not bodily torture. Something mental. Or behavioral."

"Behavioral."

Hap thought a long time, his eyes half-lidded. Then he nodded: "He was the one who tried to make me eat cooked meat, wasn't he?"

Selena gaped. "You remember that?"

"Of course I do. So it *was* him?"

Selena nodded.

"So the torture you are referring to: he wanted to—how would you say it?—humanize us?"

Selena sighed. "Something like that. But higher powers intervened shortly after you came to live with us."

"And these higher powers are the ones who want to send me back to the kzinti as a mediator, as Dieter described?"

"Yes. But they aren't really in charge of, of"— she almost said "the project" but stopped herself in time—"our actions. They only step in if something goes wrong."

"So they'll be stepping in, now."

"Yes, in a very big way." And would very probably

do so by permanently removing Pyragy, a step that was at least five years overdue.

Hap nodded. "So I take it that this administrator introduced Pretty to the oldest male, the one who almost tore into me. What did you name him, by the way?"

Selena stumbled after a lie, gave up, closed her eyes as she spoke: "Cranky Cat. They named him Cranky Cat."

When she opened her eyes, Hap's fur was rippling, but his eyes were hard. Sardonic amusement was a kzin expression she was learning to identify quickly these days. "What a dignified name," Hap slurred. "Although I have to admit it is accurate, too. So Cranky Cat didn't like Pretty any more than he liked me."

"No, he didn't." Selena shut her eyes. "It was a disaster. Because I was trying to do everything I could do to stop it, the administrator didn't inform me when the introduction was taking place. I got a panicked call from the researcher who worked most closely with Pretty, but by the time I got there, it was too late."

Selena tried to put the memory of the blood-spattered paddock out of her mind, couldn't. "We knew that kzin mating was pretty rough by human standards. So the overseers didn't know until it was too late that this was—well, way beyond that." The video ran on endless loop in her memory: the frenzied thrashing of Pretty; the pinning paws of Cranky Cat, which, as he came close to completing the coupling, began crushing, piercing, slashing— "He was coupling and killing her at the same time. And when our people realized what was happening, and tried to intervene, he finished. Both acts."

Hap's voice buzzed with a suppressed snarl. "Why did he do it?"

Selena shrugged. "There's no way to find out. Cranky Cat never learned how to speak: not our language, nor yours. He wouldn't have anything to do with us. So we'll never know why he did it. But if you want my gut reaction, Cranky Cat's drives made him unable to resist the urge to copulate, even as his speciate aversion to us made him kill her."

"And why would his hatred of humans prompt him to kill her? Because he couldn't reach you?"

"No, he wasn't symbolically killing us. It was because he could smell that she was our creature. And at a deep, primal level, he could not abide that. He didn't think about what he did; he just did it."

Hap continued to stare at her, unblinking. Then his tail switched fitfully and he rose, moving to sit alongside the mauled carcass that, two hours ago, had been a black bear. "Selena, I want to know your world. All of it."

"Hap, you've figured out so much on your own, so you've got to know I don't have the authority to make that promise."

"I know that. But if you don't convince them to let me know more about Earth, then how will I be able to help you later on? Knowing your language and your ways is not enough. The kzinti—the real kzinti—will ask me for my honest opinion, for what you would call my gut reaction, but which is better expressed in the Heroes' Tongue as *grreeowm'm'hysh*. 'Ancestral spine-whispers.' If I do not know your world, I won't be able to answer the questions that will make me useful to *them*. So they will ignore me."

Selena shut her eyes tightly, finding herself required to reject the very appeal that she herself had made so many times to the board, and for precisely the same reasons. "I cannot let you out into our world. I'm not permitted to do so. And I know they won't change their minds about that."

"Then allow your world to come in here."

Selena opened her eyes. "What did you have in mind?"

"Give me free and unrestricted access to your public records, your library, your news: all of it."

Selena smiled. "Relying on any one of those sources could give you a very distorted view of our world."

"That is why I want—why I *need*—to see all of it. I presume no one voice will speak a complete truth. So I will get to know your world in the same way I get the full measure of each new prey animal you provide: by studying it from all perspectives." Hap's fur rippled slowly in a show of good-natured amicability. "Is it not a reasonable request?"

Selena stared at him. "It is. Quite reasonable."

Pyragy was putting on a good show in front of the admiral and the associate executive chair: to watch and listen to him, you'd never have guessed that he was doing everything he could to get Selena discredited and drummed out of the scientific community. "This is an excellent turn of events. You might even say that this has produced a silver lining greater than the darkness which started it: the unfortunate death of the female."

Admiral Coelho-Chase shrugged, suppressing disgust at Pyragy's increasingly obsequious mannerisms. "Dr. Navarre, much as I regret admitting it, the director does make a good point: it seems that Hap is now interested in the mission for which we've been grooming him, and that he's coming back around to us in general. By any objective standards, those are excellent changes in him."

"Yes, Admiral, they are quite excellent. But I'm afraid you are dead wrong about him becoming interested in his mission. Or rather, yes, he's interested now—but not for the reasons you think."

"Oh?"

"Admiral, Hap intends to betray us. At the very first opportunity he has to do so."

"What? You mean this is all a conceit?"

Pyragy seemed ready to rub the admiral's arm soothingly. "Dr. Navarre is exaggerating, at best, or prevaricating, at worst. She is just trying to diminish the new opportunities which have arisen from the unfortunate incident involving the female—"

"No, I'm quite serious. And I know my subject: Hap means to betray us."

In the nine years she had known him, this was the first time Admiral Coelho-Chase had ever sputtered. "This is outrageous, if it's true. After we've cared for him all these years—why, if he wasn't a kzin, it would be treason, pure and simple."

"But," Selena explained levelly, "he is a kzin and therefore it is not treason. In fact, it is probably not as much a political action as it a developmental action."

"What?"

"Admiral, look at his age. At this point in his growth

phase, it is entirely natural for kzinti, like humans, to buck authority. Buck it hard. In the case of young kzinti, this takes the shape of suiting their actions to their words: when they start to talk the talk, they expect that they will be called upon to walk the walk. It is a phase of high aggression and a need to distinguish themselves from their parental and mentor figures by pursuing opposed paths, by separation, and frequently, by turning upon those who supported them."

"And that's natural?"

"Yes, just like rebelliousness in a teenager."

"But he is almost full-grown and is now, according to you, determined to work as a confidential agent for the natural kzinti."

Pyragy squared his shoulders dramatically. "Then, if this is true, we must euthanize him. Immediately."

Selena surprised herself with the speed and vociferousness of her rebuttal. "Why? Because he won't join hands and sing *kumbayah* with us? Damn it, he *has* to go through this if he's to become an adult. Our own human children do. Or did, until lotus-eating idealists neutered them. But at least that's over with."

Pyragy's upper lip contracted as though he had caught a whiff of dung. "Yes. The Golden Age of Peace is indeed behind us, and we have allowed our children to be raised with the knowledge of war and violence. With terrible results."

"If speciate survival is a terrible result, then I guess you're right, Director Pyragy. But this new generation has—thank God—the gumption and aggressiveness that comes from having a few fistfights growing up, and trying cases with their parents."

"Yes," Pyragy retorted, "and in all probability, by

the time those children are as old as I am, they will no longer need to fight the kzinti, because they will have become as kzinti, themselves." Pyragy looked as though he might spit. "It is horrific, barbaric."

"A lot of real-life situations are, Director—horrific and barbaric. And having some familiarity with those realities is necessary if you're going to have a reasonable chance of surviving a serious encounter with any of them. That's part of the advantage of having kids, human or kzin, grow up in contention with their own parents, as well as their peers. It teaches kids not only about the limits of change, but also about conflict itself. They learn when its appropriate and when it's not. Which battles to fight, which to avoid, which warrant biding one's time. And every scrap of evidence we have says that the kzinti need that experience more than humans, much more. So before we declare Hap an irreclaimable turncoat, let's remember this: we're all he's got, which means we're his only scratching post. So, of course, he's going to go through this phase. And a valid point of contention like this one—to whom he owes his first loyalties—is a natural lightning rod for those impulses and emotions."

Associate Executive Chair Dennehy was studying Selena closely, as if he were making several decisions at once. "And what if this isn't just a teenage phase, Dr. Navarre? After all, Hap has more reason to rebel against authority than any teen ever born."

Selena nodded soberly. "Now that's truth, plain and simple, Executive Dennehy. And yes, in turning away from us now, he could be starting down a path that ultimately makes him our permanent, sworn enemy. It might be that he never turns back toward us the way most human kids do when they overcome the tempests of their social and hormonal storm season that we call adolescence. And that's too bad.

"But it was always a risk, one we knew and articulated right at the outset of this project. And, after all, he's right to feel the way he does. He's been brought up to be a traitor to his own people, insofar as he is a creature of our making and interests. So we can only hope that, when his wisdom catches up with his intelligence, he will also realize that we were as honest as we could be throughout, eschewed the tactics of coercion, and have always worked not just for our own best interests, but for his, and his people's, as well."

Pyragy snorted. "You give him entirely too much credit. He will not stop to think about these things. This is why he had to be civilized—fully and effectively civilized—first: by remaining a creature driven by his primal drives rather than thought, he will remain insensate to these higher appeals."

"Then, Director Pyragy, you should be glad that he is turning away from us, here and now. Because if he's not smart enough on his *own* to reflect upon his upbringing in the years to come, then he's not the right person for the job of being our voice to the kzinti. A person incapable of autonomous reflection or insight would be disastrous to our diplomatic efforts, whatever their end."

Pyragy grumbled but said nothing loud enough for anyone to hear.

Dennehy was nodding, though. "Dr. Navarre, however else these events might play out, I think you're absolutely right about one thing: we can't make a being what he is not. If a kzin, or at least this kzin, is capable—as you posit—of one day seeing our actions in perspective, then this is just a bump in the road, and possibly a necessary one. But if he is not, then you're right again: he never would have been any good to us as a liaison."

Selena nodded. "So does this mean that we can start giving Hap increased access to news, to libraries, to—?"

Dennehy nodded back. "Show him our world, Dr. Navarre. Starting today."

2406 BCE: Subject age—ten years

Selena twisted the strand of silver-gray hair around her finger again and again and again.

"What is that?" Hap's voice was throaty and deep.

"This? Oh, nothing. This is nothing."

"You don't toy obsessively with nothings, Selena." He sniffed speculatively. "It's a lock of Dieter's hair, isn't it?"

She felt a hot blush rise high on her cheeks, looked away: *schoolgirl-stupid, that's what I am.*

Hap's fur pulsed once, slowly. "Don't be ashamed. I wish they still allowed Dieter to come in to see me. I miss him, too. A lot."

"Really? Why?"

"Because Dieter had true *strakh*, honor."

"There was a time you couldn't abide the sight or smell of him."

Hap swung his head slightly from side to side; an instinctual gesture, not learned, that was the kzin equivalent of a shrug. "It wasn't as straightforward as that, Selena. I just didn't know how to deal with what he had done."

"And now you do?"

Hap's eyes partially narrowed in easy acquiescence. "Yes. He was a warrior, doing a warrior's work. But when I was no longer part of his warrior work, he became a friend. He watched over me, even when your rules said he wasn't supposed to." And Selena could feel, or at least imagined, the unuttered rebuke: *which was more than* you *ever did for me.* Which was, sadly, bitterly, true.

"So you've come to see Dieter as having more than one role in your life, as having a multifaceted identity?"

Kzinti rolled their eyes much as humans did: Hap did it now. "No, Selena, you don't understand at all. Dieter doesn't have a 'multifaceted identity.' *Eeyaach,* even I understand him better than that, and I don't mate with him." Selena didn't know which she found more arresting: Hap's patronizing tone or the notion of Dieter and a kzin mating. "Dieter is a warrior: that's a single identity, not one of many. Seeing him as having many identities is just a by-product of your culture's squeamishness. You're trying to excuse his violent actions by pointing to all the other, gentle parts of him. Rubbish."

"Always nice to have another chat about the infinite failings of the human race," Selena muttered, with a good deal less good grace than she had intended.

"Oh, your failings aren't infinite, just very plentiful."

"Thanks for yet another correction. It's amazing that you consider us worthy of your improving efforts."

"Well . . . I don't; not really. But some of you are worth it."

"Dieter, for instance?"

"Dieter. And you."

"No one else?"

"I don't exactly have a wide circle of friends, Selena."

"Well, I doubt you're missing very much, then. We humans are, as you imply, hardly worth the time. Unlike kzinti, who are sterling examples of altruism and are surely treating their human slaves on Wunderland so much better than we are treating you."

One lip rippled away from a tooth momentarily. "The kzinti say what they mean and do what they say."

"Ah, so honor is the only virtue worth having?"

"It is the core virtue, at any rate."

"And so you can school us in the nuances of honor?"

Hap shrugged like a human. "It is rare that kzinti lack honor. It is rare that humans have it."

"Which is why you've decided that we are your enemies."

Hap's ears trembled and twitched backward. "Selena, don't put words in my mouth. I'm simply not in a rush to help the people who destroyed my life and family and who've been lying to me ever since. Well, most of them."

She could see the sacred, sainted image of Dieter Armbrust almost swimming in his eyes. It was a face she was imagining a lot, too: a face she would not see for at least two years, according to his most recent orders. Something was afoot, something he either did not know or could not tell her about. He had departed this morning. Whereto? Unknown. Mission? Unknown. Time until next contact? Unknown.

When she emerged from her own brief reverie, she saw that Hap was staring at the holding paddock again. "It's really quite large," he commented, nodding toward the immense bear that was walking the two-hundred-meter perimeter of the enclosure. When it reached the part closest to them, the massive creature put up its nose, growled, and tried the strength of the barrier. Defeated and disgruntled, it returned to its perambulations.

"Magnificent," purr-buzzed Hap from deep in his throat. "*Arctodus simus*, or the extinct short-faced bear, courtesy of Earth's best reverse-genetics. Last specimen thought to have died about thirteen thousand years ago. Shoulder height of one point eight meters when on all fours, four meters when upright, and all muscle. Almost a full metric ton of unrelenting carnivorous fury." He paused, drew in a deep breath. Then he exhaled: "Magnificent."

Selena looked at Hap sideways. "Hap."

"Yes?"

"Don't get any smart ideas."

"Smart ideas are the only ones I have, Selena."

"I'm not joking, Hap. No tricks, now."

"Tricks? What do you mean?"

"You know what I mean. For now, just leave that bear alone."

Hap stared at her. "And just what do you think I might do? I can't pull down the fence, and you've never been kind enough to give me a key to the gate. So just let me appreciate and savor my next challenge in peace, Selena."

She looked at the bear; as big as Hap was, the bear was simply immense, larger than any mammalian predator had a right to be. "Okay, Hap. But—"

"But what?"

"That's one big bear. And I—I worry about you, Hap."

He looked at her, his ears like pink half-parasols, his

eyes wide. One smooth ripple coursed the length of his pelt. "I know," he said.

Selena, still in her nightshirt and sweatpants, grabbed for a siderail when the floater rushed down from thirty meters, having cleared the perimeter fence of Hap's preserve.

"Go there—" she screamed, pointing, "there: the holding paddock."

The pilot nodded curt understanding; the floater swerved so sharply that Selena had to hold on to the siderail with both hands, partly to keep from flying out of the vehicle, partly to keep from vomiting.

"What are you seeing with thermal imaging?" she shouted above the wind.

The senior of the two security specialists shook his head. "Nothing yet."

That was the same moment that the pilot switched on the forward floodlights, and the paddock gate jumped out of the darkness in high contrast: a sudden, vertical blue-white mesh that scalloped itself out of the surrounding black.

And it was open.

Selena saw the reason faster than she could blink her eyes: cracked wedges of stone—mostly slate, from the look of it—littered the area around the shattered lock. Hap had wedged them in, tighter and tighter until the lock had burst.

But no, that didn't make any sense: the lock was rated for far more pounds per square inch than either Hap or the bear could generate on their own, even if they threw themselves headlong against the gate with a running start . . .

Yes, it was strong enough to thwart either one of them—but not both.

The monstrous genius of Hap's plan now unfolded before her. He had baited the bear into charging against the fence repeatedly. And every time that mountain of muscles, bone and fangs crashed into the gate, Hap had jammed a slightly wider wedge into the space between the frame and the lock until, adding his own strength, the gate was sprung.

"Damn it," the senior security specialist snapped, "how did this happen? Where are the drones? Where are the—?"

And then Selena saw the telltale signs of the rest of Hap's careful handiwork and planning. He had built the equivalent of a lean-to about two hundred meters away from the paddock: the semi-autonomous drones were littered about it. He had evidently watched how they operated, had discerned the one constant pattern: one was always close, three were farther off. So when he went into the lean-to, the closest drone lost access, tried following him in—and had been smashed with the discarded cudgel Selena saw in the doorway. One after another, the smart 'bots had demonstrated just how titanically stupid they really were. Why there had not been better oversight, she would inquire later: someone had evidently taken a very long coffee break. Which, now that she thought about it, was yet another pattern that Hap had probably figured out by testing the responsiveness of the drones. He had obviously learned to distinguish when they were receiving overrides from a live operator in comparison to when they were simply following the predictable commands of their expert system. Meaning that he had been able to put his plan into action when the odds were high that he was under automated, rather than live, surveillance.

"I've got a thermal bloom—there." The security specialist pointed up toward the ridgeline. "Downloading coordinates."

"ETA?" Selena demanded.

The pilot looked back; he and the security specialist exchanged glances. The latter coughed deferentially: "Dr. Navarre, the safety protocols are quite clear on this matter. When we do not have clear visual lock on any of the predators in the preserve, we are to assume—"

"I wrote those protocols, damn it, and now I am ordering you to disregard them. On my authority." She faced the pilot. "Fly. Now."

He did.

They could hear the melee almost three hundred meters away, even over the attitude fans and screaming engine of the floater: a constant counterpoint of basso-profundo bellows and high-pitched kzinti yowls of what sounded like ecstatic fury. She had heard Hap fight predators before, but the sound had never been like this. She leaned over the pilot's shoulder and shouted: "Hurry!"

The floater sped forward and then swerved into the steep-sided arroyo that cut lengthwise into the ridge, paralleling the crest before narrowing to a dead end. The pilot reached for the floodlights. Selena put a restraining hand on his shoulder.

"Don't you want to save him, Doctor?"

"Yes, but if we're going to be sure of doing that, we don't dare blind him."

"Then use these, ma'am." The junior security specialist, who was not much more than a kid, handed her his combo-goggles: light intensification blended with thermal imaging, software-integrated to provide maximum visibility under changing conditions. She slipped them on.

And her breath caught in her throat. Hap was doing something she had never seen before: he was retreating. His fur sticking slick against his body from the sweat pouring out of him, he scanned the surrounding slopes, looking for a way out.

The bear rushed him, so large that even before it got to him, Selena was unable to see Hap over its shambling bulk.

There was a flash of bioheat on shadow—Hap dodging toward the canyon wall—as the bear lunged, raking long claws at the evasive kzin, who, grazed, spun like a top, his yowl echoing up out of the ravine.

But Hap never really fell; tumbled by the glancing blow, he landed and jumped in the same moment, and was suddenly attached to the bear's right flank, all four paws spread wide, claws buried in the thick hide, his jaws reaching, snapping up toward the spine.

Which was when the bear rolled, but not away from the attack: rather, the bear rolled into it.

Hap had never encountered such a move, possibly because he had never encountered so large and comparatively invulnerable opponent. Even the modern brown bears had instinctively pushed themselves away from the teeth-bristling kzin jaws. Which had made for a predictable endgame: Hap was so much faster that, by swinging himself aggressively into the roll, he always came down on the far side of the bears, his body wide of their dangerous jaws and arms. That was always the beginning of the end: the only variable was the time required to finish the job.

But the prehistoric bear had no fear of Hap, and if it felt the need to protect its head and neck from the kzin that had attached itself to its left side, that need was not stronger than its impulse to roll in the direction of its attacker, thereby crushing him beneath his metric ton of mass.

Which squeezed a scream out of Hap that sent a needle of fear-pain lancing down into Selena's bowels and which she realized was a stab of maternal terror. Until the senior security specialist grabbed her shoulder roughly, she didn't realize that she had also moved next to the railing, one leg already rising to clear it. She didn't notice the specialist's startled stare: she saw nothing but the battle down in the arroyo.

The bear, feeling Hap's grip weaken and his teeth release into a scream, twisted so that the kzin was now mostly under him. The beast's immense head, as large as a small refrigerator, bore Hap down, struggling and squirming as he was pinned in place by the snout. The jaws opened like those of a small steam-shovel and then snapped closed, locking down on the kzin's upper left ribcage.

The sharp splintering of kzin bone reminded Selena of a sound she had heard years ago, sailing with Dieter down in Florida: their four-inch fiberglass mast had snapped in a sudden gale off the Keys. Hap's ribs sounded like three of those masts breaking in rapid sequence.

Hap squirmed, thrashed, yowled, blood welling up out of his throat, staining his maw.

"Do you have a shot?" Selena coughed through the bile in her throat and mouth.

The senior security specialist shook his head. "Steady

this damned floater," he growled at the pilot. Knowing, as they all did, that the thermals here were just enough to put a dangerous, unpredictable quiver in the vehicle, no matter what the pilot did.

And there wasn't the time, anyway. Selena could tell, seeing with eyes that had learned to read such actions and understand their portents millenia ago, that the bear would soon attempt to shift to a final, mortal bite. It was in the sideways slide of the creature's shoulders, the sudden rigidity of the head as it prepared for the kill.

But, whether it took the bear longer to get better purchase for that next bite, or perhaps the unexpectedly alien taste of a creature that did not share its genetic rootstock, the bear opened its maw a fraction sooner than instinct had instructed. Then the massive jaws pushed in quickly again, looking for a bigger mouthful of kzin to crush.

Selena gasped—not at the bear's lunge but at Hap's blinding speed. In the half-eyeblink that the ursoid's viselike jaws relented, the kzin became a writhing corkscrew-blur of orange and black. The bear's jaws snapped down resoundingly on thin air. Hap's blood, trailing behind as he made his almost balletic escape, landed in a wide, dark arc upon the dry ground.

Selena thumped the driver on the back. "Now! The floodlights! NOW!"

The pilot complied, and the bear flinched away, the lights full in its eyes. Hap, half-facing the other direction, was not so completely blinded, and reacted with extraordinary speed and tactical presence of mind.

As the bear tried to avoid the light, obviously uncertain what to do next, the kzin quickly scanned the sides of the arroyo, and found what he was looking for: a rocky outcropping. Knowing it to be too steep and small to be useful as a perch, Selena did not understand Hap's intent—until, gauging the bear's half-blind approach, he leapt straight at the stony protrusion.

But instead of landing on it, Hap used it like a springboard: all four limbs were extended like ready shock absorbers when he hit it. In the split second before gravity could pull him down, he looked like a bug, fantastically affixed to the wall of the arroyo. Then he pushed off with savage force, propelling himself at the bear: he twisted in mid-air and landed square on his adversary's back.

Normally, this would be when Hap would go for a killing bite to the back of the neck. But judging from the torn fur of the bear, he had already tried that tactic and had discovered the almost armored skeleton residing beneath that thick hide: even for the manic strength of a combat-stimulated kzin, the skull and neck bones of *Arctodus simus* were simply too hard to snap or even dent.

So Hap adapted: holding on with his teeth and rear claws, he used his front paws to rake down across the bear's face, from over the top of its head. The bear shook, seemed about to reprise its defensive roll, and then howled as a razor-sharp kzin claw found its mark: an eye. Forgetting the roll, the bear tried breaking away, running. Hap hung on, slashed, slashed again—and another, even more piteous roar announced the loss of the bear's other eye.

Hap wasted no time, ripping with mouth and claws at the side of the bear's face. It flinched away, stumbled: Hap was there again, teeth sinking deep into one of the steady legs.

The bear went down. A flash of black and orange was quickly at the side of its throat, well wide of the bear's killing jaws, and behind the sweeping arc of its front paws. Hap buried his face deep into that part of the neck that would have housed the carotid artery in a human...

...Four of whom watched, speechless, from the airborne platform of the floater. Then the young security specialist retched. A moment later, his superior muttered, "Jesus Christ."

Selena tapped the stunned, motionless pilot lightly on the back. "Kill the lights," she said.

2408 BCE: Sol System, Asteroid Belt near Ceres

Dieter Armbrust knew he had lost the last smallship in his command group a moment before his SensorOp reported it. "Jiang just bought it, sir. Orders?"

Well, thought Dieter, *now, commanding the 128th Squadron just means I have to fight my ship. For as long as I can. Which might not be very much longer*, he conceded, with a glance at the plot.

The three remaining kzin Raker IIs were closing in on him from three points of the battlesphere: high to port, low on the bow, dead astern. The starboard side was occluded by a planetoid whose identifying number he'd forgotten. It wasn't one of the major ones: it showed some evidence of old robotic prospecting, but no active mining. Not surprising: judging from the densitometer scans, it was just dead rock.

But that dead rock had kept him alive, shielding him from counterfire while the last two ships of his command—Jiang's and his own *Catscratch Fever*—concentrated their fire on one half of the kzin squadron that they had baited into this part of the Belt. But now the other half of the ratcat formation was coming in on him, pinning him against the planetoid. Or so they intended.

Still, the kzinti had recovered quickly from Dieter's ambush, a skill at which they had been steadily improving since their invasion force had arrived insystem twelve days ago. Scream-and-pounce was no longer the full measure of their tactical repertoire. They had become canny hunters, too, and this group had been the canniest yet.

And Dieter Armbrust would know. He had been in the thick of the fighting since this fourth kzin fleet had made its real objectives clear: to smash the defenses of the Belt as a preliminary to attacking Earth. The ratcats had become smarter, analyzing the unfolding game two or three moves in advance, instead of being constrained to their prior engagement doctrine of "damn the torpedos; full speed ahead." Almost two weeks' worth of human ruses and decoy ships, double-reverses, and delayed envelopments had taught them not to ignore the torpedoes (or any of the other human toys in the battlespace) and to proceed with a judicious mix of decisiveness and caution.

But I've still got one trick left up my sleeve, thought Dieter. "Ms. Hitsu, ready at the helm: we are bringing the auxiliary thrust package on line within the minute. Until then, slow to one-quarter, feathering the gravitic planer to simulate battle damage."

"Should I engage the damage simulation subroutine, Captain Armbr—?"

"Not entirely. Use occasional overrides. I'm worried that our automated damage mimicry is becoming predictable enough that their computers can detect it. It was a great trick a week ago, but it's getting old. Time to revivify it by throwing in some random human overrides."

"Yes, sir."

"Mr. Paraway?"

"Engineering here, sir."

"If we dump the current charge stored in our capacitors, how fast can we initiate the auxiliary thrust package?"

"About two seconds, sir."

"Then prepare to do so on my mark."

"Awaiting your mark, sir."

On the plot, Armbrust watched as the three motes designating the kzin ships closed in, the one astern closing the gap most rapidly, the one on his bow coming fully out of the shadow of the planetoid alongside which the *Catscratch Fever* was making its now unsteady way. The bogey to port was keeping distance: she'd taken some beam damage at the start of the engagement, and might not be so ready to mix it up at closer ranges anymore. All the better.

"Helm: range to bogey astern?"

"Fifty klicks, sir. Full launch of missiles detected."

"Full power to aft shields, as well as all active defenses that can bear."

"Missile launch from the bogey dead ahead, sir. Should I take evasive—?"

"Steady at the helm, Ms. Hitsu. Remainder of active

defenses are to concentrate upon those missiles. Range to bogey astern?"

"Uh—thirty klicks, sir. They're coming up our pipes, closing to the point where shield effectiveness will begin eroding."

"Which is what I'm counting on. Tell me when they are at ten klicks."

"Uh—now, sir!"

"Mr. Paraway, engage the auxiliary thrust package."

The *Catscratch Fever* bucked as kzin missiles and beams hammered at her stern, almost pushing through the defenses there. Shocks from the other direction announced the close intercept of the bow-bogey's missiles. Meanwhile, a thready tremor rose up through the deck of the heavily modified smallship. Possibly, on the bridge of the stern-chasing *Raker II*, kzin eyes opened wide as they beheld the blue glow of an initiating fusion thruster—right before the star-hot exhaust came out and vaporized them like a moth caught in the flame of an acetylene torch. It had not occurred to this invasion's kzinti that, apparently, the humans would not rely solely upon the gravitic planer drives: fusion still had a place as a thrust agency. And as a surprise weapon at close range.

The thruster's extra propulsive force shot the *Catscratch Fever* almost straight at the bow-bearing kzin bogey. Armbrust turned to his weapons officer. "All tubes and beams on that ratcat. Cascading fire: don't stop 'til she's gone."

Which took less than four seconds, during which exchange the *Catscratch Fever* took a few heavy hits herself, tumbling both crew and electronics. When the jolts and jerks ceased, the viewscreen was flickering, the sensors were offline, inertial damping sketchy. Armbrust swung himself up from the deck and back into the commander's chair. "Damage report?"

"Coming in, sir."

"Helm; do you have control?"

"Yes, sir, but I'm flying without sensors."

"Do you have visual?"

"Scope-relays only, sir."

"They'll do. Take us back around this rock; we need to have its mass screening us as we sort ourselves out—before the third kzin ship arrives."

"Aye, sir; flying by eye," announced Hitsu.

Who was unable to see that the kzin had indeed learned all sorts of devious tricks from fighting the humans. Invisible in the great, dark reaches of space, Lieutenant Hitsu had no way of detecting the minefield that the now-destroyed kzin bow-bogey had sown just in the lee of the planetoid. Into which the *Catscratch Fever* now blindly flew.

At best speed.

2408 BCE: Subject age—twelve years

"If it's any consolation, he never knew what hit him."

Hap did not look over at Selena. "It doesn't sound like that fact has been much consolation for you."

"No, it hasn't been. Not in the least." Selena damned herself as she felt a cool, wet line trace itself from her left eye down the long, smooth slope of her cheek. She had promised herself she wouldn't tell Hap about Dieter's death until she could talk about it calmly, with perfect composure. She had thought she was ready; she had practiced in front of the mirror for three weeks, and finally, two days ago, had been able to get through her whole semi-rehearsed speech without so much as a quaver in her voice.

But that had been without an audience, without feeling the eyes of another person who knew how she felt about Dieter, who had been around to sense the love that had existed between them, despite the separations and impediments imposed by their respective careers and duties. Most importantly, in sharing the news with Hap, she was sharing it with another person who had loved Dieter, who would feel his own loss, and in expressing it—even if only by the careful suppression of public grief—would resummon Selena's.

Of course, she temporized, *maybe I never was going to be* that *ready: maybe one never is, when the loss is as painful as this one.*

What Hap was feeling was unreadable. He was perfectly still, except for the faint expansion and contraction of his immense ribs: ribs which still bore the ragged scars of his first battle with a prehistoric short-faced bear.

"I have something for you," Selena said. "Two things, actually."

Hap did not look at her. "Oh? What are they?"

"Documents. One is a letter from Dieter, which he left with me years ago, and then recently updated." If that had any impact upon Hap, she could not detect it. Then again, there was something in his posture and the set of his jaw which made her suspect that he would probably not have reacted to an incoming artillery barrage.

"I am grateful for it. And the other document?"

"It is the transcript of the debriefing of a man from the Wunderland system. His name is Kenneth Upton-Schleisser. The kzin occupiers attempted to use him to gain control of the slowship *R. P. Feynman* prior to their recent invasion of this system. You might find it interesting reading."

"Why? Because I will therein learn of the horrors of war the kzinti have brought to the Alpha Centauri system?"

"Well, yes, but not battlefield horrors."

"What do you mean?"

"Well, in addition to often using children and innocent persons condemned on thin pretexts to populate their live hunts on the surface of Wunderland—"

That got a reaction from Hap: the faintest flinch, but clearly this was not in alignment with the "noble-warrior" view he had constructed of his own race, in comparison to humanity.

"—he reports how the kzinti convinced him to commit treason: they presented him with the severed hand of his wife. As an added incentive, his children would be used in a Hero's Hunt if he did not succeed. He did not." Selena stretched weary muscles; news of Dieter's death had made her suddenly feel every year of her age. More.

"And so you have told me this. Why do I need to read the full transcript?"

"Because you won't really believe the story unless you do. If I were in your position, I would suspect it was a propaganda narrative; a few unpretty truths amplified and bloated until they enrage readers, but bearing little resemblance to reality. When you read what

Upton-Schleisser said, and how he said it, you'll know he's telling the truth. And he's offered to meet with you personally: to come here, without guard if you prefer, so that you can look into his eyes and hear his words from his own mouth. He tells me that this is the sort of personal accountability that the kzinti admire. Back in Centauri, he stood up to them, told the truth, and they respected him. They still used him ruthlessly, of course, but apparently they held him in some esteem."

"They would, I think. But why would he be so willing to speak to me? I'm half worried that if he can get close enough to me, he hopes to kill me."

"No: that's not his reason at all. Actually, Upton-Schleisser grudgingly admires the kzinti, at least enough so that he believes there could be a foundation for communication. And maybe, in some distant time, cooperation."

"So he's a raving idealist, then."

"Hardly raving. He hasn't expressed this opinion to anyone other than me and Dr. Boroshinsky."

"Why?"

"Because he knows that, in the wake of the fourth invasion attempt—in which over five million Belters died, and we lost almost two-thirds of the Home Fleet—that he'd be muzzled. No one wants to hear any talk about future peace: they want their own pound of kzin flesh. Almost every family lost someone in the Battle of Ceres and the aftermath engagements, so right now, they are focused on vengeance. But he wants to share what he experienced with you because, as he puts it, you both know what it's like to have your life stolen by an enemy who wants to use you for their own purposes."

Hap finally looked over at Selena: a stunned stare. "I'm surprised that you're even willing to allow a person with those opinions in here to speak with me."

Selena shrugged. "You may not feel it right now, Hap, but if, in some future time, you choose to look back at how we treated you as you grew up, I think you'll find we have been as honest as we could be at any given moment. There were lapses, I know, and I'm sorry for those, but in general, we've been guided by the proposition that honesty is the best policy. Bringing Upton-Schleisser here to talk with you, that's just an extension of that policy."

Selena laid both documents on the flat rock table that Hap had crafted for himself: a dolmen that served him as a desk. She turned to leave, but paused. "Hap, you haven't said one thing about Dieter's death. Not one. And no physical reaction except silence. Why? Is this how you think kzinti face personal loss?"

"I really don't know how natural kzinti face personal loss, and I really don't care. My lack of reaction, as you perceive it, is more a consequence of being suspended between two completely contradictory feelings."

"Which are?"

"You will not like them—at least not one of them."

"And they are?" Selena insisted.

He looked at her. "I am proud of my people. They came back a fourth time, and from what I can read between the lines, they very nearly beat you; they came much closer than on any of the three prior invasions. And this time, they weren't swatting down tufted monkeys who'd evolved into clever accountants: they grappled with a new generation of your best warriors. Because that's certainly what Dieter was: one of your

best warriors." His voice faltered; it had a hum at the
back of it and became thicker. "And that is the other
feeling: great loss. I remember Dieter from—well,
from the moment I can remember anything. And then,
later, when it seemed like the world around me began
to shift, when the simple truths of cubhood changed
into the intricate lies of my life as your specimen,
there was still Dieter. He always found ways to tell
the truth, or at least distance himself from the lies. I
did not always see and understand what he was doing
when I was very young, but I do now." His large,
dark eyes looked into hers. "You have always cared for
me, Selena, but allow me to be frank: we kzinti have
spent untold millenia not having mothers beyond the
first few months of our lives. But we have always had
male mentors and role models, often more powerful
than merely that of a father. Dieter was the only one
I had. And he was worthy of it. Yes, he killed my
family, but he was a great warrior, and had a great
heart: he mixed great resolve and great regret in one
soul and was not torn apart by it. Instead, it defined
his greatness. And now he is gone. And I mourn
him. And I am glad that he died a Hero's death.

"And then, in the very next second, I feel that it
is wrong to be sad at his passing: he *did* destroy my
family; he *has* killed my Hero brothers. So how can
it be right to grieve him?"

Selena put out a hand to touch Hap on one rock-
hard arm, made soft by the layer of fur. "How can it
be wrong?" she asked. "Yes, he was fair, and honest,
and tried to help you, to compensate for the hurt and
losses he had inflicted upon you. But those are just a
bunch of words: you miss him because he was the first

being to do this"—she squeezed his arm gently—"and you imprinted upon him. You came to know his smell and his movements and his voice and you treasured them in the very center of your soul. So how could you *not* mourn him?"

The arm beneath Selena's hand was trembling very slightly as Hap looked away. He was quiet for several seconds. Then he swallowed and said, "I will be happy to have Kenneth Upton-Schleisser as a visitor. Good-bye, Selena."

2412 BCE: Subject age—sixteen years

Selena stepped off the transport: the chill Far South Sea wind set her teeth on edge. Hap was waiting, staring at the endless inbound waves, the serried ranks of breakers making a perpetually futile assault upon the scree-lined coast. *Well, perpetual as far as we humans measure time,* she thought.

As she approached, he stood and his fur rumpled in glad greeting. "Welcome to Campbell Island, Selena. It is good to see you."

My Hap has grown up. His voice was level and calm. Years of intensive reading, viewing and study had put a high polish on his diction: had he been a human, he would have been called urbane. "It's good to see you, too, Hap."

He waved at the one tilting streetlamp perched just beyond the high-tide waters: it had already been old when the last of the whalers had abandoned the island in the twentieth century. It was a true museum piece now. "We can have our chat in the shadows of the one remaining sign of human habitation, if you'd like."

Selena considered the rust-eaten metal pole and shook her head. "I'm fine here. Still enjoying your freedom?"

He looked around. "Yes. And no. The constant buzzing of your observation drones really does spoil the illusion of solitude and self-determination. Then again, so do your monthly shipments of my new opponents and prey. But I am grateful: without them, I'd lose too many of my skills. About which..."

She waited for him to resume; he did not. "What about your skills?"

"Is it true that the project's overseers intend to send me along with the return mission to Wunderland?"

She shrugged. "That's their intent."

"And what about the rumors of a faster-than-light drive: are those accurate as well?"

Selena considered. Technically, she had been asked not to reveal the details on this bit of information, that the hyperdrive craft from We Made It was not merely a hopeful rumor but a fact. But just who was Hap going to tell? And honesty was, as she had always claimed, the best policy. "Yes; the stories about the hyperdrive are real."

"Then I will accompany your human fleet to Alpha Centauri, at such time as it is ready."

Selena felt the cold air rush in her open mouth. She didn't care. "You're serious."

"Of course I am. I would not waste your time, summoning you out to the ends of the Earth as a joke." He reflected. "I do not think my pranks were ever *that* inconsiderate... were they?"

"No, no." She couldn't even remember anything she'd rightly call a prank: Hap had found ways to circumvent authority and security on occasions—the scars on his ribcage were a reminder of that—but a "prank" implied frivolity. Frivolity had never been one of Hap's traits. "I'm just surprised. Why the sudden change of heart?"

"There is nothing sudden about it. I just have not been willing to speak about my 'change of heart,' as you call it, until now."

"And how long have you been ruminating on this?"

"Before your last trip here, when you told me about the readying of the fleet."

"Really? Before that?"

"Selena, after Dieter died, I turned from absorbing information to using it. To think for myself. And that was why I asked to come here: I needed solitude to think about what I should do next. I thought I might commit suicide."

"Suicide?" Selena all but leaped over to his side. As if she could prevent any physical course of action that a full-grown and clever kzin might be contemplating.

"Yes, of course." Then, seeing the horror on her face, he snapped his head in the half-shake that was the kzin negation-reflex. "No, not because I was depressed or anything so pointless and melodramatic. I am happy to observe that this seems to be a purely human pathology. But when I thought about my duty to my race, I wondered."

"Wondered if the time had come to make sure you couldn't be used as a tool to further human interests?"

"Exactly."

"But,"—she poked him—"you're still here."

He looked down at her and his pelt stirred through one long, friendly ripple. "Yes, I am still here. Not due to a failure of courage. Quite the opposite, actually: I realized that the true test of my courage—the path that had fallen to me as a Hero, if I had such aspirations—was to keep moving forward. And that I would have to do so knowing that my actions and perspectives would probably never be understood, no matter which race was considering them." His sigh drowned out the surf's susurrations for a brief moment. "Both human and kzin philosophers, at least according to the translated materials you provided me, have pointed out that there are some deeds that require more courage than facing certain death. I do not know if I am about to embark upon an existence which is one long example of such a deed, but I foresee it as a distinct possibility."

"That still doesn't explain why you've decided to go with the fleet."

He stared at the ocean again. "I have heard the death of my people in the voice of your news presenters. I have heard it for about a month now."

"What do you mean?"

"I mean that the hyperdrive is probably the worst-kept secret in human history. The news presenters have smelled its presence, and they know it portends sating your race's gnawing desire for vengeance. For years, the kzinti had the advantage of the gravitic planer drives. In the most recent war, you finally fielded models with sixty-five percent the performance of the kzin engines. But still, in a war of attrition, you would have eventually lost. The populations of many kzin systems are arrayed against you, producing ships and sending Heroes in one fleet after another. And every time, you had to invent a new trick to save yourself. And so you did. And so you taught us a lesson that we would not forget."

He looked at Selena. "How much longer before you inevitably run out of new tricks? Many of your commentators seemed fairly sure that a fifth fleet could not be stopped. But this—a faster-than-light drive—changes everything. It gives you the initiative. You will be able to act so quickly, recover and act again, that my people will be hard put just to fight you to a standstill. And a system such as Centauri, where there is a large human population, will almost certainly fall to you. And then all the stories of our so-called atrocities will become widely known upon Earth and you will convince yourselves, maybe accurately, that the universe is not big enough for both kzin and human. You will reconceive your war of defense into one of preemptive genocide."

Selena nodded. "So you are doing this to ensure the safety of your own people."

"Yes. And possibly yours." His whole body rippled. "I have not decided that humans are in the right: that is a moot point. At least to me. But what I have seen is that the future of the kzinti could resemble what occurred to many of the peoples of this planet, the Zulu and the American Plains Indians, in particular. They too, were hunters like us kzinti. But they were washed away by the flood of your dominant society. Drowned and purged from existence."

"Yes, but those peoples were also terribly outnumbered by the nations who took their lands. They were overwhelmed."

"We, too, will be overwhelmed."

Selena shook her head. "That's just not accurate, Hap. The kzinti have many worlds, with a total population that is much greater than—"

"You misunderstand. I do not mean we will be overwhelmed by your numbers; I mean you shall batter us down with the quantities and powers of your innovation. I have been studying the culture of natural kzinti: they adopt pirated technologies very quickly, but they evolve and amplify them very slowly, if at all. It is the opposite with humans. And with your ARM relinquishing more and more of its control, and the UN releasing more and more of the technologies it repressed over the centuries, all constraints upon innovation and change have been lifted, and you are now making up for lost time. And the kzinti will neither be able to foresee, nor react to, all these new weapons and technologies quickly enough. But in the final analysis, it wasn't just the sudden changes in your rate of innovation which showed me the necessity of my intended course. It was the changes in you, in your species, which ultimately decided me."

Selena shook her head. "I don't understand. What changes?"

Hap sat. "When was the first attempted invasion of Earth?"

"2383."

"Correct. I came on the third fleet. A fourth was destroyed just four years ago. And the reason you defeated that one was not due to innovation, certainly not so much as was the case with your earlier victories." He looked straight at her, almost searching for something in her face. "You humans have changed, before my very eyes. I didn't realize it until I started thinking about what I had experienced as a cub, how the world had felt then, in comparison to now. It did not just *seem* to be a gentler, safer place: it *was* a gentler, safer place. Back then, all the sharp edges were padded: there was still a strong reflex against violence, even against displeasing people. Including me.

"But the wars have changed you. The young of your species do not have the same gentled reflexes of your generation. They are more direct and decisive, and understand that some matters cannot be settled with conversation and ever more conversation. Sometimes, a blade or a battle cruiser is required. In short, you are warriors now. Or, I should say, 'once again.'"

"So, does this mean that you respect us more now? That you feel we are worthy?"

"No. Well, yes, but your worthiness is not the reason I have decided to cooperate."

"Then what is?"

"Four fleets attacked you without success, and that was during an epoch when you had forgotten the skills of war making. Now, your current generation is bred to it: I no longer see panic or dismay in the faces around me, or on the news, when a battle is imminent." He sighed. "You may be running out of new tricks, but the dragons' teeth your generation sowed have sprouted into myrmidons. So I wonder: how dangerous are you going to be when all the living generations of man know war, remember nothing but war, and are deeply schooled in its arts?"

Selena stared at him. "I hadn't really thought about it."

Hap nodded. "I know. But I have. A great deal."

2419 BCE: Subject age—twenty-three years

Accented by its hallmark conglomeration of soaring spires and low-sweeping pavilions, the Shanghai Spaceport was a jarring mixture of extreme order and absolute chaos. All its personnel were doing exactly what they were supposed to be doing, with extraordinary competence, but usually without any greater sense of how their task fit into the greater whole. Not that this was unique to Shanghai: that kind of downstream cluelessness was pretty much endemic the world over. But here, each worker's superficial gloss of perfectly composed competence often fooled the first-time traveler there into thinking that it would be more orderly than the other great spaceports of the globe. *No such luck,* thought Selena, as she accepted that her outbound flight would be delayed yet another hour.

Which meant that she would have to sit and brood over Hap's departure far longer than she wished. That brooding would touch upon other, related losses: the loss of Dieter, the loss of Boroshinsky, the loss of her own youth and idealism. Hap had, during his later training, become something of a fan of old human fiction, and now employed a wildly anachronistic phrase to restart the flagging conversation: "Penny for your thoughts?"

"I was thinking about how strange it will be not to have you here. End of an era. That kind of thing." Her tone was not as airy as she had hoped.

"Well, if my escorts do not show up soon, we might not have to part at all."

Selena drew in her breath, then expelled it before explaining. "Your escorts are not coming."

"Oh? Why?"

"Because you are free, Hap. Fully and absolutely free. No escorts, no oversight, no observers, no 'cultural facilitators.' You are on your own. Entirely."

Hap's jaw hung slack, and Selena hoped he did not make that a habit: all those teeth were a pretty disturbing sight. He recovered his facial composure about the same moment he regained his sardonic perspective on human promises: "Yes, free to be your ambassador to the kzinti, wherever that assignment should happen to take me."

"Well, you're right—and you're wrong."

"You mean, I could simply be a minor liaison, or an informer, for you?"

"No. I mean that you don't have to represent us at all: you can declare loyalty to the kzinti, if you want. And if they'll have you. We're leaving that matter of conscience in your capable hands." She smiled down at his immense paws.

"But why—why would you do this?" Hap stammered out.

"Because it is the right thing to do. And because you spoke the truth years ago when you observed that, all too often, we humans are without *strakh*. Well, this is our way of trying to make up for some of those lapses in honor."

Hap blinked, then nodded. "This is a high honor you do me, holding yourself to a standard of behavior you did not promise. And to a mortal foe of your race, no less."

"Perhaps. But I hope you will reflect upon what it really means to have this freedom conferred upon you."

"Is it not motivated by your sense of honor?"

"Actually, no: this time, the motivation was kindness and justice."

"I suspect my kind would call that weakness and foolishness."

"Perhaps. But we would not do this for all kzinti. In your case, however, it is the only *right* thing to do. And I hope it will provide an illustration of one of the strengths of human society, in contrast to kzin society. For the kzinti, honor is the essential ingredient for cultural preservation: high oaths, and their rigid enforcement, are necessary if your state is to survive." She shrugged. "But we humans—we are not creatures governed so completely, so essentially, by oaths."

His ears expanded like the cowls of a cobra; it signaled a sharp, sudden realization: "And now I see why: you *cannot* be governed by oaths alone. Because you are not creatures of absolute values. We kzinti, our course is set as the course of an arrow: we seek and pursue objectives without question or regret, and without interminable reflection upon the ethics of our actions. Why should we? What we eat, how we breed, why we are kzin: these are not matters of debate or uncertainty. Our nature is direct, monofocal, and undiluted. We pursue excellence in those skills that help us attain those goals, and find little of interest in others. Anything else is, at best, a distraction from the quest to become a Hero: to conquer, to acquire a Name, a mate, offspring—and always, accrue greater *strakh*."

He pointed, smiling and understanding. "But you humans are not built this way. If we kzinti are a precisely aimed arrow in flight, you are ripples upon the surface of running water: moving outward, and in so many directions at once. To kzinti who have not grown up in your midst as I have, I suppose it must look like a pointless squandering of energy. It is the diffusion of the self, of potency, and superficially appears to be a kind of dilettantism toward the entire business of life itself. I, too, had often suspected that was what your restlessness signified: a simple inability to focus on what really matters.

"But now I see the difference. It is in your nature to be this way, as much as it is in ours to be monodirectional and focused. And in both cases, our natures reflect, and are suited to, how we survived, and flourished, at the dawn of our respective sapience.

"We were carnivores, hunters. We identified prey and pursued it, relentlessly and without deviation. But you were omnivores: sustenance was to be found in many places, requiring many skills to acquire it from diverse sources. So you became versatile. You used tools sooner and better than we did. Given how long it took for us to get to space in our much longer history, we kzinti should have seen this difference in you, in your space-faring history, and realized its significance sooner. But we did not, because while we are superior at keeping our oaths, we are your inferiors when it comes to facing the truth."

"What do you mean?"

"Is it not obvious? The oligarchic control, the culling of intelligent females, the rigidity of discipline: the kzin heart finds iron rules easier to tolerate than a nuanced and constantly shifting reality."

Selena twisted her mouth sourly. "Oh, you mean the way we demonstrated our flexibility by imposing three centuries of self-inflicted social brainwashing that we still call our Golden Age of Peace?"

"Nothing proves my point *more* than your Golden Age."

"What? How?"

"Because it was only three centuries long."

"Only three centuries? Apparently kzinti have an intrinsically different sense of time, as well."

Hap shrugged. "Perhaps we do. Did you mislead yourselves when you turned your swords into ploughshares and then denied that swords had ever existed? Yes, of course you did, but that is the risk of being creatures that advance through experiment and change. You try new things. Often, they do not work. Just as often, you then over-correct in rejecting them. But somehow, a dynamic equilibrium emerges. It may not be obvious until one has a perspective of far hindsight—looking back across decades, centuries, even millennia—but it *is* the truth of you humans: you improve by changing, and the process does not destroy you. Quite the contrary, it is the wellspring of your vitality."

Selena smiled crookedly when he was finished. "I thank you, Hap. We had thought to teach you, but I suspect, when I reflect upon what you just said, that it is you who will have taught us."

"And that comment teaches me, in turn."

"Why?"

"Because, unless I am much mistaken, making that kind of admission—that you humans can and do learn fundamental truths about yourselves from outsiders—comes relatively easily to your species. It does not come easily to the kzinti."

"Then perhaps that will be the greatest insight, and

example, you will bring back to your species. After all, you admitted to learning from us, just now, and you did so with great ease."

"It is simply a sign of your bad influence upon me." Hap's fur rippled in waves of mirth. "So I will have to learn to be more inflexible and stubborn." He bowed. "I will not bid you farewell, or good-bye. The Wunderlanders have a better phrase for parting: *Auf Wiedersehen*. Until we see each other again."

"*Auf Wiedersehen*, Hap. Success and good luck always."

He stood tall—tall as only a massive kzin could stand—and turned with what seemed a ruffle and flourish of his pelt. Had he been a human hero, the movement of his fur would have been accomplished by a cape, swirling to mark his long-striding exit.

"*Auf Wiedersehen*," Selena called after him again. And then, remembering one of Dieter's intimate phrases, she whispered "—*und tschüss, Liebling*," at Hap's broad, receding back.

TOMCAT TACTICS

◆　◆　◆

Charles E. Gannon

2413 BCE: Wunderland, leading Trojan point asteroids

"If you botch the insertion, the *oyabun* will have your left testicle," muttered Pytor Iarngavi over the tightbeam. "Probably your right one, too."

Moto Yakazuki snorted defiance. "Just let him try and get them." The wiry EVA expert shut off and detached the portable compressed air retro: it was old, reliable, zero-energy-signature tech. Perfect for *this* job. Yakazuki stowed the retro on the side of his life-support unit, and then shifted his grip on the small space-rock. Only four meters in length and two wide, one couldn't seriously call it an asteroid. He fired his suit jets in quick bursts to make small side-vector corrections.

"It's going to be too close to the other—"

"It's not, Pytor," Yakazuki snapped. "Now, shut up." The small Serpent Swarmer pulled himself hand over hand to the other side of the probably artificial splinter of rock. Once secured, he pulsed his suit jets, counter-boosting until he had zeroed out the inertia along its insertion vector. He pushed gently away, assessed his EVA handiwork: the tiny lozenge-like object was now motionless relative to the other rocks at the trailing end of Wunderland's leading Trojan point asteroids. "Perfect: like it's been there since the beginning of time."

"Whaddya think it is?"

"I dunno," confessed Yakazuki as he began boosting back to the small prospecting boat they had been loaned for this task. "Way too light to be a genuine rock, that's for sure. But the man didn't say what it was, and I wasn't about to ask. I'm just glad to start paying off for my, eh, overzealous lovemaking with Funikawa's prize *baishunfu*."

"Since when has 'beating a whore' become 'overzealous lovemaking'?"

"Mind your own business and vices, Iarngavi. Just how many thousands are you in debt, now? Word has it that when you couldn't pay last month, you offered your ass to the *Yamikin*'s collection goons. Who kicked it raw for you."

"Fuck you, Moto."

"I'll bet you would, if you got the chance. Open the hatch. I'm done out here."

Tomoaki Kitayama sipped at the small porcelain cup: the sake was ever so slightly less than body temperature. Not really tepid, yet, but not *correct*. However, this was probably going to be the least of his problems, today.

His gang's senior accountant, or *kaikei*, appeared at the entrance of his office, located in the back of the restaurant that bore Kitayama's name. The *kaikei* bowed. "*Kobun?*"

"Proceed."

"We have received the signal from the debtor and the rapist. They have completed their task."

"Has our spy drone verified their report?"

"Yes, *kobun*. Shall I inform the *oyabun* that the mission has been a success?"

"No, I shall do that personally."

"Very well, *kobun*. Are there other matters which need my attention today?"

"No, but tell me: the men who performed the mission—is their ship still in line-of-sight, for clear transmission?"

"Yes, *kobun*. Shall I raise them?"

"No, I shall tend to that also. You may go home. My regards to your family."

"We hope you will honor us by coming to dinner soon again, *kobun*."

"Yes, perhaps." *Please no; his wife is as dull as a potted plant. And less comely.* "However, it is uncertain when I might be free to do so. I shall inform you if my schedule becomes less taxing." *Which will never happen.*

Kitayama nodded in response to his *kaikei*'s bow, then studied the data tablet beside him. Two channels were already pulsing, ready to be activated: a red one that would send a narrow lascom transmission to the prospecting boat, and a green one that would open a secure line to the *oyabun*. Kitayama smiled, pressed the red button, and then the green one.

Forty seconds after the red button was pressed, and at a distance of forty light-seconds, the computer in Iarngavi's and Yakazuki's small prospecting boat received a lascom signal that did not route through to the communications panel in the bridge. Instead, it was a coded command that was addressed for the subprocessor overseeing engine operations. Which obeyed the command immediately.

The magnetic bottle on the plasma drive flickered out of existence. The superheated hydrogen expanded in every direction, including right through the hull of the craft. When it came into contact with the oxygenated atmosphere within, combustion occurred.

Which Tomoaki Kitayama's small, undetected spy drone duly recorded and transmitted.

Eighty seconds after Kitayama pressed the red button, a small, bright yellow flare twinkled momentarily on the synced screens of the *oyabun* and his most trusted *kobun*. They nodded in unison.

"The package is in place, then," the *oyabun* said, his eyes sharp and satisfied. "And no loose ends."

"Yes, *oyabun*, and only we know of its existence and position."

"And now it is our job to forget the package, Tomoaki."

"Forget *what* package, *oyabun*?"

Kitayama matched the *oyabun*'s smile with one of his own.

2420 BCE: Wunderland, leading Trojan point asteroids, and planetside near Munchen

Upon the dull surface of the rock-that-was-not-a-rock, reflections of Alpha Centauri's steady yellow light shone faintly. Other highlights—faint, brief—flickered across its surface: signs of the dying flares of ships and asteroids nearby. A human ship—a ramscoop traveling within a gnat's whisker of the speed of light itself— had come rushing into the system, spewing death and destruction as it came. Scores of large steel-alloy projectiles had been strewn in a wide arc as the craft made its approach: many had already ploughed into various planetoids, the debris from which had surged outward like shrapnel from anti-personnel warheads, destroying nearby kzin warships.

The remaining projectiles were now approaching various planets and planetoids located deeper in the system, several bound for the kzin subpolar bases on Wunderland itself. The Fifth Kzin Fleet, primed to begin its long sublight trek to invade Earth, could not respond in time: without any real warning, they were functionally stationary from the time the attack commenced to the time that it finished.

The magnetically induced corona that followed hard on the energetic bow-wave of the ramscoop tested the limits of the kzinti's EM shielding. Those limits, as well as many throughout the human communities of the asteroid belt known as the Serpent's Swarm, were exceeded by the next high-energy cataclysm: the cascade of coronal mass ejections triggered by the projectiles that had plunged straight into Alpha Centauri prime. Although no danger to the stability of the star, they tore huge holes down to the bottom of the photosphere, leaving nature-abhorred vacuums in their wake, as well as a brief moment of absolute magnetic disruption.

When the plasma rushed back into the empty vortices left in the wake of these warheads, and the magnetic fields reconnected, it was akin to high waves rushing headlong upon each other in the ocean: a shattering torrent sprayed upward from the thunderous collision of these two opposed forces. But, in this case, it was particles and radiation that sprayed outward through the system, due to arrive at Wunderland within a day, and the center of the Swarm within two.

Amidst all the destruction and streaming particles and energies, the kzinti missed detecting two subtler, but ultimately more destructive actions taken by the human ramscoop vessel. Firstly, it deposited a small infiltration/commando ship which, equipped with a stasis field, would soon wreak legendary havoc across the system. Secondly, and functionally undetectable since it was but one emission among countless others, the main vessel sent a brief, powerful omnidirectional signal, which was backed up by transmitters in two of the near-relativistic projectiles. Around the system, as the signal spread outward, a variety of dormant systems awoke in response to its summons.

One such system was embedded in the small space-rock drifting serenely with the rest of the rubble that comprised the trailing edge of Wunderland's leading cluster of Trojan point asteroids. Low-power electronics, aided by bioelectric relays that generated no discernible signature, awakened automated systems. Motion recorders and atomic clocks compared data with beacon triangulation systems and visual trackers. Having confirmed its precise location within the Alpha Centauri system—and, in that same act, having determined Wunderland's relative bearing—navigational computers calculated trajectories, thrust and duration. The moment the flight solution was confirmed, the low-power plasma thruster ignited. The pseudo-rock accelerated backward along its orbital track toward Wunderland.

The man in the protective tube at the center of the pseudo-rock awoke to the smell of fried circuitry and an alarm which both rang in his ears and pulsed in his mandibular implant. He tried to rise up, couldn't, groggily tried looking around, couldn't really do that either. But he slowly made his eyes focus.

They showed him a small screen at the far end of a compartment so tight that it reminded him of when, as a preschooler, he had hidden in a mossy, narrow-gauge culvert to stymie the bigger kids during an epic game of hide-and-seek. They'd never found him. Of course, he had almost failed to extricate himself, too. *What price glory?*

Despite the smoke and tocsin that both warned of impending catastrophe, he realized he'd almost nodded off: the cold-sleep grogginess was not out of him. He triggered a stimulant autoinjector, felt a needle pierce his thigh: he needed all his wits and all his training to figure out what was happening, right now.

He was unsurprised that the news was not good. This cryopod-capsule was the same one into which they had stuck him three months after the kzinti invaded. The top brass hadn't been sure of very much, back then: the only thing they could agree upon was that, when the time was right, he'd be awakened and sent back to Wunderland to resume the fight against the kzin.

However, it was the method of his return that was now instilling a modest measure of anxiety in him. The small screen located only thirty centimeters in front of him was displaying status reports from his primary systems. Most of the indicators were orange, with a smattering of red and green tags. Thrust and manual systems were okay, but the more sensitive systems—such as automated guidance and sensors—were either unreliable or dead.

Another circuit fried and as the acrid smoke wafted around him, he wondered, *how long before something catches fire?* Fortunately, that wouldn't be him: the unipiece combat suit he was wearing was nonflammable. On the other hand, even if live flame couldn't reach his skin and roast him, the narrow space could easily enough become a pressure cooker. So far there had only been shorting wires, but soon enough, now—

A new, more urgent klaxon superimposed itself on the multiple malfunction tones: a collision alarm. Which, without the sensors, didn't tell him much: it could be a basketball-sized rock at short range, or a whole planet at long range. He toggled the screen over to simple visual pickup, which rolled bars of gray and green for a moment before it straightened out into an incompletely colorized image. But despite the distortions, he immediately knew what he was looking at.

Wunderland. He was going to crash into Wunderland.

Which was a pretty sizable problem. He should have been awakened hours before reaching this point—except, now that he checked, the automated revival system had failed completely. So what the hell had happened?

The answer popped up when he checked the astrographic plot and position logs. They had been pretty good up to an hour ago. Then, right in the middle of a data-line, the positional reporting feed went haywire and stopped. And now that he was looking at it, all the other failed systems had gone down at the same second.

The reason for that simultaneous failure became clear: the external sensor archives showed a more or less normal electromagnetic and radiant soup outside, until an hour ago. Then the readings went completely off the scale for the better part of twenty minutes. The peaks of the rad and solar wind readings were like nothing he'd ever seen. And so he knew: he'd been caught in a coronal mass ejection. The worst ever recorded. He was lucky anything was still working, but was damned unlucky to be auto-deployed right into the biggest solar storm on record.

But no, he realized: it might not just be a matter of bad luck. This immense coronal mass ejection was probably the result of something big and fast crashing into the sun at near-relativistic speeds. Which might be a fast STL craft from Earth, since there wasn't much else he could think of which would approach at such speeds, and since that would also be the logical means whereby humanity would respond to the kzin attack upon Wunderland.

Great. So he had visuals, manual guidance controls, and thrusters. Not much else, but then again, those were all he really needed to land.

Well, those and a whole lot of luck. Eyeball guidance would be hard enough in terms of getting near the preferred pre-planned drop zone. The real challenge was making sure he came in at the correct angle. Too steep and he'd burn up. Too shallow and he'd bounce off, without enough juice left to counterboost, come about and push in for another try. So the learning curve on this task, for which he had received not quite one hour of simulator training, was fairly daunting: one strike and you're out.

Which reacquainted him with the adrenaline-fueled truth that nothing focuses one's mind so much as imminent mortal danger. Luckily, he didn't need to tumble his rock into a counterboost position: the automated attitude adjustment system had taken care of both that and the braking thrust sometime yesterday when he was still in cold sleep. But about an hour ago, the computer watchdogging that system had gone down for good, which meant that he now had to counterthrust immediately and hard in order to compensate for the lost hour.

He brought the plasma engine online, taking note of the rate of volatile consumption and the time. Then he shifted over to the viewscreen again, pinged the planet with a laser, pinged again after five seconds, and a third time after yet another five count to confirm range, his initial rate of closure, his absolute velocity, and the rate of its decrease given the current counterboost setting.

And in performing these tasks, he got his first bit of good news: he had enough fuel left to make a clean deorbit at a survivable speed, and still retain a sizable reserve. Which meant he could afford to spend a little main thruster fuel to selectively vector the exhaust for gross corrections to his descent attitude, and thereby save the dedicated but short-duration attitude control thrusters for terminal, detailed adjustments. If he was any judge of such things—and he really wasn't—he guessed that the probability of his making it to the ground alive had just jumped from unpromising to pretty good.

And that happy change had come just in time: grain-sized debris started buffeting his pseudo-rock, requiring brief corrections, and leading him to wonder: where did this debris field come from? This was clean space on the charts, and there was no way regular use could have—

The answer to his question came in the form of moonrise: one of Wunderland's two very small satellites came around the terminator. Suddenly bathed in the yellow glow of Alpha Centauri, it showed a markedly different reflection pattern. Even its shape looked different, as if—

Then he understood. Whatever had arrived in this system, and had probably caused the coronal mass ejections, had savaged planetary bodies as well. The moon's new, somewhat lopsided shape was evidence that much of it had been blown free, and that the lighter debris was beginning to migrate out into various orbital tracks surrounding Wunderland. Such as the one he was traversing now. The planet itself was flickering at the poles—probably impact sites—and wreathed in dark, slowly expanding clouds.

Cheating the nose a little closer to the planet, he held the rock more or less on course, noting two bright flares ahead of him. What? Counterfire? Kzin interceptors juicing their afterburners? But no, he realized after another moment: it was simply a pair of meteorites, glowing and flaring as they entered Wunderland's atmosphere. As he watched, he saw almost half a dozen other descending streaks of light, bright against the dark clouds below. Chunks of the moon, those blown inward or close enough to quickly succumb to the planet's gravity, were being pulled in

to their fiery death. Which was good news: his own
falling rock would not even be an anomaly under
these conditions, and thereby, warrant no special
investigation. Presuming that there were any kzinti
down below who still had the operational leisure to
investigate just one more shooting star.

Which, he realized, was what his rock was starting to become. The backup skin-temperature sensors
showed a growing thermal spike: he was hitting dense
atmosphere and starting to buck. He felt, more than
read from the screen, that his angle was a little too
shallow. Using the attitude control thrusters, he brought
the nose into a steeper descent. He had allowed the
rock's descent angle to remain slightly shallow up
until now, because it was relatively simple in the early
reentry phases to push the ship's vector closer to the
planet's line of gravitic attraction. Conversely, if one
started with too steep an angle of descent, it took a
great deal more energy to correct into a more oblique
trajectory. And in doing so, it was too easy to over-
shoot the proper point of correction and skitter off the
atmosphere like a flat stone skimmed across a pond.

As the rock's rate of descent increased, the cooling
systems started making an ominous ticking, which
rapidly escalated into a knocking, accompanied by
smoke. No, not smoke: vapor from the overtaxed
condensers—overtaxed because several of them had
gone off-line. The remaining units were overloading as
they struggled to meet the minimum environmental
demands. It started to become stiflingly hot in the
capsule.

The ride became bumpier, but the pseudo-rock was
well into the viselike grasp of Wunderland's gravity,

which now impeded further side-vectoring. In fact, he was fairly certain that there was hardly any further danger of catastrophe unless one or more of the drogue chutes failed, or there was a problem when—

The external ablative coating, which also served as the capsule's pseudo-rock exterior, peeled off with a thunderous clatter, followed by a slight tug that started the nose of the capsule drifting away from its drop trajectory. Another half-degree, and the increased drag on the nose would swing it further off the descent line, which would further increase the drag, and then the capsule would start—

Tumbling meant death. He gingerly brought the best-situated attitude control thruster back on-line, ready to deliver the faintest nudge of correction. Too little and he might not have the time to try again; too much and he'd swing out of descent alignment in the other direction, and again, begin tumbling ass-over-eyeballs down to a very kinetic demise. He brushed the thrust toggle so briefly that he wondered if the system had even engaged . . .

But the nose swung slowly back into stable alignment. Two seconds later, the cooling system died with a roar, and genuine smoke started filling the capsule. Checking his watch, he sealed the faceplate of his combat suit, and waited for the first drogue chute to deploy, hoping the fire in the cooling system would not spread too quickly.

The expected bump was so hard that his faceplate banged into the screen and blanked it. But it told him that yes, indeed, the first drogue chute had deployed. Two more bumps meant he was now at an altitude of 2500 meters, and moving at a paltry 500 kph.

He flared the main thruster briefly, the slaved ACTs joining in, maintaining the drop trajectory against any marginal side-vectoring. Again, he found himself slammed sharply against the capsule's screen as his final braking burn dropped the speed to 300 kph. Ironically, the burn he couldn't control was internal: he was pretty sure the comfort liner of the capsule was now starting to spark and flare.

Which meant that even if he survived landing, he'd do so with a live fire aboard. And he still had almost twenty percent of his volatiles in tankage. In short, he was now riding a bomb with a lit fuse down to a hard landing. Typical landing protocols dictated retaining the fuel as an insurance against terminal chute failure, but at this point, chute failure was only a dire *possibility*. A hard landing with a live fire and fuel aboard was currently a dire *certainty*. He flipped the cover back on the emergency manual overrides, and depressed the third button from the left. The fuel tanks vented with a sound like a suddenly punctured aerosol can, meaning that he was now completely in the hands of fate. And if the main chute did not deploy—

A sudden jerk and sense of sustained deceleration signaled that the main chute was out and full: the predictable, faint swaying motion was the harbinger of a gentle ride to the ground.

Gentle, but hardly a relief: the flame in the capsule was now steady, working its way up the liner and causing further short-outs. The heat in his combat suit suddenly increased, became intense, soared toward unbearable—

—just as, with sudden thump, the capsule jarred to a rough halt. In the same second, there was a creaky wheeze, and then a blast of explosive bolts blew the top of the capsule off. The flames around him roared up, greedily feeding upon the abundant oxygen in the atmosphere.

He tumbled out of the coffinlike remains of the capsule, turned about and leaned back into the conflagration, the combat suit setting up a desperate warning squall: complete failure was imminent—

Rummaging about under the control panel, he sprung open a small, armored cargo receptacle, and yanked out the four-liter secure container he found there.

Then he ran deep into the sparse scrub-lands in which he had landed...

A twig snapped a moment before a voice came from the bushes: "Hands up. Don't move."

"I won't," he answered. "I've been waiting here for you."

Two men and two women emerged from the thick brush that lined the southern perimeter of the small clearing; to the north, sand pines shot up like feathery stalagmites into the cloud-darkened dusk. "You were waiting here for us?" asked the smaller and older of the men.

"Yep. Saw you about two hours ago, following my trail from the crash site."

The man raised his weapon a little higher. "You seem pretty casual and self-assured for someone—some human—who just landed in a meteoritic assault capsule. You connected to today's activities out in space?"

"Look: I've been gone from Wunderland for a long time. Just woke up from coldsleep today. So I'm not exactly up on the most recent news: what activities in space are you talking about?"

Long looks bounced from face to face among the four armed people. The apparent leader spoke again. "Seems Earth finally did something about the kzin occupation. Looking at that suit of yours, and the timing of your arrival, seems logical you were part of the package they sent. Arrived early this morning at nearly light speed; wreaked havoc throughout the system. We figured you must have come from Earth as part of that attack force."

"Nope. To the best of my knowledge, I've never been further from Wunderland than the Serpent Swarm."

The larger of the two men, and clearly the youngest of the group, brought his weapon up quickly, sighting along its barrel. "Which means you wouldn't be alive unless the kzinti wanted you to be. Which would make this a trap."

"Nope, not the case. When I say I've been asleep for a long time, I mean a *long* time. They corpsicled me three months after the ratcats showed up."

"And so where were you all that time?"

"Can't tell you the exact location, because I have no way of knowing. I was in cold storage, so to speak."

"I ain't laughing, stranger. Who put you in storage, and for what reason?"

"The who is the local UNSN command staff. The reason was to strike back at the ratcats, but only once we had an effective weapon."

The leader of the group looked around the area, finding nothing large enough to contain the aforementioned effective weapon: just the man, his gear, his charred combat suit, a sidearm, and a small secure case. "I don't see any miracle weapon. And why wait all this time if you've been in system for—what?— more'n forty years, as you claim it."

"Yes. Forty years is how long it took to gather enough information about the kzin, pass it on to the facilities on Earth, and then back here. That meant two research labs working together with a four-point-three-seven-year message delay between them. So it took a little longer than a conventional counterattack. And the weapon they came up with is right here." He laid a long index finger atop the secure box.

The leader frowned. The young man smiled, but it was not a friendly expression. "Well, thanks for explaining things. So either everything you say is utter bullshit, in which case you're a kzin plant, trying to sneak into the ranks of our resistance. Or you're not a plant, but we've got your miracle weapon, anyway. So the logical alternative is that we take no chances: killing you might be a damned shame, but we still get our hands on the mystery weapon, and haven't taken any risks with our own security." He leaned over his tangent sights. "So sorry, but war is hell and all that."

"No," said one of the women sharply.

The young man looked at her. "C'mon; can't you see what's going on here? He's a collaborator, a traitor. And even if he's not, we have to work as though he was. We have no way to find out if he's telling the truth or—"

"No. We do." She turned and studied his charred combat suit again. Returning her scrutiny, he saw she was unusually, even strikingly, beautiful. Not in a soft or delicate fashion; her face was severe, with high cheekbones, dark eyes, almost white-blonde hair and a strangely square chin for a woman. He thought he might have seen a painting of a Valkyrie that looked like her. "You," she said. "What's your name?"

"Smith."

"Oh. Really. And let me guess: your first name is Joe."

"John, actually."

"So: John Smith. And are you a captain, like your namesake?"

"Well, it so happens that I am."

"And tell me, Captain John Smith, why did it take so long to research this wonder weapon of yours?"

"Hey, it isn't mine. But the main development problem, as I understand it, was that while there was plenty of opportunity to observe kzin behavior here, and gather physical samples and specimens, there were no underground research facilities that were really equipped to do the hard number crunching, or diverse lab work, to make any headway with it. So the information had to be gathered on site, here and in the Swarm, relayed off-world, and then sent back to Earth for—"

But she wasn't listening anymore: she had turned to her four comrades. "He's for real."

"What?" squawked the younger man. "How can you—?"

But she was looking at the older man, their leader, who had fallen strangely silent. "You know I'm right," she insisted. "You told me how, when you started with the resistance, there was a central cell—not an ops group, but an intelligence branch—that kept gathering data on the kzinti. Always wanted specimens, even live prisoners, to sneak off-world."

"It's true," he admitted. "And it fits. But what if the kzinti found out about that operation? What if they got their paws on whoever was behind it, extorted or tortured the info out of him, or her, and realized that this was the perfect ploy for getting someone inside our organization?"

She thought. "No, that doesn't fit. Even if they were going to launch that kind of operation, they'd have scrubbed it today, given the events out in space. On the other hand, if information has been going back and forth between researchers here and on Earth, then the UNSN or ARM would have seen that this was going to be the perfect day to slip in an operative. The local researchers could have had him pre-positioned so that, when the ship from Earth arrived, they'd send a signal to trigger his drop. And in the midst of all the chaos, who'd notice?" She turned back to look at him. "Well, John Smith, welcome home. I'm sorry to say you'll find it rather changed."

"So I've heard," he said, standing and picking up his gear. "Let's go: if my space-rock didn't fool all the kzinti, then we'll want to put as much ground as possible between us and the crash site."

Hilda Stensgaard looked away from the distant back of the sleeping man who insisted his name was John Smith. "Everything he's told us checks out with what we know."

"Which is almost nothing." Large, young, eager Gunnar Baden turned toward their leader. "Mads, let's not get soft-headed just because there were some pretty lights in the sky today and the ratcats got their tails a little singed. It's clear this was a one-off strike, not a prelude to invasion. We're still on our own, and that means we can't afford to take chances."

"We can't afford to ignore opportunities either, Gunnar." Mads Klinkman scooped the last of the cold beans out of his mess tin. "And I think Hilda's right: he's genuine. But I'm convinced for different reasons."

"Oh? And what are they?"

Mads spoke around his last mouthful of beans. "If the kzinti had learned that we were taking samples of them and sending them off-world, I think we'd have had some pretty vengeful indications of it long before now. Even given their new tendency toward increased patience, their outrage would have had them storming around to get to the bottom of what was going on and who was behind it. At the very least, you can be sure that their response would not have been an elaborate counterintelligence ruse, complete with a human commando from the past. And from what I can tell, he really is from the past."

Hilda nodded. "He'd have to be an exceptional actor to pull off what he has so far. He really doesn't seem to know about anything that happened more than three months into the invasion, other than what he read in the briefing materials he showed us."

"Must be a pretty quick reader," grumbled Gunnar.

"Oh, he is." Hilda nodded at the hard copy they would burn shortly after first light. "Haven't you noticed? He remembers everything after hearing it just once. And he's very alert: he picked out the trace Jotuntalander accent I picked up from *mein Mutti*. Just from listening to me convince you not to shoot him, Gunnar."

"So he has an ear for accents; so what?"

"So don't you notice how he verges into Uni slang, from Munchen, on occasion?"

"And that proves what, other than that he has an intolerably high opinion of himself?"

Hilda ignored the hostile tone and undercurrent of

envy. "It proves a lot, since the Uni slang just about died out when the kzinti came. There were years of disruption, and the professors and students bolted until it became clear that they weren't going to be slaughtered, or forced to collaborate. But when they came back, the institutional memory was gone; the links to the past were shattered. You hear a little of the old Uni slang these days: a few words, here and there. But back before the kzinti came, it was almost a dialect unto itself. And he speaks it."

"Yeah, a dialect for *herrenmanner* only."

Mads smiled slowly. "Do I look like an aristocrat to you, Gunnar?"

"No, but you—"

"Then shut up. I went to Uni for a few years, before the kzinti found my family sheltering resistance fighters."

Gunnar not only became silent; he looked away, abashed.

"Probably the only reason I'm alive is because I was *at* Uni, at the time," recalled Mads in an increasingly flat tone. "As it was, they yanked me out in the middle of a class, and grilled me until they were sure I didn't know anything. Made damned sure. Made me damned sure I wanted to join the resistance, too."

Hilda let her eyes drop, rather than see the look on Mads' face. He didn't talk about his early days very much, mostly because they were simply too painful. He had been nineteen when the kzinti had caught his parents red-handed, aiding and abetting the resistance. They had been condemned to die in the invaders' "Sport Hunts," usually held to sharpen the tracking and killing skills of cubs on the cusp of maturity. His whole family had been held in a pen, for Mads to see. And then, one per day, the bastard ratcats drove them out, to run as long as they could before a young kzin caught and eviscerated each one in an ecstatic kill-frenzy.

And after each one died, the kzinti reapproached Mads, offering to spare the remaining members of his family if only he would provide them with some information: *where are the headquarters of the resistance? Who are its leaders? How many are there?*

And of course, Mads had no answers. He was not a member of the resistance; indeed, his parents had carefully shielded him from even knowing they themselves were involved.

But the kzinti were not interested in excuses, and when, in desperation, he started saying anything to get them to stop, they simply continued to flush his remaining family members out of the pen and into the fields: they knew he was lying. In the end, they apparently realized that the reason Mads had not answered any of their questions accurately was because he couldn't. By that point, only one of his nuclear family remained: little Anneliese, the "surprise child" who was all smiles and hugs and whom his parents called Fall-flower, since she had arrived later in their life than anticipated—a full eleven years after Mads.

He had never recounted whether, when her day came, Anneliese had shrieked or was mute; was agitated or still; pleaded or spat defiance. Hilda only knew that the kzinti had shooed her out of the pen as a "free target," almost as an afterthought, a tidying-up. Anneliese didn't even make it halfway across the field; the fastest of the young kzin chased her down and took his trophies from her body. Right before Mads' eyes.

Which were now dull. "Smith isn't lying about how long he's been asleep: he knows those days too well for it to be something he learned for a role. Little bits of outdated vernacular, the long-past details of his hometown, Neue Ingolstadt, the particulars of sports rivalries back then: some are so minor and old that I barely remember hearing about them as a *bub*. No: he's who he says he is."

"Okay," Gunnar muttered. "But that doesn't mean he's a soldier for our side. He could still have sold out to the kzinti."

Hilda shook her head sharply. "*Nein*, that's nonsense. You could hear that almost everything he knew about the kzinti came from the materials he had just finished reading when we found him. He's still trying to piece things together and not look like the newbie he is, at least when it comes to kzinti. He's a fast learner, and he's drinking in all the tactically relevant materials with incredible speed, but he doesn't know what it's like to live with them."

Margarethe, the group's sniper, and almost always silent unless there was something truly urgent to say, wondered aloud: "So what's the real backstory on this weapon of his, do you think? How could a research program have been going on all this time, without the kzinti tweaking to it?"

Mads shrugged. "Oh, that's not so hard to imagine. The kzinti don't lack energy—God knows—but, lacking patience, they're not always very tidy. And that's all a smart intelligence operator needs: the messy parts of the kzin occupation are where intel operators could live and breed. For instance, look at the ratcats' policy of minimum involvement in our commercial affairs.

They clearly know that they are permitting all sorts of black-market operations to thrive, and must know just as clearly that, like remora attaching to Old Earth sharks, intelligence operatives will seed themselves into that community, using it as a conduit to move equipment, information and orders without the kzinti ever knowing."

Gunnar flicked a stone from his sleeping bag. "Which I just don't get: why do they permit any of it?"

"Because we're the geese that lay golden eggs for them, and they know better than to rearrange our nest: we might stop laying. Besides, they don't worry about problems until the problem becomes obvious. Which means they have a target. Which allows them to do what they do best: jump into the very center of that problem and lay about, destroying everything they find."

"Killing untold numbers of innocents when they do so," spat Gunnar.

"They don't worry a lot about collateral damage or due process," agreed Mads.

Margarethe nodded slightly. "Okay. But the research Smith refers to wasn't done in some backroom, underworld lab. This whole operation obviously had a lot of forethought and long-duration planning built into it."

Hilda nodded. "Absolutely. I'm thinking that the research facility in this system is not on Wunderland, or out in the Swarm. Anyone seeing that the system was going to fall to the kzinti would anticipate that those areas were going to be closely watched. So they'd go further out, to Centauri B, maybe. Possibly all the way out to Proxima."

"Proxima? That's damn close to a wasteland."

"Which would be perfect, Gunnar. It's just a small gas giant and rocks. Lots of rocks, most of which are uncharted. That would be perfect for the construction of a secret base. Or maybe one already existed out there, put in by the ARM before the war."

"And why would they have done that? They weren't expecting any trouble from the kzinti, then."

"No, Gunnar," Mads drawled. "They would have built that base because the ARM was designed to worry about trouble from us humans."

After a long pause, Gunnar scratched his ear and mumbled. "Oh. Yeah."

Hilda smiled. "So I'm guessing they've got a commo system distributed across the rocks out there, or maybe across all the systems, as a huge phased array."

Mads nodded, apparently seeing the deduction toward which Hilda was driving. "So that, when the researchers on Earth found a means of striking back at the kzinti with a really game-changing weapon, they could relay that information back here, so it could be built on site, ready to go. That way, using it did not necessarily mean having to wait for it to be brought by a fleet from Earth."

Gunnar wrapped himself in his bag against the unseasonable chill. "Okay, but how did they get 'Captain Smith' from Proxima back into the main system, presumably someplace close to Wunderland, so they could send him planetside with the weapon?"

Hilda shrugged. "I'm guessing he never left the Serpent Swarm. All they had to do was stick him in a cryo capsule along with the weapon and insert the completed package into a holding orbit. And wait for a prearranged activation signal."

"Which almost surely was sent by whatever craft from Earth came ripping through the system today."

Margarethe nodded at Mads. "Meaning that he may not be the only person—or operation—that got a preprogrammed wake-up call today."

"Or will get one in the days to come." Mads nodded. "If this is part of a larger plan, some of the systems awakened today may simply be countdown clocks. When they run to zero, they'd send a second, third or fourth set of wake-up signals. So like I said, we'd better be alert to the possibility of new opportunities springing up around us."

"Speaking of being awake and alert," added Margarethe, "where's Captain Smith?"

Damn it, thought Hilda, *what is Smith up to? If he was going to go running off into the bush, why wouldn't he have at least—?*

Panting almost as heavily as she was, Gunnar ran past, small branches rasping and snapping around him. "I am going to kill the son-of-a-bitch when we catch him."

"You'll do no such thing." Mads' growl was pained: he was getting a little old for two-hour jogs. "We need him alive."

"Why? We've got his box."

"Which we can't seem to open." Hilda pushed an aptly named whipweed away from her welted face. "I suspect he either means to come back to us or is hoping we'll follow."

"Yeah, follow him right into a kzin ambush, probably."

"Makes no sense for him to do that," gasped Mads. "He could have killed us all right there in camp."

At first, Hilda was so surprised at the idea that she

couldn't even pant, and then she realized the simple truth of Mads' observation. Captain Smith had been no more than fifteen meters away from them while they sat chatting about him as if he were on the other side of the planet: they had been sure that he was sleeping, exhausted after the ordeals of his day. But somehow, he had slipped away from them, leaving behind the secured case with the mystery weapon. However, in its place he had taken a long-arm, one of the high-rate-of-fire *strakkakers*. What he intended to do with that weapon, which could spit out almost eight hundred tiny glass lances per minute, was anybody's guess, but it seemed unlikely that he would train it upon his rescuers. Had he wanted to, he could have riddled them all as they chatted idly about whether he was who he claimed to be. The ridiculousness of Gunnar's suspicions seemed to double.

Gunnar stopped and turned to face Mads. "Okay, then if he's not leading us into an ambush, why the hell did he run? He claims his objective was to link up with human resistance on Wunderland, in the greater Munchen region. So meeting us should be 'mission accomplished,' right?"

Hilda started understanding why Smith might be running. "Meeting us only accomplished only his first objective. Remember what he said he wanted to do next: hit the kzin compound at Neue Ingolstadt."

"Yeah. Revenge. I get that."

"No. Not revenge. He said he needed to do something to get the ratcats furious, to make them follow him."

Behind her, she heard Mads stop. "What are you saying, Hilda?"

"I'm saying that I don't think he's running from us,

or setting us up to be ambushed by the kzinti. He's preparing to ambush the kzinti himself."

Gunnar scowled. "And so he picks his old hometown? That isn't a mission: that's collecting a blood debt. While committing suicide."

"I think he's heading toward Neue Ingolstadt because, of all the places on the planet, he'll still be most familiar with that region, despite all the changes over the last half-century."

"So why wouldn't he just tell us that?" Gunnar complained. "Hey, I'd even have helped him to—"

"It's my fault." Mads' voice was low.

"What?" Hilda and Gunnar chorused.

"Right before he bedded down, Smith asked me to lead a raid on Neue Ingolstadt. Tomorrow. I told him we couldn't, not yet. We had to bring him and his weapon back to HQ first. He just nodded: I figured he understood. Now I think he realized that once we got back to our main camp, he couldn't be sure he'd get his raid approved there, either. Probably he'd be penned up and grilled about his mystery weapon and where he had come from. And he knew if he argued at all, we might start realizing we had to watch him, guard against him running off on his own."

Gunnar shook his head. "Still doesn't make any sense. What does he think he's going to do with a single *strakkaker*?"

"He's going to make the kzinti madder than hell," Hilda said as she realized how Smith was going to do it with just one shoulder arm.

"How?"

"I know the area a bit too, because I went to Uni—"

"Yeah." Gunnar's arms were crossed. "We know."

She felt herself ready to launch into the old rebuttal against his self-conscious class bigotry—*I'm not herrenman stock; we just had enough money, and then I got a scholarship*—but she turned aside from that impulse. "There was a satellite campus out in Neue Ingolstadt, which is about sixty kilometers to the north of Munchen. I went there once, for a field study."

Gunnar affected boredom. "Is this story of old school days going somewhere?"

Mads' voice was quiet but sharp. "Shut up, Gunnar. Hilda, what's in Neue Ingolstadt?"

"The old governor's mansion, about fifteen kilometers to the north. It's one of the first places the kzinti took over. It's reserved for the use of their territorial governor."

Gunnar looked like he'd bitten a lemon. "The territorial governor lives in the *schloss* outside of Munchen. Everyone knows that." Then his face cleared. "Even you know that. So why are you saying—?"

"I didn't say it was the territorial governor's residence, Gunnar; I said it was reserved for his use. As a preserve." She prompted a little more directly when she saw the blank look on his face. "A hunting preserve."

"Oh, shit," he said.

"*Ja*," affirmed Hilda with a sharp nod, reshouldering her rucksack.

Mads was already back in the lead, setting what promised to be a shattering pace for them. "Hilda, do you happen to remember hearing how frequently they run their Hunts out of that lodge?"

Hilda increased her pace, moving past Mads. "Every day."

The rest, understanding, ran after her.

What none of them anticipated was that, despite being less than forty-eight hours out of decades-long cold sleep, Smith would outpace them handily. Which was probably why he made no effort to break trail at any point; he left a clear path for them to follow. *Because that's what he wants,* Hilda thought, ignoring the wind-stitch in her right side, so high and tight that she found herself tilting in that direction as she ran.

Oddly enough, it was Mads—"old" Mads—who was slightly in the lead when, heading east, they crested the Eel's Spine: a rampart of low ridges that marked the western limit of the rolling expanse of sward that sprawled and undulated northward from Neue Ingolstadt. Although the day was hazy, made so by the approach of the high-atmospheric dust clouds, the land stretched out before them in varied shades of green, hemmed in by the dark, forbidding forest to the north. That distant tree line was the inevitable first flight objective of the humans who served as prey in the kzin Sport Hunts. Few ever made it that far.

Surprisingly, Smith's trail led down the slope in that direction. Hilda started down—

—and felt herself pulled back by the left shoulder: Gunnar's hand. She shook it off.

"Wait," he panted. "Don't go. No cover. Kzinti will. See us. For sure."

Mads squinted into the distance, studied the land. Then he pointed, down to where the northern end of the ridge they were on dipped down before reaching the next low rise: a small wooded dale was sheltered in that notch. "He's heading there. It's close to the forest and protrudes out onto the plain: he'll have a clear shot at the Hunters as they cross the open ground."

Gunnar shook his head. "I thought he was going for the leadership, was going to hit the lodge. Maybe from an overlook."

Mads shook his head. "*Nei*. Look." He pointed in the opposite direction, this time down the southern line of the Eel's Spine. Far off, so small that it was not much more than an angular brown wart upon the shimmering green grass, lay the squat lodge. "That's where the leadership is. They don't come out to help or watch the Hunters. It would dishonor the cubs and undermine the notion that it is a test of personal worthiness."

Margarethe, who had been silent behind them, sucked in her breath sharply. "So he's not going after the adults."

"No," Hilda said, reversing her steps as she realized the truth of Mads' conjecture. "He's going to shoot the Hunters, the young kzinti." Recrossing the ridge line, she walked back down the westward slope and then turned north again, paralleling the crest and using its lip to shield her against any eyes that might glance in their direction from the flatlands.

"*Gott in Himmel*," breathed Margarethe. "When the adults find out, they are going to be blind with rage."

Mads made his laconic observation from the rearguard position: "That, I think, is exactly what Captain Smith wants."

Hilda was panting. Sweat had soaked her loose-fitting field-tans to a dull brown-black. Mads pointed a shaking finger down into the wooded dell. "There."

Hilda squinted, saw a faint bit of motion next to the broad trunk of a ten-meter-high allweather fern:

Captain Smith was settling the *strakkaker* into the crook of a branch protruding from the main stem of the treelike weed.

Margarethe, the only one of the four who seemed to have any physical reserves left at all, stared down the steep switchback that would have to be navigated before getting down to the same level as Smith: "Mads, what do we do? He's setting up to fire: he must have acquired his target."

Mads pointed again. "We do nothing. Because you're right: he has chosen his target and he's going to fire before we can get to him. Not sure he'd cease and desist even if we told him to."

Gunnar rubbed the forestock of his rifle meaningfully. "That depends upon how we tell him."

"Stow that crap. I don't like what he's doing, but mostly because I don't know what he's up to. But we're not going to start shooting down our own people."

"But he could—"

Hilda started moving down the trail that would eventually bring them to Smith, but she did so at a leisurely pace. "Might as well start moving."

Gunnar did not move to follow. "Why not wait here?"

Margarethe almost sneered. "Because, Gunnar, he won't exit the area by the same path he entered. And the closer we are when he finishes, the less time we spend linking up before un-assing this place. How long do you figure we'll have before the ratcats are after us, Mads?"

"At least a couple of hours, maybe half a day. If one of their young bucks is late, they'll presume almost anything—lost scent, tricky or lucky prey, laziness—before they'd imagine that he's been killed."

"So we just might get away clean?"

Mads rubbed his chin. "Clean? As in, they have no idea where we went? I doubt that, and I doubt that fits in with the captain's plans, either."

"Whaddya mean?" asked Gunnar.

Hilda shrugged and almost lost her balance at the edge of a fifteen-meter sheer drop. "Mads means that Smith probably wants the ratcats to be able to follow our trail. Why else rile them up like this?"

"But that's insanity, it's suicide—"

"Whatever it is, it's happening right now." Margarethe stopped, pointed. "Look."

Smith was hunched over the *strakkaker*. Following along the trajectory implied by its muzzle, they could see a slight perturbation out in the sward, perhaps three hundred meters beyond the edge of the tree- and fernline: a young would-be Hero, tracking his prey. Even at this range, they could see the kzin confirm the scent: he put his head up, an orange-furred protrusion that lifted over the rippling sea of meadow grass, tipped by the twitching black dot that was his nose. Far off, nearly a kilometer to the east, they marked the progress of yet another indistinct rustling in the green: that was the next closest Hunter, and he was moving farther off.

Hilda was able to predict the moment when Smith fired, having spotted for Margarethe, who was a formidable sniper. The wind came behind them from the west, and as it shaped the sward into undulating currents, it made a whispering rustle: nature's own version of white noise. Also, with the breeze blowing from behind, there would be minimal azimuth drift when the *strakkaker* fired—

A growling hiss rose up out of the dell when the young kzin put his head up again; the weapon was just barely audible given the distance and the breeze. Out on the plain, the black-tipped orange snout was obscured by a spray of red; the grasses around it seemed to shudder fitfully beneath a less calm and steady force than the breeze. Then silence, stillness.

Hilda had not, however, foreseen what Smith did next: he snatched the weapon out of its support and raced headlong into the grass himself, heading directly for the target he had presumably slain. "What the—?"

"Fuck!" Gunnar finished for her, although his was an angry exclamation where hers had been a baffled query. "He's going to bring the whole damn lot of them down on us!"

Mads said nothing, just launched himself down the switchback at a full run, Margarethe right behind him.

Hilda followed. "Damn it," she hissed at Gunnar, "get moving."

"Fine, but we're going the wrong way. We should be un-assing this place, and right now. Back over the ridge. And as far away from Captain Kzin-magnet as possible. He's going to—"

"He's going to need us to be right there waiting for him when he gets back from whatever he's doing out there."

"You mean, we're going to follow this *verrückter*?"

"*Ja*—what else? He's the only one who knows what he's up to, so we follow him, or abandon him."

"Yeh? Well I vote for—"

"Gunnar." Mads panted over his shoulder, gray-faced. "You don't vote; I give orders. And Smith isn't crazy. He has a plan."

Hilda grimly noted the return of her wind stitch. "Wish he would have told us what it was beforehand." She half-ran, half-stumbled around a steep-shouldered corner and kept sprinting deeper down into the dell.

By the time they reached the spot Smith had used as his hide site, they saw stealthy movement in the sward. Approaching.

Mads ducked low. "Damn it. Gunnar, fan left. Margarethe, to the right. Stay low. Target confirmation before you fire." He paused. "What did I say, Gunnar?"

"See it before you shoot it."

"Damned straight."

The closest thatch of chest-high grass veed apart and spat out Smith, who was running at a crouch, *strakkaker* held loosely in his right hand. And in his left he held—

"That's our death warrant you're carrying there," Mads exhaled.

Hilda stared and gulped at the large pink half-parasol ear that Smith was stuffing into a plastic ration-wrap. "You know what they'll do when they find him dead, and with his ear removed. They can't let it stand, can't let a human kill one of their Hunters and carry the ear away as a trophy, as defiance." She swallowed again, met his dark brown eyes. "They're going to come after us with everything they have."

"Which is just what I want them to do." Smith cleaned his knife on the grass, shouldered the *strakkaker*. "Now, let's see how well they do in a real chase."

The longer the kzinti searched, the more hyperactive they became. Hilda had no way of knowing how quickly they had discovered their slain Hunter, but she was the first to hear the spaceplanes screaming across the skies, the dim echoes of their passage echoing all the way down into the limestone tunnels that they had entered only ninety minutes after having left Smith's hide-site. In the following hours, and then days, the frequency and diversity of noise seemed to build steadily; towards the end of the second day, the breathy rush of tilt-rotors combing the ground in a slow, methodical nap-of-earth mode were clearly audible on several occasions. Smith paused when he heard that, and then moved them deeper into the caverns.

Hilda had been able to maintain a sense of direction and relative position for the first twelve hours, but after that, she relented and accepted that she simply had no idea where they were. None of them did, anymore. Except, apparently, Captain Smith. Gunnar had tried to learn a little bit about the caves: how extensive they were, where they resurfaced. Smith simply shook his head and tapped his ear meaningfully: in these caves, traveling as they did with relatively low-intensity cold-lights, they were far more likely to detect the approach of an enemy via sound than sight. Gunnar, frustrated both in his desire to learn about the caverns and his clear desire to start an exchange which would allow him to needle Smith, consoled himself with surly, guttural comments, until Mads scolded and shamed him to silence.

Hilda picked up her pace until she was trailing Smith by no more than a meter. "You're not really from Neue Ingolstadt proper. You're from right around here, aren't you?"

Smith swept his light in a quick arc across the

irregular walls, found a side-branching tunnel they would have walked straight past otherwise: he slipped into it. "I was born just a few klicks south of the lodge the kzinti are using for their Hunts."

"Farm boy?"

He half-turned, smiled: he had fine, straight teeth and features to match. "Not really. Dad was a town official."

"Security? Police?"

He snickered. "Procurement. Don't tell Gunnar, though: he'll be sure to crack a joke about my *Vati* being a pimp."

Hilda grinned back at him. "So, procurement?"

"Yeah, you know: vehicles, maintenance supplies, work suits, screwdrivers, demo charges. Soup to nuts and the kitchen sink in which to keep them."

"That's a pretty broad mandate for one official."

"Well, we lived in a pretty small town. You know how it is: you don't need much of any one thing, so you assign one person to be your all-around expert on 'needed stuff.'"

"So that's the official terminology used: he procured 'needed stuff'?"

"Something like that."

"Just the same way your official name is John Smith."

Smith smiled and didn't insult her by disputing or wisecracking. The new passage had widened out; small bits of limestone growled and rasped beneath their feet; a fine white mist drifted up to obscure their lamps.

"So that's how you know these tunnels," she persisted. "Fled to them to escape having to work alongside Dad?"

"No. Nothing as sensible as that. We just came here as kids because it was dangerous. You know: one wrong turn and you're lost forever." He went silent. "Actually, two kids were lost forever. Never found them. But there are really only a few turns you have to watch out for when you're heading north like we are. It twists a lot, but almost all the secondary tunnels branch out behind us, to the south. So as long as we don't do something stupid, like taking a hairpin turn, it's all pretty straightforward until we come out the far side."

"Which is where?"

"North of the Grunwald, which was where the Hunters were heading, trying to catch their prey before it could get in among the trees. That can slow things down for them, and young kzinti haven't really learned to savor the thrill before the kill, evidently."

Hilda shuddered. "You took a big chance."

"How do you mean?"

"Counting on these tunnels being unused by the resistance, and unexplored by the kzinti."

"Oh, I was pretty sure your resistance didn't have access to these."

"How?"

"From talking with Mads the first night. I didn't ask about the tunnels, but I asked about your operations: how much lead time for retreat you needed, refuges, bolt holes. Everything he told me indicated that these tunnels did not figure in your broader tactical picture."

"They might have." Hilda put up her square chin stubbornly. "Could have been that the very first resistance fighters used them, and the kzinti flushed them out."

"In which case I would have seen the automated monitors the ratcats would surely have left behind in the region, and possibly live patrol spoor. But when I neared the ridge line and the entrances to the caves, there was nothing there." He smiled back at Hilda. "C'mon, now, admit it: this one time, aren't you actually *glad* to be wrong?"

"What do you mean, 'this one time'?" She sniffed. "It's not like you know me."

"No, I don't know *you*." The way he emphasized "you," she was sure he was going to conclude his comment with "—but I know your type." He didn't, saying instead: "However, it seems to me that you're pretty clever and strong-willed. Meaning you're usually right, and you usually get your way, which is why Gunnar resents you so much. And is probably smitten with you, too."

"Gunnar likes his women big and dumb, just like himself."

"Ahhh . . . I suspect he'd make an exception, in your case."

Hilda elected not to reveal that she'd had a similar sneaking suspicion herself. "Besides, Gunnar's got a real class-consciousness issue. He's convinced my folks were *herrenmanner.*"

"Huh." Smith did not sound surprised.

"What do you mean, 'huh'?"

"I mean it's funny how some things change, and some things don't. It was the same in my day."

She considered that. Considered his accent. Considered his familiarity with Neue Ingolstadt and Munchen, despite being from a little *Dorf* up near the hill country. "You went to live in Munchen long before Uni, didn't you?" She considered the possibilities. "A sponsored invitation to the *Gymnasium* there?"

He almost missed a step. "You're good," he allowed

after a moment. He raised his voice so the others could hear him. "We're coming to the end of our subterranean stroll. They shouldn't be waiting for us on the outside, but—"

"—but you never know." Mads nodded, snapped his rifle off safety.

Following Smith's lead, they shut off their cold-lights. Up ahead, a dim gray patch stood out from the blackness. He turned to them. "I'm going up ahead. I'll be gone for a few minutes so I can scout not just the exit, but some of the surrounding terrain. It's far more likely that they'd be in the vicinity by chance, rather than purposely sitting right on top of the exit, waiting."

Even Gunnar didn't have any answer other than a single, sober nod.

Smith faded into the gray, stooping lower as he went.

Mads came closer to Hilda. "Did I hear him mention that we're coming out north of the Grunwald?"

"*Ja*. Why?"

Mads scratched the back of his sunburnt neck. "That puts us well outside of our operations zone. It's a long way home from here. And with all the kzinti combing the countryside for us, we wouldn't stand much chance of making it back."

Hilda nodded. "I suspect he knows that. In fact, I suspect he's counting on it."

"Why?"

Gunnar's voice was tight, sharp. "Because he's a crazy, arrogant bastard, that's why."

"Gunnar, you are an ass. Smith is doing all this because he doesn't want, or doesn't have the time, to negotiate with the resistance cadre. He's got a secret weapon to test and everything he's been doing is almost certainly driven by that mission."

Mads shrugged. "Hell. He should've pulled rank on me and taken command. Then at least he could have let us know where we were going instead of trailing us along this way."

Margarethe remained in the shadows, invisible, but her words were clearly coming out of a smile: "Sure, Mads. And you'd have let him pull rank over you. Sure."

Hilda sighed. "Look, let's walk in his shoes for a moment. It's pretty clear his orders prohibit him from revealing what's going on: I don't think he's playing mystery theater with us just for fun. But at the same time, he's got orders to test this weapon, something he probably can't pull off on his own. And it's also a mission which I'm guessing cannot afford to fail. The folks with the fleets and the power need to know if this weapon is going to work or not.

"So he looks at the situation when we catch up with him and he rightly concludes that if he goes back to our HQ with us, his mission is going to be buried in procedural haggling. He also knows that if he comes right out and tries to usurp command over you, Mads, all of us would have told him to shove his orders and his rank where none of the three suns shine. And what could he have done in response? Reported our mutiny to higher authorities that are light-years away? Besides, he's no idiot: he knows that our resistance has worked on its own for almost half a century. We have our own values and ranks and traditions and protocols. So he knew that, just because he arrived in a flying refrigerator with an official uniform and rank, we weren't simply going to snap salutes, fall in, and pretend that the last fifty years hadn't left us with ideas and a command structure of our own."

Gunnar rested his own *strakkaker* on both knees, put his elbows atop it, put his chin atop his cupping hands. "Ten gets you one he's got a bioweapon in that case."

Hilda reflected that when Gunnar was not busy demonstrating how big his mouth and biceps were, he was actually not the idiot he seemed. "I won't take that bet. Fact is, I'd put my money on the same horse."

Margarethe's voice was cool, level. "Because of the size of the case?"

Hilda looked at the object, which Mads had entrusted to her. "That, and the fact that this is one tricked-out puzzle box. And also because the kzin life sciences tend to lag far behind the others: it could be an area where they're particularly vulnerable."

Mads nodded. "*Ja*, medicine and genetics are not their strong suit, probably as much due to impatience as all the other reasons combined. I wonder how many Heroes aspire to earn their Names by conquering a gene code with a computer and a microscope?"

Gunnar's tone had become more surly. "So if following Captain Kzin-magnet doesn't get us sliced and shredded by the kzinti themselves, we can look forward to coughing up our lungs in great piles of gooey slime, courtesy of some new viral agent of our own manufacture."

Hilda sighed. "Gunnar, neither side has shown any willingness to use that kind of broad-spectrum agent: they're too indiscriminate, and there's always a chance that, once you let a bug out of its test tube and it starts replicating in a target population, it could mutate and come roiling back in your direction. That's particularly true if the agent is retroviral, and in this case, it would almost have to be."

Margarethe sounded genuinely interested. "Why's that?"

Mads shrugged. "Because any bacteria or non-viral microorganism designed to do them in would almost surely find us tasty as well. But Hilda, even a new retrovirus would be dangerous for the same reason: we're similar enough in terms of our chemical building blocks that a virus made to harm the kzinti could hop the genetic divide and come for us, just like bacteria."

"Not quite, Mads: they don't have our genetics. Hell, their biological blueprint isn't even encoded on a braided double-helix structure. So if the bug was something that went strictly after the proteins of their gene-analogs, maybe we'd be safe."

"That's a pretty big maybe," observed Gunnar.

"No argument, but it's hard to imagine what else he's got in the box."

"So why don't you ask me?" inquired Smith's voice.

The four of them—even sharp-eyed and -eared Margarethe—started violently. Smith emerged from the near-darkness. Hilda was tempted to look down, half-expected to see that he had removed his boots, just to creep up and scare the feces out of them. "You mean, you'll actually tell us what's in the case?"

Smith smiled a bit. "No, not yet."

Gunnar scowled. "Then when, damn it?"

"When the time is right, Gunnar. Now, let's get going." He began moving back toward the gray patch at the end of the passage. "It's dusk out there, but darker and cooler than usual, due to the high-altitude dust. I heard a fast mover heading east to west but it was too far to the south to see. It looks like they landed a few troops here a day ago to look around; the bush is tramped down in a few places, but not more than you'd expect from a fire team."

Mads nodded. "Sounds like we're on the far edge of their search perimeter. They dropped a few Heroes to snoop about for a few hours, maybe half a day, then gave it up and moved them elsewhere."

"That's how I see it."

"And they didn't leave sensors behind?"

Mads shook his head at Margarethe's question. "*Nei, 'chen.* Hell, the local ratcats aren't equipped for this kind of search, not out here in the boonies. And their local administrator won't want to admit that humans have eluded him, not right away. So by the time he realizes that he should have sucked up his pride and taken the prudent step of asking for help and more resources, he'll also realize that our possible escape radius has become impossible for him to cover, even with additional assets."

Gunnar nodded. "So they're ramming around the search perimeter with whatever they've got on hand, trying to be in twenty places at once."

Smith nodded. "And probably doing a fair job of it, too. But I was pretty sure they wouldn't find us here." They neared the mouth of the cave, faint light picking its way in through a chaotic filigree of vines, roots and branches.

"And what's so special about this place, that the kzinti wouldn't be looking for us there?" Gunnar asked.

"See for yourself." Smith pushed through the tangled growth, held an armful back so the others could exit.

Hilda squirmed out, felt a gnarled branch scrape her face, wondered why she suddenly cared how the scratch would make her look, and slowed to a stop two steps beyond the mouth of the cave. She felt, rather than heard or saw, the others drag to a halt around her.

"Oh, Christ," Gunnar groaned.

"*Gott verdammt*," profaned Mads, as Margarethe ground her molars audibly.

"*Scheisse lei*," whispered Hilda. "We're running there? To this hemisphere's own natural cesspool?"

"It's called the Sumpfrinne," Smith supplied patiently.

Freay'ysh-Administrator's mouth sagged open slightly in violent frustration, then he snapped it shut. Not that he was enamored of Chuut-Riit's endless object lessons in patience, but rage was of little help when coping with human resistance fighters. The leaf-eaters were innate cowards but, being omnivores, had just enough opportunistic cunning and duplicity to be dangerous. As his patrols had learned on one or two occasions, when venturing into the small hamlets that were known to shelter the resistance.

Which was a misnomer, he mused, since the humans did not resist in the physical sense of the word. They struck and faded away, always fleeing, yielding before the kzinti could meet them in battle. Wherever his security patrols went, the humans were not there: having the sympathy of the region's populace, they also enjoyed timely warnings from multiple sources. Freay'ysh-Administrator had been sure that burning a few of the more troubling hamlets to the ground, inhabitants included, would deprive the monkeys of much of their support. The tactic backfired. If anything, the support had increased.

The administrator let his jaw sag open again and

did not care: the stiff wind of riding in a fast floater was invigorating when it hit his teeth, chilling them, awakening a semblance of the same sweet ache that Heroes felt in the immediate anticipation of biting a long-elusive prey animal. However, today's prey—the humans who had left Shraokh-Lieutenant's first-born cub earless upon the sward—was more than merely elusive: it was defiant, arrogant, taunting. His lips rippled as he fought to control the fury that brewed down deep in his belly every time he reflected upon the audacity of their actions, and the signal dishonor of having it happen on his own lands.

Worse yet, those lands were, more formally, Chuut-Riit's lands: Freay'ysh-Administrator was both direct vassal of, and regional overseer for, the Patriarch's most august offspring. Chuut-Riit did not spend an immense amount of time on his estates near Munchen, but still tarried there enough to be aware of what was transpiring even in this far-flung holding. The Dominant One's teeth were sure to show over this incident unless Freay'ysh-Administrator found and exterminated the patch-furred vermin who had—

"Freay'ysh-Administrator, Zhveeaor-Captain urgently requests a meeting."

"There is progress in the hunt?"

"It seems so."

"Then do not fiddle aimlessly with the controls; fly to a suitable point of rendezvous—at once!"

The floater banked steeply and came around, the waist-gunners leaning into the turn, the pintle-mounted heavy beamers loose in their heat-gloved hands. Freay'ysh-Administrator quickly spotted what had to be Zhveeaor-Captain's command sled. The flat, angular wedge was making the kind of low-altitude speed that only a comms-and-control chassis could sustain. Down on the ground, small orange faces looked up at its screaming approach: it was the first sign of promising urgency since the hunt had begun almost a week before.

The administrator's and captain's vehicles slowed as they drifted toward a bare hillock, which was set at the northern end of the Eel's Spine like the dot of an inverted exclamation point. The command sled's top hatches popped open, two kzin officers emerged and Freay'ysh-Administrator felt his ears go back. One of the officers he had expected: Zhveeaor-Captain. But the other was a complete and uncomfortable surprise: Shraokh-Lieutenant himself, the sire of the slain cub. But there was nothing to be done: Freay'ysh-Administrator had summoned Zhveeaor-Captain in all haste, and Shraokh-Lieutenant was one of the captain's subordinates. The two craft settled onto the sparse grass that tufted the top of the hillock.

Shraokh-Lieutenant was out in a single leap. However, despite his bodily energy, the kzin's mouth hung slack, his pelt was unkempt, and the air audibly rasped between his teeth: he did not radiate fury so much as a form of savage distraction. Apparently, when the human perpetrators had not been swiftly found and eviscerated, he had lost something even more irreplaceable than his oldest offspring: some essential component of Shraokh-Lieutenant's reason had been swept away, left behind in the meadows where his first cub had been butchered.

Zhveeaor-Captain followed his subordinate at a brisk but dignified pace and touched noses briefly with the

Administrator. He snarled lightly at the lieutenant, who evidently recalled that some sign of fealty and subordination was required of him. Shraokh-Lieutenant leapt up and grazed a sloppy nose across the Administrator's own. Who resisted the urge to bat the ill-mannered offender, because remonstration would be pointless. Logically, no insult could have been intended, since no thought or attention to decorum seemed to remain in Shraokh-Lieutenant: just a restless, subcognitive monomania to tear apart the murderers of his progeny. *Well, the sooner this is over*—"You have news, Zhveeaor-Captain?"

"I—we—do, Freay'ysh-Administrator. We know where the humans have taken refuge."

So suddenly? So certainly? "Their scent is fresh then, their trail clear?"

Zhveeaor-Captain glanced anxiously at his distracted subordinate. "We needed no scent or trail."

"Truly?"

Zhveeaor-Captain licked his lips as he produced a small leather pouch with a flap. "The humans showed us where they are."

Freay'ysh-Administrator's ears flicked forward, then snapped back in rage and loathing. "They openly indicated their location? And they still live?"

"Freay'ysh-Administrator, it is not so simple as that. I will explain."

"You had better. And quickly."

"We were patrolling at the far northern tip of the search perimeter, coordinating the floater patterns, when two of the crews saw a bright arc against the sky."

"A weapon discharge?"

"No, Freay'ysh-Administrator. It was a flare. Shortly after it was fired, we approached and our lead unit saw a fire burning: we could not tell if it had been ignited by the flare, or—"

"You investigated, did you not?"

"Yes."

Freay'ysh-Administrator was tempted to cuff Zhveeaor-Captain for his failure to report quickly and clearly, but rethought that impulse. The captain was his best officer, had attracted the special notice of Chuut-Riit himself, and was the epitome of both ferocity and efficiency. Noticing the quick, measuring glances that he shot at his distracted lieutenant, Freay'ysh-Administrator realized that the captain was either fearful of, or fearful for, his subordinate. But there was no time to untangle interpersonal nuances: duty was duty and there were humans to catch and rend. "Zhveeaor-Captain, what did your investigation reveal?"

"Just the fire, Freay'ysh-Administrator. And this." He proffered the leather pouch to his superior.

Who crossed his arms and shook his head. "No; you open it."

With a nervous glance at Shraokh-Lieutenant, the captain undid the clasp. Carefully, as if reaching in to handle a venomous serpent, he removed its contents:

One half of a young kzin's right ear.

Freay'ysh-Administrator drew in a rapid, surprised breath. Then, suddenly unsure of what reaction this object might provoke, he shot a fast glance at Shraokh-Lieutenant.

Who, eyes unfocused, let slip a long, thin stream of drool; it spattered on his foot. None of the three kzinti moved or made a sound.

After a long moment, Zhveeaor-Captain shrugged a shoulder away from his subordinate, whose downward stare was evidently focused upon the very core of the planet itself. Administrator and captain moved aside, walked to the far rim of the hillock's crest.

"How long has he been like this?" the Administrator demanded.

"Just since we found his cub's—since we found this."

"And you will answer for his behavior?"

Zhveeaor looked as though someone was removing his claws with red-hot iron tongs. "Freay'ysh-Administrator, I must. I do not wish to. But our duty to those whose heads have been beneath our hands must come before our own preferences."

The administrator rumbled approval deep in his chest; it was clear why Chuut-Riit liked this Hero so much. He spoke and acted as the kzinti of Old. "Very well. Now: you say that this token tells you the location of the humans. How? Was it near a stronghold?"

"No, Administrator: the ear was—well, it was on a threshold."

"What do you mean? The threshold to what?"

"It was at the very mouth of the Susser Tal."

Freay'ysh-Administrator leaned back. "They've gone in there? Into the swamps of the Sumpfrinne?"

The captain shrugged. "So it would seem. We found their tracks leading that way."

"And you did not pursue?"

"The trail we found was a false one, Freay'ysh-Administrator, and the swamp was unsafe for a small probe."

"What do you mean, unsafe?" It sounded like evidence of cowardice to the administrator, and he would have presumed it to be the case had the speaker been anyone other than Zhveeaor-Captain.

"Freay'ysh-Administrator, the trail split five times within the first two hundred meters. At that point, the overhead cover from the trees was too thick for aerial reconnaissance, and floaters would have been easy prey for ground fire. And I lost one of my Heroes to a deadfall trap."

"Set in anticipation of our probe?"

"No, Freay'ysh-Administrator: it was a game trap. And quite old, probably several years. But there were too few of us, the light was failing, and we are entirely unfamiliar with the terrain. Our chances of finding prey whose scent had been lost were slim, at best. Conversely, the chance to suffer further casualties, by enemy action or misadventure or both, was rising rapidly. Seeing that a more concerted effort would be required, it seemed that the best course of action was to bring this—object—back to you as soon as possible, and prepare for a more determined pursuit."

"And the lieutenant compelled you to bring him along when you made your report?"

"He was insistent, but I was also fearful of his being shunned if I left him behind. His behavior has degraded precipitously. He cannot effectively command, and his demeanor dishonors his rank."

"Yet you do not relieve him of his command."

"Freay'ysh-Administrator, with respect, how may I do so? He would impale himself upon our collective claws if we try to remove him from the search: his thirst for his cubslayer's blood has driven him beyond mere fury into the Unknowing Rage."

Freay'ysh-Administrator shook his great head sadly:

reduced to an animal by incessant, uncontrollable rage. Humans had similar psychological ailments, although rarely so extreme as this: their obsessive-compulsive disorders were more common, but infinitely more benign and passive afflictions. Obversely, losing control by slipping into the Unknowing Rage could not always be cured. And invariably, if a cure was possible, it required the satisfaction of the thwarted vengeance that was usually its cause. "So what do you recommend, Captain?"

Zhveeaor-Captain sighed. "That he be assigned special duty as a lone tracker and a rogue-killer."

"Do you really believe we should make him a *hseeraa aoshef*? Would that not be suicide for him, pursuing the humans on his own, and in his current state?"

"Perhaps, but better he should have a chance to avenge himself or die trying than being slain by us should he become uncontrollable when removed from his command. Besides, given the prospect to engage his energies and anger in a vengeance hunt, I believe much of his current distraction will be replaced with intense focus."

Freay'ysh-Administrator nodded sad approval. "Perhaps we can use him as a means of conducting advance reconnaissance into the Susser Tal and its swamps. Shraokh-Lieutenant will no doubt move quickly and range far, disdaining obstacles. If he were to be rigged with an adequate sensor cluster—"

"I have already ordered one be brought up from stores, Freay'ysh-Administrator."

"Your foresight is admirable, Zhveeaor-Captain, as is your tactical thought. Speaking of which, we have a campaign to plan."

"Yes, sir: that is why I returned in haste. A successful pursuit now becomes far more involved and costly."

Freay'ysh-Administrator let a growl echo in his throat. "Some treasure spent now—teaching the humans that they cannot dishonor us with impunity—is better than whole vaults of it spent later on. Because that is what will be required if the leaf-eaters become emboldened by our lack of resolve in pursuing and punishing the perpetrator of this outrage."

"My thoughts precisely, Freay'ysh-Administrator. What do you command?"

"First, an assessment of the larger tactical picture. I am not so familiar with these regions." It galled him to admit it; it galled him even more that the humans had chosen to lose themselves in the hellish morass that were the swamps of the Susser Tal. It was hard to tell whether their choice had been motivated by desperation or inspiration, but either way, it set a further challenge before the kzinti: since the biome was particularly unfriendly to their physiology, they had little experience with the region, and even less interest in it.

That was obviously soon to change. Zhveeaor-Captain had apparently prepared for this eventuality; he commenced what sounded very much like a prepared briefing: "The microclimate of the valley will undoubtedly be our greatest obstacle and adversary. It features the most dramatic shift in temperature and humidity on the entire planet, relative to the surrounding climate zone." He called up a map on his data slate. "Down here at Munchen, with an elevation of about eighty meters above sea level, average daytime temperatures in the current season range between nineteen and twenty-four degrees centigrade, with humidity of seventy-five percent being considered somewhat high. Moving north eighty kilometers to Neue Ingolstadt, we find modest change. At one-hundred-ninety meters above sea level, average temperatures dip slightly, as does humidity. Then we go sixty kilometers further north, across the plains, and beyond the forest back there"—he pointed to the southeast—"which the humans call the Grunwald. Average temperatures and humidity remain relatively unchanged. Until we get here." His finger thumped down on a valley mouth that looked like an opening into an eastward-stretching worm's gut. "This is the entry to the Susser Tal, which, in the first three kilometers, descends over four hundred fifty meters to a valley floor that is nearly two hundred fifty meters below sea level."

"A drainage ditch without any run-off," growled Freay'ysh-Administrator in disgust.

"An apt characterization," agreed Zhveeaor-Captain. "It is bordered on the north by the Grosse Felsbank, a mostly sheer escarpment that climbs rapidly to two thousand meters above sea level, with a few alpine spurs set further back in massif-groupings. The southern extent of the Susser Tal is bordered by a slowly rising upland, which reaches almost six hundred meters above sea level. It is neither very steep nor very high, but more than enough to make the valley resemble a trench between two highlands."

Freay'ysh-Administrator traced the swampy trench that was the floor of the Susser Tal back to its narrowing, dead-ended eastern terminus. "A strange place to choose as a refuge. Despite its advantages, the humans have no way out. Unless they can get over these southern hills."

Zhveeaor-Captain shook his head. "Actually, the southern highland is more impassable than the Grosse Felsbank. It is very jagged and barren, even though the average per-kilometer elevation increase is not so great."

"A strange formation."

"Not so strange, Freay'ysh-Administrator, when its origins are taken into account: it lies right along a tectonic contact front. These low jagged hills—like teeth sprung from other teeth—follow along the fault line where the southwestern plate is breaking, buckling and snapping up through the surface of the ground. Made more treacherous by winter ice-cleaving and wind erosion, even the locals deem these highlands impassable except to professional mountaineers."

"And yet the valley itself has a surprisingly temperate climate, does it not?"

Zhveeaor-Captain looked sidelong at his superior. "I would say that its climate is much more than merely temperate, Freay'ysh-Administrator. It is punishing. At this time of the year, the prevailing temperatures are in the high twenties and low thirties centigrade. The air is almost perpetually at one hundred percent humidity, with some rather unusual supersaturation effects reported. The prevailing biome is therefore a half-swamp, half-jungle microecology."

"But certainly, this must change in winter?"

"Not as much as one might expect, Freay'ysh-Administrator. Because it lies along an active tectonic faultline, the valley is riddled with hot springs. These factors, in combination with a slight elevation of ambient temperature from widespread vegetable decay, makes snowfall extremely rare. Also, the prevailing winter winds from the Grosse Felsbank tend to shoot straight over the valley without depositing much moisture. It is only seven kilometers across at its widest point."

"How strange."

"Yes, strange and uninviting. In addition to the stink of dying vegetation, the sulfur-reek from the springs is as pervasive as the local flora is pungent. I doubt we will have much luck sorting out human scents in that environment. Furthermore, the tree cover makes conventional aerial observation almost useless, and the attempt to compensate with thermal imaging is only effective picking out biosigns that are fairly distant from the heat-blooms of the hot springs."

Freay'ysh-Administrator twitched his ruff, vexed at the implicit mystery: "Then it is strange that the human resistance has not made use of it before now. In many ways, it is an ideal hiding spot."

"Yes, Freay'ysh-Administrator, but as you observed at the outset, it is also a cul-de-sac. Except for a handful of narrow, forbidding passes through the Grosse Felsbank, the only way out is also the only way in. Which is quite easy for us to patrol and hold."

"Could they not exfiltrate through the northern passes you mention?"

"Not swiftly enough to be tactically feasible. The Grosse Felsbank cannot be navigated by ground vehicles, and we would detect any aerial movement with ease. For a human on foot, it is almost a two-month trek through the mountains to the great northern plateau, where there are few settlements, and to date, no resistance activity or suspected contacts."

Freay'ysh-Administrator gave the one-shouldered toss that was the kzin equivalent of a human shrug. "This cesspool isn't in practical range of any useful targets for them, anyhow. And not a lot of local support, either. If I remember correctly, wasn't the valley used as a compound for various social outcasts?"

"There is a small community of locals, although they are not exiles so much as they are separatists."

"Political antagonists of the human state?" Freay'ysh-Administrator felt the glimmerings of an advantage. If the indigenous population of the region disliked the human authorities, perhaps he could entice them to—

"Not political antagonism," Zhveeaor-Captain said, and the administrator felt his hopes deflate. "Cultural and class disaffection."

"Explain."

"Before our arrival, all the human settlers avoided this region except for a few Hinterlanders, as they were called: people who preferred to dwell at the far fringes of the larger communities. Many of them had radically different religious beliefs and family structures; others felt alienated by the majority of the human settlement groups."

"What? Why?"

"They were from different cultures."

"What do you mean, different cultures?"

"Evidently, Freay'ysh-Administrator, the homeworld environment of the humans was once extremely heterogeneous in terms of language, traditions, philosophies, economies, ethnicities."

"Logical: it explains their chaotic multi-focal society today. So: how did these self-imposed exiles survive? Hunting? I seem to recall that there are some excellent, and quite dangerous, prey animals in the swamps, no?"

"There are. The scant reports we have indicate that the locals rely heavily upon the meat of those creatures for their own protein intake. But this was not the basis of their external trade. They subsisted on collecting biobounties."

"On collecting what?"

"Biobounties, Freay'ysh-Administrator. It was discovered that the swamps and jungles of the valley were rich in rare plants and insects prized for the unique compounds they contain. In particular, many of these substances proved to be very useful to the pharmaceutical corporations that were attempting to produce improved anti-senescence formulations."

"Which we have largely suspended. So how have the Susser Tal's inhabitants survived since we occupied Wunderland?"

"Poorly, Freay'ysh-Administrator. And we only know this because there is still some rare contact between the swamp-dwellers and distant relatives they have in the villages around Neue Ingolstadt."

The administrator nodded at the dataslate, signaling that he no longer needed its displays. "So, Zhveeaor-Captain: how many companies do you think it will take to find the human lickers-of-feces and root them out?"

Zhveeaor-Captain let his tongue wash slowly over his nose: his statement was to be understood as a carefully considered opinion. "Freay'ysh-Administrator, I think that two *battalions* might be enough."

Freay'ysh-Administrator stared at his subordinate.

Who twitched one shoulder slightly: "Maybe three."

"So just where are these swamprats you were talking about, Smith?" Gunnar spat. "We've been slogging through this shithole for two days and haven't seen a single—"

"They call themselves Sumpfrunners. And as for where they are—" Smith gestured to the quagmires through which they were slowly wending their way "—they've been paralleling us for a while now. Probably about three hours."

"Four, actually." The voice seemed to emerge from a plant that looked like an upward-writhing mix of Spanish moss and cactus. A spare, sallow man of middle years wriggled out of what had looked like the solid folds of the cactus trunk. Dressed in much-patched overalls, spattered in swamp muck, and his hair a receding skullcap kept slick by humidity and infrequent washing, he was not a particularly welcoming sight. His attitude seemed a match for his appearance: dour and uncongenial. "Seems like you drylanders are a *lang wegs* from home. *Nichts* for y'all here." He spat with meticulous care and deliberation atop Gunnar's own spattering of saliva.

"Actually, we came here quite intentionally—" Hilda began.

"Zat so, li'l *'madchen*? Sorry to disappoint, but there's still *nichts* here fer *du*."

Smith stepped forward. "You're here. We came for you."

The Sumpfrunner looked Smith up and down. "*Und* whad'ud you want *mit* me, officer? Yeh, I can smell it: you got goverstink comin' outta ever' one of yore pores. Police? No, military."

Smith nodded. "That's right."

"Well, you come to de wrong place, *hauptman*: you comin' fifty years too late, and one army too short. You turned your back on us; now we turnin' our backs on you."

"I didn't turn my back on anyone. I've been in cold sleep for fifty years. And I'm here to fight the kzinti."

The Sumpfrunner's sideways glance might have been sympathetic or merely pitying. "Then you got a lotta catchin' up to do, *hauptman*. But you won't do it wandering in here; thayz all out there. Kzinti don't like the Sumpfrinne very much."

"Maybe not. But they're coming."

"Then lettum come." Other Sumpfrunners emerged from similar hiding spots. All were armed; some were carrying much-refurbished or homemade bolt-action rifles that would have inflicted a case of bore envy upon any self-respecting twentieth-century elephant gun.

"Those are mighty big rifles," Mads said appreciatively.

"Theyz *gut* fer killin' ratcats," the 'Runner answered with a narrow smile. Hilda, seeing the teeth, wished he had settled for a close-lipped grin.

"Bet they are," Mads nodded. "But they won't be enough."

"We got lossa bullets," the other offered.

"I'm sure you do, but they still won't be enough."

For the first time, the 'Runner's easy, dismissive confidence faded. "How many you think are comin', drylander?" He looked from Smith to Mads and then back to Smith.

"As many as they can bring. At least a battalion. Maybe two. Maybe more."

The 'Runner stared at Smith. "*Scheisse.* And what got them so riled up to come pouring in here?" He followed Mads' quick glance at Smith. "Oh, so we have you to *dank* for their visit."

Smith shrugged, nodded.

"And just what did you do to them? Take one of their ears and laugh in their faces?"

"Actually, yes."

The 'Runners looked simultaneously aghast and envious. "What? How?"

Smith told them. Hilda could see the factual knowledge of the event and the birth of a legend growing in their eyes at the same time.

When Smith finished, the spokesperson of the Sumpf runners whistled, the sound made three-toned by the plentiful gaps in his teeth. But then he shook his head. "*Schlaffin'* through fifty *jahr* muss've made you eager to join all yore dead friends from back then. And so now you run here to hide." He spat again, but this time it was fast and angry. "So nice of you to think of us—now."

"We thought of you fifty years ago."

Again, the 'Runner squinted, suspicious, but Hilda saw that he was also intrigued. "Whaddyu mean, that you thought of us fifty *jahr* ago?"

Smith squatted down, and Hilda admired the posture change: without sending any message too overtly, it signaled that this was to be the beginning of a story, told in a casual fashion. *He's good,* thought Hilda, *maybe too good, the way he manages to slowly draw more and more people into whatever ultimate scheme he's hatching.*

"So," Smith began, "fifty years ago, when it was pretty clear the ratcats were going to overrun Wunderland, there were some folks in the ARM and UNSN who were thinking ahead to how humanity was going to come back and kick their furry butts off our home."

A few smiles sprung up around the group; Hilda folded her arms, thought: *and once again, Smith gets*

the measure of his audience and begins to work them.
He could've made a small fortune peddling snake oil...

"There were a lot of ideas tossed around. Most did not survive close eyeballing by the experts, but a handful did. And most of those were going to take time: time spent watching the kzinti, learning about them, their habits, their biochemistry, their society. You all hunt, right?"

The slick, unwashed heads all nodded in unison.

"Well, how well could you hunt an animal if you didn't know its habits, where it liked to sleep, to feed, to rut, to run?"

Now the same heads shook from side to side. "Might as well stay home and stay hongry," drawled one of Smith's audience; a few snickers followed it.

"Exactly. And that's what the war-planners realized: that they'd be damn fools trying to put any plans into motion until they knew more about the species they were hunting. And when it comes to kzinti, we've got to have the advantage in smarts, because they've got it all over us in speed and strength."

Somber, even grim nods followed Smith's assertion, as well as one solemn, "*Ja, stimmt.*"

"So, fifty years ago, the war planners put long-range projects in motion. And they put a bunch of people like me down for the longest nap in human history, without even telling us what the plans were. That information, along with whatever tools and weapons we'd need, were added to our cryo-capsules years later. That way—"

"That way, if the ratcats found you before the plans were ready, they couldn't learn anything about what was in store for them." The 'Runner who'd completed Smith's sentence was quick-eyed, clean-shaven and lean.

Smith nodded his agreement and appreciation. "Exactly: just like he said. So when I woke up early last week, I had no idea of what I was supposed to do. But there was a briefing packet with me: hard copy only, which was lucky, since my capsule's electronics had been fried. In that, I learned that I was to land in any one of four locations that the experts said would be the best place to try out a brand new weapon, which is in that box right there." He pointed at the safe-case that Hilda was carrying: all eyes turned toward her. She resisted—barely—the impulse to sheepishly wave at them all.

"What is it?" shouted one of the 'Runners.

"He can't say, not yet," countered the quick-eyed lean one.

"I ain't fighting for people—outsiders!—fifty years dead and a weapon no one will tell me about," a third rebutted.

"*Stille!*" shouted their gap-toothed spokesman, who looked back to Smith. "You tell a mighty *schon* story, *hauptman*," he said quietly, "but maybe that's all it is: a story." He and Smith watched each other: neither blinked. "I don't see, and I haven't heard, anything that proves that your experts chose four locations or that the Susser Tal was one of them."

Smith nodded, reached into his pocket, and pulled out a slim strip of plasticoding. He read from it: "42.68.2113 by 89.61.4532; do you know where those planetary coordinates are?"

The spokesman sat up as if someone had jabbed a spear into his back. After a long moment, he said, rather formally, "Yes. I know the location of those coordinates." His followers looked stunned, first at him, then at each other, murmuring as they did. Hilda couldn't tell if it was his sudden loss of local accent, or knowledge about the global coordinate system that had surprised them most.

Smith was nodding. "Then here's what you do. Go to those exact coordinates, which, unless I am very much mistaken, are about a day's march further east. Then dig. You'll probably need to go down at least a meter or maybe a little more, given the fact that this valley is like one big compost heap. You'll find a box. In the box, you'll find a plasticoding strip like this one, and there will be a single word on it. Don't tell anyone else what the word is; just come to me. I'll tell you the word on the strip."

The group was completely silent. The spokesman rose, nodded soberly and started down the trail to the east. After a moment, he turned, stared at Smith and the resistance fighters: "Well, you comin' with us or waiting here to get snatched by the ratcats?"

Later that day, when the pace of the march had slacked off, and during a brief lull in the wave-attacks favored by the local mud-mites and swamp-flies, Hilda caught up to Smith. "Quite a performance you put on back there."

He stared at her. "I had the choice to make the truth interesting, or dull. I chose interesting. But it was the truth, every bit of it."

His sudden seriousness took her aback. "Hey, I'm sorry: I didn't mean to offend you."

"No, not exactly. But you figured a little needling wasn't out of line."

"Well—" she wondered if it was right to feel suddenly defensive, and decided she didn't care. "Well, maybe it isn't out of line, after all. You're dragging more and more of us around by our noses, without ever telling us what we're up to, or why we're doing it."

He looked away. "We're doing it to kill kzinti. To kill a lot of kzinti." His cheeks bunched as he said it.

"Yeah, we figured that out. But it would help if you could share a little more—"

"Look." His voice was calm, but low. "I don't like keeping secrets, but it's part of my job. What if this weapon doesn't work? What if it does but the kzinti capture some of us, now or later? This isn't the start of the Great War of Liberation: this is only the test of a new weapon. Which will only be effective later on if it remains a surprise, a *secret*, after it's been tested."

"So what does that mean? That you'll kill all of us after you've tested the weapon? Otherwise, every one of us that walks away from your apparent suicide mission is a potential security leak, right?"

"Wrong." His expression and tone softened slightly. "That won't be necessary. You won't be security risks."

"Oh? And why is that? No, wait: let me guess; you can't tell me."

"See?" Smith's jocularity had returned. "You *are* starting to get the hang of this."

"Ha ha. But what about you? You know about this weapon, and you could be caught. That seems like a pretty significant secrecy risk. Unless, that is, Captain John Smith has his own private poison pill, ready to go." She had meant it as a jibe, but seeing his expression, Hilda suddenly realized that her wild fabulation had actually brought her face to face with the cold hard truth of the matter. "*Gott in Himmel!* I—I'm sorry. I didn't know—I didn't mean to—"

"Of course you didn't. Look: I'm sure a lot of my old mates would have been happy to have a 'final option' rather than get captured by the kzinti, and be diced up or Hunted for sport. Besides, this mission ends one of two ways for me: success and hiding, or failure and death. So if I fail, I'd rather the death be quick, painless, and at the time and place of my choosing."

In the silence that followed, Hilda sought desperately for a new conversation-starter and discovered that no such rhetorical beast existed: "Well, that was all a bit awkward."

He shrugged.

"And continues to be so," she added. That got a genuine smile; *handsome, even through the swamp muck,* she had to admit.

"Having a kill-pill in your pocket is only a big deal if you let it be one," he said gently. "Taking a mission like this—well, let's just say I made my peace with all possible outcomes the day I said 'yes,' and they cut my orders." He drew to a halt when the local that Hilda had come to think of as Papa Sumpfrunner put up a hand, listened and then made a leisurely, palm-down motion. Sighing, the whole contingent sank to the ground, except the three that Papa selected with a pointed finger; they uttered sighs of resignation, not relief, and wandered outward toward the perimeter.

Watching Smith's easy motions, Hilda took a stab at starting a different conversation: "You seem pretty comfortable here: have you been in the Susser Tal before?"

"Not in it, but at the entrance to. A couple of times. Back when I was a kid, and my dad dragged me along on his provisioning trips, we had to make runs up here. Ours was the closest town that got regular deliveries of supplies and spare parts, so the 'Runners came to him with their orders."

"But I thought your dad only 'procured stuff' for your town."

"Yeah, but areas as far off as the Sumpfrinne fell into a special category. Technically, they are in *someone's* backyard, and in this case, it was my dad's. Could've been a few other towns just as easily, but my dad wasn't a bigot or a classist prick, so he didn't mind being their conduit to the cities and supply sources. And they were pretty grateful. Not that they showed it much: people back in these swamps don't show much of anything. They're a careful bunch. But still, you could tell they liked him."

"Oh? How?"

"They teased him a lot."

"And that's how they show they *like* you?"

He stared at her. "Of course it is. It's their way of saying, 'you're okay; you can take a joke.' You have to have a certain basic level of trust, of comfort, between two people before they can start to really tease each other."

Hilda nodded, tried to simultaneously study his features but not get caught looking at him: every time she spent five more minutes talking with Captain Smith, she discovered things about him that were surprising. In this case, the surprise was not how he had learned to manipulate 'Runners so well, but rather, the obvious affection he had for a father now long-dead, and the genuine sympathy he had for the 'Runners themselves. As well as a sharp dislike of bigots. *You're not half-bad, Captain Smith, inside or out . . .* "And so if the 'Runners don't like you?"

"They don't tease you. At all. They don't do anything: they just stare at you. And spit at the ground. A lot. Not right at you, or where you're standing. But you'd have to be a low-grade moron not to get the message."

"So how did these people come to live in the Sumpfrinne?"

Smith shrugged. "It was better than being constantly reminded that the *herrenmanner* think you're subhuman. And the rest of the Teuto-Nordic immigrants followed their example; the poorest of them were the most outspoken and harsh in their prejudice."

"When you're next to the lowest spot on the totem pole, you fight pretty hard to keep the one guy lower than you are in his place."

"*Ja, wirklich.* A lot of these folks either traced their roots to *gastarbeiters* or signed on the colony ships as the equivalent of indentured servants: a lot were poor folks from the Balkans, South America, South Africa. And of course, anyone foolish enough to marry into that kind of family was encouraged to spare their high-blooded kin any further embarrassment by wandering out here to join the rest of the *untermenschen*. To become swamp rats, hillbillies: your choice of derogatory terminology."

"Upon whose bioharvesting skills the anti-senescent pharmaceutical firms depended, if I recall correctly."

Smith nodded. "Until the kzinti arrived, who apparently decided that the earlier each human dies, the better they like it."

"*Ja*, sure seems that way. But how do the 'Runners survive at all, now?"

"Hey, you're the one who was born into this time period, not me." Smith turned to look at their shabby clothing and much-repaired guns. "Looks to me like

they're just managing to hang on. Maybe not even that."
He looked away. "I don't want to know what their infant
mortality rate has been since the kzinti arrived. Nor the
prevalence of malnutrition-related diseases."

Hilda followed his gaze, saw the same things, wondered a further question she decided not to ask: *so why
would they stay?* The answer was in front of her, plain to
see, if difficult to grasp: they didn't leave the oppressive
stink and miasmas of the Sumpfrinne because it was
all they knew, and was what their parents had known
before them. In almost every face, she could detect
the sullen resolve of squatters. These were the faces of
true parochialism, of the unfathomable intransigence of
insular communities that had, since the beginning of
recorded history, doggedly inhabited the most marginal
and isolated of environments. Even unto their own,
slow extinction.

Papa Sumpfrunner had risen to his feet again;
about half a dozen of his followers drifted into the
bushes rather than lining up on the trail. They wielded
machetes, wore heavy gloves, carried hide sacks that
they started to fill with cuttings. If there was a rhyme
or reason to their action, Hilda could not discern it.

Smith nodded in the direction of the harvesters.
"That's Burn Bramble they're harvesting."

"Burn Bramble?"

"Yeah, the smaller branches and leaf-stems have tiny
pockets of nitric acid stored in them: really discourages grazing by the local fauna."

"And the 'Runners harvest it because—?"

"'Cause nitric acid be the main ingredient in smoke-
less powder, *'chen,*" muttered Papa Sumpfrunner as
he drifted past, seeing to the assignment of their

rearguard and the laying of a few choice traps. "Can't live without it. Easier to blow things up than cut them down here in the Sumpf. And even before the kzinti come, we stuck with old-style cartridge guns. Reload our own brass, make the powder from the Bramble."

"And the bullets?"

He smiled at her quick understanding of their real challenge. "*Ja*, well, we make bullets from whatever metal works and is handy. Thayz not always so *gut* as we'd like, but they get the job done." He waggled his heavy-barreled rifle.

That was the first time Hilda noticed the desiccated kzin ear attached like a tribal fetish to the trigger guard.

Papa saw her staring and nodded. "*Ja*, '*chen*—they get the job done."

Hilda did not doubt him in the least.

Early the next day, they arrived at the closest thing to a town that the Susser Tal could boast: about three dozen families, whose huts were perched on stilts sunk into rock pilings. Hilda stared at the spindly structures. "Spring floods come down from both sides," Smith commented at her elbow. "And the rest of the time, the problem is the rain, which has nowhere to go but down. Slowly."

She nodded. "How many people are—?" She stopped: again, how would Smith know, after having been asleep for half a century? Handily, wiry Papa Sumpfrunner was about to pass them, moving at a good clip.

"*Bitte*—" she started.

He turned, apparently agitated. "*Schnell* or nothing,

'chen: I got a message to dig up." He glanced at Smith.

"Uh—how many of you are there?"

"You talking here, or the whole Tal?"

"The whole valley."

He shrugged. "Seven hundred, maybe seven hundred twenty. Why?"

Hilda was going to confess idle curiosity, but Smith jumped in before she could. "Because that's how many people will need to be informed that the kzinti are coming. And that's how many may have to leave this valley as a result."

The spokesman glared at him. "I guess we'll see about that, hey?"

Smith shrugged. "I suppose we will."

"And if I don't agree, then what? You gonna make us go, you an' your army of four?"

Smith shook his head. "They sure aren't my army: hell, they don't even like me. But that's not who's going to convince you to leave the Susser Tal."

"No? Who then?"

Smith pointed to the dried kzin ear hanging from the trigger guard of Papa Sumpfrunner's rifle. "They will. Believe me."

"Well, we'll see whether you can be believed at all, first." He waved the plasticode strip Smith had given him and stalked away.

He stopped directly under the center of what appeared to be his own house, given the questions that were being shouted down at him, and which he momentarily ignored. He started prying up rocks, rather than digging. When he saw Smith's look, he spat, grumbled: "I thought my PeePaw was *verruck*, insisting we keep this pile clean and the plastic sheeting over it." He paused, glared more fiercely. "Well, come on, you soft-skinned drylander; you ain't as tough as me, but you got decent-sized muscles. Help me move these damned rocks."

Smith joined him in his labors; four other 'Runners drifted over to pitch in, as well. In less than twenty minutes, they had moved the rocks, thrown back an all-weather tarp and heaved up an old vacuum-rated shipping crate. They opened it and found a plastic-wrapped footlocker inside. Within that was a box. And in that box was a single plasticode strip. Papa Sumpfrunner stared at it as if he were holding a live viper. Then he studied the characters scored into its impervious surface, folded it up, and jammed it in his grime-lined pocket. He turned to Captain Smith. "What's the code, drylander?"

Smith looked him straight in the eye. "The word on the plasticode is 'distemper.'"

The spokesman blinked, looked down in the hole, looked away. "Well, shit," he said.

Mads looked from Papa Sumpfrunner to Smith. "So? What does it mean?"

The senior 'Runner looked at Mads with eyes that were prematurely rheumy. "It means that your friend is exackly who he says he is." He sighed, his shoulders sloped. "Well, come on in with you all. We might as well have supper while we talk about the end."

Hilda blinked. "The end? What end?"

Papa Sumpfrunner looked around himself sadly, and then at her. "The end of this, *'chen*: the end of our world."

Shraokh-Lieutenant heard the splashing slither again, this time closer behind him. He froze in place as quickly and completely as only a Hero could.

But the sound was gone, and the other incessant buzzings and whirrings and sloshings and ploppings of the accursed swamp reasserted in his ears.

In his ears. His ears. No longer distracted by the demands of his hunt-mission, Shraokh-Lieutenant felt the sudden, torturing itch in his middle ear return. He dug at it with claws half-extended, gouging and scratching in his urgency to get relief.

Which was impossible to obtain. On the third day of his vengeance-hunt as a lone-tracker, the mud-mites had swarmed and found a warm, moist nesting place next to Shraokh-Lieutenant's eardrum. Two days later, the senior battalion doctor, Nriss'sh-Healer, had fiddled with the afflicted audial canal for the better part of an hour, spraying one noxious potion after another into what felt like the center of his head. All to no avail: the mud-mites proved impervious to the antibacterials and insecticides the kzinti had ready to hand, and were now busily laying eggs in the cavity. Which, according to the Healer, meant he would lose hearing in that ear sometime within the next four days. So he had to find his prey before then, because his nose was of almost no use in this midden-heap of a valley, and with his hearing diminished—

More noise, this time in the bushes to the left, moving steadily from his front flank to his rear.

Shraokh-Lieutenant swung his beamer—a carbine-sized model—off his shoulder and snarled, squeezing the trigger as he spun to put his aim point in front of the target, sweeping back toward where he had heard the sound.

The welding-bright beam sliced into the jungle like a blinding scythe, decapitating ferns and bushes, toppling a pair of trees, torching a few patches of (rare) dry grass, and eliciting a single, abruptly silenced scream. Matching that sound with his own high-pitched screech of triumph, Shraokh-Lieutenant sprang forward: an eight-meter leap from a standing start. He landed at the source of the death-sound.

At his feet lay a feral boar, bisected lengthwise, half a meter beneath the spine. The smell of the seared meat made him retch through his fury and frustration. He turned his back upon the creature and sprinted further down the trail, in search of his real prey: humans. Leaf-eating, urine-gulping, cub-slaughtering humans. He felt the emotional upsurge toward the Unknowing Rage, and fought back hard. Distracted, he consequently forgot the caution which he had rigidly imposed upon himself since setting forth to avenge his cub as a *hseeraa aoshef*, a solo rogue-killer. He forgot to move carefully rather than swiftly.

As he ran, paralleling the bubbling hot springs to his right, he remained focused on his left flank and the ground beneath his feet—and so missed the catch-wire that was looped down among the hanging mosses he pushed out of the way to his right. He heard the unmistakable sound of a mechanical release, instantly twisted away from it, and felt darts whistle past his chest, missing by a centimeter. But he did not hear the sigh of a heavy weight beginning to swing down from above his head to the left.

As the spiked, rock-laden warhead of the pendulum

trap swung down faster, its sigh became an accelerating rush. Shraokh-Lieutenant heard it now, but, with his feet still committed to the fast leaping sidestep he had used to dodge the darts, he was unable to react, other than to avert his face and put out his arms. He knew, even through the building Rage, that this was what the humans had intended: that they had known the darts were not faster than his reflexes, but that they could force him into an evasive maneuver that would make it impossible to avoid the true, killing component of their doubletrap.

The sharpened, dung-smeared stakes on the pendulum-bob swung into him with a sound of slicing leather and shattering kindling. He felt multiple punctures along his left side, and then he was airborne: the impact of the warhead threw him five meters to the right, halfway into the murky, fetid water he had been paralleling.

Shraokh-Lieutenant howled, partly in pain, but mostly in a fury that quickly blotted out the pain, washed over his senses, even disintegrated the shame of having been so dishonored by the humans. In place of all that was not merely rage, but the Rage. Thought was now extraneous. Wounds were now extraneous. Caution was now extraneous. Killing was the only thing that mattered. Only killing.

Consequently, he did not hear, until the very last second, the stealthy wet rush behind him: he spun, bringing up the beamer. And found himself looking into a maw full of teeth: a maw even wider, with teeth even longer, than his own.

It was, he dimly realized as he pulled the trigger and converted his roar of rage into one of murderous aggression, what the humans called a swampadile. However, it did not really resemble their homeworld's much-storied crocodile. This creature, although every bit as large, was more akin to a flattened eel with stunted legs and wide, almost spatulate jaws. But whereas the crocodile was surprisingly fast over short distances on land as well as water, the swampadile's limbs were too rudimentary for such pursuit. On the other hand, its feet were wide and webbed, and so, although not a good land predator, it had extraordinary speed in the water, being propelled both by its limbs and the sinusoidal motion of its body.

As the creature's teeth seemed to leap toward Shraokh-Lieutenant's face, the kzin's beamer sent out a brief actinic stab—and died. Whether the power pack was exhausted, or fouled by immersion in water, was of no importance to Shraokh-Lieutenant. More important was that he had missed: one of the pendulum's stake-points had lodged and broken off in his left shoulder-joint, throwing off his accuracy.

The swampadile was badly injured, nonetheless: the momentary beam flash hit the water in front of the creature, sending up a gout of hissing, reeking steam. Scalded, the swampadile writhed back. The kzin cast aside his spent beamer and pulled his *w'tsai*: a shortsword with a nearly monomolecular edge.

His overhand cut coincided with the swampadile's forward lunge. The weapon dug in, well behind the rear of the creature's jaws, which snapped down on the kzin's warding left arm. A medley of splintering bones and shearing hide counterpointed the contending screeches of the combatants.

But only for a moment. A second heavy blow from

the undaunted kzin was a message that even the almost brainless swampadile understood: its current grip upon the orange-furred creature was not killing it, at least not fast enough. Even the left arm of the biped, although almost completely severed and halfway down the monster's gullet, evidently had claws on the end of it: they ripped and tore at the amphibian's upper gut. The swampadile coiled back, releasing the mauled arm, eyes fixing instinctually on the kzin's head, and it came forward with a warbling screech—

—only to impale itself on the *w'tsai*, which the kzin plunged deep into its mouth, the point ripping out through the creature's faint dorsal ridge, just behind its eyes.

But the swampadile completed its attack even in death; the fang-crowded jaws snapped down on Shraokh-Lieutenant's last good arm.

The kzin tried to extricate himself, found his arm held in a death-vise, pierced by half a dozen of the creature's long, tapering teeth. Frustration, pain, triumph, and, oddly, rut-aggression boiled up out of him in a long, thready scream.

When he fell quiet, the jungle and swamp rewarded him with a moment of perfect silence. And then, he once again heard the slithering burble that had presaged the swampadile's attack. Shraokh-Lieutenant's kill- and rut-addled brain focused for the briefest moment, noted the sound, wondered, hypothesized—

At that moment, he learned a fundamental and important lesson about the swampadiles of the Sumpfrinne:

They always hunt in pairs.

Freay'ysh-Administrator could tell from Zhveeaor-Captain's rigidly erect posture that he bore bad news. And he suspected he knew what it was. "Shraokh-Lieutenant has fallen in the hunt, I presume?"

The other kzin nodded tightly, but said nothing.

So, something worse than death? "And what else?"

"We found him like this." Zhveeaor-Captain handed a dataslate to his superior.

Freay'ysh-Administrator looked at the image on its screen and felt his fur tuck flat, his ears snap back against the rear of his head, his lips ripple open to release a deep, primal growl. Somewhere, from miles away—or maybe only a meter: all distances were suddenly the same—Zhveeaor-Captain's voice explained: "He had met his Hero's End before the humans nailed him up in this fashion. Most of the damage to his body was done by swampadiles: they killed him when one of humans' traps wounded him and knocked him into the water."

"And did the swampadiles bite off his right ear, as well?"

"No, Freay'ysh-Administrator. They did not. If you look carefully down here, you will see that the humans pinned his ear onto his—onto his—"

"I see clearly enough, Zhveeaor-Captain. But—" he peered more closely, not wanting to do so, but wishing to confirm the full magnitude of the human atrocity "—this is not his whole ear, is it?" When the captain did not reply, he looked up.

And discovered a hide pouch being held out toward him. He turned away. "I do not need to see its contents," he growled, a screeching buzz edging into his voice, rising up from the rage, the shame, the rut-aggression—

He stopped, sniffed mightily, shook his head: how odd. Rut-aggression? Yes, it was there: he could feel it, but he smelled no female kzinti. Which was manifestly impossible here, being so far from any harem. So why—?

"There is more," Zhveeaor-Captain said calmly.

How could there be more than this? "Yes?"

"It seems the humans killed the second swampadile so that it would not consume Shraokh-Lieutenant, so that they could create this monument of defiance."

"And have we responded?"

"We have."

The lack of extrapolation told Freay'ysh-Administrator everything he needed to know. "But our response was repulsed."

"Not repulsed, Freay'ysh-Administrator: lost. No Heroes returned. The coursing squad assigned the task of tracking down the humans drew ahead of the main body—"

"And they were ambushed."

"Freay'ysh-Administrator, I take this on my own head; I offer up my Name and females in expiation of my failure. I should have known. The short sight ranges in the undergrowth made it simple for them to ambush us. And exhaustion must have led to our Heroes' obvious distraction. I suspect they were overheated by the mud coating their fur, which cannot be removed except by extensive grooming."

The administrator stared at the captain. "Our Heroes were distracted? In what way?"

"When the humans retreated from their ambush, our Heroes gave chase."

"Is this not customary?"

"Yes, Freay'ysh-Administrator, but not until the main body has arrived, so that the pursuit can be made along a broad front, with secure flanks. But our Heroes, hot and enraged as I must imagine they were, completely disregarded that protocol, as well as communication discipline. They seemed to be on the edge of the Unknowing Rage themselves. And so, following the trail of the retreating units, they did not detect the second ambush, lying close along that path."

Freay'ysh-Administrator closed his eyes. "Have our reconnaissance assets located the leaf-eating shit-lickers who destroyed our Heroes?"

"No, Freay'ysh-Administrator. The tree cover is too thick, and the heat from the springs makes thermal imaging useless down in the lowlands. Perhaps if we had more aerial drones to seed down under the forest canopy—"

The administrator negated that notion with a toss of his head and flex of his ruff. "Impossible. With the recent incursion by the human ship from outsystem, the fleet has concentrated out in the Serpent Swarm, bringing most uncommitted ground assets with it in order to quell the scattered insurgents who were evidently emboldened by this recent human attack. The two battalions we have on hand are all that we are going to get."

"With a full company providing base security, here at the mouth of the valley, I am uncertain that the remaining numbers will be enough."

"They will have to be, Zhveeaor-Captain. And they will be. They are kzin Heroes."

"They are, but they still have no target. Our short-range patrols have found nothing but a few abandoned observation posts. And our rogue-killer, and now our subsequent scouting teams, are all dead, with little to show for their Heroes' Ends."

"Then the time has come to conduct a reconnaissance in force. You are to coordinate a rolling series of company-level sweeps, all along our front, pushing constantly deeper into the valley. Our minimum objective is to move the lines of our safe zone ahead at least five kilometers a day." Freay'ysh-Administrator saw Zhveeaor-Captain's uncertainty, felt rage—and again, that odd hint of rut-aggression, as if the captain was a mating rival. "This is what is required of our Heroes!" he asserted. "This they must do!"

"It shall be as you order, Freay'ysh-Administrator."

"Make sure that it is." He paused. "Or you may yet forfeit your Name and females."

The three surviving kzinti came bounding through the brush, pursuing Gunnar and one of the 'Runners, closing the gap with sickening speed. Hilda held her breath as the two humans vaulted over a fallen fern-trunk, then crouched down rather than continuing to run.

The kzinti pushed harder, one of them firing his beamer as he sprinted and shrieked like a scalded tiger. The beam danced unsteadily along the fallen trunk, slicing chunks off, starting one brief, guttering fire, but not focused enough to cut through it.

The kzinti were within five meters of the trunk when their leader evidently noticed something odd about the brush ahead: specifically, that parts of it had been cleared. He paused, probably seeing the faint, narrowing avenues that had been cut through the foliage.

From Hilda's reverse viewpoint, though, they were sightlines into the widening fields of fire that the kzinti had now entered. "Optimum," she said, sharply enough to be heard up and down the line. From concealed positions in the densest brush, five roars—almost as loud as light artillery—boomed out at the kzinti: an equal number of meter-long muzzle-flashes marked their sources.

The lead kzin had a leg blown clean off: as it cartwheeled into the underbrush behind him, the Hero yowled and exsanguinated in great arcing gouts of dark red blood. The second of them staggered, then stopped, and lasted just long enough to look down and realize that a sizable red divot had carved away half of his right lung. He never realized—but revealed as he fell, senseless—that the exit wound in his back was a crater so wide that it had partially exposed his spine.

The third was marginally luckier: one shot took off half his tail, another clipped through his gut at an angle. The pulped coils which flopped out of this belly wound signified it as mortal, but kzinti did not die quickly or easily. He struggled back to his feet as the five human snipers reloaded their home-brewed, single-shot elephant guns.

That was when Gunnar and the 'Runner popped up from behind the fallen fern-trunk and sent streams of *strakkaker* fire into the slowly rising Hero. Bits of fur, blood and bone flew in a haze of carnage: as the weapons fell silent, magazines expended, the tattered remains of the third kzin toppled backward.

"That's the last of them," shouted Gunnar in savage glee.

"And it will be the last of us if we don't get the hell out of here now," Hilda shouted back. "No talking:

move. Back to waypoint Foxtrot." Hilda jumped up, grabbed her gear, and, as she launched herself full speed down the narrow path that was her personal bug-out route, she wondered: *And again, where the hell is the heroic Captain Smith?*

By the time they got back to their combination camp/refuge/hideout nine hours later, Gunnar had exhausted his considerable creative energies for thinking up new insults concerning Captain Smith's courage, commitment, leadership skills, choice of aftershave, and female ancestors. And what galled Hilda most was that she had to endure hearing it in silence.

Because, in terms of leadership, and maybe even courage, Gunnar was right. Or at least he seemed to be.

Which was what Hilda was thinking when she stormed into Smith's lean-to and stared not at him, but the secure box he'd been carrying for days now, wandering and staring about as though he were some uber-macho version of Van Gogh looking for the perfect field—or, in the Sumpfrinne, fetid bog—to paint. "So, have you had a productive afternoon, Captain?"

He stopped his infernal map plottings—his favorite activity these days, after wandering around with his purported secret-weapon-in-a-box—and looked up at her mildly. "Pretty fair. How about you?"

"Well, we had a great day, Captain. Shot up two squads of kzinti that were poking into the village we evacuated yesterday. They came after us, as they always do, and burned down Shindle and Milsic with beamers. Which left the ratcats feeling so wonderfully confident that they charged straight into another L-ambush. Killed about a dozen there."

Smith had an almost dreamy look on his face. "That never gets old, does it?"

"I can't see how *you'd* know, sir, since you haven't been on a single god-damned op since the second day we got the 'Runners organized. But if it matters to you, the last of the kzinti came after us, straight into the firing lanes of our hidden rearguard's elephant guns." She threw her empty canteen down and realized she stank. Just like the whole Sumpfrinne stank. And she resented Smith for stinking less—a lot less—than she did. "All told, we got a whole section of them today. No thanks to you, Captain."

His right eyebrow arched. He had never made himself the official CO: Mads and Papa Sumpfrunner would probably have bristled at that. But the de facto reality was that he was in charge. He never gave orders: he simply pointed out what needed to be done, maybe put in a word or two on how best to do it, and faded away, resuming his love affair with his goddamned secure box. "Well, it seems like you don't really need me out there," he said. "You folks are doing a fine job all by yourselves."

"Yes, but what for? Smith, you said that your plans for success included survival. But we're trapped here. There's no way out of this valley except through the kzinti. Which is to say, there's no way out of this valley."

"There are the passes up through the Grosse Felsbank."

"Yeah, an exit where we have to walk two abreast, with a horde of angry kzinti on our tails. That's not a retreat. That's volunteering ourselves to be the victims of a box-canyon slaughter."

Smith shrugged. "I'm not sure it would turn out that way. But tell me, why do you think the kzinti are unable to adapt to the ambushes you've been setting up?"

"Damned if I know, and damned if I care." She lurched across the rickety card table that Smith used as a desk. "Listen: this can't go on. We need you out there. At least so we can stop the rumors that the 'Runners are starting to whisper back and forth. Rumors about how you don't really have a master plan, how we're all going to die in a last stand, because word has it you're building an oversized pillbox at a chokepoint in the eastern half of the valley."

"I promised them we'd escape, and I mean it: we're building that pillbox with a big escape tunnel that will—"

"Screw escape tunnels! Escape to where, Smith? Have you lost your mind? Wait: is *that* the secret weapon inside the box? That it has the power to make a human leader so insane that even the kzinti can't predict the tactical idiocies he's going to think up?"

"You could not be more wrong," he said. And then he smiled. "Or more right."

"*Quatsch!* Enough with the mysteries: when are you going to use this *verdammten* secret weapon? When are we going to start seeing some results?"

Smith paused, and Hilda had the strange sensation that he was trying to decide which of her two questions he should answer. "You'll see the effects in time."

"In time for what? In time to save us? In time for any of us to survive? Or in just enough time to witness our pyrrhic victory as the last of us to keel over from exhaustion, or heat, or wounds?"

Smith smiled. "Long before that. Hell, if that were to happen, then I'd screw up my other objective."

She reared back. "What? Another objective? What the hell is this one? Global domination? Mastery of the universe?"

Smith suddenly looked serious as he came around the table. His eyes lowered for a moment: she thought he was going to sneak a glance at the map, but instead his gaze came up, directly into hers. "No. My other objective is to make sure you get out of here alive."

Wha—? She swallowed; her facetious rejoinder was hoarse, weak: "Yeah, right after you've seen to your own—"

"No. You come first."

"But what about—?"

"No. No 'buts.' This has top priority. Commander's discretion."

Hilda wasn't sure if she grabbed him or he grabbed her. She only knew, as they kissed long and hard:

Damn it, I do *stink more than he does . . .*

Freay'ysh-Administrator stared at the map. *We're gaining only three kilometers a day and they are still getting in among us, occasionally, in our rear. And we almost never catch them.* He pounded the field table with his fist: the frame-metal legs screeched as they bent under the blow; they did not spring back. *And now I've ruined this piss-for-steel table.* He batted it aside, charts and datachips spraying in a wide sweep against the south side of his hab-shelter.

Staring at the mess, he noticed shadows protruding through the open flap hole: "Enter," he growled.

Zhveeaor-Captain and a young Hero, one he had not seen before, entered. Both waited upon his gesture to approach, which he signed gruffly. They entered, leaned forward, touched noses quickly, lightly, stepped back. The administrator looked at the young kzin again: he could not have been six months beyond the Hunt that elevated him into the ranks of the Heroes of the Race. He faced Zhveeaor-Captain. "And where is your usual adjutant?"

Zhveeaor-Captain's shoulders sagged for the first time in the years he had known him. "He was slain by the humans this morning, Freay'ysh-Administrator."

The administrator calmly reached out for the table, intending to right it, but instead, snapped off one of its steel legs and started bending it. "Unfortunate."

The other two kzinti looked at each other, then Zhveeaor-Captain stood a bit straighter. "You asked for a report, Freay'ysh-Administrator."

"I did." The steel leg was now horseshoe shaped.

"The new tactic of inflicting maximum casualties upon the humans instead of taking more ground has proven ineffective, also. Our new, reinforced hunter-killer sweeps are inflicting few—and mostly unconfirmed—enemy KIAs."

"So you believe we are not finding all the bodies of those that we kill."

"It is probable, Freay'ysh-Administrator."

"I must have answers, information, Zhveeaor-Captain, to know if this strategy should be continued."

The new adjutant spoke, voice buzzing with throaty anxiety. "Freay'ysh-Administrator, perhaps I can be of assistance in this matter."

"You?" The chair leg was now a hoop. "How?"

"I have studied the hum—the leaf-eaters' history, Freay'ysh-Administrator. One of their great pre-unification powers faced a problem akin to ours."

"A leaf-eater solution is not a kzin solution."

"Not normally, perhaps, but their problem was identical: determining how many leaf-eaters were actually killed in a battle when it was not possible to find all the bodies."

"Hmmm." Freay'ysh-Administrator's hands were still upon the tortured table leg. "And what was their solution?"

"They used ratios, Freay'ysh-Administrator."

"Ratios?" His hands flexed; the steel squealed faintly.

"Yes, Freay'ysh-Administrator: ratios. The method was devised by the power's senior war leader at the time."

"And what was this war leader's Name, for I assume he had a Name as well as a title?"

The young adjutant lifted his chin in the throat-exposing gesture of deference. "He did, Freay'ysh-Administrator. As best we can tell, he was known as McNamara-SecDef." The adjutant's tone became distracted: "He apparently had many titles over the course of his life, some of which are now only preserved as the shorthand address-forms which the humans..." Zhveeaor-Captain jabbed a warning elbow into his adjutant's ribs. The young kzin's voice terminated with the suddenness of a machine being switched off.

Freay'ysh-Administrator's hands absently worked the steel hoop more tightly upon itself. "And before sharing this battle-wisdom, McNamara-SecDef had himself led armies in many wars?"

"No, not exactly." Seeing the administrator's look, the adjutant added hastily, "But, in his youth, he planned bombing missions."

"Hmm. Hardly deeds worthy of earning a Name." The chair leg now resembled a pretzel. "Tell me, Adjutant, what were these magical numbers that made this leaf-eater so canny a war leader?"

"His numbers indicate that one can determine the total enemy dead without actually counting their bodies."

The administrator felt scorn vie with dark curiosity. "I do not understand. How can one know the number of relevant objects without counting them?"

"By estimate, Freay'ysh-Administrator. If our tactics and doctrine remain constant, we can arrive at a ratio of how much firepower we expend per human killed by studying the enemy casualty count in those battles where we know that none of the leaf-eaters have escaped. Thus, in less-controlled engagements, even if we find only one human body, then we may infer how many more we have killed, based on the control data. Once the system is perfected, arguably you only need to count the number of shots you have fired to determine how many of the enemy you have kil—"

Freay'ysh-Administrator whipped out his fist— the one holding the steel pretzel—and smashed the adjutant across the nose: the sharp snap and spurt of blood ensured that he would have a lasting reminder of how his crooked logic had earned him a perpetually crooked snout. "Moron! Imbecile! Eater of *sthondat*-dung! This is not an answer: this is a delusion."

"But," whimpered the young adjutant, "Chuut-Riit urges us to reflect upon problems, attempt to devise new solutions which employ thought, rather than brute force or overly simple—"

"The only thing here that is 'overly simple' is you, dolt." Freay'ysh-Administrator swept back his hand: the adjutant flinched then fell flat on the ground in the most abject of honorable submission gestures. Freay'ysh-Administrator had thought staying his raised hand would be easy, but it was not: a sudden surge of deeper anger, almost like rut-aggression, peaked, proved unusually hard to quell. In order to physically defuse the strange, persisting rage, Freay'ysh-Administrator heaved the steel pretzel at the far side of his shelter: with a brittle popping sound, it burst through the blend of synthetic sheeting and carbon-filaments and out into the spoiled-egg stink of the Sumpfrinne's marshes. "These ratios are foolishness," he growled at both of them, "and cowardice. A war leader may need the skill of estimation, but this is saying that shit is meat, and piss is blood. There is no help in such numbers, for they are not real. Allow me to hypothesize, learned adjutant: this McNamara-SecDef lost the war he was fighting, did he not?"

"Well, there are some who say—" Seeing Freay'ysh-Administrator's look, the adjutant cowered back down, one paw held protectively over his bent and bleeding nose. "Yes, Freay'ysh-Administrator: he lost."

"*Rrrrsh'sh'ch.* Of course he did. His was a science of opiating lies, not truth." Freay'ysh-Administrator reflected: *truth. The truth of Heroes. The truth of Heroes is that the great should lead, not sit in an office like this McNamara-SecDef obviously had. Nor in a shelter like this one. I must lead.* And the powerful aggression impulse surged again. By leaving behind the cursed numbers and reports and analyses, he would be the Hero he should be. He strode to the squat locker that held his combat gear. "Here is a truth for you both: not many mathematicians make great Heroes, and vice versa. And so I have the Hero's answer to our quandary in this campaign."

Zhveeaor-Captain's ears came forward quickly. "And what is that, Freay'ysh-Administrator?"

"To lead from the front. And no more maneuvering. We have enough forces to push the humans to the other end of the valley if we are bold enough, strong enough, fierce enough: if we listen to the Heroes' blood of our sires, singing in our veins."

"But Freay'ysh-Administrator, we have been trying—"

"That is the problem, Captain." He left out his subordinate's Name purposefully: the veiled threat of Name revocation teetered on the edge of actualization. "We have been 'trying.' Trying is for kits and cubs: we do or we die. That is the truth of the Hero. Now, I shall reaffirm that truth. You will stay here, Captain, with the support services section and this number-loving leaf-eater's spawn." The adjutant whimpered, but also struggled to keep his lips together over his gritting teeth. "You will coordinate with the rear. That seems a fitting job for you both."

Zhveeaor-Captain reared up. "If the failure is so completely mine as you deem, Freay'ysh-Administrator, I again offer my Name and my harem—"

"Keep your Name so that we may better attach your shame to it. And what mangy collection of females would stay in a harem of yours rather than scratch open their own veins? None that I would deign to *ch'rowl* with." Aggression pheromones streamed out of Freay'ysh-Administrator: he could smell them pouring out of his body. He felt alive and vital once again.

He noted Zhveeaor-Captain's rigid stance and his suddenly muted pheromones: he elected to interpret it as cowardice rather than a further sign of the captain's almost preternatural self-restraint. Teeth bared at his two subordinates, Freay'ysh-Administrator reared up to his full height and closed the side clasps on his ballistic armor. "I will go into the valley at the head of all our forces, find our foes, defeat them and suck the marrow from their bones. Stand aside, you nuzzlers-of-genitals: make way for a true Hero."

Mads came stumbling into the CP, out of breath. Hilda knew what his message was before he opened his mouth, knew it because Mads was too old to run flat out for anything less than a crisis, and because John Smith had been expecting the news for two days now. "How many and how fast?" Hilda asked, shouldering the cut-down kzin beamer that was her new personal weapon. Most of the large kzin weapons took two humans to hold and operate, even after the grips, forestocks and other outsized furniture was reduced. But the 'Runners had been able to modify a few of the carbine-sized beamers they had captured so that they were no more unwieldy than a big human assault rifle.

"They're coming fast and on a broad front. As for how many—" Mads took a deep breath "—damn me if it ain't all of them, Hilda." He looked around. "Where's Smith?"

The perpetual question and, now that she and the captain were lovers, her own secret embarrassment: *where's Smith?* What could she say? The most martial occupation Smith had undertaken in the past week was to supervise the construction of the pillbox-fort two kilometers further east, then oversee the excavation and concealment of defilading trenches on the flanking heights. But, then, toward the end of each day, her hero-paramour would once again steal away to contemplate the flowers, trees and bushes in some intense myopia of fascination that might have been appropriate for a botanist or Romantic poet but not for the captain of a guerilla war band. It was as if he went into the jungles and marshes looking for a sign, an omen. One that was apparently very slow in coming.

"He's off being nature-boy again, isn't he?" Mads' voice had edged into pity for Hilda: he was one of the few who was aware of her relationship with Smith.

"Not anymore," announced a voice from the doorway.

They turned as Smith entered at a brisk pace; he was wearing the secure box like a backpack now, and moved purposely to the trunk that was his gun and ammo locker. "How long until they get here, Mads?"

"An hour, maybe two if we give them a stiff fight."

Smith turned, eyes sharp. "No, Mads. Pass the word: no one runs, but no one is to hold a clearly compromised position."

"Damn it, Smith, the moment the kzinti start attacking a position in earnest, it gets compromised. Pretty quickly, too."

"That's fine. We've drilled this for weeks. Our troops are to fall back, each defensive line leapfrogging to the rear and into the next open set of defensive positions."

Mads looked grim. "So: no secret weapon to save the day, after all."

Smith smiled. "Oh, the secret weapon is quite ready. Fully deployed."

"What? When did you—?"

"Doesn't matter. It's in place now and primed."

Mads frowned. "Well, what is it and how do we use it? Is it remote-activated? Or remote-operated? Do we have to—?"

Smith had his *strakkake*r in hand: on his back was one of the three kzin fire-and-forget missiles they had taken. "Mads, listen to me: we don't need to worry about the weapon. It doesn't require our control."

"Okay, but—but how do we coordinate with it? We need to know its area of effect so that we can adjust our own—"

"Mads." Smith smiled, waited. "Mads. You're listening, but you're not hearing me: the weapon takes care of itself. Entirely. We don't need to control it, or adjust to work with it, not beyond the preparations we've already made. Now, get those orders to the unit runners. And Hilda, have Margarethe take the snipers to the bolt-holes in grid box delta-tango. They're to stay fully concealed until the kzinti have gone past."

"And then hit them in the rear."

"Under no circumstances are they to hit them in the rear. Not until they hear three shrills of my whistle. Again, just the way we drilled it."

"So what are they to do? Follow the kzinti and watch the fun?"

"Yes, from a safe range. Beyond detection."

Mads shook his head. "And you think that's going to work? That the kzinti won't have rear-area security units watching for that kind of trick?"

Smith's smile widened. "That's exactly what I think, Mads. Now: you have your orders. And remind our people: final fall-back is to the bunker."

"It isn't big enough for all of us," Hilda said in a hushed voice. "You must be expecting a lot of casualties."

Smith kept smiling. "Are the civvies already there?"

"Sent at the first sign of the new attack. They're already inside the walls."

"Good. Send them into the underground shelter."

"And then what?"

"And then the civvie group leaders we've trained will help Papa 'Runner take it from there. Now scoot."

A sergeant, whose name Freay'ysh-Administrator suddenly could not remember, bounded to his side. "Success again, Freay'ysh-Administrator. We have driven the humans back from another line of defenses."

"Yes, yes, but how many have we killed?" Freay'ysh-Administrator gnashed his fangs at the mere thought of seeing ruined, gutted, dismembered human bodies. In a brief moment of calm between the quick, pounding waves of fury and bloodlust, he knew that this was bad command image, that the sergeant might believe his commander was verging over into the Unknowing Rage.

But evidently the sergeant did not notice, or did not care—possibly because his own exposed teeth, stooped posture, and intense pheromonal secretions indicated that he was even closer to the mind-blanking fury that his commander was narrowly holding in check. "Not as many dead leaf-eaters as we would wish, Freay'ysh-Administrator, but that is only because they are running like terrified, self-soiling *sthondats*."

Freay'ysh-Administrator let his pelt ripple wildly and his lips roiled away from his teeth. "Let them run. Because there is no way for them to get past us, and this valley is a dead end. For them, a truly dead end.

We must wait a little while longer, but—the slaughter at the climax! The slaughter!"

He imagined himself coated in human blood, mounting endless throngs of kzinretti: his own, Chuut-Riit's, every kzinrett he had ever seen or smelled. The rut-aggression surged; he would kill the females which did not please him, which did not writhe against him with enough desperate fear and eagerness—

Apparently overcome by the flood of both his own and his superior's pheromones, the sergeant tilted back his head and unleashed a screech that was both mating cry and war howl.

They both stopped, panting, and looked at each other. Freay'ysh-Administrator wondered if his non-commissioned officer was as deep in rut, as rigidly and uncomfortably tumescent, as he himself was. He blinked; the sergeant looked away.

"Orders, Freay'ysh-Administrator?"

With a profound effort, Freay'ysh-Administrator kept his voice low and level: "All units to the line and advance. We shall push the humans as hard as we can. We will overrun them before the sun sets. We will taste their marrow tonight, Hero; this I swear."

"I bear your words to your Heroes, Freay'ysh-Administrator." And the sergeant bounded off into the underbrush, moving awkwardly, stiffly.

Hilda serpentined her way through the final set of tripwires and saw Smith standing at the entry to the pillbox like he was directing traffic. His voice was loud, clear, unhurried: "That's the last of the civvies, Papa. Get the team leaders moving. Yes, now. Everything's going to be okay, but only if they start moving *now*."

To the slightly battered but still intact squads that had already fallen back to the pillbox, he pointed them up the slopes to the defilade positions. "Morena, Keibel, take your squads up to the left flank overlooks. Varsic, Mbele, head up to the right. Missiles ready; if they have any vehicles to commit, they're going to do it here where they've got a clear field of fire and comparatively safe flanks." He looked around to see if anyone else was waiting for orders, saw Hilda, walked over. "Hi," he said.

"Hi. They'll be here soon. Not more than ten minutes, possibly as little as five."

"How many losses did we take?"

"Once they started coming on strong, we couldn't keep our heavy weapons positions secure or our lines dressed. We lost about two dozen in the last hour, and the last line will be coming under fire any minute."

A set of rapid explosions told them that even that estimate had been optimistic. Somewhere overhead, there was a rapid, shuddering rush that echoed strangely in the saturated air of the valley: loud but muted, like listening to a sound system with all the treble removed. Explosions—large ones, starting five hundred meters behind the pillbox—pounded their way further east.

"That's not good," Hilda observed.

"Yeah, but that's probably as close as their air units are going to come for now," Smith speculated. "They know that the detection and tracking systems on the missiles we captured can't see up through the clouds here, but that we can prang them if they drop down beneath the murk."

And murk was not an exaggeration: the pillbox, built and dug out of an upthrust bulge of rock, was flanked by perpetually bubbling hot springs. A constant upward drift of water vapor created a ceiling haze that was nearly opaque at fifty meters altitude, and largely trapped in place by the prevailing temperature gradients about three hundred meters above that. Real fleet sensors—downlook densitometers and the like—could have picked out the basic terrain features well enough to generate targeting solutions, but to the rear-echelon, battalion-level gear that the kzinti had been using in the Susser Tal, the murk was functionally impenetrable.

"Do you think they'll eventually bring their attack craft down into the valley?"

Smith nodded. "When they see the last of us run into the pillbox and shut the door, they'll want to bring down the fire. I would."

Hilda looked up the gentle upward slopes to north and south; both highlands pinched somewhat tighter here, putting the pillbox astride the valley's narrowest bottleneck. "And the 'Runner marksmen that you've sent up to the defilade slit-trenches; how are they going to get inside in time?"

"They're not."

"What? They'll be slaughtered out here."

"No, they won't, because they're going to stay in hiding. Until they get their signal to fire."

"But when the kzinti fan out and check their flanks, they'll find them."

"Tell me, Hilda, how well have the kzinti been following their standard tactical doctrines today?"

"Well, they—" She looked at him, wondering. "In a word, they weren't following any doctrine at all. They were coming straight at us."

Smith nodded. "So trust me for just a little longer; I'm pretty sure our troops up on the slopes are going to be fine."

Deep within the tree line, a ripple of heavy reports—'Runner elephant guns—was drowned out by several stuttering roars and a supercharged whine-hiss: kzin automatic weapons and a heavy beamer, respectively.

Hilda swallowed. "They're coming. And our troops won't get here much sooner than they do."

Smith touched her cheek with a grimy, sulfur-reeking hand. "I know. So, get inside the pillbox."

"What? I'm an officer; I've got to stay out here and help—"

"It's because you're an officer that you're needed inside the pillbox; it's the most crucial position."

"Why?"

"Because without radios, we need someone with excellent judgment inside."

"Excellent judgment about what?"

"About when the kzinti are going to bring down the tacair hammer and blow the whole upper level to dust. If we don't have someone in there who's shrewd enough to anticipate that airstrike at least half a minute before they make it, we'll lose all our combatants. Hell, we'll lose anyone who isn't already underground in the bomb shelter. So. Get inside the pillbox. Now."

The humans ran like so many startled *veerthsas*, one of the prey animals that the kzinti brought to every world they settled. Small and fast, the *veerthsa* was quite challenging to bring down, but, ah, the satisfaction when the spindly beast was finally pinned beneath an irresistible paw...

So it felt now, watching the humans scatter away from their prepared positions, their tattered clothes streaming behind them like the shredded flags of a lost battle. Each defensive line had crumbled faster than the one before it, his Heroes gathering inertia and more bloodlust with each successive triumph. The evasive human foes had finally stood and fought: they had been forced to, Freay'ysh-Administrator told himself, since they were trapped in a valley with no exit. A small voice, that belonging to the weakling trait that Chuut-Riit bombastically liked to call "higher reason," whispered that today's success was also puzzling: the kzinti had tried this tactic before, led by the very capable Zhveeaor-Captain. But those offensives had bogged down every time, gaining only three kilometers a day. The double-envelopments, the L-ambushes, the stay-behind attack teams, the cunning use of mines to guide kzin assault forces into cleared fields of fire: the humans had not made such extensive, or effective, use of these ploys today.

But the voice of Freay'ysh-Administrator's rage and bloodlust shouted down these observations into mute oblivion: why question what was working? The answer could be as simple as this: he, Freay'ysh-Administrator, was a more inspiring leader than Zhveeaor-Captain. Also, he had been willing to sacrifice more kzinti in a sustained assault in order to achieve his objective. Two hundred eighty kzinti had started the offensive this day, and slightly more than a third were either dead or incapacitated. Many of those still on the line were severely wounded; he had personally seen three Heroes amputate and cauterize their own ruined arms with beamers and move forward, carrying whatever weapon they could still wield. It was a day of loss and blood and terror and fierce fierce fierce exultation: it was akin to living in the time of the Ancient Heroes, of being in one of the sagas, of . . .

"Freay'ysh-Administrator, our scouts have come upon a hard point: a large pillbox partially built out of an immense tooth of stone straddling hot springs."

Freay'ysh-Administrator looked around for the source of the voice; a Hero, his left side bloody and partly shredded by a human mine, waited upon his reply. Freay'ysh-Administrator wanted to shriek in joy and rage, and order a general charge—but the small, interior voice reasserted momentarily, just long enough to compel him to ask: "This pillbox is in a clearing, yes?"

"Yes, Freay'ysh-Administrator."

"How much open ground from the edge of the surrounding cover to the pillbox?"

"Rangefinders put it at eighty meters, Freay'ysh-Administrator."

Eighty meters: not much, but on the other hand, the humans had achieved quite a lot, just clearing that much brush and building this pillbox. Whatever their disgusting habits and contemptible inferiorities, the leaf-eaters did not lack industriousness. Or inventiveness: somewhere off in the distance, a whistle shrilled three times. A signal of some sort, obviously, but for what? The Ancestors themselves would not have known. "Is the fort equipped with heavy weapons?"

"Impossible to tell until we probe it. So far, all we have seen is that they have adapted some of our own beamers to personal use. And we know that some of our missiles are missing, and probably in their hands."

"Yes, that is true. Do you have a clear signal to Captain?"

The Hero blinked at hearing his superior's title stripped of his Name. "We have a clear signal."

"He is to call in our two dedicated attack craft

immediately. They are to fly to these coordinates and await our signal to come beneath the mists and strike at the pillbox, if necessary. Choose three steady Heroes for laser designation."

"And then, Freay'ysh-Administrator?"

Freay'ysh-Administrator heard the eagerness in the kzin's voice, felt his own hunger for rending the humans limb from limb leap up to meet that excitement—but mastered it. *For the last time,* he promised the best, fiercest and truest part of himself. *After this, the Rage. Just the Rage. Until the humans are no more.*

"Freay'ysh-Administrator?"

Freay'ysh-Administrator struggled back out of his visions, out of savoring the carnage to come. "Security teams to the flanks. Assure we are safe. The rest encircle the hardpoint. Concentrate fire. If the humans are weak enough, we shall not risk the attack craft. If they are stubborn, one airstrike will ensure that their fort becomes their tomb."

Through old-fashioned binoculars, Smith watched the five kzinti trudge up the hill. Like almost everything else the 'Runners used, the binoculars did not rely upon batteries. And in this brief campaign, that had been a welcome feature: there had been enough other logistical needs to contend with.

One of the 'Runners in the defilading trench whispered, "Captain, I see 'em, too. Should we—?"

"Stay down. Stay quiet. Stay calm. Those are orders."

A stunned silence was followed by a whispered chorus of "Yes, sir."

Smith watched the five ratcats scan the slopes, saw two glance longingly behind, in the direction of the firefight and the fleeing humans. The intervals between the Heroes of this flank security patrol had started well, but now they were pulling apart: the two back-lookers had begun to drift wide of the other three. Predictably, back down toward the battle unfolding on floor of the valley.

Remonstrations that Smith could not hear were obviously uttered. And ignored. The kzin on point in the upslope group raised a weapon, pointed in the direction of the two malcontents. One roared something: the posture could have meant outrage, challenge, frustration, impatience, or any mix of them. The point-man's gun wavered. The other two did not move directly away, but their distance widened. Within a minute they would be out of sight of the three who were still ascending the slope, and it was plain to Smith that the pair's course would then shift even more radically back in the direction of the valley floor and all the excitement there.

Which, twenty seconds later, became an almost irresistible lure. The main kzin force, having gathered in a wide ring around the pillbox, tried to send a team to work through the misty margin between the flank of the strongpoint and the southern hot spring. Weapon fire erupted from the pillbox; two kzinti went down immediately. A third was clipped in the back of the leg as he tried to reach the safety of the tree line again. Stumbling to a knee, he rose up, was swatted down again by a shot from a hunting rifle, staggered, got both legs under him—and his back fairly exploded in a cloud of small bits of blood and fur: the work of a *strakkaker* on full auto. The mauled kzin finally fell over. In the meantime, the final, fourth member of the kzin probing team leaped into the underbrush and vanished.

The response along the kzin line was both spontaneous and unanimous: the surrounding perimeter of covering brush erupted in weapon fire, all directed inward upon the pillbox. Beamers slashed at it, autoguns peppered it with the force of jackhammers. When that first wave of fire relented, and the smoke cleared, the pillbox still stood. It certainly looked worse for wear, but it was structurally intact and defensibly sound.

Smith swung his binoculars back to the kzin flankers coming up his slope. The two who had already been veering away were now sprinting pell-mell back in the direction of the battle that had been joined. Of the remaining three, their pace slowed, not due to argument, but to indulge in a wistful appreciation of the same martial spectacle. One of them started pointing in that direction as the gunfire began again: not so concentrated this time, but steady and loud.

Which was why none of the three slope-scouting kzinti heard the reports of the elephant guns that fired into them from the rear. Two of the Heroes went down immediately, one missing his head before he even started to fall. The third staggered against a tree, then fell into the brush, left arm dangling uselessly, his right leg washed in blood: not quite an arterial wound, but a bad one.

His tumble into the bushes was probably what saved him in those first seconds. There was no movement in the undergrowth for a five count, then a ten count—

At the count of thirteen, the kzin came rushing out with a severe limp, but the real shock was that he could force himself to move at all. Smith saw one flash and then another jump out of the dark wall of the undergrowth some seventy meters behind the kzin.

Both shots were misses. Another ten meters, and the kzin would reach the cover of a granite outcropping and be within shouting distance of—

Two more flashes licked out of the distant wall of tangled vegetation, and the last kzin fell over, three meters short of the outcropping.

Smith exhaled through a smile.

The fellow next to him in the slit trench—a 'Runner named Tip and their best guncotton brewer—cocked a quizzical head: "What's up, *hauptman*?"

"Our odds of success," Smith replied, "our odds of success."

Freay'ysh-Administrator waved away the two scouts who had just returned from scouting the left, or northern, flank. They claimed there had been nothing to report on the northern slopes. So why were the other three in their team continuing to search? Nervous glances had gone back and forth between the two of them: because they were going higher, just to be sure. Yes, that was what they were doing.

In his earlier and weaker days, Freay'ysh-Administrator would probably have clouted them across the nose for what was obviously an abandonment of their assigned duties: there was no way they could have gone high enough up the slopes to conduct a full security sweep. That, no doubt, was what the other three, including the team leader, were still doing.

But Freay'ysh-Administrator could not bring himself to punish them for heeding the savage summons singing in their blood, since it was the same one he was following as well. Indeed, the scouts on the other flank had abandoned their mission en masse as soon as the barrage was unleashed upon the pillbox. When asked to explain themselves, they had looked down, abashed—a cub's reflex—and admitted that they had forgotten the mission they had been sent to carry out.

In the moment, Freay'ysh-Administrator had had to struggle to keep his pelt from writhing in sudden amusement, because he knew they were telling the truth. When the siren-song of combat drew them back, it wasn't an act of insubordination. It was a strangely intense, almost irresistible attraction to a veritable orgy of violence, of sating a bloodlust almost as arousing as the promise of *ch'rowl*. The need to weed out insurgents, to show mastery, to exact vengeance had long fallen aside as the primary motivations of their struggle in the Susser Tal: it was to satisfy their hunger—both individually and as a group—to drench themselves in the gore of the humans. Nothing else would do, for nothing else remained in their minds.

The kzin known as Communicator approached him. "Latest reports, Freay'ysh-Administrator."

"Yes?"

"Still no word from the last upslope scouts, sir, although it is still somewhat early to expect them to have—"

"I am unconcerned: if the humans had significant forces up there, they would have intervened by now. They would have a clear field of fire down upon us here, and would not be so foolish to miss taking advantage of it."

"As you say, Freay'ysh-Administrator. Our attempts to outflank the stronghold itself have been repulsed. There are only a few meters between the flanking faces of the pillbox and the hot springs to either side. And there is no cover."

Freay'ysh-Administrator waved his acceptance of the situation: he had watched three of the attempts himself. They had been futile—and costly—tactical probes. "What else?"

"We confirm at least half a dozen defenders killed inside the pillbox, but there must be at least fifty more leaf-eaters sheltering behind its walls."

"Have you tried to fire through the embrasures with the beamers?" It would be a difficult shot, of course, but the effects, if successful—

As if to illustrate the futility of that option, a beam lanced out at the pillbox. It was focused on the horizontal slit in the front face of the structure, but then it seemed to double back on itself. The resulting explosion threw out a jet of dust and debris, occluding the embrasure, and making it impossible to keep the beam fixed on the initial aim point. At the same instant, one of the defenders' elephant guns barked, and the kzin who had been wielding the beamer yowled piteously.

"That has been the result so far," explained Communicator. "Although we cannot see it in the shadows, the embrasure is stepped, and irregularly so. Consequently, if the beam is not perfectly aligned, it will graze against the stepped surfaces. This deflects part of the beam's energy back upon the beam itself and obscures the aim point with debris. Also, to hold the beam on target for more than two seconds both threatens to burn out the weapon from overheating, and also attracts the attention of the enemy's marksmen, as you just saw."

So. Half a dozen of the humans killed. Maybe. At least thirty of his Heroes had been lost in the trade; more, if you counted the wounded. Working around to the rear of the structure would mean an all-night hike up the slopes and down again on the far side. And once there, if his guess was correct, they would find rear-facing embrasures in the structure, built to frustrate just such an attempt to get in behind it. He turned his gaze on Communicator. "The attack craft are on station?"

"Awaiting your orders, Freay'ysh-Administrator."

"Pull our Heroes back from the tree line. Once they have found adequate cover, call in the air strike. Let us throw open the gates that we may drink their blood without losing any more of our own."

Hilda noticed it before Gunnar could shout it out. "They're pulling back! *Gott sei dank*, they're—!"

"No. They're not." She grabbed her gear, gave a high sign to Papa Sumpfrunner, who dropped through the narrow hatchway in the floor of the pillbox.

"Whaddya mean?" shrieked Gunnar, almost as loud and enraged as a wounded kzin might have sounded. "They've stopped firing. I can see them un-assing their positions. They've had enough, they've—"

"Shut up, Gunnar. They're not giving up; they're clearing the zone."

"Clearing the zone? For what?"

"So they can bring in their strike package. Now: everyone down the hole. We're getting out of here."

The kzin fast movers were in and out so quickly that Smith doubted he could have launched a self-guiding missile at them, even if he had wanted to.

Clearly, the kzin pilots had been warned that the humans had nabbed a couple of dual-purpose missiles in the early stages of the hunt-become-a-campaign. When the two ground-attack birds roared down out of the low-hanging murk, their internal bay seals were already open for munitions deployment. A cluster of missiles dropped out of each one's belly. As their rockets ignited and they streaked toward the pillbox, the attack craft were already nosing back up into the mists: they disappeared just as the strike package hit its target dead-on.

Smith had not thought that, at more than half a kilometer's distance, the sound would be too bad, or the destructive force so considerable that he should suspend observing the area of operations. So he was not prepared for the deafening roar, nor the concussive wave that slapped him against the rear wall of the trench so hard that it winded him. And the six bright after-images of the warhead flashes, which moved around with his point of view, had the look of a retinal imprint that would not disappear for quite a while.

His men, who had obeyed his precautions to remain under cover, were smiling at him. Tips, the powderman, drawled with a grin, "Seems like someone forgot to take his own advice, Captain."

Smith grinned back. At last: they were calling him Captain.

And best of all, they were teasing him.

Freay'ysh-Administrator stood as the grit and rock shards that had been blasted skyward by the strike package began to fall around them like monstrous hail. As it did, the thickest drifts of the ground smoke began to clear, revealing a shattered, rocky shell where the low, sturdy pillbox had been. Piercing screams of triumph and victory rose up all along the arc of kzin attackers, who now sprung to their feet, weapons ready, bodies hunched forward, each eager to be first to find survivors, bodies, pieces, anything human that they might further rend and despoil.

And why shouldn't they? If the cleared area around the pillbox had been seeded with mines, the concussive ground wave would certainly have triggered them. If there had been booby-traps in the structure, they would have been either tripped or disabled. And if there were any survivors in that smoking framework of waist-high remains, it was best to be upon them swiftly, before they could fight back or flee.

The Rage was poised within Freay'ysh-Administrator just as his body was poised to run. Was there anything left to consider? It was hard to think beyond the desire to attack, to rend, to rape—and so he did not bother to think.

The long, ululating shriek that rose up from him was like an engine, propelling him forward. Shifting his beamer to his left hand, he drew his *w'tsai* and bounded—five meters per leap—toward the ruined human pillbox.

With a chorus of cries akin to Freay'ysh-Administrator's own, his remaining troops rushed from their hiding places, a ring of snarling orange fur converging upon the smoking pit that was their final objective.

"Stink!" came the sharp call sign whisper from the bracken to Smith's rear.

He gave the response—"Pot!"—and watched as Hilda came low-crawling into the slit trench. "Did everyone get out?"

"Yeah, but just barely. The tunnel collapsed about ten meters behind me."

"Behind you? You were the last one out?"

"My post: my job."

He smiled and touched her face. The men in the trench stared, then looked away awkwardly: almost all were smiling; the youngest one was blushing.

Freay'ysh-Administrator leaped from smoking rockpile to smoking rockpile. Here and there a hand, a leg, part of a torso, a few human implements twisted and scorched beyond easy recognition. Cordite and sulfur and guttering fires completed a tableau that some human mythologists associated with the punishment-place that they called hell. But—

"There are not enough bodies, or material," he snarled. The Heroes around him growled and snapped their agreement.

But one yowled sharply. "Here! A trapdoor! They must have crawled away through a tunnel, like the shit-burrowers that they are."

Freay'ysh-Administrator felt his fur standing straight out, partly from rage at being thwarted again, partly because it meant there was more hunt left to thrill him, and the promise of rending more humans—live ones—at its conclusion. He reached the flimsy door in two great bounds, felt his troops gathering close around him. He tried to remember his training, to think what would be wisest at this point. Tunnel attacks were a risky business, but they were Heroes, and their adversaries were skinny, swamp-grubbing humans who were outcasts even amongst their own contemptible species.

"Down! After them!" he shrieked, and his Heroes roared approval and struggled with each other to be the first down the hole.

◇   ◇   ◇

Hilda almost sighed when Smith removed his gentle hand from her face and his tone became businesslike again. "So what about the wires?"

"Well, I'm glad we laid three sets," Hilda admitted. "And we still have the wireless relay, if it comes to that."

"Guess we'll find out. You wanna do the honors?"

She stared at the wire-wound, inverted alligator clips—adapted from jumper cables—that had been pressed into service as a contact detonator: "No: it's your show."

"Freay'ysh-Administrator, we can go no further: the tunnel is too narrow for us beyond thirty meters, and it has caved in. But there may be another exit."

"Yes?"

"We have found another door—much better hidden— in the floor of this subterranean shelter."

"Well, open it!"

"Yes, Freay'ysh-Administrator. But perhaps we should start by cutting the wires running down through the floor alongside it?"

Far at the back of Freay'ysh-Administrator's lust-besotted consciousness, a small voice rose one last time, crying for one last moment of caution.

A cry that came one moment too late.

Smith smiled at Hilda, squeezed the makeshift contact detonator, and, bringing her down with him, ducked into the trench.

The entirety of the Sumpfrunners' reserve stores of explosives went up with a roar nearly equal to the kzin strike package. But this explosion was longer, lower, louder, and it hoisted up great slabs of rock and gouts of dirt.

It also vaporized or splattered all but forty of the kzinti that had intended to slaughter the humans as completely as they themselves were now being slaughtered.

As the first vertically ejected rocks came down, some easily large enough to be lethal, Hilda looked up over the edge of the slit trench. The surviving kzinti were littered in an arc around the smoking hole that remained, moving feebly. Most were trying to roll or crawl away from the epicenter of destruction, thin lines of blood running out of their ears and nostrils. One or two actually staggered upright.

Hilda felt, rather than saw, Smith stand up. When she looked over at him, he was clenching a starter's whistle between his teeth. He blew it once, paused, blew it twice—

—the kzinti, shaking their heads, stared around dumbly, as if vaguely aware that, despite their shattered hearing, there was some new sound in the air around them—

—Smith blew the whistle three times.

The troops in the slit trench rose up, leaned over their weapons, adjusted their sights. Across the valley, Hilda could just barely make out subtle hints of the same movements being performed in that defilade trench, too.

And then—one slow, deliberate shot after the next— the turkey shoot began.

Papa Sumpfrunner—who now insisted that they call him by his given name, Maurice—looked back down from the Grosse Felsbank's Schwerlinie Pass into the Susser Tal. Hilda, seeing the melancholy look on his face, stopped to join him. Smith slowed to a halt a little further along the trail, standing to one side so that the refugee Sumpfrunners could still pass two abreast into the narrowest part of their journey: a crevice only four meters wide, but with walls almost two hundred meters high. Once on the other side of it, they would be on the reverse slope of the Grosse Felsbank and unable to see the valley anymore.

"Seems wrong," Maurice grumbled, looking down at the Susser Tal. "Birthed there, lived there, loved there, chapped there, fought there. It'd be rightways that I'd die there. *Ja, stimm'.*"

Hilda put a hand on his narrow, wiry shoulder. "But you'd die too soon, Maurice. You know the kzinti are going to go in again, and this time, no half measures. They lost the better part of two battalions in the Susser Tal; that makes it more than a regional problem. Chuut-Riit or one of his inner circle will take charge and bring in all the resources at their disposal." She shook her head. "You fought a good fight for as long as you could fight it. Now it's time for you—for all of you—to leave."

"Shouldn't never have fought at all," he retorted. "Warn't our fight. Not worth it. It was outsider doings, an outsider war. We coulda waited until—"

"Until someone came to save you, or the kzinti owned the world so completely that they decided that even the Sumpfrinne had to be forced to bow down before them." Smith's voice wasn't exactly harsh, but it certainly wasn't gentle. "There are no outsiders anymore, Maurice. Flatlanders, Belters, *herrenmanner*, 'Runners: we're all fighting the kzinti, fighting for our lives, for our species. And sometimes, in order to keep doing that—to survive to fight not just another day, but throughout all the years that might follow—we have to leave things behind. Our families, our lives, our homes. I came from around here, too, and I don't know if any of my family is left alive. I don't even know if I'll ever see them, or my home, again. But I cope and keep fighting."

Smith looked back at the Susser Tal; the mists thinned, thickened and roiled in futile bids to escape. "That valley made you 'Runners tough. Tougher than drylanders, I used to hear your relatives tell my dad. So now you tell me: are you tough enough to do what I'm doing? To leave your home to fight the kzin? At least this way, you get to stay together with your families." Smith waved to take in the winding stream of refugees, making their way slowly through the passes, some being carried on litters. "Because you know what would have happened if you had stayed behind. Instead of watching your young and your old and your wives and children taking a hard passage over hard mountains, you'd be watching them—one by one—fleeing through the bushes, through the meadows, flitting among the trees, before the kzin coursers finally catch them and rip them limb from bloody limb. For sport, mind you: for sport, practice and a little ratcat thrill. So tell me: is living in your valley worth that? Is that what you want to stick around and see, just so you can hang on to that piece of land a few weeks more?"

Maurice looked back toward the Susser Tal. "My *gros'vati*, he was willing to fight and die to keep that patch of swamp." The mists thinned, revealing the festering Sumpfrinne. Maurice shrugged. "I guess he wuz the hot-headed type." He tilted a cracked smile at Smith, patted Hilda on the arm, and then resumed trudging up the path.

Hilda turned to look after Maurice, let her eyes slip over to Smith. "So, about that secret weapon—"

"C'mon, you've figured that out already."

"The basics, *ja*. It altered the kzinti's behavior, but in such a way that it must have felt—well, normal to them. So I'm guessing it was a pheromone or a hormone."

Smith nodded. "Both, actually. Specifically, a pheromone that activates their rut-aggression hormone."

"Rut-aggression? Is that any different than plain old aggression?"

"Actually, yes, it's very different. Whereas we human males have pretty much just one main aggression hormone—testosterone—the kzinti have several. And unlike testosterone, which performs a lot of other functions in the body—like growth regulation and muscle development—kzin hormones tend to be one-purpose compounds."

"That must make for a much more complicated system."

"I'm no biologist, but it's a very *different* system, certainly. Rather than relying upon a single big gland secreting a single hormone that handles a bunch of related functions, the kzin physiology separates the same functions into many smaller glands. In addition to better loss-resistance through organ redundancy, this also gives their bodies the opportunity to employ a lot of finely tuned hormonal effects."

"And that's where all their various aggression hormones come in?"

"Right. When our scientists started doing comparative studies linking kzin biochemistry to kzin behavior, they started wondering: if kzin males will unthinkingly and often uncontrollably fight to the death over females because of a surge in aggression hormones, then how do they exert the self-control they show during military operations, when their aggression hormones are also at high tide? So the researchers started looking very closely at the kzin aggression hormone and discovered that what looked at first like one compound was actually a family of related compounds, each of which evinced subtle differences from the others. What they identified as the 'rut-aggression hormone' was by far the most powerful of them all. But it was also the one that was most selectively and rarely secreted, since it is only released when a male is exposed to the pheromones of a female in estrus."

Hilda nodded. "So the other aggression hormones still permit some measure of flight-or-fight discretion, whereas the rut-aggression hormone is, essentially, a berserker drug."

"Exactly. And because of its evolutionary connection with mating, their brains find it an especially thrilling high, so much so that they don't really care if they live or die."

"I guess that was pretty much an evolutionary necessity, given how deadly kzinti are, even to other kzinti."

"*Ja*: they needed something that was going to trump common sense during the mating season if natural selection was going to favor maximum combat power and aggressiveness. The weaker ones had to fight—and die— in order to maintain an optimal breeding population."

"That's a grim picture," commented Hilda.

"Yes, but it turned out to be a very pretty picture for us. Once the researchers had isolated this hormone, they started to realize that it had extraordinary weapons potential. Yes, it made the kzinti extremely aggressive, but it also made them more impetuous, harder to control, incapable of self-restraint, and too impatient to formulate or follow complicated plans."

"In short, you reduced them to the kzin equivalent of cavemen."

"Right."

"And so where does your little silver case come in? Were you spraying the female estrus pheromone in the places you expected them to be? That doesn't seem very effective."

"You're right; that wouldn't be effective at all. And that was the real challenge of the research project: to design an effective delivery system."

"Which was?"

"Which was not to deliver the estrus pheromone like a weapon, all at once, but more like slow poisoning: something that increased slowly over time."

Hilda shuddered. "So what did they come up with?"

Smith smiled and opened the case. Inside was a canister for compressed gases, a temperature-control system, sensors and a small data-reader.

Hilda gawked. "And that's it?"

"That's it. The trick is that the canister doesn't contain the estrus pheromone: it contains a geneered mold that remains inert when at or near zero Celsius. However, when it is released into a warmer environment, it quickly activates. When it reaches maturity it releases several different chemicals into the air, one of which is a slightly denatured form of the pheromone that the kzinti females release during estrus. When it comes into contact with a kzin male's mucosa, it is too weak to generate the smell they associate with the female, but it is still potent enough to trigger the hormone production cascade that results in the release of the rut-aggression hormone."

"You mean, they're running around angry and horny?"

Smith laughed; it was a pleasant sound. She'd only heard it a few times before, and very much looked forward to hearing more of it in the months to come. "No, they're not horny. Not exactly. It's more like they're . . . well, on edge."

Hilda raised an eyebrow. "As you have now learned, I'm not a prude. I believe the common term you're looking for is 'blue balls.'" And to her utter delight, the redoubtable Captain Smith actually blushed: very slightly, but the glow was there. *Hilda, even your* mother *would like this one—*

Smith was pointing to a small aperture in the side of the case, mated to the narrow nozzle of the canister. "I just pressed this button under the handle, here, and the mold was discharged through this hole. Although I started by seeding the key parts of the valley, the mold spread far beyond them, flourishing in the environmental conditions of the Sumpfrinne: hot, humid, lots of decay. Mold paradise."

She nodded. "And then as you walked around, that sensor package kept track of the amount of pheromone that was being released. And I'm guessing you seeded the entry to the Susser Tal lightly, so that the kzinti would be advancing into areas of steadily increasing mold density. That way the effects would grow slowly enough that they'd never notice them, particularly not if it felt good, and their own powers of observation and cognition were being undercut."

"Yes, that was one of the reasons. Also, I had to measure the type and intensity of kzin behavioral change at different levels of exposure. The experimental data are guesstimates at best: there was no way to control for continuous versus intermittent exposure, or for the effects of exposure incidents of different duration. But what we did learn is that it works, that the kzinti don't feel the onset, and that their sensors don't detect it as a toxin or biohazard. And why should they? It's a natural product of their bodies, and one that they seem to consider a positive hormone."

"So now what? Grow the mold and share the joy with our kzin visitors all over Wunderland?"

Smith shook his head. "*Nei.* That's the last thing we want. One of the other reasons that the brass chose the Susser Tal is because of the spring flooding from the mountain runoffs. Sustained immersion in water kills the mold, and we don't want to leave any long-term evidence behind, or worse yet, have started a crèche from which the stuff can spread naturally."

"I don't get that; so how—or more to the point, when—do we get to use this as a weapon?"

Smith reached out and held both her hands in his. "As soon as we get the coded signal confirming that the counter-invasion fleet from Earth is in the system. We, or whoever is around to use it, will spread the mold, ensuring the highest possible densities in the landing areas."

Hilda nodded. "Makes sense to keep it as a surprise weapon for when all the cards are on the table.

Once we release it broadly on the planet, it will not only help our forces retake Wunderland, but will be a permanent planetary defense. And I am presuming, of course, that the mold will be seeded on Earth itself?"

Smith shrugged. "That's supposed to remain classified, but given what you've seen here, I don't think it's much of a secret."

"No, it isn't. In fact, as far as I can tell, there's only one more secret that needs revealing."

"Oh?" Smith looked genuinely perplexed.

Could he be so smart—and so dumb—all at the same time? She pulled her hands out of his, put them on her hips, smiled up into his still-wondering face: "How about your name? What's your *real* name, Captain Smith?"

"Oh, that." He smiled. "I'm Wulf. Wulf Armbrust."

She put her hands on his chest and stood on her toes to kiss him on the cheek. "Nice to meet you, Captain Wulf Armbrust. Now, let's catch up with the logistics staff: we're going to need to rework the portage roster to redistribute the food and water."

Together, they turned their backs on the mist-filled Susser Tal and resumed the long trek between the snow covered peaks of the Grosse Felsbank, so impossibly high above them.

AT THE GATES

◆　◆　◆

Alex Hernandez

Righteous Manslaughter

Righteous Manslaughter dived into the dust and asteroidal grit of an aborted solar system choking a brown dwarf star with only a string of cryptic numbers for a name. There was no escape. The human dread-naught, Pick of the Litter *Alaric*, pounded them with lasers, missiles and, as the telepath felt, blazing hatred. Humans had come a long way in the three wars and kzinti were dying—courageously as always, but dying.

"The humans are going to exploit a slowly spread-ing hairline fracture on our starboard hull," *Righteous Manslaughter*'s Telepath screamed in terror. "We have to leap into hyperspace!"

"Silence, you subkzintosh, I am in command of this ship! Our orders are to hold this Fanged God–forsaken system even if the molecules of our ship join the thick orbiting haze," Fnar-Ritt roared at the Telepath, trying to maintain some semblance of dominance in this insane situation. Telepath, like all his kind, had no dignity to forget, but his abject fear could not be allowed to infect the remainder of the crew.

All surviving warriors had come together on the bridge as other sections of the ship were abandoned to the devouring vacuum. *Manslaughter*'s Telepath, pumped full of the *sthondat* drug, tried to push out of his mind the young Heroes' panic and focus on the savage cunning of the humans. One more well-placed missile and the *Manslaughter* would be slag.

He knew that the incompetent Fnar-Ritt had no intention of withdrawing and no skill for a fight. He had been handed the captaincy of this ill-fated vessel only because he was of the Patriarchy's line and had been bred with the rare ability to navigate in hyperspace.

The mind of Tdakar-Commander, a battle-weary veteran who had no particular fear of attempting the impossible, brimmed with stratagems, but he knew his place and held his muzzle shut.

As the humans launched the killing missile at the dying ship, *Manslaughter*'s Telepath felt Fnar-Ritt's fear swell almost beyond reason. This was the telepath's only chance for survival. With the speed of thought he tore at the stretched-thin film of duty and honor that barely held back the vestigial flight response and let the captain's own overriding terror spill over him. In a last act of cowardice, Fnar-Ritt threw himself onto the crackling console and activated the hyperdrive.

The missile hit and everything flooded with blinding pink light.

The Raoneer Wilderness

The plains of Raoneer were chill under the shifting light of the aurora. A heavily muscled kzintosh watched as a small pride of hunters waded through the feathery lavender grass. They approached the black-furred dome that had been his home for several years as he had roamed the savage land. Healer-of-Hunters had stalked and killed the hefty animals that early human explorers had named wombadons for their supposed resemblance to an Earth animal called a wombat and made their thick hides into a shelter. He had studied wombats when he was still at crèche and found very little similarity between those cute little creatures and these fiercely territorial monsters. Also, these beasts were no marsupials: like all higher life forms on Sheathclaws, they were neither mammals nor reptiles, but a deadly synthesis of the two. The planet was at an evolutionary stage roughly equivalent to the Permian period on Earth. The advancing pride dragged the heavy carcass of one behind them. Healer thought that he would eat well tonight.

"Are you Healer-of-Hunters?" The leader of the small band asked in Interworld. Three cautious females, one clearly his daughter, circled closely around the male. They kept their distance from the wild-looking young kzintosh. These hunters were too well-groomed to have been living wild for long. They were recent arrivals from Shrawl'ta.

"Yes," he growled.

"I am Maintainer-of-Communications; at least, I was back in Shrawl'ta. My idiot son has been attacked by a pack of alliogs while on a hunt. One of them took a chunk clean out of his side," the father said, pulling back the obsidianlike hide of the wombadon, revealing a mutilated kit, almost a kzintosh. The adolescent stoically bore the pain as a kzin should.

"Take him into my hut. I'll see what I can do."

Inside the structure of animal bone and rawhide was an impressive array of chirping diagnostic equipment and a blinking new autodoc. "You've got a field hospital here," said the father, sniffing the antiseptic chemicals in the hut.

"You'd be surprised how many kzinti injure themselves on the hunt or in duels in these backwoods." Healer examined the kit sprawled out on the pallet. "Well, perhaps it would no longer surprise you. Please wait outside."

Healer connected the juvenile to the doc and immediately administered a strong painkiller. The kit's writhings ceased. He sighed through clenched teeth in instant relief. The kit was missing a U-shaped chunk of flesh under his right arm. Luckily, the bite hadn't penetrated through the bony mesh of the kzinti skeleton. Healer sprayed synthetic skin, cultured from the adolescent's own DNA, onto the bloody hole. "You're going to be fine. It was a small alliog." He wrapped the kit's torso in a tight bandage.

"It didn't feel like a small alliog."

"Why did you leave Shrawl'ta? Your father held an important position there."

"Everyone is saying a kzinti warship has entered our system. My father had always dreamed of living free in the Raoneer country. He said now was his chance before the Patriarchy exterminated us all for breeding like vermin."

A kzinti warship? Surely, thought Healer, we would all be dead by now. This thriving amethyst planet would be reduced to a dusty disc of debris, but being Maintainer-of-Communications, this kit's father would be privy to the truth of such information.

He adjusted the flow of anesthesia and sedated the kit. He called for the waiting kzintosh to return to the hut. The former Maintainer-of-Communications entered and made appreciative prostration. "Is the stupid kit going to survive?"

"Yes."

"Thank you and the Maned God!" He prostrated himself a little lower. "Please, Healer-of-Hunters, take my daughter into your harem. We are of praiseworthy stock, sired of Shadow."

Healer had instinctively breathed in the young, attractive kzinrett as she approached his hut, but her pheromones carried the uncomfortable tinge of the incestuous.

"Thank you, brave Hunter, that is a most generous offer, but I do not wish to complicate my life in these uncertain times." He scratched his scruffy neck, hoping the excuse and change of subject were not too obvious. "If what I've heard is true, this small hut will be swollen with the bodies of wounded Raoneers."

The kzintosh rose quickly. "You know of the ship?"

"Your son purred about it while under the influence of the autodoc. Is it true, a warship?"

"Yes, it's true. Ceezarr himself met with the human Triumvirate about the matter. According to their analysis, and ours, the ship is unresponsive, probably wrecked."

"That is somewhat of a relief."

"Yes, still the threat was enough for me to reevaluate my life."

"Indeed." Healer was no longer listening to the other kzintosh. He pawed at the possibilities this ship presented. Were there survivors? Perhaps frozen in coldsleep caskets, unaware that their ship had been attacked? He grabbed his wristcomp and moved toward the flap in the tent. "You can sit with your son until he wakes. I am going on a hunt."

Healer-of-Hunters dashed through the wispy purple reeds as though in hot pursuit of quick and cunning prey. "Get me Daneel Guthlac," he hissed into his wristcomp, and kept running until he had reached the gravcar he'd tucked away beneath blood-colored brush.

The image of a human male with a mane of sandy, wavy hair, a close-trimmed beard and strong jaw line winked over Healer's wrist.

Harp, Angel's Tome

Dan lay on the floor of his lab calibrating the compact gravity motor of his car for the eighth time. Its hum was so perfectly pitched that it purred like a newborn kit. He had reached the limits of what he could squeeze out of this ancient kzin-derived technology and he was becoming bored with it.

His wristcomp pinged and he pushed himself from under the triangular gravcar. The grainy hologram of a kzin with black markings lost in dark orange, almost chocolate, fur beamed out of his wristcomp. Its piercing amber eyes scrutinized him for a long second.

It took just as long for Dan to place this savage-looking face. "My God, I haven't heard from you in ages! Where the tanj have you been?"

"I'm out in the Raoneer wilderness, hunting and providing medical care for other kzinti out here."

"All that academic excellence back at the crèche and you've gone bushcat!" Dan couldn't suppress a smile.

"I need your help. I've just got word that a kzinti warship was sighted in our neighborhood. Can you verify that claim?"

"Yeah, there are media rumors circulating that a scout ship was detected in our system. Anyone with any sense knows that's got to be false because our planet is not a cinder."

"Agreed."

Dan could hear his old friend panting like a thirsty dog. "But something's got the A.T. Triumvirate all in a huff."

"Word from Ceezarr's mansion says the ship is incapacitated."

"Is this why you called me?"

"I want to pounce on it, but I'm going to need your help. I need all the information the Triumvirate has on the ship and I need an engineer once I get to it."

"Whoa, I'd love to get my hands on a modern warship with technology one hundred years ahead of anything we've got in this miserable marooned colony, but the risks seem a bit too high. I'd hate to be the guy that points the Patriarchy to our doorstep."

"I believe the risk is acceptable. I plan to fly the barge my father has set up as a useless museum piece and tow the derelict back here. Will you join me?"

"Come on, I haven't seen you in years. I don't even know what you're called now! And you drop this on my lap all of a sudden?"

"My provisional Name is Healer-of-Hunters. I don't have any other friends. You're an engineer and you have poor judgment. I figured you'd leap at the chance to sink your blunt little nails into state-of-the-art technology."

"Nice to meet you, Healer-of-Hunters. What do bushcats care about advanced technology?"

"Absolutely nothing. You can have the ship and open it up like a fresh kill."

"So why are you so interested in this ship?"

"Do not worry about that."

"Dishonesty comes across as stiff and unnatural on kzinti. You lack the neurological architecture to shamelessly lie."

"I'm sorry. I was informed you worked at Harp University's engineering department, not in neural science." Healer's ears rippled at his own joke, and Dan imagined his tail whipping around. "Besides, I'm not lying. I'm withholding information."

"Sarcasm? Humans are ruining a proud and unflappable species!"

"Will you help me? If not, I'll do it alone, but the odds of success will be greatly reduced."

"I don't know, you're not exactly convincing me to give up my cushy life as a researcher to go on a potentially world-devastating endeavor."

"Remember back when we were kits and you used your monkey wiles to talk me into eating Mrs. Davis' pug. I didn't question you, I simply attacked. I need you to attack."

"I remember your dad tore you up when she showed up at his mansion blubbering. Was it really worth it?"

He absently licked his lips. "Oh yes, that plump little dog was utterly delicious."

"Alright, who am I to argue with a million years of kzinti killer instinct?"

"Can you get an audience with the Triumvirate?"

"With a name like Guthlac? I'll be sipping tea with them by noon."

"How much time do you need to get the information and get to Shrawl'ta?"

"Give me four hours."

"That fast?"

"I have a very fast car."

The bushcat abruptly cut off the transmission.

Dan's arrowhead of a car shot around the city of Harp in a wide arch. He saw the gleaming white skyscrapers topped with radiant blue domes that tastefully hid beam cannons and rocket launchers, all pointed toward the sky. The coastal metropolis was a Byzantine sprawl of culture and commerce. Its wide and bustling walkways were lined with plants like black orchids the size of grand palms. Of the three human settlements in Angel's Tome, Harp had become the richest and largest. It imported meat from Raoneer and exported seafood, which the kzinti loved. The University of Harp had finally unraveled the captured alien technology and churned out lucrative spin-offs, like his gravcar. He circled the extravagant Triumvirate House and remembered one of its architects deliriously describing it as what the Hagia Sophia would have looked like if they'd had ultra-light building materials with the tensile strength of carbon nanotubes.

"Triumvirate House accepts your request to land. Please direct your vehicle to the south parking garage," his onboard computer chimed.

A security officer marched him toward a private elevator. When he finally entered the massive indoor amphitheater, its grandeur floored him. The underside of the luminous blue dome displayed a high-resolution image of what Earth's sky would have looked like on a sunny spring day. Its clarity had a charm Sheathclaws' complex sky lacked. The vast space was empty but for three stern humans. They radiated a haughty annoyance.

He sat in a central chair surrounded by an azure half-moon desk. Facing the three politicians, he quickly scanned them with his weak empathic powers. "Thank you for granting me the honor."

"The Triumvirate has a tough decision to make, and since you called us about this mysterious ship, we thought it natural the only native of Raoneer in Harp should partake in the discussion," Jibunoh, the spokeswoman told him. "We might benefit from your unique input. Your heritage was also a factor, of course."

"Thank you again, Triumvir, but there are quite a few people from Raoneer here."

"Correction, as the only human." She looked at the unruly specimen before her, as if she didn't quite believe in his humanity. "What do you know of the matter at hand?"

"Only that what appears to be a damaged kzinti ship penetrated our sensor swarm not too long ago." Dan's mind prowled around the three heads of state like a predator trying to pick out the lame prey.

"A month ago, to be exact, every sensor in the system began screaming when a Patriarchy warship suddenly appeared in our system's heliosphere. The three of us and Apex Leader of Raoneer quickly gathered to strategize and ready our defenses, but all subsequent scans show that the ship is indeed badly damaged and currently tumbling toward the sun. Ceezarr lost interest when the chance for battle became remote, and returned to Shrawl'ta."

"You attempted to communicate with it?"

"No. This meeting is precisely to determine our next step. Images of the ship indicate that it's far more advanced than the ships our founders confronted."

"They've had about a hundred years to improve."

"Exactly. The question is, do we want those upgrades or do we let the derelict go on its way."

"There are barbarians at the gates and you talk of trinkets?" murmured Triumvir Bhang. The woman had aged rather well, but her dark almond-shaped eyes were filled with fear. She wanted nothing to do with kzinti, local or otherwise.

"Well, the up-to-date information held in their computers would be incredibly valuable," he said, ignoring the anxiety of the three leaders. "The fact that the ship just popped up suggests to me as an engineer that they have one of those FTLs we've been hearing about for the past twenty years."

"Are you a Rejoiner, Mr. Guthlac?" Anxiety was suddenly laced with suspicion.

"I don't subscribe to bipartisan rhetoric. I definitely understand the Separatists' pragmatic reasons for keeping Sheathclaws hidden. We are uncomfortably close to Patriarchy space."

The only male Triumvir in the room spoke for the first time. "For the past twenty years, we've been bombarded with stray radio signals announcing human victories over the Patriarchy in several wars, because of hyperdrives just like the one that has landed on our doorstep. The time is ripe to regroup with the other human worlds in Known Space!"

"We've all heard your arguments, Triumvir Delmar. The one flaw is the word 'several.' It's only a matter of time before another war flares up, and if we've revealed ourselves we'll be the first planet conquered! Simply because of proximity!"

Not to mention the value of a planet full of potential kzinti telepaths, Dan thought.

He sensed Triumvir Delmar's unabashed interest in the ship. The other two minds of the trio were already made up. He needed to delicately appeal to Delmar. "Just because we bring in the ship doesn't mean we'll all hop on the next flight for Earth. The information in those computers as well as the FTL would go a long way in strengthening our defenses."

"That is a very valid point, Mr. Guthlac," exclaimed Delmar.

"We're not here to discuss the theoretical capture of this crippled warship, which I have no intention of voting for," Triumvir Bhang said, slamming the palm of her hand on the podium. "What I'm interested in is the kzinti reaction to our letting their brethren glide into the sun."

"The kzinti of Raoneer have no love for the Patriarchy. I don't know Ceezarr personally, but I was crèchemates with one of his sons."

Bhang flinched at the outright inhuman term. "So you don't believe there would be unrest among the kzinti of Sheathclaws?"

"You said so yourself, Ceezarr lost interest when reports of the ship's state came in. I believe that's how most kzinti and humans will react, with vast collective indifference."

"Thank you, Mr. Guthlac, for your singular insights on the matter," said Jibunoh. He knew, in her mind, the discussion was over. "Let's vote, shall we? All those in favor of letting this ruined craft continue unmolested raise your hand."

Triumvirs Bhang and Jibunoh stylishly raised their hands. Triumvir Delmar simply shook his head in obvious disgust.

"Wait a minute, that's it? You're going to reject an enormous boon for Sheathclaws after one meeting? You're not going to put it to a popular vote?"

"Our pronouncement may seem swift to you, Mr. Guthlac, but I assure you that we've been weighing the issue for a month now. As for a popular vote, you yourself said that the general public would be indifferent to the final fate of the ship."

"Can I at least have all the information on the ship obtained from the probes? Maybe I can study those and find something useful to us."

"Absolutely not, Mr. Guthlac. A young, intelligent man such as you could cause all manner trouble with that data. I believe it will remain safely classified."

Delmar burst out of his chair with explosive frustration and stormed out of the meeting chamber.

Jibunoh turned to Bhang and said, "We can even spin the situation as not wanting to sully this ship out of great respect for the fallen Heroes aboard."

Dan knew he was already dismissed.

Minutes later, no longer having access to the private elevator, he jogged up the wide marble steps leading to the garage. His mind chewed on the state-of-the-art kzinti ship. The technological treasures that were found on the ones a hundred years ago had taken eights of years for the colonists to decipher. How long would it take him to reverse-engineer this one, a lifetime?

"A word, Mr. Guthlac," Triumvir Delmar sat on a

bench near his car, watching a few leathery pteranobats languidly circle the sapphire-domed spires of Harp. Dan had known he was there.

"I'm sorry I couldn't be more convincing," Dan said in the absence of any real salutation.

"Don't be too hard on yourself, young man. We didn't summon you to our meeting because of your Raoneer citizenship or your impressive engineering degree. We invited you because of who your grandmother was. Jibunoh and Bhang didn't want posterity to say they made a crucial world-changing decision without consulting a Guthlac! No, you were there simply so that the record could show that you were there."

"That's ridiculous."

"That's politics," he waved a dismissing hand as if they've talked enough nonsense and it was time for business. "The truth is we need that ship and everyone is too afraid to go and get it."

"I agree." Although not about joining the rest of humanity. Not yet anyway.

"Excellent!" Delmar handed him a tablet scrolling with information and displaying a red elliptical line spiraling through their system.

"Is this the warship's current position and its projected circuit toward our sun?"

"Correct. As the leader of Hem, I would like to extend our full support if you decide to mount an expedition to this ship. We can't provide you with shuttles, of course; my hands are tied as you witnessed back at the House, but I can give you data and will run interference with those two."

"If I don't have access to a shuttle, how can I get to the ship?"

"I was hoping you could use your name and connections to Raoneer elite."

If Dan possessed the flexible ears of a kzin, they'd be beating. *Got you.*

Shrawl'ta, Raoneer

Dan tore over the hourglass-shaped landmass at a roaring mach 5. The vantage point always gave him a healthy sense of perspective. From up here, the rambling megalopolis of Harp and the adjoining green and gold agricultural fields seemed a tiny freckle on the plum-colored rain forests that dominated Angel's Tome.

The original colonists, being severely traumatized by their hideous encounters with kzinti, decided that cohabitation would be too much for them. So the commanding personnel of *Angel's Pencil* and *Gutting Claw*'s rogue telepath agreed to divide the large Panunguis continent between the two species: humans took the subtropical and tropical southern bulb because its fertile jungles provided excellent soil for farming and the kzinti had taken the colder, northern bulb with a wide open steppe teeming with therapsidlike creatures to hunt.

He zoomed above the volcanic mountain range of the connecting land bridge. Dan found it appropriate that the two bulbs, once separate islands, were being ground together by unhurried geological processes. After a century of mutual segregation, the two species had begun to mingle: industry, education, sport, tourism had all blurred the hard isolating line.

After a couple hours of contemplative driving, his onboard computer jolted him, "You are now crossing the border into Raoneer. Your passport has automatically been stamped. Welcome home, Daneel Guthlac." The cool mauve tundra that hugged the open plains of Raoneer greeted him like a stern and proud father. His car spooked large herds of iguanalope and sent them racing across open territory. His pride had been part of Raoneer from the start. His grandmother, Selina Guthlac, had decided to stay with the kzinti and help build Shrawl'ta. Of course, she did her part for the human population of the planet as well, having children from the genetic stock frozen aboard *Angel's Pencil*. She even got the ship's geneticist to clone four kzinti kittens from the bodies salvaged from the *Tracker*, including *Tracker*'s Telepath, and raised them along with her biological children.

From the air, Shrawl'ta looked more like a colossal star fort on the shores of a great lake than a proper city. Its tall stone and steel walls surrounded the squat settlement. The highest structures were massive gun turrets emerging from each star point, and Ceezarr's mansion, the Hall of Harmonious Dominance. The estate was the largest living space in Raoneer, a square edifice the color of sun-burnt gold rising some thirty meters above all other surrounding buildings except for the laser towers. It was the practical and ceremonial center of kzinti power on Sheathclaws. Dan had grown up in its shadow.

He landed his car in the plaza near Healer's gravcar. His old friend paced fretfully.

"Did you get anything useful?" he asked, as Dan exited his car.

"I got all the data captured by the sensor swarm, courtesy of the Triumvir of Hem. Now all we need is a ship." The frigid breeze of his native Raoneer stung Dan's nose and burned his lungs. He went back into the car for a leather jacket.

"Let's go see my father." Healer-of-Hunters' fur flattened on his muscular body, as if expecting a fight.

They walked up to the wide, red, arched entrance of the Hall of Harmonious Dominance. The head of a lion, its mane blazing like the sun, was carved into the keystone. Two full-grown alliogs snapped and clawed at each other while chained on either side of the gate. The sparsely furred reptiles looked a lot like alligators with the fast frames of wolves. The result was something like prehistoric pristerognathus, although all Earth analogies failed to match the truly alien biology of these creatures.

They crossed a spacious, echoing vestibule. The interior of the Hall was no less lavish than Triumvirate House but it was warmer, less airy, like a medieval castle. The hide and heads of worthy game and rivals hung from the walls. They paused respectfully before the crystal sarcophagi that enshrined the remains of Selina Guthlac and Shadow.

"They died too young," Healer said, noticing his ancestor's small, frail body. Selina too was rather young despite the gray in her blond, curly locks.

"Shadow had one foot in the grave, even before he got to Sheathclaws, and his rapport with my grand-mother was much too strong. When he died, she simply faded away. Do you think our remains will rest in this great hall?"

Healer slapped a large paw across Dan's back,

breaking the reverie. "Oh, I assure you we will rest in this hall; the question is will we be honored relics or trophies?"

They continued on their way to Ceezarr's office and passed an elderly orange-and-white kzinrett who gave Healer an affectionate lick from chin to cheek. On any other world, she would be severely disciplined for showing a kzintosh such tenderness in front of a human. Healer nuzzled her head. "Grandmother-aunt, Rilla, please make sure my stubborn father takes full advantage of the autodoc after our discussion is over."

"I will," she purred in her limited Interworld.

"Autodoc?" Dan looked to Healer nervously, but before he got an answer, Healer pushed open the heavy double doors that led to Ceezarr's private den.

The office was a simple and elegant affair of polished cherry wood and dark leather furniture. Four kzinti pelts hung from the red brick walls, mockingly referred to as the senate, trophies from his unification of Shadow's competing heirs. He chose the Name Ceezarr after that battle and built the Hall of Harmonious Dominance.

"If it isn't my first-born son, the bush doctor!" Ceezarr roared, his luxuriant black-striped ochre fur showing distinguished silver streaks that Healer didn't remember from before. How long had it been? He studied them as a geologist might examine the ancient bands of sedimentary layers in exposed rock. Ceezarr poured vodka into the coagulated blood of an alliog and gave it a quick stir. "Want a drink?"

"I don't drink," Healer snarled, thin membranous ears flattening on his head. The essay he had written back in med school postulating that the early human settlers had intentionally introduced alcohol to the kzinti in order to keep them docile (and the interspecies controversy it caused) had been one of the major ideological wedges between them.

The older kzintosh took a hearty swig. "What do you want, Healer-of-Hunters?" He ignored the human in the room.

"Honored Ceezarr, I know about the kzinti warship that suddenly appeared at the edge of our system."

"It's dead. The robotic sentries around the system aren't detecting any active signatures. I say give them the fiery end these brave Heroes deserve." Dan understood that the Great Ceezarr wanted absolutely nothing to do with the Patriarchy. He was as eager to be rid of this ship as the leaders of Angel's Tome.

"Those sentries are a hundred years old. They could be faulty!" That came out dangerously close to sounding like the derision tense.

Dan could feel the situation quickly spiraling into fury. He needed to splash some cold reason on these potential fires. "Dominant One, I've met with the Triumvirate and I feel they aren't fit to claim this prey. The Separatists will stifle all research and the Rejoiners will foolishly bound into the jaws of the Patriarchy. I believe this ship would be better off here, in Shrawl'ta, where we will use its secrets to further strengthen Sheathclaws as a whole."

"Do not presume to dictate to me, boy! You are not your grandmother." Fear flew off this mighty kzin like cosmic rays from the sun.

Healer hesitated for a second, then leapt into what would surely end up as a word-duel, or worse. "I mean to lead an expedition to the ship. I need *Shadow's*

Chariot. If I can rescue anyone aboard, my mission would be complete, but if I can bring back much-needed technology to our young civilization—"

"Civilization!" The old kzin gulped the rest of the drink and slammed the glass down on the bar. "Since when does my savage son, the one who abandoned an honorable career as a brilliant doctor to chase down game in the wilds of Raoneer, care about civilization?"

"You know many of my generation, of yours too, chose to live as kzinti should, hunting the brutal creatures of this untamed world. There is no shame in that!"

"No, there isn't. Normal kzintosh are allowed the luxury of roaming the cold steppes of this world and live as the Maned God intended."

"Am I not a normal kzintosh?"

"No, you are the direct descendant of the Ancestor. You have a duty to Shrawl'ta, the settlement he founded on Raoneer." He glowered at Dan with ember-colored eyes, "Your ancestor too, boy."

"Don't be so proud, Ceezarr! All kzinti on Sheath-claws are descendants of Shadow! The original refugees amounted to barely two eights. We're already having to abort fetuses with severe health problems! If I can bring back any survivors, we can deepen our gene pool." Dan sensed the acute single-minded sting of primal emotion springing from Healer. It was almost a biological imperative, like the fundamental passions of pteranobats on their long, arduous journey from one end of the Panungius continent to the other to mate.

"Do not speak of our Ancestor's blood with such insolence!" The tips of teeth poked out from Ceezarr's jaw. His ears virtually disappeared.

"Careful, father, I believe Shadow would disapprove

of your creating a new Patriarchy around his lineage."
Four sicklelike claws raked across Healer's face as the
last syllable rolled out of his mouth. The powerful
blow threw him clear across the room. Years of living rough allowed him to quickly recover. He'd been
thrown off wombadons too many times. He poised
himself, ready to pounce on the graying kzintosh,
purple blood dripping on the lavish carpet.

"If you believe you can kill me, leap now and take
Shadow's Chariot!" Ceezarr bent his knees, digging
his protracted hind claws past the carpeting and well
into the floorboards, his thick tail cracking like a whip,
an impressive show of dominance. "If not, go back to
your miserable hinterland and don't return until you've
earned a proper Name!"

The rational part of Healer, telling him that this was
his father, receded with his lips leaving behind only a
mouth full of sleek, pearly teeth. They screamed and
leapt. Dan backed away against the wall. It wasn't the
two massive bodies tearing each other and the office
apart; it was the raw inhuman emotional emissions
coming from the blazing tornado of fur.

Ceezarr mangled his son's blocking arm with no
visible sign of restraint. Despite the awful pain, Healer-
of-Hunters struck with the speed of a killer and the
conviction of a surgeon. With four black scalpels, he
sliced muscles and tendons, punctured vital organs
and severed fat oozing arteries. Twenty-three precise
incisions later, the leader of all Raoneer dropped like
a limp orange pelt.

"I wasn't asking permission to take the ship," Healer
growled in the venomous Menacing Tense. He stalked
out of the room, leaving a sprinkled trail of urine in

his path. Dan scurried out behind him, careful not to step in the victory piss.

Several long minutes of crippling pain and fury passed. Ceezarr breathed deeply, carefully contemplating each stinging gash and aching bone. Then he clawed his way up to his desk and slammed on the holocomm. He snarled the voice command for the Triumvirate offices in Harp.

The crisp holographic portrait of Trimunvir Jibunoh appeared standing next to him. Horror spread across her perfectly rendered face. "Ceezarr! What happened? Has there been a coup?"

"Of a sort, Triumvir, my son, Healer-of-Hunters and Daneel Guthlac are taking control of *Shadow's Chariot* and plan to rescue the smashed warship. We can no longer ignore the problem."

"This is terrible!" She looked away as if absently listening to an aide, then turned back to Ceezarr. "Why are your ears flapping like a giddy old fool?"

"Because, Galia, my wayward kitten has finally become a grown kzintosh."

Shadow's Chariot

Healer hastily spritzed artificial epidermis on his shredded arm as they made their way toward the great plaza where *Shadow's Chariot* had been reverently parked. Dan didn't speak. He simply processed all the primal sensations he had just bathed in.

They entered the flat, ovoid vehicle as kzinti and human tourists gaped in horror at their sacrilege.

"If it was this easy to jump into the ship and take it, why did we bother confronting your father?" Dan finally mustered.

"That would have been disrespectful."

"But maiming him wasn't?"

"No."

Shadow's Chariot had a small command bridge consisting of a plush, crescent-shaped couch hugging an intricate command console clearly designed for massive paws.

"I know why you're so focused on this warship," Dan said finally, plugging his data tablet into the barge's control panel. All information on the warship immediately downloaded into the antique ship's navigational computer. New charts and figures appeared on the surrounding screens.

"Do you?" Healer played at the controls and the long-atrophied gravity motors hummed to life.

"Yeah, you're lonely." Now that Dan had said it, he felt the waves of loneliness languorously rolling off his companion.

"Kzinti don't require the complex social structures of primates."

"Still, at your age you should already have a couple mates and a few kittens running around."

The museum artifact that had lain dormant for a century achieved escape velocity in impressive defiance of inertia. Tight laser communiqués were pouring in from all over Angel's Tome, particularly from Harp. They ignored them.

"I could say the same for you."

"I do alright. I work at a university, have a dangerous Raoneer accent and drive a sexy car."

A new red line had appeared on all the displays of the solar system, this one cutting a straight path directly toward the other wandering line of the warship.

"Really, the accent?" Healer's ears flicked like the elongated thoracic ribs of the small gliding pangolins found all over the indigo canopies of Angel's Tome.

"The females love it when I turn my S's into Z's and roll my R's."

"To be honest, since deceit is apparently physiologically impossible for me, I'm finding it difficult to find a compatible mate. They smell uncomfortably familiar to me."

"That's because they are," Dan said, but noticed that Healer's ears stopped flicking. He knew he had touched a sore spot. "Look, it isn't a problem for other kzintosh. It's got to be mental with you. I think because of your medical training, you know that genetically all kzinti on Sheathclaws are closely related, so it's become a thing for you."

"Possibly," he said, scratching the tan fur on his chin. "Why did we stop being friends, Dan? I believe kzinti are better off with humans calling them out on their quirks."

"You grew up too fast. You were out picking off wombadons while I was still picking my nose."

"Perhaps there's a harem of foreign kzinretti on that ship waiting to be rescued."

"You know females aren't allowed on warships."

"Unless there's an Admiral aboard." Healer dialed up four scarlet meal bricks and demolished them in two gulps. "Hungry?"

"Yes, but I'd rather have a medium-rare steak and a glass of wine."

Healer and Dan stopped talking a hundred kilometers away from the derelict, their radar bounced back a significant ping. They toggled the screens to video view. The blast-smeared crimson ship looked like the jagged disc of a crab's discarded carapace.

Shadow's Chariot warily approached the drifting ghost ship and matched speeds with it. It was so immense that it could easily swallow their barge whole. A series of blackened commas and dots were emblazoned on its side.

"What is that, the ship's name? What does it say?"

Healer looked at it for a moment and said, "I have no idea. My written Heroes' Tongue is horrible. My instruments confirm that there are no life signs. Although, some basic system is still running because I can detect an active power flow."

"Yeah, I'm not picking up any emotional activity at all." He felt Healer's deep disappointment and added, "But I wouldn't if they were frozen. The good news is that the long-range communications antenna has been destroyed. The bad news is that all that mysterious machinery that seems to be part of their FTL also looks damaged."

"Look there." Healer highlighted the area on the screen. "That gash on the starboard side, that's what killed it. If we can seal it, we can repressurize the whole upper deck and get access to the bridge."

"Alright, I'm releasing a repair robot now." Dan typed the instructions into his tablet. A fat robot the size of a pregnant wombadon jetted out from the underbelly of *Chariot* and proceeded to work on the fissure in a blur of quick and numerous articulate manipulators.

"I'm going to take us in. We can land in the hangar

bay and simply walk to the bridge without excursion suits."

"Is that wise?"

"Perhaps not, but I want to inspect the ship first before I tow it any closer to Sheathclaws."

Healer sent ancient override codes from *Shadow's Chariot* archives until one managed to coax the hangar bay doors open, then they deliberately burrowed into the wrecked craft, like a scavenger digging into a rotting carcass. The *Chariot* touched down in the cavernous boat deck amid rows of smaller, long-dead fighters.

The repair robot finished spraying the gash with epoxy, and Healer and Dan waited impatiently for the warship's resurrected life-support systems to slowly refill the chamber with atmosphere.

Righteous Manslaughter

"We have air outside," Healer reported at last, and grabbed a supply pack. "Let's go. We can move behind the wave of life support activation."

Dan grabbed a beam gun. It was manufactured for big dexterous paws, but he'd hunted with them extensively in his teens.

"You don't think any frozen passengers we thaw might find the weapon a bit provocative?"

"Well, I was going to have claws and fangs genetically implanted, but I don't think I could pull off the look."

"Point taken."

It took an arduous hour of trekking through murky, labyrinthine corridors and service tubes. The corpses of kzinti warriors, contorted by explosive decompression, were scattered everywhere. Healer stopped here and there, taking DNA samples from the bodies showing the least amount of cellular damage from space.

"The bridge should be through here. It'll take a minute for the atmosphere to build up, then—"

A detonation of emotions shook Dan. He bashed the back of his head on the floor repeatedly and his limbs flailed about wildly. He vaguely felt Healer restrain him before he thrashed himself to death. With great effort, Dan pulled himself together and croaked, "There are kzinti here. Alive! It's like they just sprang into existence, radiating rage, confusion and terror."

Healer looked at the tablet that was slaved to *Chariot*'s sensor array and saw that seven individuals had suddenly appeared on the bridge. "Rest. I'm going to talk to them."

"Talk to them?"

Healer ignored the protestation and punched up the bridge, relaying the signal through *Chariot*. Instantly, the furious face of a warrior showed on the screen. Three black stripes ran down his face like war paint. "Who is this?" he snarled.

"I am First Medic. Are you in need of medical assistance?"

"I am Tdakar-Commander. Our Captain Fnar-Ritt is a corpse honorably still at his post. There are six of us wounded Heroes and one telepath sheltering on the bridge."

"And the Admiral?"

"There is no Admiral aboard *Righteous Manslaughter*. Fnar-Ritt was the highest ranking officer and now that honor falls on me."

Healer felt a knot tighten in the pit of this stomach. *There are no females here.* All he could hope to accomplish now was boosting Sheathclaws' general gene pool, if not his own. He pushed his loneliness aside and asked, "Where were you a second ago? My ship's sensors failed to pick you up."

"Obviously in stasis!" The stupid question roused suspicion in the commander. "First Tech tells me you are aboard an outdated Admiral's Barge. Explain."

"No, we are outside the bridge, but we're relaying the transmission from the barge. We lost our ship in battle and this was all that was available to us, but we continue to perform our duty of search and rescue."

"What are you doing?" Dan whispered. He could feel the velvety footfalls of a powerful alien telepath prowling in his mind. He tried to push it out.

"Lying through my teeth, despite my neurological handicap," Healer hissed to the side, then continued speaking to Tdakar-Commander. "Permission to enter the bridge and attend the crew?"

The commander scowled at Healer through narrowed blue eyes for a chilling moment, then barked, "Permission granted!"

"The telepath scanned us, but I don't think he'll report us. What's the plan?"

"We go in there and I deal with the injured warriors. Since you're the only one with any kind of active telepathic ability, you need to appeal to the telepath. Tell him that if everyone is to survive, he needs to mentally persuade all the warriors to cooperate."

"Failing that?"

"We kill everyone in that room and clone them afterwards."

When Dan didn't reply, Healer allowed his ears and fur to sleek over with fear. "If I am permitted a moment of weakness, Dan, I dread these warriors may be too fierce for me. They are truly of the Heroic Race."

"Trust me, it's not their ferocity we should fear, it's their philosophy. I sense nothing but utter contempt for humanity in that room."

Healer forced his ears to ripple. "A barrel of bloodka would go a long way in pacifying them."

"You're a hypocrite."

The door to the bridge slid open, exuding the foul stench of kzinti blood and sweat. Seven badly injured creatures, miraculously still at their stations, all bared slobbering canines like dripping icicles. Dan was acutely aware that he was the only human in the room and reflexively held his heavy gun a little tighter.

"What is this pathetic *kz'eerkt* doing on my bridge? No filthy monkey slaves are permitted here!" Tdakar-Commander roared at the rude affront to his ship's honor.

"He is not a slave. Daneel Guthlac is a valued companion. He's here to help."

The wounded warriors' ears flapped like a flock of migrating pteranobats. Healer controlled his withdrawing lips and used the break in tension to begin examining the kzinti. Not one of them was older than the foolish youngster he had healed back at his hut.

Dan stayed focused on the empty-looking, shriveled kzin that sat in the far corner of the room. He looked like the many corpses they had passed on their way to the bridge. Slowly, the wraithlike kzin reached over to a stand near his couch and plucked a needle from a wide assortment of syringes arrayed like instruments of torture. He thrust it into his arm.

"Who . . . What are you? I've examined both your minds and you are neither man nor kzin, but an abomination," *Manslaughter*'s Telepath directed the thought toward Dan.

Dan, not used to direct mental communication, transmitted his response. *"We come from a planet colonized by humans and an escaped kzin telepath. We're here to offer you sanctuary."*

Healer cracked a leg of a kzintosh that had started to heal wrongly and set it right. The warrior only winced at the excruciating pain. He tore away sheets of charred flesh from the muscles of another Hero who had suffered third-degree burns over his body and drenched him in synthetic skin. All the while, he subtly delivered a mild sedative to each one. Tdakar-Commander watched him like a hungry predator. Healer-of-Hunters continued until all the wounded were taken care of. Then he warily moved toward Tdakar-Commander. "These warriors are mere kits. Their spots not yet faded."

"The grand campaigns against the humans have left us scrounging for war-ready Heroes," Tdakar-Commander replied, eying his motley assortment of bloodstained warriors. "These kits, as you call them, hail from all over the Empire: First Tech from a moon orbiting Hssin, Weapons Master from Ka'asai, Navigator from the habitats of Sårng, Chief Programmer from Shasht, Systems Controller from W'kkai. Young perhaps, but Heroes all."

"Can it be that against all odds, in my desperation, I've landed us at the gates of paradise?" The telepath silently asked Dan, his body slouched lifelessly, as if his disembodied spirit had spoken.

"*I wouldn't call it paradise. It's more a boondocks full of scared people who just want to hide. You'll be safe there and free to earn a Name and a harem, but it'll take hard work and cunning,*" Dan thought back.

"You've got a serious gash running down your side," Healer moved to look at the commander's oozing scar.

"Do you think me a fool?" Tdakar-Commander unsheathed eight long, black claws. "Your strange accent and odor, your whole demeanor screams impostor, yet you know your craft well."

"I really am a doctor."

"I don't doubt that, I doubt your Heroic nature."

"Let's cut the crap then, commander. I am not a Hero. In fact, I come from a world free of the Patriarchy, a world with wide wintry steppes and tundra the color of venous blood. Our multihued sky lights up under constant bombardment from our orange, subgiant sun. Strange and challenging beasts are plentiful for the cunning hunter, and many of us have chosen to live as kzintosh were intended."

"*Are you telepathically calming the warriors?*" Dan asked the telepath when he didn't get a mental reply.

"*Quit jabbering, monkey, I wish to hear more of this savage utopia,*" the telepath snapped, without moving his jaw.

"It sounds glorious, Imposter, and I believe you. I can taste sharp, sylvan molecules rising from your fur. I would like very much to hunt on these alien moors, but I am bound by Honor to continue the war with humanity until we're victorious or I die."

"I can provide you and your warriors with two females each and enough land to lose yourselves in."

Dan wasn't getting anywhere with the telepath.

"Can you psychically persuade Tdakar into coming to Sheathclaws? It should be easy, I can sense his desire to abandon this futile war and live the simple life of a hunter."

"Tell me about this Maned God I read in your minds."

"It's nothing. A local superstition, a religious syncretism." Dan failed to see how the question related to their immediate predicament.

"I see that Gutting Claw's Telepath had a vision of the human's Bearded God merged with the kzinti Fanged God."

"It was a drug-induced hallucination."

"I sincerely hope this Maned God is more merciful than the Fanged God."

Suddenly, Dan felt something deeply wrong with *Manslaughter*'s Telepath. Years of suffering and drug abuse had left his mind critically scarred and twisted.

"My tormentors and slave masters will not lay a hind claw upon the soil of paradise." It was the last coherent thought sent by the telepath. After that there was only mental static.

"I take it you will not give us any other choice?" Tdakar-Commander said to Healer.

Healer protracted his own claws, sharpened on the bones of animals far larger and less injured than Tdakar-Commander. "I'm sorry. I cannot allow you to escape and reveal our position, but your ship is severely damaged and you wouldn't be able to leave even if I allowed you to."

"A death-duel then." Tdakar flipped out his gleaming *wtsai* with well-practiced elegance. "If I die, my warriors are ordered to stand down and retire to your primeval hunting park." Tdakar's tail moved in a way that subtly told Healer this was as far as he was willing to yield. At least the kit warriors under his command would have a better life.

"He's mentally ill!" Dan screamed. "He's going to kill them all!"

Tdakar plunged his blade into Healer's gut. Healer let rip a terrible, shrill whine. He staggered as the skilled Hero pulled it cleanly out. Blinded by pain, Healer-of-Hunters lashed out instinctively, chomping down on Tdakar-Commander's neck and pulverizing his spine. Steamy purple and orange blood gushed out of Tdakar's yawning mouth, black nostrils and limp ears. His body went rigid, then fell into Healer's arms. They both collapsed to the floor in a jumble of damp fur. For a second, Healer sat there, horrified.

"Do not mourn the good commander, Healer-of-Hunters. If you'd been born on another world, around another star, he'd have bound you in the unbreakable chemical shackles of the *sthondat* drug and enslaved you without a moment's hesitation." *Manslaughter*'s Telepath spoke verbally for the first time. His voice was harsh and raspy like mauve grass during the dry season. He lurched out of his couch and paced the bridge without taking his eyes off Healer. "These common brutes are not worthy of, what is it, Sheathclaws?" He bent over and took the sidearm from Fnar-Ritt's burnt corpse.

"What are you doing?" was all Healer could say before his lips and ears pulled back in unrestrained rage.

"Calm yourself, Healer, I have a proposition for you. I can sense your lust for unrelated females. The

Patriarch is desperate to breed more Heroes able to use a mass pointer for navigation, so he conceded two females aboard this ship, in Fnar-Ritt's quarters. They were probably locked in a stasis field once that deck decompressed."

He fired a shot at one of the young warriors, the tall, lanky one from Ka'asai, sending him sprawling over his console. "Allow me to cleanse this vessel of butchers and we can all go down to Sheathclaws victorious." None of the other lame Heroes moved. The cadaverous telepath dulled their already distressed and anesthetized minds. Another beam ignited Systems Controller.

Dan felt Healer waiver. He'd have mates and DNA samples, his friend would have all the technology he wanted, and this poor wretched telepath would finally find refuge, but as he looked at the remaining spot-spangled adolescents, frightened and vicious, he couldn't let them be simply slaughtered. Was it his training as a doctor or had a century of living with humans infected this carnivore with crippling humanity? "No," Dan heard his friend hiss through still-gritted, exposed teeth. He tried to push Tdakar off him.

"I've read your minds and I know their continued existence is not necessary for your mission to succeed. You can always grow them in a vat later. Is that not what you said?"

Healer could no longer speak, so Dan shouted for him, "This is murder! We had them sold! A simple push would've been enough!"

"No, monkey, this is vengeance!" The psychotic telepath turned his awful power on Dan's meager defenses. "I can mow you all down and pilot this ship to your planet if I have to. Take the females for myself!"

Dan's verbal ability was torn from him along with shreds of his higher brain functions. His frontal lobes pulsated with slashes of pain. With what little control he still possessed, Daneel Guthlac bared his teeth, raised his gun and squeezed out a neat blue shaft of light that scorched its way between the telepath's eyes. The preternatural din died at once. Dan's quivering husk buckled.

Hours passed and *Righteous Manslaughter* continued on its tumble toward the hungry orange sun. Healer-of-Hunters woke with a pounding headache and excruciating pain in his stomach. The wrecked bodies of kzintosh and Dan were tossed helter-skelter across the bridge, an occasional twitch the only sign of possible life. The faint scent of cooked brains still lingered in the recycled air.

Chief Programmer loomed ominously over him. "Can you really deliver on all your promises?"

"Yes," Healer said, trying to get up, readying himself for another fight.

"Take it easy, Imposter. While you were unconscious we agreed to abide by Tdakar-Commander's last order. We cleaned and bandaged your wound from the supplies in your medical pack. Your brave monkey is still out cold. Also, we checked on the kzinretti. Once we got life support working down there, the stasis field winked off."

Healer sat on his haunches at the center of the bridge for a long while, like a hunter waiting for prey to amble by. He ignored the pain shooting through his abdomen. All this chaos had been his fault. He had a responsibility to salvage it somehow.

"Thank you, Chief Programmer. I will take my friend

and go back to our ship. I can tow us to Sheathclaws with it." Healer took careful tissue samples from the two fallen kits, then from Tdakar-Commander and *Manslaughter*'s Telepath. Perhaps the two bitter enemies would be reborn on Sheathclaws as allies. When Healer-of-Hunters was done, he threw Dan's body over his shoulder like a fresh kill.

He noticed the innocuous little tray with its collection of needles. He was, in theory, a powerful telepath, the product of uncontrolled breeding (inbreeding) with the genes of two telepaths in his pride. He had no training in the Telepathic Arts, but maybe he could make up for that in raw talent. Without a moment's hesitation, he walked to the tray, selected the largest dose of the *sthondat* drug and left the bridge.

Healer marched back down long twisting corridors toward his ship. The insubstantial weight of his friend was heavy on his mind. He entered the cramped bridge of *Shadow's Chariot* and carefully laid Dan's unconscious body on the command couch. Although the damage was not physical, he hooked Dan up to the barge's autodoc.

He piloted his ship out of the hangar bay of the colossal derelict. Healer took hold of it with magnetic grapplers and began steering the wreck toward his planet. Healer-of-Hunters had won. He had taken an advanced warship for Sheathclaws and mates for himself. He saved four young kzintosh from certain death. His triumph felt utterly empty. When he was sure they were on course, he administered the *sthondat* drug into the crook of his arm and sat next to Dan.

The Eleventh Sense burst within his skull and his awareness of the universe blossomed into pure satori. It was a near impossible task to focus on the pale, dismembered mind lying before him. He took a deep breath and set to work on the tattered mind of his only friend. He mended memories and reattached loose bits of personality. After the initial high, Healer's body began to shiver and his fur became matted with sweat, but he continued to toil with the resolve of a dedicated physician. He diligently stitched intellect, instinct and soul as close as possible to how it had been before the attack. As the massive dose of the unfamiliar drug bled from his system, he hung on long enough to seal Dan's mind, then fainted.

When Healer came to for the second time, his mouth was parched and his long pink tongue hung from his jaw like dried leather. He pushed himself up and waves of nausea swirled in his belly, the taste of sour, half-digested meal bricks in the back of his throat. Dan still lay unresponsive on the couch. He looked more at peace, but the doc registered no change. Had he dreamed his telepathic surgery? Healer dialed *Manslaughter*'s bridge, and two of the warriors, First Tech and Navigator, came on the commscreen. "What's going on?" His booming roar came out a hoarse whisper.

"We've established a parking orbit around the planet," First Tech said formally. "We're receiving many messages from the surface, but we decided you should be the one to answer them."

Healer-of-Hunters stood and paused a minute, letting the queasiness subside. "In a minute," he said, and the silent juvenile waited. He switched the view to the barge's external cameras and looked at the magnificent bruise-colored world, still new and untamed. Despite an overwhelming sense of loss, Healer's ears weakly flitted. A young Hero could be happy down there.

ZENO'S ROULETTE

◆　◆　◆

David Bartell

Phase one of the mission had gone without a glitch. Phase two began in the cramped armory of the *Catscratch Fever*, a dark, sleek pitchfork of a ship, serial number long since removed, now in mercenary hands. Adjacent to the yawning launch tubes, Flex Bothme helped Annie Venzi wriggle into her battle armor. He knew well how to bear hug Annie's square frame into it; not only had they worked together on a swindler's dozen missions, but as a fellow Jinxian, Flex was built the same way, and knew the pains and pleasures of a custom suit. It was a shame to fold the wavy brown billows of her hair into a helmet, but he had to admit, she looked sexy in armor too.

Together they ran her suit's readiness checklist until the green light came on, then repeated the procedure on his. Flex thumped a fist on his chest, expecting Annie to return the gesture. Instead, she made a wan smile, and then punched his cubical fist in half-hearted solidarity.

"You in this?" he said, studying her hazel eyes as if they were another item on the checklist.

"I'm tired of this so-called war," she said.

"Then you're lucky, because the stars we earn

from this job will set us up for life." Flex, freshly thawed from near-death at Brain Freeze, was anxious to get this over with, too. It sounded like a routine affair—infiltrate a kzinti resort compound, obtain some specific intelligence, and get out. If some cats were killed in the process, well, it's a cold universe, isn't it? "I don't know why the Pierson's Puppeteers are paying so handsomely for a little intel on some exotic wormhole," he said, "but what a break! This one's for us."

After he kissed her, she drew in her lips. "Just remember my terms," she said. "Don't kill any kittens."

He smiled deviously. "Accidents happen." He tore a slab of protein from a synergy bar dispenser and offered it to her. Its musky odor whispered of their past adventures: hunting for sugar shrooms on Gummidgy, making love in a floating fountain over Paris... He drew the odor in heartily, and smiled.

She wasn't having any of it. Her expertise was kzin psychology, not felinicide. "Promise me you won't kill the kits."

"Look," said Flex. "Let me tell you about your bleeding heart. When those kits grow up, your heart will bleed all over them as they unzip you from your pretty throat down to your..." He winked.

"This kitten can take care of herself."

"That's the only reason Zel lets us work together," Flex said.

"All right already, time to kiss and ride!" said Zel Kickovich, the captain of the *Fever*. He pushed them both on the back toward the tumbler capsules where four other specialists were already sliding into place. Flex gnashed at the synergy bar, gave the rest to Annie, and they both washed it down with water from a squeeze bulb.

"Launch in thirty seconds!" Zel turned to lower the canopies onto those who were ready. "We're picking up some positron streams along your trajectory," he added as a parting shot, "so watch out for thunderheads."

Flex nodded at Zel, but Annie kept him in a locked gaze. "Promise me you won't kill the kits."

"All right already, I promise. Now let's go!"

"Swear it."

"I swear. I won't kill the flea-bitten kits."

Annie thumped her chest, and any doubt in Flex's mind of her readiness fell away. He smiled and thumped, and with the aid of a pull-up bar, they hopped into their respective tumblers. Flex could no longer see Annie, though she lay not two meters away. A hoist lowered the opaque cockpit cover over his tube, and it hissed as it was squeezed into place.

In the dark space above the gravid world Meerowsk, *Catscratch Fever* yawed to a new attitude, ready to propel the tumblers while at the same time adjusting her orbit, thus disguising the recoil from the tumbler launch. These six tubes carried little more than enough fusion power to make safe planetfall—a controlled crash, to be generous—so the initial thrust came from the ship. The tumblers would be aimed against the current orbit, which had the effect of de-orbiting them. The ship's job was then to distract and survive until phase three, extraction.

Extraction was going to be dicey, Flex knew. This was supposed to look like a suicide vendetta, so that if things went wrong, the kzinti would not suspect the true mission.

A loud roar shook Flex's tumbler, and as it kicked him out of the *Fever*, the G forces made it feel as though he were standing upright inside the flying coffin. To a Jinxian accustomed to increased gravity, it felt good. "Tabam!" he said, a victory cry from Jinx that derived from "to be a man."

"Tabam!" came Annie's voice through his helmet speaker. The phrase had become unisexual, as had many such on a world where women had long been recognized as men's equals in all things physical.

"Do you think this planet will make lucky number eleven?" Flex asked her.

"You mean ten. I don't count Jinx, because we're both from there."

"Which is beside the point that we did it there, too."

"Not to interrupt, lovebirds," said Zel, "but what are you talking about?"

"We're going for the record of making love on the most worlds."

"Well, this won't be one of them. This is just an in-and-out mission."

A dozen voices broke into laughter.

"On that note," Zel said, audibly grinning, "it's time for data silence."

"Love and money!" was Flex's parting shot.

"Tabam!" Annie said, and the voice com ran silent.

Six fusion tumblers pitched in unison, end over end, until they were heads-up. They were quickly dropping into the atmosphere of Meerowsk. Despite the tiny size of his viewer, the images of the other tubes slicing into the stratosphere made Flex shiver. He knew exactly which one was Annie's by the painted red diamond on it—her mark, stylized from the A and V in Annie Venzi. No doubt she was noting the X on Flex's tumbler, so they could watch each others' backs.

The tubes sliced through atmosphere, howling like a pack of morlocks in heat. The braking engines came vigorously to life, roaring against the wind. Flex had no intention of letting this become a suicide mission. As an intelligence specialist, his job was to extract certain information from a certain kzin character he knew little about, and get out with it and his precious red diamond. The first challenge in avoiding suicide was to keep the tumbler from burning up. Since they were adapted from interplanetary ballistic missiles, the tumblers could not be made of indestructible material. Instead, they were made of schwartzite, a material made from asymmetric carbon crystals that had been a staple in construction in centuries past.

Annie was going in hot. Why didn't her computer slow her down? "Annie!" Flex shouted, knowing she could not hear. She should switch to manual.

"Annie!" No change. Her engine discharge went white-hot, and her tube pulled back with the others. Flex cut to manual just long enough to steer a little closer to her tube, then back to auto. She rocked her fiery tube to signal she was all right.

"Tabam!" he said.

With fusion rockets firing there was no way to see what lay below. Based on his topographic display Flex knew that they were angling in over a continent, on target for the vacation den of one Jarko-S'larbo, a rich kzin who had built a reputation as a luxury resort owner. The plotted route was low and stealthy, and with some planned distractions from the *Fever*, they should be able to slide right into Slarbo's backyard.

The four mercenary soldiers with them were to subdue S'larbo long enough for Annie to implant a coma collar on the cat. Then they could spirit him away. Failing that, Flex's job was to extract whatever information he could from the compound's data systems.

The tumblers cut across the terminator and slid into night and then into clouds. Lightning flashed and crackled around them, triggering a warning alert. Usually not a problem, but Zel had mentioned positrons from the storm system…

Through the schwartzite hull, Flex heard a loud booming. Then he felt a violent rumbling as they hauled ass through storm. Another thunderclap, and more flashes.

In the stroboscopic light, Flex went manual to check on Annie. He had to roll to one side to aim a camera in her direction. He found her, red diamond against the cobalt, just in time to see a powerful bolt of lightning forking below her craft. Breaking formation, he fought the turbulence so he could keep the sensor trained on her capsule. Annie would understand his maneuver and rock her tube to show she was all right.

Her tube did not rock. The lightning did not seem to have adversely affected its engine or navigation, but the detection of positrons from orbit meant that the lightning from the storm was probably giving off gamma rays. That could cause any number of problems. The disposable tumblers had no redundant systems, since they were built for single, rapid strikes.

A signal indicated that the power landing would commence in five minutes. The tubes would pitch 180 degrees again, tails up (which really meant tails behind in this case), and cruise over the terrain like guided missiles, until final braking. Flex prayed to the closest thing he had to a goddess, Annie, that her tube would tumble properly. Meanwhile, Annie's tube had slipped closer, and a proximity alarm sounded.

"Tanj!" Flex instinctively switched to manual, just as his tumbler moved to a safe distance automatically. He wished for daylight, so it would be easier to see his companion.

Another alarm. Again, a proximity warning. Flex steered clear, but now the two of them were veering from the group. Why didn't she go manual? Why didn't she rock her tube? He didn't want to admit it, but Annie must have been hurt in the lightning hit.

It was time for the power approach, and Flex returned to auto, making sure he had a clear visual of Annie. His tube tumbled head over heels, the thruster no longer braking. Now it accelerated him forward, low over the ground that was still hidden by darkness. Annie's tube also turned, right on schedule, as did the others, which were now fifty-three meters away. Still manageable, but they had a lot of ground to cover before final braking.

They glided into badlands seeped in pre-dawn mist, the guidance systems keeping them low, between the hills, and then threading them through sandstone canyons and monuments that leaped from the shadows as if they were shoots seeking light. Flex's tumbler dodged and weaved, leaving him free to scrutinize Annie's.

Her tube was negotiating the labyrinth, so its maps and guidance were operational. But execution was sluggish—it was slow to evade on all planes. These mountains and rocks provided perfect cover for tiny personal craft to sneak in, but there was no room for the kind of slop that Annie's tumbler was exhibiting. He watched with horror as Annie careened toward an outcropping, only to avert it at the last minute.

"Not while I'm here," Flex said, adding a choice swear word he overheard in an isolated vacuum plant while still a boy on Jinx. That was not far from Brain Freeze, where he later learned what the word really meant.

A large stone pillar loomed ahead, and he felt his tube adjust for a tight pass. That's how this course had been charted, as a geographilic caress of the landscape. Even though they had strayed from the plan, the guidance system adjusted. He felt his thruster ease off some, but noted that Annie's did not.

That was the problem, then. Somehow her tube was not modifying its speed properly, so its steering was wild and uncontrolled. She was going to hit that mountain.

In desperation, Flex kicked over to manual and gunned it. His tumbler shot ahead, directly toward the rock wall. He caught up with Annie and pulled alongside. With a hearty "Tabam!" he nudged over, physically knocking her tube away from the death ahead.

It worked. He saw her tube shoot off to the left, to a relatively open area. His own tube had yawed to the right, so to avoid the mountain, he had to shoot around the other side, losing sight of Annie. He found her again, this time sliding dangerously toward a rock-ribbed plain.

"Come on, Annie, wake up!" he said. "I can't steer for both of us!"

He zipped in her direction, taxing the poor maneuverability of the tumbler. The only evident way to keep her from crashing would be to get underneath her, and jostle her upward. He straightened out in front of her and cut power. Annie's jet was pegged, and as she passed above him he bumped her just enough to level her off. Then he allowed her to move ahead again.

"Wake up, Annie, we need you! You're the only one who can get S'larbo out alive!" A calculated exaggeration.

Ahead, the ground sloped slowly, sinking into a verdant morass. The kzin backyard was somewhere in that jungle, and somehow he had to get them safely grounded there.

Twice, Flex kicked Annie's tumbler this way and then nudged it that. One last time he saw the other four tumblers kilometers away. Then the green hills separated them from sight.

Trees seemed to shoot into the sky, the tumblers rising above them, Annie's with a little kiss from Flex's. It was impossible to steer the speeding tubes between such dense obstacles.

An alert signaled the final tumble. Flex's tube pitched 180 degrees back to the braking position that had countered the planet's gravity a while ago. Annie's followed suit and their thrusters beat at the steaming air above the forest canopy. Flex predicted that if her thruster did not modulate it would overbrake, and she would drop into the ground like a hot javelin through snow. So with his own retro roaring, he again slid beneath her and gave her an upward push, their hulls grinding together like teeth.

Too much. He contacted off center, too close to the engine. Her tube rose into the air, while his own, scorched from her flaming exhaust, began to shut down. The last thing he saw was her tube, still on a defective autopilot, tumbling back into braking attitude, but yawing and rolling like a snuffed candle discarded into a cloud-spackled sky.

Completely fried, Flex's tumbler lost power, and the crash net deployed prematurely, draping uselessly over his legs. In utter blackness, he felt the tumbler chopping branches away from the canopy.

He wished that he had broken silence before losing power, if only to say good-bye. What more was there to lose?

The benefit of autopilot is that the organic pilot is free from complicated tasks to focus on tasks more reliant on a natural intelligence. Yet the human mind has its own autopilot, wherein autonomic bodily functions or rote activities continue without conscious management. In Flex's case, his autopilot was shock-induced, his full consciousness deferred. His legs moved him through the kzinti recreational area, his throbbing head unaware of his surroundings. When he came upon a running stream, a decision was forced upon him, and that kicked him back into manual.

Flex remembered where he was. Slowly, his vision widened, and with a lone breeze that meandered through the trees, he heard the multitude of sounds of the jungle. Insects circled him, distant unknown animals barked and cried, and overhead, the whir of a motor grew faint and was gone. A bird began a sweet chirping that invariably ended in a mock-death scream. Its *warble-warble-tweet-tweet-YAAAGH* neatly encapsulated the beauty and horror of any number of jungles in known space. The sun slanted through the steamy air, slicing the contours of gray-green foliage into confusion.

Born and raised in the nearly doubled gravity of Jinx, Flex Bothme was short and stocky, a knotted muscle of a man. Such a knot might slip at any moment, and he often had. He was wearing cammo flight togs, and his wristcomp still worked. Apparently, he had been walking for only a few minutes. He thought to back-track to his tumbler, but suddenly he remembered Annie Venzi. If she was still alive, she was in mortal danger, so he had to find her immediately. Had he, in his traumatized subconscious, calculated which way she must be? He'd been walking northeast before encountering the stream. That would be about right, so he decided to continue.

A large winged insect dared a pass at his neck, but before he could swat it, it changed its mind. "Guess I don't smell right," he muttered. On Gummidgy, Annie and Flex chased pests through the air with a sizzler, and then swung lazily in a hammock. They watched the wan light of the little moon bobbling on Circle Sea, and then made love. That was number nine on their "worlds to make love on" list. Flex swore to himself that if he found her alive on Meerowsk, he'd make love to her there and then, even if it meant *mission interruptus.*

In the sandy loam at his feet, fresh footprints from a small clawed animal with at least four legs ran along the stream. Flex was not a tracker, but he was not the stereotypical dull-witted Jinxian either. It was obvious that the thing had lingered for a drink and then bounded downstream, to his left. This might be important if the animal was being tracked by kzinti hunters. After all, this was a recreational park designed for their amusement. Flex might suddenly find himself the prey of known space's finest hunters.

He scanned the shallow stream up and down. He had a sidearm, but would be no match for a kzin in this situation. Even if he survived, there would be no way to rescue Annie. Come to think of it, his best chance to find her was if the kzinti found her for him. And there was one way he could help them do that.

Flex used his wristcomp to estimate the direction of Jarko-S'larbo's lodge. His comp calibrated to the planet's magnetic field, and he bounded off in that direction. If he could surrender to the kzinti, he might be able to bargain for her life, mission be damned. Annie had always said it was a bad idea to serve together. Despite all the fun and profits they'd had, she was right. What good was it earning money to buy expensive treatments to try to extend their short Jinxian lives if you got killed in the process?

Only bruised here and there, Flex made good time through the forest, but he was far from stealthy. He heard the crashing of limbs behind and above him—something large but elusive was leaping from tree to tree, chasing him. He darted behind a thick mossy trunk, drew his flashlight laser, and chanced a look back.

Nothing. Whatever it was, it was clever. His eyes darted around, but could not detect a trace of the arboreal predator. He hadn't studied the native fauna, because they were supposed to have landed nearer to the kzin compound, and there was no time to look them up now.

A tentative rustle from above. No doubt that by

hiding, Flex had signaled a disadvantage that the beast above sensed. If it's eat or be eaten, Flex's choice was clear, and he broke cover, crouched and took rough aim.

The thing growled, a marbled, choking sound. Flex's sidearm could out-growl that. He shot at the thing in the shadows, missing but making his point. Before he caught so much as a sight of it, the creature's growls were echoed from all directions.

There were a lot more of the things closing on him. So much for growling. Flex stood and ran like hell in his original direction, laser in fist. He heard rustling above, like a hurricane whipping at the trees. Maybe Annie was lucky; if still unconscious, she would be in the safety of her tumbler.

He thought to turn and fire, but hearing the beasts both behind and above, he knew it wouldn't buy him a quantizer's nano. It might, however, get someone else's attention.

He made for an open area where the predators would have to come down from the heights, improving his odds. In the center of the clearing was a rocky knoll, and he climbed that, turned, and fired at will.

The creatures were cats the size of kzinti, but they were not kzinti. Flex had never seen them before, but they reminded him of saber-toothed tigers from pictures, except that these were green and gray, and stout. Black stripes ran straight back from the eyes like tears peeled from the eyes by racing the wind in the treetops.

He took two of them down with one slow sweep, but one got back up, and a dozen more appeared at the forest wall. The laser wasn't powerful enough to take out these cats quickly—it would take a concerted beam. Now the tigers were wary, but they quickly circled the clearing. Their ears were long and laid back, their jutting teeth curved like scimitars.

"Can anybody hear me?" Flex shouted to the trees. He repeated the call in the Heroes' Tongue.

The cats roared, and he fired at will, wheeling from his rocky roost. This cowed them only for a moment, then they moved closer, still circling. No solitary hunters, these. The green cats were methodical and organized. Perfect prey for the kzinti, who were ever thirsty for more challenging sport. Probably genetically created just for this purpose, Flex thought.

He fired more shots, taking out several tigers. He also took some random long shots in the direction he thought the kzinti were. "Come on, you ass-lickers!" he shouted at the kzinti. "You're missing some good *killzerkitz* hunting here!"

One of the tigers leaped at Flex. He took his best shot, hitting it square in the chest. At the same time, he whirled to find a second cat attacking from his rear. He had anticipated that, and took it down, too. But sooner or later, he would miss, or would be overwhelmed. Sooner, he knew. Even his fellow tumblers could not help him now, and they were doubtless continuing the mission elsewhere.

Angry, Flex fired randomly at the monsters, trying to break up their formation. They slunk back and forth—he had bought a few more seconds.

Then, words, unexpectedly screamed from the shadows. "Hold your fire, you stupid monkey!"

The tigers turned on the speaker, a large kzin hunter who screamed and leaped from the jungle onto the back of one of the green things. Flex expected a furious cat-on-cat fight, but the kzin had the beast in a choke hold with one powerful arm, anticipating its reaction. The startled tiger snapped in that direction, lunging its body around to try to throw the kzin off. The kzin hunter let the tiger toss his legs around, and he used that momentum to advantage with his free arm, clawing a deep gash in an arc across the tiger's throat.

Before the other tigers could react, he had torn open the furry neck of the tiger and thrown the bleeding carcass onto its back. At the same time, a dozen more kzinti screams, and as many dead tigers, and Flex, staring breathless at the slaughter around him.

But three kzinti stood prizeless at the jungle edge, glaring at Flex with eye slits as sharp as their claws. "You stole our prey from us," one snarled, kicking one of the cats Flex had shot.

Flex exhaled deeply, relieved that the tigers were all lifeless, and certain he could not escape or fight his way out of this jam. He shrugged and dropped his weapon, thinking hard of a ruse to save his skin, and Annie's.

"You're wasting your time toying with these pussies," he said, grinning carefully so as not to show his teeth provocatively. "I know something more challenging for you to hunt, and far more rewarding."

Flex stood in the den of Jarko-S'larbo, stripped of weapon, wristcomp and clothes. The three kzinti hunters whose game he had killed stood around him, constantly poking and clawing at him, gently by their standards, but with the successful intention of drawing a little blood.

The den looked vaguely like a hunting lodge, if only

because Flex knew that was its function. It was a long, tall hall with windows on the left, tall tiers of blue carpeted couches on the right, all empty. At the far end was a massive iron fireplace the size of a small lander, burning only a modest fire to one side. Most telling were the numerous trophies, huge toothy creatures stuffed in the most horrific poses. These formed two lines of the grand hall, standing fierce on pedestals carpeted with live grass, perhaps as an eternal insult. They were guardians of an old way of life, preserved by the modern kzinti as evidence of the deep instincts that had not been bred out of them despite centuries of attempts by other spacefaring species. The angry kzinti forcibly marched Flex through the gauntlet of taxonomic terrors to the great hearth where the puffy Jarko-S'larbo sat on a cushion, looking like nothing less than an overweight tabby cat curled in front of a fireplace. Next to him purred a *prret*, a female concubine. Not only was she sleeping, she was also loosely bound with red leather leashes, the purpose of which Flex did not want to know. To the left rose a wall of windows, dripping on the outside with condensation that distorted the view of the jungle playground.

"Jarko-S'larbo, I presume."

"Should I get up?" growled S'larbo, wuffling his tattooed ears.

What a fat, lazy puss, thought Flex. "Not on my account," he said, in the Heroes' Tongue.

With a hiss, and rapidity surprising for his size, Jarko-S'larbo bounded to his feet, baring his teeth in Flex's face. "In my den, you do not speak unless ordered to, *kshat*."

Flex put a hand over his mouth in deference, and

S'larbo stepped back, arching his back and curling his upper lip in minor victory. At his full height, S'larbo did not appear so fat and lazy. He had flattened his fur to show off his musculature, and he turned his back dismissively.

Wheeling back, he said, "I already know what you are doing here, and I am going to stuff you for it." S'larbo paced around Flex, whipping his hairless tail cruelly across the cuts already inflicted by the hunters. So much for the myth that the tails were useless vestiges. Flex knew better than to wince. Besides, he prided himself on his rhino hide, the extinct rhinoceros being his martial-arts totem. S'larbo inspected his trophy gallery, stopping at the smallest, least-imposing creature. "I think I'll put you here. A monkey isn't so threatening as this pitiful specimen, but if I pose you properly, perhaps with a bigger weapon than that piss squirter you came with . . ."

"Do you think hunting these overgrown fleas is compensation for fear of real predators?" Flex said, deciding it was time to risk speaking. He used the mocking tense of the Heroes' Tongue, to ruffle the fur.

One of the hunters knocked him to his knees, but S'larbo snarled a "Belay!"

"You know what I'm talking about," said Flex, not getting up. "The Puppeteers are essentially hunting you to extinction. However cowardly they are, and however unfair they fight, the end result is the same."

S'larbo licked his whiskers. "It is you humans who have hunted us for them. If they are puppeteers, then you are the puppets. And by the way, you have just confirmed that you have infiltrated this place to kill as many of our offspring as you can."

Just as well that S'larbo bought the cover story, thought Flex. He could negotiate on that basis. "That is only partly true," he said. "Some of us came for that purpose." He watched for reaction, unsure whether the kzin knew about his human companions. Using the most formal words in the Heroes' Tongue he knew, Flex said, "I myself have sworn not to kill any of your kittens on this mission."

"We killed the other monkeys," S'larbo said. "They landed in a secluded place nearby, while your decoy in space tried to fool us." He hissed and spat on Flex. "You stupid monkeys! You think we are so foolish as to fall for that trick? Your cunning ways have served you long enough, but we are onto them."

"You killed all three men?" Flex said, probing.

"There were four!"

Good, thought Flex. Not that he felt good about the others being killed and eaten, but at least they hadn't found Annie yet.

"So you see," S'larbo continued, "we have enough human meat to satisfy our customers' wildest dreams, leaving you for my gallery."

"You'll let me go."

S'larbo leaped into the air, turning full around and lashing Flex's face with his tail in the process. "Ouch," Flex said sarcastically.

"Why should I let you go?"

"Because I am not really part of this operation," he said. "I was planted with them for a different purpose. That's why I broke away from them before landing. In exchange for my life, I will give you whatever information you wish."

Jarko-S'larbo turned to stoke his fire, gazing into it

the way humans have done for centuries when lost in thought. Flex had S'larbo intrigued. Before the kzin came to some decision, he had to play another big card, to gain what advantage he could.

"There is one more human with me," he said. "She's injured, and I want you to help me find her and let us go. If you do that, I promise you will find what I have to tell you well worth it. Remember, we still have a big advantage orbiting your establishment."

"She?" S'larbo repeated, turning back to Flex, his interest piqued. Flex regretted the word instantly. "There was a female with you out in the park?" To the hunters, S'larbo said, "Go find her, before the sizzle-teeth do!"

And to Flex, "I have never tasted a human female before. She will make tonight's dining a one-in-a-million experience for the hunters. Then maybe it will be the humans that will become extinct, starting with her."

All three hunters pounced out to initiate a search, leaving Flex alone with S'larbo. Two guards paced at the back of the room, their hind claws clacking on the stone floor. Flex weighed his chances and concluded that he could not fight his way out of this one. His only hope of saving her lay with this whiskered slob.

"We're not done yet," Flex said. "Have you ever heard the saying, 'If you need information, you need a Jinxian'? Well, that's me. That's how I earn my kibbles and cream."

"My grandfather had a saying, too," S'larbo said. "'Monkey lie, monkey die.' Why it took so long for us to realize that you don't think honorably the way we do I don't know. But you can give up your feeble attempts to deceive me. I have already caught you in a lie about your numbers."

"What if I just show you then?" Flex said. "I cannot only prove I have information that will save you from the conspiracy we both know is out there, but I can do it without leaving your den. You have nothing to lose."

"I don't believe for a whisker that anything you are saying is true. What kind of boneless prick begs for its life with pure deceit?"

"If we wanted to kill you and your kittens, we could have done it with heavy weapons without trying to sneak in here. Think about that. Isn't it possible that we cooperate with the Puppeteers to learn more about them? Keep your enemies close, and all that?"

"The only information I need from you is the location of the Puppeteer home world." Jarko-S'larbo kept his eyes narrowed on Flex, but Flex could tell that he was mulling things over. He could have ripped Flex in half at any time. "On second thought, I would also have your title."

Names and titles were of utmost importance to kzinti, especially those who had particularly good ones. Jarko-S'larbo was a full Name, earned from a successful career as a rich businessman. S'larbo had made his fortune attracting other rich kzinti to his pleasure palace, replete with big-game hunting and, evidently, kinky kzinretti.

"I have no official title," Flex said, "because I represent no government or organization. All I can tell you about is my name."

"You are a mercenary then," the kzin concluded.

"My full name is Argumos Bothme, but growing up, people called me Arri. Now they call me Flex," he translated, "because of my fighting style."

"A warrior for hire then. Not the sort to go on a suicide mission." S'larbo growled over the thought.

This cat is smart, Flex thought. Fewer lies, always wise.

"What is the history of 'Bothme'?"

An odd question. The only reason Flex could imagine for the kzin's curiosity was that he wanted to know how to label the pedestal that would soon hold Flex's stuffed carcass.

"Bothme derives from the old English words 'both' and 'me.' My great-grandfather Argumos was an organ-legger, and he had an illegal clone of himself made, so he could harvest the organs when his failed. There's a black market for those on Jinx. For some reason the clone grew up as an independent citizen. I don't know why; maybe Argumos was caught. Anyway, the family split from two ancestors, which Argumos called 'both me,' to avoid legal battles over inheritance. To this day, none of his descendants knows which was from the original or the cloned line."

"So you are not even a bastard, but an artificial one!" S'larbo's hooded ears perked.

Flex shrugged. "Maybe. Or maybe I'm from the original line."

"To be uncertain is the greatest shame imaginable. But let's cut to the quick. If you monkeys have quick inside those pink beetles that pass for claws. Why are you here?"

"Right now, the only thing I care about is my mate, who is injured somewhere out in the jungle. She and I have a secret mission that even the mercenaries we came with didn't know. All they knew was that they were to help kidnap you. It was to be a surgical strike."

"Not to kill as many kzinti as possible?"

"I'll be honest with you. No one was concerned about collateral damage. It happens. But no, the clients that funded the mission only wanted you alive. There's something they need from you."

That was mostly true. Flex did not know the details, only that a Puppeteer named Hylo wanted information from S'larbo. He knew little about the peculiar two-headed creatures, and had only seen Hylo on image screens, and then only in silhouette. The information sought was about something called Zeno's Wormhole, whatever that was. How this pompous puss came upon such esoteric data was a mystery. But then, with so many ranking kzinti passing through his lair, it made sense that he might be involved in some far-flung enterprises.

"And you don't know why they wanted to capture me?"

"You're rich, aren't you? I can imagine any number of reasons."

S'larbo roared. The sleeping female stirred, but did not wake. She only purred louder. "Do you honestly think that paltry bit of disinformation would free you?"

"Of course not. But the Puppeteer home world might."

"Your ship has scampered away," S'larbo said, "though that could be a ruse, just like your transparent offer. You don't know where that home world is."

"Not yet, but there's a way to find out. It's dangerous, especially for you."

S'larbo bared his teeth and inhaled, but held his breath, ready to hiss. Good, thought Flex. He had to get through to this overgrown housecat somehow; time was running out for Annie.

"The Puppeteers targeted you for some reason," Flex said. "I have no idea why, but we were supposed to shanghai you and turn you over to them."

Jarko-S'larbo hissed, spattering Flex's face. The Jinxian wiped it off and continued. "Suppose you go along with that plan, sending a decoy in your place. Then you can track the decoy right back to the Puppeteers' home world. We've already got data to suggest where it is."

"Do you now," S'larbo said, still hissing. "Why don't you just give me that?"

Bait taken. "I can do that here and now. Get your best astrogator in here."

S'larbo eyed him suspiciously, but paced to a com console next to the fireplace. He pushed a button and muttered something Flex could not hear. At the same time, one of the hunters who had captured Flex returned to the gallery, and with a guard ready to cut Flex open with a beam rifle, S'larbo conferred in gruff whispers with the hunter. Then the hunter left, and the guard moved next to Flex. In a moment, another kzin entered, smaller than most. He wore a helmet on his head, not for protection in battle, but for virtual computing.

"I'd be a fool to allow you access to my network," S'larbo said. "But First Technician can check out your story. Can you do this securely, First Technician?"

"Certainly, sir. I am familiar with every cyber-trap the humans have conceived."

That's what you think, Flex mused. The time was ripe for him to fulfill his mission, and he was intent on doing it, whether he got out of this or not. "Start with the code for the Institute of Knowledge," Flex instructed the technician. "But do not commit the request."

"Done," said First Technician, as a series of connection indicators lit to life. Then, to Jarko-S'larbo, "No risk yet, sir. Everyone uses this portal, kzinti included."

"Now," said Flex, "cancel the last three digits of the code."

"Cancel them?"

"Yes. The system treats the cancel codes as additional entry codes. It doesn't actually erase the previous three."

First Technician looked impressed, and he exchanged glances with S'larbo.

"Now re-enter the last three digits, and commit. That will get you into the back door, and I'll give you my personal code. Of course, the code changes each time, so you'll need me..."

"Technician?"

"It may be as the human says, m'lord. It would not be a trivial conquest to penetrate the Institute of Knowledge at this level."

"But?"

"It could be a mousetrap."

Flex saw his opportunity waning, so he tongued his lower left molar and released a capsule that had been implanted there prior to the voyage. Then he stifled a sneeze.

Flex held a hand to his mouth. "Sorry," he said. "I must be allergic to your technician's fur. Some kzinti have that effect on me."

With Annie, they might still have a chance at their first plan, to catnap S'larbo. Without her, he would at least carry out his part of the mission. Flex sneezed, then covered his mouth politely.

"Monkey tricks!" said S'larbo. "Sever the connection."

First Technician turned a hard switch on his helmet, and the row of blinking indicators went dark.

S'larbo hissed. "My grandfather was right. Technician, dismiss! As for you, Argumos Bothme, I have decided to kill you only after you have been my guest for dinner. You see, my warriors have found your female, dead in her metal coffin. I want her on tonight's menu while she is still fresh. What kzin can say he's tasted a human female?"

He spat a command to someone outside the hall, and two kzinti guided a chrome-finished gravity sledge into the hall. Flex tensed as he saw Annie Venzi, still in her armor, atop the gurney. Her helmet had been removed and her eyes were closed. The sight evoked the memory of how he had fallen in love with her when they had wrestled over the last spacesuit during a decompression emergency, and his horror as she floated in vacuum, looking dead. Now her body was truly lifeless. Flex choked in horror, and felt the blood flee from his head.

"Doesn't she look positively succulent?" S'larbo said, gnashing his fangs in mockery.

Flex shivered. He chewed the inside of his mouth, and then let out a scream of anger. At the same time, a shrill klaxon blared, and everyone leaped in alarm. Jarko-S'larbo whirled around, and the guards ran out of the hall, raising their weapons.

Rifle beams fired outside the steaming windows, and Flex came to his senses. He ran to Annie, placing one hand on her head, and the other on her suited arm. Her skin was cold.

The sounds of a firefight echoed outside, and two of the tall windows shattered. Flex heard an engine whining. It was the extraction team from the *Catscratch Fever*. His message had gotten through.

Flex raked Annie's hair, then reluctantly cut loose. He threw Annie over his broad, naked shoulder, and hauled her to the shattered opening. Amidst gunfire and chaos, the kzinti were least worried about an unarmed monkey.

But S'larbo's slumbering kzinrett had awoken, and took notice. She took to all fours, and with an earsplitting shriek, she arched her back, sliced her leather bonds with painted claws, and pounced.

Flex bolted for the nearest shattered window and somersaulted through the opening. Something caught, and he fell hard, his face impacting on a stone walkway. Dazed, he swore and tried to figure out what had happened.

"Annie!" The female kzin had stripped her from his back. Flex tried to stand, but his vision was clouded. From his knees, he looked frantically for the help he knew was nearby.

His sneeze had worked, sending a shower of nanocomps into the technician's data port. The tiny components coalesced into a homing beacon, signaling good old Zel Kickovich and the *Catscratch Fever* to commence extraction. Eight armored men had swung in from a roaring lander, beams blazing. Flex was thrown bodily into a stealth shuttle, still calling for Annie. But there was no time. The shuttle rose above the palace.

"So it's only you," said the pilot grimly.

Flex huffed an affirmation. He'd lost his Annie.

"I'm sorry." The pilot ducked the shuttle under some ground fire.

"Just a sec," Flex said, grinding his teeth until he could feel the pain. "We haven't killed any kzinti yet."

"You planted the spybot?" said the pilot.

Flex nodded. "But the Puppeteers expect some collateral damage, to maintain the ruse. Do you know where the kits are?"

"Easy enough to figure out. I saw their jungle gym on the way in. The kittens are all over the place. Even under attack, the kzinti can't herd their own cats to safety. You want to scratch some of them?"

Annie's admonition burned in his mind. *Don't kill the kits.* He had promised he would not. But that was before. Another image seared his brain—that of the kzinti eating his beloved Annie.

"Drop a butt-breaker on them."

The pilot smiled. "Can't do it. That would make us unbalanced. I'm going to have to drop *two*." He pushed two release switches, and made for the sky.

Below, an enormous fireball grew to engulf half of the palace.

As they made orbit, joined by two other strike shuttles, the pilot pointed to a flashing yellow indicator. "I've been ignoring that," he told Flex. "A com request from the kzinti."

"This I gotta hear," said Flex, still grinding his teeth furiously.

The pilot opened the line, and the screaming voice of Jarko-S'larbo graced the shuttle mid-sentence. "...And I'll kill you and every shit-flicking monkey that has ever breathed your bastardized name..."

"He's a real sweetie," said the pilot.

Flex said nothing, but resumed grating his teeth until they began to crack.

◇   ◇   ◇

Most battles are cold and impersonal, especially for a data puller. You sit at your station reading data and instructions, pushing buttons and relaying information. Somewhere out there maybe a million klicks away is a faceless enemy, claws and jaws atrophying for lack of flesh on which to gnaw. You have to remind yourself who your enemy is and what they've done. That is most battles, for most people. This battle was personal, and Flex was a field agent as well as an ops researcher.

A hundred days passed, filled with thoughts of Annie. He had done everything in his power to save her, but could not. Her lifeless face haunted his soul, and thoughts of what the kzinti might have done to her sickened him physically. On top of all that his broken promise gnawed at his gut because it was the one thing that he had done willingly.

His supervisor sympathized, but eventually felt obliged to growl, "Get to work!"

As if on cue, Flex's nanos began to report in, giving his ingenuity something tangible to gnash at. Jarko-S'larbo obviously had designs on a more honorable station than that as a tour guide. If Flex could rob him of his wormhole prize, Annie would rest easier.

The nanobots hidden in Flex's tooth were much more than homing signals. They were the latest tool in the kit of the professional information spy, of which Flex was the best. His sneeze had deployed millions of microscopic vectors, electronic germs whose first task was to unite in as many numbers as possible inside the target device—the kzinti technician's data helmet in this case. Once the nanobots organized themselves into functional units, they deployed their malicious programs. Sending the homing signal was simple, but incidental. Their primary function took fifty standard days to bear fruit.

On Jinx, Flex returned home to downtown Sirius Mater where he had access to equipment best suited for receiving the precious fragments of intelligence. The Puppeteers were waiting patiently for his report, but Flex was no longer motivated by their money or promises to increase his longevity. Nor was he consumed by the fire of revenge. What was working its way under his skin and into his bones was his broken promise to Annie. Her most strenuous desire was to complete the mission and collect the intelligence without resorting to feline infanticide. A fault of hers, perhaps, but he had sworn to her. Worst of all, his breach of her trust cast a dark shadow over her death.

He did not know how to make it up to her, other than to proceed as originally planned and make good with the Puppeteers. Perhaps in the process, he would find some way to redeem himself. If not, a real suicide attack might be a very good idea, kits be damned.

When the nanobots began feeding stolen data to Flex's collection system, co-opted from forgotten coldputer cycles, he did not immediately inform the Puppeteers. Better to figure out just what this wormhole thing was all about first, so he would know the full value of his efforts.

In fact, there wasn't much data to be had, but the information the cat Jarko-S'larbo had dragged in was very specific. There was reference to something that translated to a "non-transversable wormhole," which he managed to correlate with something called Zeno's Wormhole in some esoteric mathematical literature.

The intelligence implied that such an object had been found, and its location was given. The importance of this object was not known, but the information had cost the lives of at least one entire expedition.

With that as his basis, Flex commenced his private research in two directions. First, he learned all he could about the theoretical Zeno's Wormhole. He did not understand much of the detail, but he compiled it for future use. A non-transversable wormhole was a natural vortex that could form in space connecting two places with a shortcut through hyperspace. Possibly the offspring of an interaction between two black holes passing in the night, the wormhole could remain stable long after its parents had moved on. What made a Zeno unique was that it didn't lead anywhere—the far end was pinched off. If one entered the wormhole opening, one would eventually hit a dead end. The literature was unclear whether one could exit from such an object, and Flex guessed that this may have been the little snag faced by previous expeditions. In any case, it was clear why the Puppeteers were interested in Zeno's Wormhole. It would be a groundbreaking scientific discovery, if nothing else. Still, Flex couldn't shake the suspicion that there was more to it than just that.

His second line of inquiry was concerned with Jarko-S'larbo. He surmised that the wealthy kzin had bought the information from someone who did not have the means to mount another expedition, and that S'larbo intended to do so himself. The sweetest revenge would be to rob the kzin at the moment of his finest glory. Flex set about orchestrating his own trip to the wormhole.

With access to all public information in known space, and great skill at piecing together seemingly unrelated data from the great rumor mill in the sky, it was not difficult for Flex to outline S'larbo's plan. What ships come and go at Meerowsk? Where had they come from, and where did they go next? Who had been talking with whom? What statistical anomalies were there in com logs that might lead to S'larbo's co-conspirators?

The art of intelligence is to assemble bits of information, make deductions, draw a coherent big picture. At best one might *plant* information designed to reach a desired outcome. As such an artist, Flex Bothme fancied himself as a pointillist, seeing a broad pattern emerge from the bits. Ultimately, this painting would have his signature on it.

The light was wan, most of it coming from the lights of two landers. Overhead, the bright arm of the Milky Way was cold and remote.

Flex stood next to the spacesuited Jarko-S'larbo, on the dead moon of a gas giant circling a spent sun beyond 18 Scorpii that was gasping its last breaths of exhausted hydrogen. He had timed his arrival just ahead of the kzin. To his surprise, S'larbo had landed alone, presumably to claim his prize for himself. Perhaps not so surprising after all. Flex had a beam rifle leveled on the cat, who *was* surprised, though he did not yet recognize his human adversary. Spacesuits and vacuums work wonders to mask odors. It was too late for the cat to call for reinforcements and preserve his honor.

The dead moon was larger than Earth, orbiting in a leaden march as if looking for a more pleasant site to be buried. It was a wonder anyone found it. Flex suspected that the Outsiders had tipped someone off, but since the information had been bought and sold several times already, it was impossible to determine.

At nearly twice the gravity of Earth—a bit more than Jinx—Flex felt quite at home. The burden on the kzin helped even up the odds, should there be a fight. Then again, S'larbo's gloves were tipped with metal claws twice the size of his natural ones. Overhead, *Catscratch Fever* and the kzin ship, *Sizthz Chitz*, circled in wary orbits. Zel Kickovich had reconfigured the *Fever* so as not to be recognized from the cat-and-mouse game back at Meerowsk. It got no trouble from the kzinti ratliner—so called because of the fresh game allowed to scurry the dim corridors as food and sport.

Zeno's Wormhole? Flex stood at the mouth of an artifact, a cylindrical tube of something like a General Products hull, but showing signs of scarring from what must have been hundreds of millions of years of exposure to the cruel elements of space. The tube was sixty-four meters long, according to data collected shipside (and downloaded into Flex's in-helmet knowledge well) and just under ten meters in diameter. It floated above a gravity polarizer that had been set up below it by the unnamed party that had vanished from record.

The only other features on the airless surface were piles of rocky rubble that outlined what were once walls. The moon had never had an atmosphere; it was likely that the natural regolith had once protected an underground compound. No doubt the ruins would be worth digging up, but for now, the prize hovered half a meter above the contemporary lift system.

Even with two lights blazing into the tube, Flex

couldn't see a thing inside. "After you," he said to Jarko-S'larbo through his com unit.

"I don't trust Jinxians," S'larbo said, and Flex didn't blame him. "For example, those protrusions on your helmet look like weapons. Then again, since you are a coward, they are probably antennae, linking you to your precious Institute of Knowledge."

He was referring to the horns. Flex had a horn affixed to his helmet's forehead, and a smaller one just above it. The horns represented the weapons of Flex's self-adopted totem, the rhinoceros. They also contained not a link to Jinx, but a complete data set from the Institute, bootlegged, of course. S'larbo was more right than he knew.

"Bad guess," said Flex. "Are we going in there, or not?"

"After you," said the ratcat-in-a-can.

Maybe not such a bad idea, thought Flex, depending on what was inside. If the earlier expedition lay dead in there, the disarmed S'larbo might find a weapon. On the other hand, he would be foolish to go in alone.

"We go together."

They climbed a portable stair that had been erected at the left end of the metal cylinder. One long stride from there, and they were inside the cylinder. Its surface was a charcoal gray, so that helmet lights revealed no internal detail. Flex expected to at least see the star glow at the far opening, but it was blackness.

They continued ahead, walking cautiously down the inner length of the alien artifact. It seemed safe enough, and there was no trace of the prior expedition. They reached the far end, at which point they could see outside. The nearby midden heaps had blocked most of the light from that side.

"It's inert," S'larbo said. "There's no stasis box here!"

Stasis box? Now that's a rather important bit of information to have missed, Flex thought. "Maybe someone beat you to it."

"You!" shouted S'larbo.

Flex was about to deny that when the great cat made his move. Kzinti were notorious for announcing their attacks with a scream, but evidently this fellow had enough sense to attack first, and scream later. He went for Flex's rifle, but only succeeded in knocking it to the curved floor. Fighting in a spacesuit usually had less than satisfactory results.

Flex scrambled for the weapon, and once the kzin realized he would get it, the cat bounded away down the corridor. By the time Flex raised the rifle, S'larbo was nearly out of the artifact. He would undoubtedly return, with a weapon from his lander. Unable to catch him, Flex opted to stay put, saving his strength. In this gravity, the kzin would tire out quickly. Besides, by staying at the far end of the corridor, Flex could fire, while maintaining an escape route at his back.

He kept an eye on that opening, in case S'larbo tried to sneak in that way, but there were no stairs to allow an easy approach.

After a while, Flex heard a blip from his warning system. His sensor had detected the priming of a beam rifle. Flex could see S'larbo silhouetted at the far opening of the tunnel. He cut off his lights and stepped up the curving wall to his right, to get out of the line of fire. He left his data display up, but covered the lower part of his visor with an arm, to block the light.

"What's wrong, you hairless coward?" S'larbo was gloating.

"Is that the honor of the kzinti, to hunt with over-whelming force? I thought you hunted with bare claws."

"Your gibbering spews like bandersnatch dung. Too long have my people faltered at the lies of you bony worms."

Flex could not keep his position so high up the wall, and slid down. As he sought better footing, two strange things happened. First, he felt the entire cylinder roll slightly under his foot. While the cylinder hung stable over the ground, it was free to rotate on its long axis without friction. And Flex's weight was enough to set it in motion. Second, as it moved, some hidden mechanism must have awoken, because a dull amber light emanated from an area at the center of the structure.

Jarko-S'larbo grunted with surprise, not knowing that Flex had triggered the device. Flex stepped higher up the rounded wall, and the tube cooperated, rolling down under his weight.

Time to shake things up a bit, Flex thought.

S'larbo fired two bolts down the center of the tube, missing Flex, who continued to climb up the wall. He heard the kzin grunt again, and guessed that the ratcat had momentarily lost his balance.

"Is it true," said Flex, stopping the roll and reversing it as hard as he could, "that cats always land on their feet?"

"Grrraaarr!"

Flex again turned around and treaded hard up the opposite wall. Once the tube got going, he stopped it, and ran the other way. More bad shots from S'larbo, but they were getting better. Sooner or later, one would connect, and that would be it. Not content to die at the hands of this furball, Flex pounded full-bore up one wall, to get the cylinder spinning as fast as he could. It was more fun getting the kzin dizzy, storming him and fighting hand-and-claw. He wanted to beat the shit out of that bastard before boring a hole in him.

The cylinder rolled at a good clip, so that if Flex stopped too long, his feet would be swept out from under him. Not a problem; at a mere meter and a half, he'd have a better time of it than a knock-kneed feline twice his height.

"Let's go even faster!" he said.

"You're doing this?" S'larbo hissed, unable to suppress his astonishment.

Flex worked his way to the center, but slowly, because he wanted to reverse the direction at unpredictable intervals. An image from history formed in his mind: that of two men rolling on a floating log, until one fell into the water. No doubt a competition from the Olympic games of ancient Greece.

Meanwhile, the light at the center of the tunnel was growing, and Flex feared that the keen eyes of the kzin would have no trouble seeing him now. Yet, in the growing light, an object seemed to descend from the ceiling, blocking most of the tunnel at its center. It made no sense, since the "ceiling" was constantly rolling around. When the object—or group of objects, as they now appeared to be—reached the "ground," the light shot back upward. The beam seemed to reach through the cylinder, forming a shaft of light reaching up at a right angle to the tunnel, extending beyond it, where there was once a curved ceiling. The new shaft appeared to be another cylinder like the first, but Flex could see only a little way up into it.

The objects under the new tunnel were bathed in the amber light. They were solid rectangles of differing sizes, open on their tops. Where the two tunnels joined above, a series of armatures hung, perhaps waiting to re-hoist the empty boxes, or to bring new ones.

"Hey, Slobbo!" Flex said, to see if the kzin saw what he was seeing. No answer. He tried again, but the changes to the cylinder seemed to have cut off their communication.

Flex stopped revving up the cylinder, letting it coast. He had to keep walking up one side, or side-stepping to avoid falling down. He turned his lights back on and did a quick query of his knowledge well. Nothing was forthcoming until he correlated "Zeno's Wormhole" with "stasis box." This produced an obscure monogram with the intriguing title: "The Spontaneous Generation of a Quasi-Quantized Stasis Field inside a Rotating, Non-Traversable Wormhole: A Proposal on How the Slaver Stasis Boxes Might Have Been Manufactured." It was not a quick read.

Wisely, Flex had been studying related material, and as a professional collector and collator of information, he got the gist of it while skimming his display and side-stepping at the same time.

Finagling mist demons, he thought. This artifact is a factory for stasis boxes, and I've turned the damn thing on!

While he was coming to grips with that, he was slow to notice something else. His lower legs tingled, from the feet up past his knees, and he found difficulty in walking toward the intersecting tunnel. He took a step with his right leg, to make sure he wasn't imagining things. He wasn't. There was an unmistakable increase in resistance as he progressed toward this small wormhole's pinch point.

Flex scanned some basic material on "the dichotomy paradox," whereby ancient Earth mathematicians such as Zeno noted that for an object to move from point A to point B, it first had to reach the midpoint between the two. But to reach that midpoint, the object first had to reach the quarter point, and so on. The paradox was that if one had to overtake an infinite number of intermediate points, one could never reach the destination. The mystery took thousands of years for mankind to unravel, by the invention of calculus.

One speculation about non-traversable wormholes that caught Flex's attention concerned time traps. One theory supposed that because space was squashed inside, time literally slowed as one progressed inward, until it stopped completely at the pit of the wormhole. So, he concluded, this was how the Slavers built and stocked the variety of stasis boxes found scattered throughout known space. This could be the most important technological advance since the conquest of hyperspace.

Thank you, Institute of Knowledge, he thought.

The wormhole was only about ten meters in diameter, so there was a distracting sort of Coriolis effect—a differing temporal disparity between his head and feet. It was manageable but caused the tingling in his legs. He felt bloated, and his heart raced to pump blood to feet that plodded through congealing time.

Flex heightened his awareness of things unseen ahead, but doubted the kzin could make it to the stasis boxes, much less past them. The cylinder was open on both ends, and its contents symmetrical, so it was logical to assume that a mirror wormhole stretched out in the opposite direction.

Flex stumbled as he turned back to face the center, and he realized that the spin of the tunnel had slowed. The kzin! He was running himself, trying to de-spin the thing. As the cylinder slowed, Flex helped it, blindly running the same way around as his opponent. The rolling slowed, then picked up rapidly in the other direction.

The phantom tunnel above widened, and then another one opened up at an odd angle to it. Tempted, Flex ran as hard as he could, spinning the cylinder to a breakneck pace, clockwise. As if on cue, three more lighted tunnels opened up, each at an equal angle of separation from the others, forming five spokes of a wheel around the axle spun by Flex and S'larbo.

"Tabam!" said Flex to himself. *This isn't just a Zeno's Wormhole, or even two or three. It's a roulette of wormholes meeting at the hub, feeding into the machine.* But feeding from where? He wanted to get nearer to the center to be able to peer into one of the adjoining tunnels—he'd be the first to see into them in over a billion years—unless the expedition that had discovered the artifact had already been sucked into eternity.

He pressed on, feeling a thickening of space with each latent step. His left foot kept straying outward, and his right would tend to trip into the left, so he crouched to lower his center of mass and lessen the Coriolis effect.

The next step was a toughie. To his eyes, the tunnel ahead appeared level, but his muscles told him that the floor sloped up like a summitless mountain. *Just a few more arduous steps for mankind,* he thought, *and I should be able to get a look into the other tunnels.* Then retreat.

Another step, as through thick mud, then another, through hardening cement. "You're a Jinxian," he told himself, "the strongest race in known space, by weight. Now move your Finagling feet."

Aside from the difficulty in walking, Flex could only assume that the nearer he was to the stasis boxes, the slower time must be moving for him, relative to home. It was a sobering thought, but he recalled an old Jinxian adage: Only a fool wastes time worrying about time. Wisdom for a race of short lifespan, his father once said.

When he was a swindler's dozen paces from the center, he craned his neck to look up into one of the other spokes in the roulette. As it rolled away and out of sight, he thought he saw inside a huge vehicle of some kind, so huge that it should not have been able to fit inside. It was a transport laden with dozens of terra-movers with mounted guns. Or so it appeared to Flex. Whatever it was, it looked like it was meant to build entire worlds—or destroy them. He could analyze the fleeting image later because his helmet imager was recording.

He gazed into the next wormhole as it wheeled into view to his right. Inside was a star field, and against that, what looked like a fleet of ships in an attack formation. The ships matched the configuration of those he had seen in a research project many years back: Slaver battleships. How a fleet of ships could fit in a tunnel not much larger than a personal yacht he did not know. Perhaps the wormhole could compress space as well as time. The fleet may have fallen into a larger wormhole that pinched into the roulette an eon ago.

Flex kept his feet apace with the rolling floor, and tried to peer into another tunnel. To do that, he had to step aside to see past a trio of the largest stasis boxes that were large enough to hold a groundcar. He ran opposite the tunnel's rotation, slowing it into darkness, and then picking up speed counter-clockwise. The light from the other spokes returned, only this time their contents were different.

In the tunnel directly above, the mechanical armatures began to move, and Flex watched in horror as a huge spindly gray creature—or robot—darted through the lowering arms like a bizarre monkey in high steely branches. The leggy creature grabbed two of the crane arms and beat them together until they came untangled. Immediately, the crane separated into two parts, each a cage of curved girders. No longer binding together, the cages lowered until they were just above the tumbling metal boxes ahead. Arms protruding from the cages unfolded to corral the boxes, holding each in the vacuum above the turning floor. What the crane was attached to up in the vertical tunnel was a mystery; it could not be affixed to the inner surface of a rotating cylinder.

I'll be damned, Flex thought. The robot just repaired this whole thing.

He realized that not only had the wormhole been harnessed into a stasis factory, but that he had the opportunity of a lifetime—if he didn't end up frozen in the jaws of time. No, it was Jarko-S'larbo who would be caught!

Humans hold a great part of their reflexes in the spinal cord, so that a hand may be pulled from fire without even thinking about it. On the other hand, humans also have instincts to freeze and to flee. Kzinti had a larger part of their reflexes in the spine, hence the "scream and leap" before thinking. Sometimes freezing or fleeing was better than charging. This evolutionary difference was to determine what happened next. With all the technology, knowledge, wisdom and experience, what matters most at times is a construction of nature that was intended for primordial worlds, not rotating wormholes.

Flex calculated what might make Jarko-S'larbo leap, and decided it was time to reveal himself. He backpedaled, gradually slowing the tunnel's rotation until the roulette faded into darkness.

"Ratcat!" he said.

"I see where you are now, Jinxian. You're dead!"

"Don't you want my name and title first, so you can claim bragging rights? I'm Flex Bothme, the guy who dropped the bomb on your kits!"

"*Skalazaal!*" bellowed Jarko-S'larbo in a cry meant to freeze prey. "Flex Bothme?"

Flex ran hard, pounding up the wall to set things spinning again. His feet hurt like hell, worse than the frostbite at Brain Freeze, but he ran even harder, conjuring up the roulette, and the mechanical arms overhead.

He only heard the kzin shout, "—you shitflick—" as the cat leaped toward him, and froze in mid-air, amidst the repaired machinery.

When the icy-eyed monkey thing went into action, Flex needed no other warning. He made the most of that human flight reflex, taking the path of decreasing resistance.

As he reached the mouth of the tunnel, he realized he might be able to turn off the machinery, so he jogged the cylinder down to a halt. The roulette spun away into unseen dimensions and the lights went out. Cautiously making his way back to the center, Flex beamed his light around. There was no sign of the Slaver fleet, the monster monkey, nor of Jarko-S'larbo.

Unless you count the neatly packaged, kzin-sized stasis box that lay sealed on the floor.

"Well happy birthday to me," said Flex.

Zel Kickovich folded his arms and looked Flex hard in the eyes. "What took you so damn long?" he said. "We nearly got fried by the *Sizthz Chitz*."

"You try lugging a metal box the size of a groundcar through a tunnel, down eight stairs, across a pile of rubble and into a cargo hold," Flex retorted. "With a kzin in it. Then try evading the *Lisp Kzinship*—"

"*Sizthz Chitz*."

"—however you pronounce it, in a lander with half the power of a wristcomp. Oh, and did I mention nearly getting stuck in a time trap? How long is it supposed to take to get out of one of those, by the book?"

Zel beamed and clapped Flex on the back. "I love it when you get mad."

That drew a wan smile from Flex.

Now that *Catscratch Fever* had reached hyperdrive, Flex was able to contact the Puppeteer Hylo by hyperwave.

"Mission accomplished," he said dryly. "I found a stasis box, but I'm keeping it."

Both Hylo's sock puppet heads bobbed up and down in silhouette, but did not make a sound.

"Don't get your necks in a knot," Flex said. "I've got something even better for you."

"It would not go well with you to renege on our bargain," said Hylo, composing herself. (At least Flex assumed Hylo was a female, based on the shimmering pitch of her alluring voice. If Hylo was male, Flex felt just a little bit dirty.)

"Trust me, when I tell you what I found, you're not going to want the stasis box anymore." Puppeteers were cowards, after all, and used humans to deal with dangerous species. For Finagle's sake, Hylo would probably be afraid of its own silhouette.

He told Hylo about the stasis assembly line, and Zeno's Roulette. "Not only can you make your own stasis boxes, there are ageless places to explore, if you can figure out how to get through. It's impossible to place a value on that."

After a pantomime of what looked like two weak-knuckled hand shadows consulting one another, Hylo could only agree. "What's in the stasis box?" she asked.

"One very angry cat I call Schrödinger, because I haven't made up my mind whether he lives or dies."

Hylo appreciated that. "You know what I would do," she said. "In any event, you may have the stasis box."

"I'll send you the data you need, and destroy all copies."

"Then this is our last verbal communication. We have no more use for you."

"Why not?" said Flex, not so much caring as curious.

"We no longer have enough stars to compensate you. Our budget is exceeded. Money aside, we find you to be motivated by sex and revenge. Both are now spent tools."

Both unlikely, sex and revenge, Flex considered. But both me. Bothme. Jinxian puns were rancid enough without being one's actual name. He harrumphed. Sex and revenge, love and money, whatever you called them, that was not him, not anymore. He had his revenge, but Annie was still gone. Maybe she could at least rest in peace now.

"Good-bye," Flex said, thinking more like "good riddance."

"I wish you well," said Hylo. "What will you do, now that you have a tiger by the tail, and a pocketful of stars?"

Flex thought that over. A pocketful of stars. "Tabam," he said.

BOUND FOR THE
PROMISED LAND

◆   ◆   ◆

Alex Hernandez

Bobcat swaggered through the seedy Orange District of Canyon like a bloody victorious warrior. If his tail hadn't been blown off in that Fanged God's anus of a planet, Wunderland, it'd be swishing around proudly. This current intelligence-gathering campaign had yielded very little data of military value. Two domesticated kzintoshi had been appointed to the City Council as representatives of the burgeoning kzin population. Of slightly more interest, those two kzinti had suggested they open up the site of the stasis-enshrined Heroes buried beneath set magma, to tourism. Bobcat's ears quivered and his stumpy tail darted around cheerfully as he imagined the Patriarchy attempting to free these savage warriors while on a guided tour of the lava fields, but he knew that was a bit farfetched.

More disturbingly, he had sensed another telepath, a human ARM Agent, poking around the fringes of his mind. They had chased each other through the white caves of thought, a monkey holding onto a tiger's tail. The tiger was caught, but if the monkey let go, the tiger would snap it up. Little did the agent know that this particular tiger had no tail! Bobcat locked down and moved away. He hadn't sensed her presence in quite a while.

Now he simply enjoyed the brisk walk. Despite the pointlessness of this specific mission, he loved Canyon. Something about this hostile planet, with its cratered and scarred auburn surface, spoke to him on a cellular level. Old, desolate Warhead had found a new life, as if the monumental disintegrator wound had become infected with glittering architectural encrustations, creating a strange human-kzin amalgam society. Sometimes in the still void between stars, he toyed with the dream of someday retiring to Canyon. That was not likely. He understood that he would be worked until his synapses sizzled and nothing remained but a drooling *kshat*. He only regretted that every time he visited this world he so admired, he betrayed it. Telepaths were by nature poetic; they relied too much on imagery and metaphor to process the intangible world of the mind, so the irony was not altogether lost on Bobcat.

He pushed the thought out of his head and continued to walk through the bright lights and salty smells of the old seaside district that predated the vertical urban sprawl. As *Devourer of Monkeys*' Telepath, he was permitted a modicum of liberty, he had been Yearrl-Captain's faithful servant since before the captain had a partial Name and his covert missions on other human-kzin worlds had made Yearrl rich and admired throughout the Patriarchy. There was a saying aboard the *Devourer*: when Yearrl bathes in blood, we all get splattered; and, in truth, as kzintoshi went, Yearrl-Captain was what humans would call a decent fellow. His Captain obliged him a few hours of leave after the operation, so Bobcat held his scruffy chin high, as if admiring the lavish balconies and clinging structures rising up the sheer cliff walls, and let the thoughts of the tall, spindly Canyonites wash over him in tune to the sound of the sea's lazy surf. Where the true warriors on his ship saw an old, mangy half-kzintosh, humans saw a leaner, meaner version of their nightmares. His long-battered ego always appreciated these jaunts.

Bobcat stopped at an old kzin building made up in garish detail to look like an ancient human sanctuary. The flashing sign above the entrance read TEMPLE OF SEKHMET in Interworld. Inside, the walls were covered with vertical lines of primitive pictorial script and vulgar murals of stiff, angular humans prostrating themselves before a kzinrett with the hairless body of a human female. Bobcat assumed the artist had never laid eyes on a true kzinrett as this representation had round, furry ears.

The smell of sex hung in the air like mist and young, nameless warriors lurked about the lobby avoiding eye contact with each other. His ears twitched as he met Iggy Larsson, the large, barrel-shaped human in charge of this outfit. If you considered your average human to be a monkey, Larsson was a silverback gorilla.

"Bobcat!" The human flashed him a lascivious smile full of blunt, plant-crunching teeth, "We got some new merchandise brought over from Kzin itself!"

"Foliage must quake in terror at the sight of those incisors," Bobcat snarled acidly.

Larsson slapped his back in a rude show of famil-iarity and the kzin's ears fell flat on his head, then rose slowly with well-practiced restrained ire. He clamped down his mind, not wanting to sully it with what passed for Larsson's thoughts. "Before you do your thing, I need to show you something I think Yearrl-Captain would be very interested in."

A slow clicking noise in Bobcat's throat began to announce his growing frustration, but he allowed the corpulent human to lead him into a small room housing a single orange female and a small, utterly black kit still suckling. All the frayed fur on Bobcat's wiry frame flattened in horror. "I thought you euthanized all kittens born here?"

"Oh, we do, except for a few females to replenish our stock, but something is different about this dusky little runt. At first, I thought it was the shock of his color. I've never seen a melanistic kzin before, but I just can't bring myself to put it down. I wanted to know if it's got some telepathic juju mucking with my brain. That's where you come in."

Larsson harshly grabbed the measly kitten by the scruff of his neck and lifted him up for the kzin's inspection. The dull female made no attempt to rip the human's arm off, so Bobcat guessed she was sedated. The telepath grudgingly loosened his mental grip and permitted a swift sweep of the kit. A low-grade telepathic cry emanated from this tiny nugget of neutron star, repeating the same reflexive message like an emergency distress beacon: protect me. Care for me. *Love* me.

Bobcat tore himself away and walked out of the cramped, suffocating room, "Yes, he's got telepathic potential."

"I knew it!" Larsson absently tossed the kitten back at his mother.

Bobcat's nostrils flared and the long-denied scent of estrous pheromones entered his body, grounding him in the material world. He tried to control his arousal in front of the leering human. "I'm going to do now what I came here to do!" he roared as his mind went blank.

The old telepath bounded like a fresh kitten down the hall and into a gaudy room unsuccessfully made up to look like a palatial harem chamber. He pounced on the three females anxiously pacing the room. Something buried deep in the back of his mind understood that these little freedoms allowed him by Yearrl-Captain were as much a part of his imprisonment as his addiction to the *sthondat* drug. At the moment, though, he didn't care.

Hours of painful clawing and biting ensued, but he savagely took each of the kzinretti like a hot-blooded warrior conquers planets. No, whole systems!

When the females were all soundly vanquished, Bobcat lay on the large fur-covered waterbed surrounded by the sweaty bodies of the females. The bed gently rocked back and forth with the rhythm of their panting. He thought lazily of the kitten and its primal, drilling petition. He imagined the kit all grown up: a drug-sick wraith aboard some ship, pitch black as a tear in the hull. The crew would not be able to ignore him as they do the rest of us. Their hatred would be sharper. *I should kill him now,* he thought. *First Telepath should have killed me in the crèche instead of training me.* The tight hold on his mind slowly melted away with the drowsy warmth of the kzinretti and the swirling *sthondat* drug still in his system. He brushed against three distinctly female, quietly desperate minds filled with thoughts he found all too familiar.

Bobcat leapt out of bed, ears erect, small nub of a tail thrashing, and he glared at the complex females like a trapped animal. "You're sentient?" he whispered in the Heroes' Tongue.

No answer. They only clustered around themselves for protection. Cautiously, he walked over to the small case buried in the clothes he had carelessly strewn about the room, took out a syringe and pushed the intimate needle into the crook of his arm. The hit was instantaneous. Tentatively, he scanned their thoughts again and noticed they were thinking neither in the Heroes' Tongue nor in the limited females' tongue. They spoke a sort of primitive cousin of the Heroes' Tongue. A more precise scan revealed that they were taken from a remote, underdeveloped region of Kzinhome. He felt their longing for a dense blond jungle nestled between majestic mountains. The priesthood that cultivated meekness in females had never tampered with their bloodline.

After decades of mastering the humans' monotonous grunts, he easily learned the rich and rumbling tongue clearly birthed by a kzin larynx, "Can you understand me?" he asked. He knew metaphysically that they could, but he still *disbelieved* it.

Fear and hope flared in them like a triple star system cascading into a supernova. The psychic blast charred his soul into a black silhouette. He desperately tried to shield himself from the torrent of their minds. Most telepaths are weakened by their rampant empathy, but Bobcat had learned early on to shut his mind like a clenched jaw. It was a trick that allowed him to do some of the more hands-on jobs of his career as *Devourer*'s Telepath, but now he was paying it back with interest. He profoundly understood their oppression; after all, was he not a despised slave himself?

After a short time one of them, the gorgeous golden one, Raxa, unaccustomed to speaking out loud, hissed, "Yes."

"Will you help us?" another female, with blue crystalline eyes, Xast, growled pleadingly, and for the first time in his long and miserable life, Bobcat saw himself as they saw him, not as cripple or a man-eater, but as a Hero.

His knees buckled and he collapsed onto all fours. "I will," he spat and braced himself for another annihilating wave of hope.

Bobcat fled the emotional singularity created by the psychic kitten and cogent females. Larsson yelled out to him, "I took the liberty of calling Yearrl-Captain and he wants that kitten, said he'll transfer payment when it's on his ship."

Bobcat hurried down the street. His mind whirled. He needed to ground himself, sink his teeth into something warm and bloody, something solid. He noticed another old kzinti building, dots and commas above the doorway read SERENGETI: AUTHENTIC EARTH GAME. Hunger welled up as the effects of his last shot of *sthondat* extract slowly drained from his system. He would never be allowed in the public hunting park, so he ducked inside the eatery.

The place was deserted except for two local kzintoshi hunched over the gleaming red carcass of an animal no longer recognizable. Bobcat entered a feeding stall and punched up something called a zebra.

Escape was the only option. Take the kitten and the sentient kzinretti and go. There was only one place in all the universe a tattered old telepath with his stolen harem could go. He had grown up with the legends. He needed help of course. Bobcat used the ebbing traces of his telepathic power and unlocked all the remaining blocks and compartments he had so meticulously put up around his mind. It was easy after the onslaught at the Temple of Sekhmet.

He instantly caught an image of the ARM Agent who had been tracking him, a dark young woman, though of course, youth could be deceptive with these humans. She wore the blue uniform of Canyon police, but her true employers were the UN back in the Sol system. Her hair and eyes were black streaked with violet, a cosmetic allusion to her flatlander past. She was all muscle, with enough body fat to make her absolutely delicious. He sent her an image of Serengeti and asked her to join him for dinner. Then, he sat and meditated on his predicament.

Varsha Khan entered the restaurant and the metallic tang of blood and wet extraterrestrial fur hit her like a slap. She breathed through her mouth and surveyed the room. A smaller kzintosh with russet, black-spotted fur and large erect ears like the junk sails on ancient Chinese boats waved her over. Varsha approached cautiously. He had ruffs of longer hair on his cheeks ending in two points on either side of his chin. She also noticed he was more ragged than most kzintoshi, like a shabby old alley cat.

"You opened up on purpose. Is this some kind of trap?"

"Not at all, Agent Khan. We're both talented telepaths

and I'm pressed for time. Allow me to get right to the point. Right here on Canyon, sentient kzinretti are being held as sex slaves."

"That's absurd," but as she spoke, a faint, guarded mental transmission passed from Bobcat to Varsha and she knew it was true.

A young man with a gaunt face and sunken eyes led a small striped horse into the stall and quickly left. "Ah, so this is a zebra," Bobcat licked his muzzle with a broad pink tongue and proceeded to chaw down on its neck with bone-crushing force. The pitiful animal *hee-hawed* in terrible pain. Varsha dodged kicking hoofs, then the beast went still.

She suppressed a sudden surge of terror and revulsion and said, "I don't think that's an actual zebra, probably a genetically modified donkey."

Bobcat didn't look up as he lacerated a large chunk of dripping scarlet meat and threw it back whole.

"How do you know about this?" she continued.

"I partake of their services." His face was all sticky and red.

Despite her businesslike demeanor, she arched a curious eyebrow, "I thought telepaths weren't allowed to breed?"

"No, not breed, but my captain allows me to *ch'rowl* until my heart's content."

"And what, some of you macho kzintoshi have a fetish for exotic sapient females? Not in proper harems, of course, but you can *ch'rowl* them in brothels, huh?"

"I don't believe those responsible know they are sentient. The kzinretti are quite scared and reluctant to talk, and even if they did, they don't speak the Heroes' Tongue or Interworld." He rent another heavy mass of equine muscle, and Varsha's skin crawled at the sound of striped flesh ripping.

"Wait. I caught that thought! You want me to believe that this is a human operation?"

"It is. Humans are an enterprising ape. They've learned to take advantage of this odd situation of coexistence with kzinti, and a sort of cottage industry has sprung up, catering to our gruesome needs." He pointed to the drain at the center of the stall's tiled floor as if that explained everything. "As a matter of fact, Serengeti is also a human establishment. Who else would come up with the idea of a restaurant that brings you a live animal, allows you to ravage it, hoses you down, and then is ready to serve the next famished kzin in less than an hour?"

"That's barbaric."

Bobcat caught the waves of nausea and denial rippling through the agent, and he decided that her smooth and supple youth wasn't a product of boosterspice. His ears twitched like the pectoral fins of a Fafnir flying fish.

"You think kzinti are the only barbarians in known space? Do not fool yourself, Agent Khan. We've had four glorious wars and you've won every one of them. We are currently sitting at the bottom of a planetwide scar etched by one of *your* claws of mass destruction. I believe the veneer of civility has long been cast off. You have soundly beaten us, and as consolation, you offer us whorehouses and fast-food restaurants."

Varsha knew he was right. The wars had changed humanity, just as much as they had changed kzinti. Now, each species met somewhere in the muddy middle. She composed herself rather quickly and said, almost in the

Menacing Tense, "Did you invite me here to mess with me? To gloat?"

"No, Agent Khan. I need your assistance." The kzin was covered in blood, and a bloated, banded cadaver lay bare on the floor.

"My assistance? What makes you think I'm not going to arrest you right now for espionage? Remember, I was tracking you before all this tanj prostitution affair came up. I know you've been selling information to the Patriarchy."

"I am just a simple tool. Would you arrest the listening device or the listener? If you help me, I can open up further and reveal the full extent of my spying on at least three worlds, as well as some colorful sabotage and an assassination." He let a trickle of information pass between them and her large, lilac eyes widened into saucers. "If you play your cards right and use your clever little monkey tricks to help me, you might even arrest Yearrl-Captain himself."

"Why now? It doesn't make any sense!"

"I'm a strung-out old telepath on his last hunt and I've just had something of an epiphany. I know now that what I've done is wrong."

The dribble of thought continued between them, and she knew he was lying about his guilt. He was quite proud, in fact. It was the closest this drug-addled kzin had come to feeling like a true warrior, but some kind of revelation had shaken him recently. Varsha caught a flash of a small, sickly kitten, black as night with aquamarine eyes, and three trapped and desolate kzinretti.

"What do you want of me?"

"Transport. I need you to pull some ARM strings and get me a ship so I can get off this fractured rock."

"Where will you go? Fafnir? Wunderland?"

"No, those are regular scratching posts along *Devour-er*'s prowl. Yearrl-Captain will have ample connections and resources to hunt me down."

"Then where the tanj else can a *sthondat*-juice junkie and his freemother females hide in the universe?"

The predatory speed with which Bobcat slammed Varsha against the blood-splashed wall made her heart stop. "That will be the last time you refer to *my* harem in such a disrespectful manner. We did not choose our horrid circumstances." The words came out hot with the stench of the fresh kill on his breath.

"I'm sorry. I really am." Varsha immediately regretted her remark, not because she could feel the prickling of reaperlike claws pressed against her jugular, but because she had touched the kzinretti's awesome heartache through the tiny telepathic feed.

Bobcat released her. "Will you assist me? All I have is one hour. By then, Yearrl-Captain expects me to be onboard the *Devourer* with the kit. When I don't show up, he'll immediately send Heroes down to fetch me."

Varsha realized that that infinitesimal filament of thought running from this creature's soul to hers had given her a taste of its bleak perspective and that of the females and even the poor shade of a kitten. She understood that, like it or not, she was becoming invested, which is precisely why she severed the connection. "I'm sorry. I guarantee you that we will investigate this prostitution ring, but I cannot under any circumstances help a spy escape. All I can give you is the assurance that I will not impede you in any way."

Varsha turned and left the gory feeding stall before

Bobcat could even process her rebuff. She thought she caught a glimpse of his lips peeling back exposing rows of deadly, ivory-colored teeth, a black hole where a three-inch canine should've been.

Rage erupted from Bobcat in the form of an explosive roar as Varsha Khan exited the restaurant. The female monkey had outright betrayed him. He had been so sure she would help. He had felt her pity, her genuine concern. After all these years, how little he understood these honorless *kz'eerkt*! He pounded the wash button in the stall and let the boiling water cleanse the blood and fury off of him.

Bobcat hastily made his way back to the bordello. He didn't stop to appreciate the dazzling human civilization scrambling up the crag. He had no plan and he was entirely alone. He had two doses of the psychoactive steroid left and he needed to conserve at least one of them. He stopped suddenly at the foyer of the so-called temple and urinated on a faux stone column. The immature warriors mulling about the lobby caught a whiff of Bobcat's musky kairomone challenge and hurriedly left, not wanting to shame their families by being embroiled in an embarrassing situation.

He ran toward the chamber holding the sentient kzinretti.

"Did you think that monkeys bold enough to work with warcats don't hoot and holler at each other whenever there's danger? I got a call the second your server at Serengeti overheard you murmuring to that cop." That *kchee kz'eerkt*, Larsson, blocked his path, brandishing an impressive fifty-year-old gun.

Bobcat slowed a bit, but only a bit. He slashed with a laser-sharp claw across the pimp's belly, and his stinking innards spilled to the carpet with an audible slosh. Bobcat jumped over the spasming body and stormed the room. The kzinretti were gone. He sniffed the air and caught their distinct spice not far off. He launched himself out of the cheap harem chamber.

Bobcat found them toward the back of the building as four of Larsson's gorilla goons were trying to wrestle them out to the alley and into a waiting airtruck. He charged. One of the wretched apes lifted a beam pistol and shot a straight red lance of light through his shoulder. Pure, blazing agony dropped Bobcat onto the filthy alley floor. The females instinctively, viciously took note and mauled their captors with such contempt that Bobcat caught sobering pangs of it despite not being on the drug. He picked himself up, screamed and leapt onto the gun-monkey, ripping out his throat (and a better part of his shoulder), exposing clean white vertebrae.

"Yara, Xast, go back and get the simple kzinrett and her black kit!" he spat in their native tongue. They hesitated for an instant, not wanting to reenter their prison, but a fast moment later, they sprang back inside. "Raxa, prepare the cargo compartment of the truck for our escape."

Bobcat took the hypodermic from its case and plunged it into his arm. The familiar rush of extra-sensory force exploded from his brain. He tracked and gulped down the necessary knowledge to fly the human vehicle from a shredded and dying human. He also knew that Larsson had already reported his treachery to Yearrl-Captain. He had less than an hour.

The two intelligent kzinretti came out escorting the dazed mother, Tirran, and her little bundle of mewling dark matter. Without question, the group jumped into the airtruck and shut the door. Bobcat shoved himself into the cramped driver's seat as electric pain spread from the burnt hole in his shoulder across his body. He blocked it, like he'd blocked other people's pain, and released the brake. The airtruck rocketed out of the alley and over the bottom of the artificial canyon. He flew the tight vehicle made for small primates with reckless abandon, nearly hitting a penthouse terrace as he raced to the spaceport.

Doubt and balconies rushed by as he flew up the nineteen-plus kilometers along the north precipice. He looked across the wide gap to the south cliff and saw shining white structures and rugged, indigenous amarillo moss running up and down its face like gold and silver veins in the rock. He grasped that, one way or another, he would never see this world again.

What did he hope to accomplish? All he had was an insystem shuttle, which was absolutely no match for the might of the *Devourer of Monkeys*. Where could he take his parody of a pride that would be safe? Another thought struck him: despite her betrayal, Varsha had kept her promise, no police had even attempted to get in his way.

He slowed near the lip of the massive ravine just enough to dip into the airlock tunnel that led to the pressurized portion of the spaceport. Once at the garage, he skidded the truck to a stop. Something was wrong. He sensed no mind (or too few) in this usually busy area of spaceport. Canyon Police must have evacuated this entire zone. He tore the cargo hold's door open and hastily pulled the females out, absorbing their fear and disorientation.

"Hurry!"

The group ran, huddled in a tight knot of flame-colored fur, down the airtight tarmac toward the waiting shuttle. Bobcat was all too aware that a second shuttle, from the bowels of *Devourer*, had just touched down nearby. His mind was so completely focused on the coming Heroes, that the sight of Canyon law enforcement officers surrounding, no, *dismantling* his ship nearly floored him. The Canyonites looked like cobalt-uniformed social insects carrying away components of his ship in single file.

His keen sense of smell and even keener telepathy discerned the presence of five fully-armed kzinti warriors before he even saw them pouring out of a passage that led back to their ship parked on the surface. His phantom tail lashed furiously. He was trapped.

"You will die, Nameless Traitor!" shouted Remover-of-Obstacles of the *Devourer*'s elite boarding squad. The black-swathed, orange warrior dwarfed the injured telepath.

"I *have* a Name!" Bobcat bared his teeth and dug in his hind claws, preparing to die fighting single-handedly and finally meet the Fanged God.

Hold your breath, a human voice rang in his mind and compelled his lungs to lock up. The Heroes were upon them. Everything blurred. He choked. His females were suffocating. He heard the distinct clank of a metal container hitting asphalt and then a blast of smoke filled the spaceport's pressurized terminal.

Don't breathe; just run to me. Varsha's spectral voice controlled Bobcat and his harem like holopuppets.

They ran, lungs yearning for air, muscles burning for oxygen. After an eternity, they cleared the haze and reached the undercover agent waiting by an old ARM ship. She finally allowed them to suck in air.

"You look like cinnamon-sprinkled shit," she said without a hint of jest.

"Trap?" he managed to gasp, ignoring the wicked monkey's verbal feces.

"No. I need you to link with me. Do that bridge thing you kzinti telepaths do," she said, helping Tirran and her kit.

"*Nwarrkaa Kishri Zaaarll?*" he coughed. "How do you know of the Double Bridge of Demons?" *Was she trying to help him? These monkeys lied too easily.*

"We had a kzinti telepath as a consultant during the wars. Do you think you're the first to defect?"

"No, of course not." In fact, he bet his life on it. "That is a permanent mental structure. We would be inextricably bound forever!"

"Does it have to be lasting and demonic? How about a telepathic pontoon bridge?" She sent him an image of a temporary military bridge. "Quickly now! You didn't give me the hour you promised and I need to explain the situation. Anything less than the speed of thought would be dangerously slow."

They both opened up to each other, much more so than the small bond they had shared back in the restaurant. Their minds bled together, but they took great care not to lose themselves in the experience. "They were listening to us at the restaurant! They were prepared," Bobcat said with the speed of a neuron firing.

"Of course they were listening to us. That's why I

made it a point to refuse you out loud. I didn't want them to know you had ARM help."

"I thought you had abandoned us!"

"Sorry, I didn't think you were going to leap into the whorehouse and kill everyone!"

"I'm a kzintosh. What else did you expect?" Bobcat looked back and saw *Devourer*'s Heroes writhing and purring on the tarmac like lunatics, frantically licking and scratching the pavement. "What did you do to them, some kind of nerve agent?"

Varsha laughed. "Nah, we tossed a Catnip Canister at them, made of a powerful strain of genetically engineered *zheerekti* plant. Canyon Police has been experimenting with non-lethal violence deterrents to break up the regular death-duels that spontaneously erupt."

She led them up the gangplank and into a chaotic ARM ship. Canyon medics gently ushered his nervous females toward the coldsleep caskets. "This is the *I Love Lucy*. I had our techs cannibalize your shuttle and moved over a kzinti autodoc and autokitchen. They're in the process of installing your command console to this ship so you can pilot it."

Bobcat looked around at the blue-garbed officers working with haste on the small ship and was entirely unimpressed. "Thank you," he said politely, sinking into the command chair. Fussy medics descended upon him, hooking tubes and cables from the autodoc to his long-abused body. The acute pain of the wound dulled.

Varsha instantly felt his dismay and added, "Trust me, this is all part of my cunning monkey plan. There is another ship exactly like this one primed to take off in minutes. These old ships are hardened against invasive kzinti scans. Yearrl-Captain won't know which one to pounce on and he won't act within Canyon space, anyway. They'll respect the Covenant of 2505."

Bobcat noticed his orange female being put under the freezer. "Bring me the kit!" he howled at the medics while trying to get up from the chair, but pain and pushy doctors held him down. "When I tell him of our fight for freedom, I want to say he sat right here on the bridge!" A tall, reluctant female medic handed him the tiny ebon kitten. Bobcat thought with great shock that this was the first time he'd ever held a kit.

"That only gives me a fifty-fifty chance. Those aren't wonderful odds."

Varsha rapidly checked the tech's work. *These local kids are good*, she thought and turned back to Bobcat, "Can't you telepathically nudge Yearrl-Captain toward the *Sun Wukong*, like I did with you during the gas attack?"

"I cannot. Will you help?"

"Hmmm, that complicates things a bit, but I'll think of something."

"I can guide you through his mind, but I cannot deposit any thoughts."

"Anyway, I should mention that we're *not* going to give you an incredibly expensive hyperdrive ship. ARM isn't a charity and no amount of telepathic manipulation on my part will change that. The faster-than-light section of the ship will separate from the crew subdivision once it has reached its destination and return to its point of origin, leaving you to navigate the system with a fusion drive alone."

"Despite my many considerable talents, piloting in hyperspace is not one of them."

"I thought of that. The *I Love Lucy* is a coldsleep troop transfer ship; you just punch in the target location, go to sleep, and it wakes you up when you get there. Are you going to tell me where you're going? I've been trying to pick it from your brain since the restaurant and all I'm getting is a vague idea that alludes to something like *the Promised Land*."

"What do you know about the *Angel's Pencil*?"

"Absolutely nothing."

He sensed her ignorance. "*Angel's Pencil* was part of the first wave of human colonization about two hundred years ago. It had the misfortune of running into two kzinti warships and plunging deeper into Patriarchy space. Somehow, this slow and antiquated vessel managed to destroy the two ships. Then it disappears. Its ion trail goes cold, but no debris was ever found. The *Dripping Crimson Saber* was sent to investigate the wreckage of the *Gutting Claw*, and it found a defiant message from the *Gutting Claw*'s Telepath to its Captain recorded on the ship's surviving backup computer.

"On the surface, it was a tirade of insults and challenges and a clear declaration of treason. The telepath had sided with the humans and escaped. The official Patriarchy statement was that the *Angel's Pencil* and its weak telepath ally were obliterated beyond any detectable trace. The techs, however, deduced that they cut off the *Angel's* messy fusion drive and were then towed by the captured kzin barge using its faster and untraceable gravity-engine to another location. The *Dripping Crimson Saber*'s Telepath also perceived a hidden vibrational message embedded within the recording. It said, *Brother Telepaths, an opportunity*

*presented itself and I pounced. I have taken a harem
and I will earn a Name. I challenge you to join me.*

"Over the years this account has become legend,
Agent Khan. Their secret location has grown into some
kind of mythical sanctuary for our kind, although I
don't know of any telepath that has heeded the call."

"Because they don't know the exact location! You
don't know that these humans didn't just shoot this
telepath in the head the second they were clear of
the Patriarchy."

"Come now, Agent Khan, you know as well as I
do that these humans went against their instincts
and helped *Gutting Claw*'s Telepath just as you are
helping me now."

"You still don't know where you're going!" She felt
that all of this had been for nothing. She should have
probed deeper into his desperate, delusional mind.
*When had kzinti become the dreamers and humans
the cold realists?*

"I have a spoor of a theory. Telepaths have a pen-
chant for the symbolic. If *Gutting Claw*'s Telepath
wanted us to follow him as his message suggests, he'd
give us an emblematic sign post. If he towed them, he
certainly had some say in their destination. I believe
they went to 46 Leonis Minoris."

"The lesser lion, the eunuch?" She grasped the
archaic *human* imagery from his mind.

"Are feeble telepaths not lesser lions? Unable to
breed, are we not eunuchs?" He flushed with emotion.

Varsha sensed that these blasphemous ideas had
been percolating within him for a long time. She also
had to admit that they carried a sort of mystical logic;
the reasoning of a drug-crazed telepath.

One of the fresh-faced medics that a second ago had waved diagnostic instruments around the kzinretti, now approached and broke the spell, bringing them back to the slow pace of the material plane. "Two of the yellow females are pregnant. I suggest they go into coldsleep before takeoff. I'd hate for them to get jostled around."

This rolled over Bobcat like a sudden storm. The concept of being a sire was so remote, so impossible, that the actual fact rocked him. Varsha felt squalls of equal parts joy and fear crashing down on him.

She turned to the expecting females and spoke in the closest approximation of their proto-Heroes' Tongue her vocal cords allowed, "First, let me just say it's an honor to finally meet intelligent kzinretti, and congratulations, you're going to be mothers." She gently stroked their cheeks, then turned to Bobcat and said in the same language so the females could understand, "Well done, champ!"

He said nothing for a while as his own personal paradigm shifted toward the paternal. "We have to get out of here," he rumbled at last.

"Right. The *Sun Wukong* is taking off in three minutes, and I want the *I Love Lucy* to be ready to launch right along with it," she barked, and all the techs ended their last-minute fretting.

Bobcat placed a massive paw on Varsha's shoulder. "Thank you, Agent Khan. I give you my word that I will name my first female kitten after you."

She smiled warmly. "You know, I've been giving some thought as to why kzinti telepaths are born scrawny."

"Enlighten me." His spotted, rust-colored fur bristled at the mention of such a delicate subject. He removed his paw from her shoulder.

Varsha continued enthusiastically, "I believe there's a battle for nourishment in the kzinrett's womb, between the kzin body, which is a high-maintenance, calorie-hogging machine, and a telepath's developing brain, which also demands more energy than most. Inevitably, the brain wins out at the cost of a fully developed body."

"An interesting theory," he spit between gritted teeth. He turned to see his two mothers-to-be being tenderly placed in freezer caskets.

"Don't you see? If you took better care of your females and perhaps gave them specially formulated prenatal vitamins, you could have big, strong killer telepaths!"

Bobcat's lips pulled back and flashed her the obscene stiletto teeth Varsha had briefly glimpsed back in the kzin restaurant. His ears fluttered like pink moth wings.

"I'm sorry. I didn't mean to offend."

"Relax, Agent Khan; sometimes a smile is just a smile. That's quite a brilliant and rather obvious observation." He wondered if the Patriarchy suppressed such knowledge.

"Thanks." She walked out and down the walkway, clapping her hands. "Alright, grease monkeys, time's up! Everybody out!"

Alone on the bridge, Bobcat took out his last remaining shot of *sthondat* lymph extract and delicately placed it on the console. He felt the insubstantial ball of soot on his lap stir and look up at him with big, powerful blue-green eyes.

"You need a crèche name, little one. Fortunately, your mother was too stupefied to give you one, so the Honor falls on me," he said appraising the kit as if it were a fine, olden trophy belonging to a great Hero. Neither Interworld nor the Heroes' Tongue seemed appropriate now that they were leaving known space.

The kitten yawned, revealing needle-pointed teeth and a small curled tongue. "A very casual attitude in the face of danger." Bobcat's ears flicked and he wondered if the painkillers from the autodoc were making him silly. "Then you shall be called Jarri, until such time as you earn a Hero's Name. It means *valiant* in the exotic language of your new den mothers."

He gave the sleepy kit a reassuring lick between the ears. "I give you my word, on what little Honor I have, that you will not be dragged into a life of slavery and never feel the sting of animal poison in your veins."

The two war-era ships lifted off the autumnal, pockmarked surface of Canyon with perfect synchronization and into the waiting maw of the immense, spherical ship. The kzin ship's armored hull plating shone like polished copper and did nothing, patiently waiting like a hunter in the bush. Bobcat entered the coordinates for 46 Leonis Minoris into the kzin computer recklessly rigged to the ARM dashboard. He sent a silent prayer to the cruel Fanged God that he reward his audacity with better territory. Then, he leaned back in the command chair and meditated on the rapidly shrinking planet.

"How's the shoulder?" Varsha asked, entering the small bridge.

"You didn't have to stay." He had known that she would before she closed the ship's airlock behind her staff.

"Of course I did. You can't get into Yearrl-Captain's head, and I can't do it all the way from Canyon. Besides, you haven't given me all the valuable intel you promised, and my superiors would be livid otherwise."

He dumped a heavy load of memories into the human's mind. It felt good somehow to be relieved of his glorious past.

Varsha faltered for an instant, all the death and mayhem wrought by *Devourer of Monkeys* . . . because of Bobcat, gross violations of the Covenants of Shasht. She placed the weighty information in a sealed compartment of her mind and steadied herself. No room for doubts anymore.

"Will you be reprimanded for allowing me to escape?" Bobcat and Varsha were still linked by the provisional psychic bridge.

"Nah, think of it as extreme witness protection."

As the two identical ARM vessels coasted along their parallel trajectories, he tried to imagine the infuriated Yearrl-Captain pacing the control deck of his ship, mulling over which prey to leap upon. "I cannot reach Yearrl-Captain! He's skirting the limits of my telepathic reach!" Bobcat moved to tear out all the tubes and lines from the autodoc. "This machine is already scrubbing the *sthondat* fluid from my system!"

"Calm down." She placed a soothing hand on his trembling shoulder. "You've crept in Yearrl-Captain's inner mind many times. Show me a layout of his psyche from memory."

The sleek and sterile command center of their ship faded around them. Varsha and Bobcat, with Jarri cradled in his good arm, stood on an ethereal bluff overlooking the wide tangerine savannah of

Yearrl-Captain's most primitive hindbrain. The illusion was so palpable that Varsha could taste the acidic aroma of the veldt rising in the morning heat. Two glowing moons hung low on the horizon, like the eyes of the Fanged God skulking behind the curve of the world. A pair of lumbering alien herbivores plodded along on their own ancient migration. A faint rustle in the grass hinted at a concealed killer.

"Wait a minute, those beasts are us! Is this how Yearrl-Captain sees the situation?" The level of detail astounded her. She had to remind herself this was a reconstruction and not Yearrl's actual mind.

"Only subconsciously, Agent Kahn. As you see, the captain is too far and well hidden for direct manipulation."

"Trust me. You've spent your entire career trying to block out other minds. Me? I'm an expert at this." She studied the primordial scene much as her own simian ancestors might have.

Bobcat got visceral insight into human thinking. Where kzin brains evolved from the low, direct vantage point of the ground, humans took in the bigger picture. He also instantly recognized the Australopithecine meaning behind the name of their small ark.

"Okay, Yearrl might be beyond telepathic tampering, but he's not above manipulation. The captain of the Sun Wukong *is close enough to mess with."*

"I don't follow . . . You wish to sway an ally into attacking a kzinti warship? That's madness!"

"No, the Sun Wukong's *captain is already nervous. I can use that to push him to speed up just a bit. Get his ship away from the constraining mass of p Eridani and into the safety of hyperspace."* Varsha stroked

the part of Captain Garcia's mind that informed his forebears to hide from Iberian cave lions during the last glacial maximum.

One of the elephantine creatures began a light, anxious trot and at once an almost imperceptible crackle in the grass moved in closer toward it. Sensing danger, the dumb animal picked up its pace.

"They're feeding off each other!"

"Exactly. Yearrl-Captain's primal instincts are telling him that the animal that shows fear is the weaker prey. His logic is telling him that the ship that's trying to run must harbor the fugitive. The closer he gets, the more Sun Wukong *reacts."*

The prehistoric scene melted away and Bobcat was still hooked up to the beeping medical machine. The little kit curled up in his lap. Varsha pointed to the display showing the *Devourer of Monkeys* gravitating toward the *Sun Wukong*, which was now ahead of them by many AU and entering the system's heliopause.

I Love Lucy's own hyperspace shutters began to slide across all windows. Before the stars were completely blotted out, they saw the *Sun Wukong*, followed by the *Devourer*, wink out of Einsteinian space. Bobcat and Varsha simultaneously exhaled. Soon after, they felt their own ship slip into hyperspace.

She patted his good shoulder, where her hand had comfortably rested the entire time, then let the pontoon bridge collapse between them. "Alright, the chief engineer's ice box is over in the second half of this ship near the hyperdrive. I'm going to sleep now before our rapport does become permanent and demonic." She smiled slyly. "What're you going to do when you get to where you're going?"

"Thrust this last dose of *sthondat* drug into my arm and give a telepathic cry for help like no other. A planet of telepaths, even latent ones, won't be able to ignore it."

Unless they've been reduced to inbred idiots by two hundred years of isolation, she thought, but kept it to herself. Instead she picked up the slumbering kit. "Here, I'll put this little warrior to bed next to his mother."

"Why don't you join us? You make a truly worthy companion." He tried to turn, but the autodoc numbed his entire left side.

"I lack your faith. Besides, I've always wanted to retire on Canyon. That's why I telepathically maneuvered my boss back on Earth to transfer me."

He leaned back in his command chair. "Treat it better than I did."

She left Bobcat to heal.

The following is an excerpt from:

SHADOW OF FREEDOM

DAVID WEBER

Available from Baen Books
March 2013
hardcover

✦ Chapter One

The wingless, saucer-like drone drifted through the wet, misty night on silent counter gravity. The fine droplets of rain sifted down in filmy curtains that reeked of burned wood and hydrocarbons and left a greasy sensation on the skin. Despite the rainfall, fires crackled noisily here and there, consuming heaps of wreckage which had once been homes, adding their own smoke and soot to the atmosphere. A faint, distant mutter of thunder rolled through the overcast night, though whether it was natural or man-made was difficult to say.

The drone paused, motionless, blacker than the night about it, its rain-slick, light-absorbent coat sucking in the photons from the smudgy fires which might otherwise have reflected from it. The turret mounted on its bottom rotated smoothly, turning sensors and lenses towards whatever had attracted its attention. Wind sighed wearily in the branches of sugar pine, crab poplar, and imported Terran white pine and hickory, something shifted in one of the piles of rubble, throwing up sparks and cinders. A burning rafter burned through and collapsed and water dripped from rain-heavy limbs with the patient, uncaring persistence of nature, but otherwise all was still, silent.

The drone considered the sensor data coming to it, decided it was worth consideration by higher authority, and uploaded it to the communications satellite and its operator in far distant Elgin City. Then it waited.

The silence, the rain, and the wind continued. The fires hissed as heavier drops fell into their white and red hearts. And then—

The thunderbolt descended from the heavens like the wrath of Zeus. Born two hundred and sixty-five kilometers above the planet's surface, it traced a white line from atmosphere's edge to ground level, riding a froth of plasma. The two-hundred-kilo dart arrived without even a whisper, far outracing the sonic boom of its passage, and struck its target coordinates at thirty times the speed of sound.

The quiet, rainy night tore apart under the equivalent of the next best thing to two and a half tons of old-fashioned TNT. The brilliant, blinding flash vaporized a bubble of rain. Concussion and overpressure rolled out from its heart, flattening the remaining walls of three of the village's broken houses. The fury of the explosion painted the clouds, turned individual raindrops into shining diamonds and rubies that seemed momentarily frozen in air, and flaming bits and pieces of what once had been someone's home arced upward like meteors yearning for the heavens.

"Thank you used a big enough hammer, Callum?" the woman in the dark blue uniform of a lieutenant in the Loomis System Unified Public Safety Force asked dryly.

She stood behind the drone operator's comfortable chair, looking over his shoulder at the display where the pinprick icon of the explosion flashed brightly. The operator—a sergeant, with the sleeve hashmarks of a twenty-T-year veteran—seemed to hesitate for just a moment, then turned his head to look at her.

"Unauthorized movement in an interdicted zone, Ma'am," he replied.

"And you needed a KEW to deal with it?" The lieutenant arched one eyebrow. "A near-deer, do you think? Or possibly a bison elk?"

"IR signature was human, Ma'am. Must've been one of MacRory's bastards, or he wouldn't've been there."

"I see." The UPS officer folded her hands behind her. "As it happens, I was standing right over there at the command desk," she observed, this time with a distinct bite. "If I recall correctly, SOP is to clear a KEW strike with command personnel unless it's time-critical. Am I mistaken about that?"

"No, Ma'am," the sergeant admitted, and the lieutenant shook her head.

"I realize you like big bangs, Callum. And I'll admit you've got a better excuse than usual for playing with them. But there are Regs for a reason, and I'd take it as a personal favor—the kind of favor which will keep your fat, worthless, trigger-happy arse in that comfortable chair instead of carrying out sweeps in the bush—if you'd remember that next time. Do you think you can do that for me?"

"Yes, Ma'am," the sergeant said much more crisply,

and she gave him a nod that was several degrees short
of friendly and headed back to her station.

The sergeant watched her go, then turned back
to his display and smiled. He'd figured she'd have a
little something to say to him, but he'd also figured
it would be worth it. Three of his buddies had been
killed in the first two days of the insurrection, and
he was still in the market for payback. Besides, it
gave him a sense of godlike power to be able to call
down the wrath of heaven. He'd known Lieutenant
MacRuer would never have authorized the expendi-
ture of a KEW on a single, questionable IR signature, which was why he hadn't asked for it. And if
he was going to be honest about it, he wasn't really
certain his target hadn't been a ghost, either. But
that was perfectly all right with him, and his intense
inner sense of satisfaction more than outweighed his
superior's obvious displeasure.

This time, at least, he amended silently. *Catch her
in a bad mood, and the by-the-Book bitch is just likely
to make good on that reassignment.* He shook his head
mentally. *Don't think I'd like slogging around in the
woods with those people very much.*

"Confirm impact, Ma'am," Missile Tech 1/c George
Chasnikov reported. "Looks like it drifted fifteen or
twenty meters to planetary west of the designated
coords, though." He shook his head. "That was sloppy."

"Was the problem at their end, or ours?" Lieutenant
Commander Sharon Tanner had the watch. She also
happened to be SLNS *Hoplite*'s tactical officer, and she
punched up the post-strike report on her own display

as she spoke. "I'm not real crazy about 'sloppy' when we're talking about KEWs, Chaz."

"Me neither, Ma'am," Chasnikov agreed sourly. "Reason I brought it up, actually." He shook his head, tapping a query into his console. "I hate those damned things," he added in a mutter Tanner knew was deliberately just loud enough for her to hear.

She let it pass. Chasnikov was an experienced, highly valued member of her department, a lifer who would stay in SLN uniform until the day he died, and every TAC officer he ever served under would be lucky to have him. That bought him a little extra slack from someone like Sharon Tanner.

Not that he didn't have a point, she thought bitterly, reflecting on all the things Hoplite and her small squadron had been called upon to do over the past few weeks. Compared to some of those, expending a single kinetic energy weapon on what had probably been a ghost target was small beer.

"Their end, it looks like, Ma'am," Chasnikov said after a moment. "It didn't miss the designated coordinates; it missed the amended coordinates. They sent us a correction, but it was too late to update the targeting queue."

"And did they happen to tell us what it was they wanted us to kill this time? Or if we got it?"

"No, Ma'am. Just the coordinates. Could've been one of their own battalions, for all I know. And no strike assessment, so far." And there won't be one, either . . . as usual, his expression added silently.

"I see." Tanner rubbed the tip of her nose for a moment, then shrugged. "Write it up, Chaz. Be sure to make it clear we followed our checklist on the launch. I'll pass it along to Commander Diadoro. I'm sure he and the Skipper will . . . reemphasize to Groundside that little hiccups when you're targeting KEWs can have major consequences. And emphasize that they didn't give us a clear target description, either. We can't go around wasting the taxpayers' KEWs without at least knowing what we're shooting at."

And I hope Captain Venelli uses that little memo to rip someone a new asshole, she added silently. *Chaz is right, we've done too damned much of this kind of shit. I don't think there's anything left down there that's genuinely worth a KEW, and anything that discourages those bloodthirsty bastards from raining them down on some poor damned idiot with a pulse rifle schlepping through the shrubbery all by himself will be worth it.*

There were many things Sharon Tanner had done in her Frontier Fleet career of which she was proud; this wasn't one of them.

Back in the shattered ruins which had once been a village named Glen mo Chrìdhe, the sound of rain was overlaid by the heavier patter of falling debris. It lasted for several seconds, sparks bouncing and rolling through the wet as some of the still-burning wreckage struck, and then things were still once more. The crater was dozens of meters across, deep enough to swallow an air lorry . . . and more than enough to devour the cellar into which the thirteen-year-old boy had just darted with the food he'd been able to scavenge for his younger sister.

❖   ❖   ❖

"They got Tammas." Erin MacFadzean's voice was flat, worn and eroded by exhaustion and gradually swelling despair. She looked across the dingy basement room at Megan MacLean and her expression was bitter. "Fergus just reported in."

"Where?" MacLean asked, rubbing her weary eyes and clenching her soul against the pain of yet another loss.

"Rothes," MacFadzean replied. "The Uppies stopped the lorry on its way into Mackessack."

"Is he alive?" MacLean lowered her hands, looking across at the other woman.

"Fergus doesn't know. He says there was a lot of shooting, and it sounds like he was lucky to get away alive himself."

"I see."

MacLean laid her hands flat on the table in front of her, looking down at their backs for a moment, then inhaled deeply. It shamed her to admit it, but she hoped Tammas MacPhee hadn't been taken alive, and wasn't that a hell of a thing to be thinking about a friend she'd known for thirty T-years?

"See if we can get in touch with Tad Ogilvy," she said after a moment. "Tell him Tammas is . . . gone. He's in charge of whatever we've got left outside the capital now."

"On it," MacFadzean acknowledged and quietly left the room.

As the door closed behind her, MacLean allowed her shoulders to sag with the weariness she tried not to let anyone else see. Not that she was fooling anyone . . . or that everyone else wasn't just as exhausted as she was. But she had to go on playing her part to the bitter end. At least it wouldn't be too much longer now, she thought harshly.

It wasn't supposed to be this way. She'd organized the Loomis Liberation League as a *legal* political party seven years ago, during one of the Prosperity Party's infrequent bouts of façade democracy. She hadn't really expected to accomplish anything—this was Halkirk, after all—but she'd wanted MacMinn and MacCrimmon to know there were at least some people still willing to stand up on their hind legs and voice their opposition. The LLL's candidates had actually won in two of the capital city's boroughs, giving it a whopping four tenths of a percent of the seats in the Parliament, which had made it the most powerful of the opposition parties. It probably wouldn't have won those races if the Prosperity Party hadn't been putting on a show for the Core World news crew doing a documentary on the silver oak logging camps, of course, but two seats were still two seats.

Not that it had done any good. And not that either of the LLL's members had won reelection after the news crew went home. President MacMinn hadn't even pretended to count the votes in the next general election, and that was the point at which Megan MacLean had listened to Tammas MacPhee, the LLL's vice chairman and MacFadzean. She'd maintained her party's open organization, its get-out-the-vote and lobbying campaigns, but she'd also let MacFadzean organize the Liberation League's thoroughly illegal provisional armed wing.

It had probably been a mistake, she thought now, yet she still couldn't see what other option she might have had. Not with the Unified Public Safety Force turning more and more brutal—and worrying less and less about maintaining even a pretense of due process—under Secretary of Security MacQuarie. Except, of course, to have given up the effort completely, and she simply hadn't been able to do that.

And now this. Seven years of effort, of pouring her heart and soul into the liberation of her star system, and it ended this way, in death and disaster. It wasn't even—

She looked up again as the door opened and Mac-Fadzean walked back into what passed for their command post.

"I got a runner off to Tad," she said, and her lips twitched in a mirthless smile. "Somehow I didn't think I should be using the com, under the circumstances."

"Probably not a bad idea," MacLean agreed with what might have been the ghost of an answering smile. If that was what it was, it vanished quickly. "It was bad enough with just the Uppies tapping the coms. With the damned Sollies up there listening in..."

Her voice trailed off, and MacFadzean nodded. She understood the harsh, jagged edge of hate which had crept into MacLean's voice only too well. They had Frinkelo Osborne, the Office of Frontier Security's advisor to MacMinn's Prosperity Party, to thank for the for Solarian League Navy starships in orbit around the planet of Halkirk. Officially, Osborne was only a trade attaché in the Solarian legation in Elgin, the Loomis System's capital. Trade attachés made wonderful covers for OFS operatives assigned to "assist and advise" independent Verge star systems when their transtellar masters felt they stood in need of a little outside support. And if an "attaché" required a certain degree of assistance from the SLN, he could usually be confident of getting it.

We could've taken MacCrimmon and MacQuarie on our own, MacFadzean thought bitterly. *We could have. Another few months, a few more arms shipments from Partisan and his people, and we'd have had a fighting chance to kick the LPP straight to Hell. Hell, we might have pulled it off even now, if not for the damned Sollies! But how in God's name are people with pulsers and grenade launchers supposed to hold off orbital bombardments? If I'd only been able to get word to Partisan—!*

But she hadn't. They hadn't been supposed to move for a minimum of at least another four months. Partisan had been supposed to be back in Loomis to lock down the final arrangements—the ones she hadn't yet discussed even with MacLean—and there hadn't been any way to get a message out when the balloon went up so unexpectedly.

She glanced across the room again, wondering if she should have told MacLean about those arrangements with Partisan. She'd thought about it more than once, but secrecy and security had been all important. Besides, MacLean wasn't really a revolutionary at heart; she was a reformer. She'd never been able to throw herself as fully into the notion of armed resistance as MacFadzean had, and the thought of relying so heavily on someone from out-system, of crafting operations plans which depended on armed assistance from a foreign star nation, would have been a hard sell.

Be honest with yourself, Erin. You were afraid she'd

tell you to shut the conduit down, weren't you? That the notion of trusting anybody from outside Loomis, was too risky. That they were too likely to have an agenda of their own, one that didn't include our best interests. You told yourself she'd change her mind if you could prevent a finished plan that covered all the contingencies you could think of, but inside you always knew she still would have hated the entire thought. And you weren't quite ready to go ahead and commit to Partisan without her okay, were you? Well, maybe she would've been right ... but it wouldn't have made any difference in the way things've finally worked out, now would it?

She looked up at the command post's shadowed ceiling, her eyes bitter with hate for the starships which had rained down death and ruination all across her homeworld, and wished with all her exhausted heart that she had been able to get a messenger to Partisan.

—end excerpt—

from *Shadow of Freedom*
available in hardcover,
March 2013, from Baen Books

MORE . . .
ERIC FLINT